No, We Can't Be Friends

BOOKS BY SOPHIE RANALD

Sorry Not Sorry
It's Not You, It's Him
Out with the Ex, In with the New

No, We Can't Be Friends

SOPHIE RANALD

Bookouture

Published by Bookouture in 2020

An imprint of Storyfire Ltd.
Carmelite House
50 Victoria Embankment
London EC4Y 0DZ

www.bookouture.com

ISBN: 978-1-83888-136-8
eBook ISBN: 978-1-83888-135-1

Chapter One

You know that creepy little kid in the movie who was like, 'I see dead people'? That was me, except what I was seeing was pregnant people.

It had happened so gradually that it kind of crept up on me without me noticing. If I thought back to maybe a year ago, I could barely recall there being any pregnant women in the world. There must have been, of course, and I must've noticed one occasionally and thought, 'OMG, what happened to that poor woman's *ankles*?', or offered her my seat on the Tube.

But in recent months, I'd started to see more and more and more of them. In the supermarket queue with their husbands, idly caressing their bellies. On public transport, wearing their little 'Baby on Board' badges, shifting uncomfortably from foot to foot until I offered them my seat. Even when I checked out celeb gossip, I'd see Beyoncé or Helen George from *Call the Midwife* (ha!) or the Duchess of Cambridge all fecund and glowing.

It was like the country was stockpiling baby bumps in the event of a no-deal Brexit.

I mentioned it to my friend Bianca one day, when we'd stopped for coffee while shopping for a birthday gift for Bianca's daughter.

'Hey, Bianca, it might just be me, but I've noticed a really weird thing…'

She looked up from her phone. 'What's that? We're going to have to call it a day, I'm afraid. Michael says Charis is missing me and feeling anxious, and I don't want her upset so close to her big day.'

I privately thought that Charis, at almost seven years old, was both too young to suffer from anxiety and too old to have her mother rush home when her father should be perfectly capable of parenting his own child, but I didn't say that, of course.

I said, 'Are there, like, loads more pregnant women around than there used to be?'

Bianca looked at me like I'd grown another head. 'Of course there aren't. The birth rate in the UK has been falling more or less steadily for the past forty years.'

'Oh. I suppose you're right. But it's really weird. It's like they're everywhere.'

Her expression changed to one of dawning comprehension. 'Oh, now I get it!'

'Get what?'

'You're thirty-four, right?'

'Right.'

'And you and Myles, you've been married for, what, five years?'

'Four years, eight months, two weeks and a day,' I said. The calculation took me slightly longer than it used to, and I'd stopped counting hours and minutes, which I have to admit I did for about the first year of our relationship. Tragic? Me?

'And you've thought about having a family, haven't you?'

'Well, yeah, of course. I mean, that was always a thing that we knew we'd do, when the time was right.'

'Well, there you go then. This is it. It's your subconscious mind, or your body clock, telling you that the time is right, right now. You've been whacked with the broody stick.'

'But I... I mean, Megan just made me a partner at work. Myles's practice is still growing. We've put the house on the market so we can move somewhere bigger. It can't be the right time.'

She shrugged. 'Tell that to Mother Nature. Here, look at these and tell me what you think.'

She pulled a package out of a Selfridges shopping bag, carefully unwrapped the tissue paper and handed it to me. She'd mentioned that, as well as looking for loot for her own daughter, she was after a baby-shower gift for a friend, but I'd said I'd leave her to browse that department while I checked out the new Urban Decay eye palette.

Now, though, I looked intently at the garment in my hands. It was a romper suit in the softest, plushest white cotton, with a hood that had little teddy-bear ears on it. On the front, where a pocket would be on a man's shirt, was a tiny embroidered bear. I lifted it up to my face and sniffed and, all at once, something in me turned to mush.

'Oh. My. God. That's the most adorable thing.'

'It's wildly impractical, of course. Annette's sprog will puke or poo on it within about three seconds and it'll never be the same again. But still. Awww.'

'Awww.' I caressed the garment again, imagining little starfish hands emerging from the sleeves, a tiny scrunched-up face surrounded by the white hood, and the heft of a new-born baby in my arms.

'Well,' Bianca said, 'you'd best get cracking then. It's not like you're getting any younger.'

It was typical of Bianca to segue seamlessly from being kind and perceptive to making a remark like that; one of the reasons why, although we hung out together sometimes, I'd never felt I could completely trust her. But now that this window into my own psyche had been opened, I realised she had a point, and alongside the broodiness that was suddenly washing over me was a knife-blade of cold fear: *what if she's right? What if I've left it too long?*

We paid for our coffee and said our goodbyes, but I didn't follow Bianca to the station. I stood on the sidewalk until I was sure she'd gone, and then rummaged in my bag for my cigarettes and lit one, feeling the blissful hit of nicotine as it met my throat.

That would have to go, of course. That would be the first thing to go.

A few weeks later, on a Sunday in early autumn, I woke up late. With Myles away, the house had felt huge, empty and a bit creepy, and I'd slept badly, every creak and rustle startling me awake or invading my dreams. Now it was almost eleven, and the looming mountain of my to-do list made further sleep impossible.

I needed to tackle the overflowing laundry basket. There were a bunch of Myles's suits that I still hadn't got around to picking up from the dry cleaner. The monthly supermarket order needed doing – we were almost out of toilet roll, washing-up liquid and, crucially, coffee. I needed to do an epic declutter of our spare bedroom, because an estate agent was coming to photograph the house on Wednesday. I needed to send an anniversary card to Myles's aunt Susan and a birthday card to his mother.

But there was another, even more important task to do first. I rolled over and found my phone on the nightstand and my thermometer in its case in the drawer. I swiped through to the tracker app and entered the numbers. My temperature hadn't risen, but that was okay – once it did, it would be too late.

I walked, naked, to the bathroom, suddenly conscious that I was desperate for a pee. But even that had to wait. I rummaged in the cupboard for the box of ovulation tests and unwrapped one, thinking how weirdly quickly I'd become accustomed to this ritual. I wondered how long it would be before I got to have a pee without there being a stick involved.

Not to mention the obsessive interest I'd developed in my cervical mucus. A couple of months before, I'd barely thought about the stuff – now, it had become the holy grail of body fluids.

Superstitiously, I forced myself to clean my teeth and cleanse and moisturise my face before checking the test. If I resisted the urge to stare at it while waiting the full five minutes, it was almost as if it would be more likely to give me the result I wanted – it would like me.

And, that time, I was rewarded with a little smiley face.

All my plans for the day were forgotten. I was ovulating. I needed to have sex before the fickle fertile window banged shut again. Only problem was, the guy I needed to have it with was a thousand miles away.

It wasn't fair to blame Myles. He was working, after all – it wasn't like he was off gallivanting or something. And, even if he had been, demanding that he stay home in order to attempt to get me pregnant would have been pretty unreasonable. Even so, I couldn't help resenting the late-running project that his architecture practice was working on, which had kept him away in Lisbon for great chunks of time over the past few months.

It would be completely crazy to fly to Portugal for one night to have sex with my husband, obviously. Totally nuts to forget my plans for the day and drive to the airport, get on a plane and surprise him, stay overnight, get an early flight back and head straight into the office to be at my desk on time on Monday morning.

Nuts. But I was going to do it anyway.

Five hours later, I was in a taxi, the driver weaving his way at breakneck speed through the winding streets towards the hotel where Myles was staying. Normally, the erratic driving would have freaked me out, but now it suited me just fine. If saying to him, 'Go faster, I need to have a fuck,' would have made him drive even more insanely, I'd have happily done it, but there was no need.

He screeched to a halt outside a grand stone building, and I paid with the wad of euros I'd withdrawn at the airport. I retrieved my bag and made my way inside, towards the reception desk, wondering what the chances were of them letting me head straight up to Myles's room and surprising him there. I might even whip off my clothes, stand there in front of him in my lacy underwear and go, 'Ta-dah!' Too much? Probably.

But there was no need. Before I got to the desk, I heard his voice behind me – that East London accent I'd fallen in love with, back when it had seemed like the most exotic thing in the world.

'My God. Sloane.'

I spun around, my face breaking into a smile. But there was no answering pleasure on his face. He looked – for a brief second before gathering me into a hug – absolutely appalled to see me.

'Hi, babe,' I said. 'Surprise visit! I'm so glad you were in – I thought I'd have to wait, or head out and try to find you.'

'Well, here I am. I've just got back. I was over on site, checking things out. They don't work on Sundays here, no chance. This is… Well, I certainly wasn't expecting to see you.'

He wasn't, of course. I hadn't called him, or texted – perhaps I should have done, I thought, looking up at his face. He still didn't look happy. There was something in his expression that was almost panic.

'I'm quite surprised you haven't bumped into Bianca, too,' I joked, trying to lighten the mood. 'She's out here this weekend for a hen do. But I was missing you, and you're not due back until Wednesday, right? So I thought… you know. Shall we go up to your room and drop off my bag? Then maybe head out for something to eat?'

'They haven't made up the room yet. I don't know why. Guess there was some mix-up with housekeeping. Let's leave your stuff down here. I'll talk to reception now and ask them to sort it while we're out.'

He looked tired, I thought. Tired and stressed. Which wasn't surprising, given he'd been working long hours, in a strange city, on a massive project with workers whose first language wasn't English. But it wasn't like I'd been goofing off at home, watching box sets with my feet up. I was stressed too, and busy, and dealing with all the stuff life threw at us – from the estate agent who was marketing our house to the man who'd tried and failed to fix the strange noise the boiler was making, to getting the car serviced – on top of my own job.

We just needed to reconnect, that was all. Just be together and chill for a bit, and then everything would be okay.

'Sure,' I said. 'We can go to that place you were telling me about, near the site where you're working. I remember you raving about the pork *alentejana* they do there. Or we could just order room service, if you're too whacked to go out. I don't care if the bed's not made.'

If I had my way, the bed would be in a state of disarray before too long, anyway.

'Yeah, I think that was Alma's.' Again, there was that brief flash of alarm in his face. 'They're not open on Sunday nights. There's a place down the road that does great *prego* rolls. Come on, let's head out.'

After he'd had a word with the concierge about the room and left my bags with them to take upstairs, and I'd been to the bathroom, wishing that I could have a shower and change out of the jeans and sneakers I'd worn on the plane into something more alluring and more suitable for the warm night, we did just that.

Sitting opposite me in the restaurant, our cold beers leaking rivulets of condensation down onto the bare wood table and a bowl of olives between us – I was starving; I'd only had time to grab a slice of toast at home, and the chickpea and avocado wrap

I'd been served on the flight had been about as appetising as the cardboard sleeve it came in – Myles seemed to relax. His phone was on the table between us, but his glances at its screen were becoming less frequent. After asking me the same question about the price the estate agency had suggested listing the house for three times, he finally seemed to have taken in my answer. He'd stopped compulsively smoothing back the wing of silver hair that flopped down over his forehead.

It had been almost six months, and I was just starting to get used to Myles's new do – his 'barnet', as he called it, using the Cockney rhyming slang I could never get my head around. When I met him six years ago, his hair had been jet black, glossy as a raven's wing. Then, gradually, grey hairs began to appear and, later, full-on streaks of pure white. It never bothered me – as far as I was concerned, my husband was the sexiest man on two legs, grey or no grey.

But it freaked him right out.

'I'm too young for this,' he'd lamented, scrutinising his parting in the mirror. 'I'm thirty-three. I can't have grey hair. What do women do?'

'They dye it, obviously,' I said. I was lucky; my own hair was still an even, rich dark brown, my best feature, and although I spent a small fortune on oils and serums and conditioning treatments, I'd never coloured it.

'But people will notice,' Myles said. 'They'll be like, "Look at that tragic fucker, who can't deal with going grey."'

'You look great, honey,' I replied. 'It suits you. It's distinguished.'

And I took him to bed and proved just how much I fancied him, and assumed that was the end of it. But then, six months ago, Myles had come home one day with the dye job to end all dye jobs. What had been slightly greying dark hair was now a blend of charcoal, ash and deepest midnight violet. I was gobsmacked, but also delighted – my gorgeous husband looked like a younger and more metrosexual George Clooney.

Which reminded me, as our food arrived – slices of spicy, just-cooked, chewy steak in floury white buns, with fries and an oily lettuce and tomato salad on the side – what I'd come here for.

'So,' I said, 'I have something for you. A surprise, to go with my surprise visit.'

Again, that brief flash of alarm crossed his face. 'What's that?'

'You know how we've been talking for a while now about maybe trying for a baby sometime soon?'

'Yeah, and you said you weren't ready, and there's plenty of time.'

I rummaged in my bag and pulled out the parcel I'd carefully wrapped for him at home, using the white paper printed with silver rattles I'd used for his cousin's daughter's christening present a few months before, and passed it over to him.

'What the…?'

He turned the package over in his hands a few times, then peeled aside the tape and opened it. Inside, I'd put an unopened pack of contraceptive pills, my cigarette lighter and a copy of *Pregnancy for Men*.

'*Pregnancy for Men*?' he read out incredulously. 'What, has there been some major medical breakthrough I don't know about?'

I couldn't help laughing. 'That's not what it means, doofus.'

'But seriously, sweetheart. You're not…?'

'Not yet. But I'm ready to try, if you are. I came off the Pill. And I haven't had a cigarette in two weeks. And I…'

I paused. *Just thinking about her egg-white cervical mucus gives me the horn*, said no man ever.

'I'm ready.'

'Sloane, that's great. I mean, I'm dead excited. You know I want kids. But there's no rush, is there? Sometimes these things take time, anyway.'

'Of course,' I lied. 'There's no rush at all. We've all the time in the world.'

He paid the bill and we walked hand in hand through the balmy darkness back to his hotel. We climbed a narrow stone staircase to the room, which, finally, had been spruced up for the night, the sheets turned down and chocolate truffles placed carefully in the centre of the pillows.

I delved into my suitcase and found my washbag, then ducked into the bathroom and showered at warp speed. But when I was done, Myles was already in bed, the duvet pulled up to his chin, gently snoring. I slid in next to him and wrapped my arm round his waist, pressing my body against the familiar curve of his back, hoping to rouse him as my hand caressed the familiar hard planes and dips of his ribcage and thigh.

But he didn't respond. Not a twitch, not a moan, not a sigh. Nothing. It was like getting into bed with a man-sized stuffed toy, only not as cuddly.

Maybe that should have given me a clue. Maybe dozens of other tiny things – little dropped stitches and snags in the fabric of our marriage – should have done. Everyone says, *Trust your gut. When something's up, you know. Don't ignore those spidey senses.*

But I had nothing to ignore. I had no inkling that anything was wrong. No idea at all.

Chapter Two

Nine months later

'It's just the most amazing space,' Bianca said, looking around the dust-filled, scaffolding-ribbed shell of our house. 'You totally made the right decision to stay and extend, rather than selling.'

'To be fair, selling just wasn't an option right now.' Myles raked his hand through his hair. 'We were on the market for months, and we only got four low-ball offers. The market's just dead right now.'

'And so we decided to make the most of what we had.' I tried my hardest not to sound bitter, but I couldn't help feeling that way – our house had been amazing, a comfortable home filled with all the things we'd built up over our life together. The antique armoire I'd found in a thrift store in Queens and lovingly restored over several weekends at a cabinet-making workshop (which, admittedly, I'd only signed up for because it had seemed like a great way to meet single men). The squashy dove-grey couch we'd chosen when we moved in and immediately christened by making love on it. The round pine table that just about fitted into our tiny kitchen, where we'd had so many candlelit dinners.

The kitchen wasn't going to be tiny any more, that was for sure. Walls had been bashed down and replaced with steel girders. The roof had been ripped off to make way for a loft extension. What had been our garden was now a builders' yard. Boards blocked the windows, and it was stifling in the summer heat.

It would be a 'showpiece', Myles said. A bricks-and-mortar advertisement for the fact that Taylor + Associates, his architecture firm, could create domestic spaces as well as commercial ones. It would feature in interiors magazines, he'd promised – and to that end, he'd enlisted Bianca's help.

She'd do the interior design on mates' rates, she'd promised, because we were among her closest friends.

Which was news to me, because sometimes Bianca didn't feel like much of a friend. She'd been Myles's acquaintance first, a contact he'd made through work, and then she'd befriended me too, first inviting us round for dinner – so, of course, we'd had to reciprocate – and later persuading me to join her for Pilates classes and shopping trips.

And now it looked like I was going to find myself living in her dream home.

'This front area can become an intimate snug,' she said. 'With Farrow & Ball Vardo on the walls – so on trend right now, that deep teal shade – and touches of pale rose in the soft furnishings. Mixed metals are so in right now – I'm thinking glowing brass with accents of copper and iron. And a reclaimed parquet floor.'

'And steel interior windows opening through to the main entertaining space,' Myles went on. 'The roof light will really open this up, so we could opt for a dark shade on the walls here too.'

'Absolutely,' gushed Bianca. 'Brinjal, perhaps, and a statement artwork on the chimney breast. I'll add some suggestions to the mood board.'

'We're so lucky to have your support on this,' Myles said. 'A real unifying vision. And of course taking care of the practicalities, while Sloane's so tied up with work.'

It was true, of course – I was tied up with work. Two weeks before, Megan, my business partner at Ripple Effect, the talent agency she founded and I'd joined when I moved to London, had gone off on maternity leave. I was delighted for her, even though I couldn't help feeling a twinge of envy that she'd found herself effortlessly pregnant when she and her husband Matt had only been trying for about five minutes.

'It's crazy, right?' she'd said. 'I mean, one minute you're just a couple and then suddenly – wham – you're going to be a family. I swear pregnancy takes so long to give us a chance to get used to the idea.'

I'd wished, privately, that Mother Nature wasn't giving me quite so much time when it came to my own attempts at pregnancy, and would get her ass in gear. But of course I wasn't going to say that to Megs.

'The timing's awful,' she'd said, 'because Matt accepted that three-month secondment to the Beijing office and I don't even know whether he'll be able to be there for the birth, never mind be hands-on afterwards. But Mum will be around. I'll manage, won't I?'

'Of course you will,' I assured her.

And now I was having to step up and manage Ripple Effect on my own, and the prospect of choosing everything from kitchen cabinets to scatter cushions for the house was daunting to say the least. So I should have been grateful for Bianca's help – but the idea of everything being chosen by someone else felt all kinds of wrong.

Besides, I wasn't sure I wanted to live in a showpiece filled with 'pieces' sourced from the interiors boutique Bianca ran. I wanted to live in a home, a home that would one day contain a family. Where in this 'design-led space' would the oceans of plastic that I knew children accumulated fit? Where in the 'low-maintenance, Tuscan-themed walled garden' would anyone be able to kick a football or play hide-and-seek? How would the expanse of polished concrete on the floor of the 'entertaining space' work when a toddler was taking their first steps and falling over all the time?

'I'm just concerned that it won't be very homely,' I ventured.

Bianca looked at me like I was speaking ancient Greek. 'Of course it will be homely. It'll be your home.'

'Yes, but, once we have a family – what about all the stuff?'

'We've planned for integral storage,' Myles said impatiently. 'Just because there's stuff, doesn't mean there has to be clutter. Honestly, sweetheart, it was all in the initial designs. I wish you'd pay more attention.'

He was right – I'd found the whole design process so confusing that I'd agreed to pretty much everything he'd suggested. The next thing I knew I was packing all our stuff away in boxes to be shipped to a storage unit, creating a makeshift temporary kitchen in what had been our spare bedroom (and which I hoped would one day be a nursery) and coming home every day to look in horror at the expanse of rubble, ladders and scaffolding.

And the dust. Oh my God, don't get me started on the dust. It was everywhere. No matter how much I tried to clean, it seemed to get into every corner, every single item I owned. Even my stockings, when I took them out of the drawer in the morning, rained white powder down onto the carpet of our bedroom.

We were three months into what Myles said would be a ten-month project, and I'd never been so fed up with anything in all my life. And I found that every time I got a call at work from a carpenter needing to know what height to position the ceiling joists at, or from the project manager wanting to know when he'd receive his next payment, or from Bianca wittering on about some wallpaper samples – because, mysteriously, Myles never seemed to be available when these crucial bits of information needed to be imparted – I resented it more and more.

My dream – our dream – of having a baby was looking more distant than ever, because we were too tired, the house was too much of a mess and my mood was on too much of a hair-trigger for me to feel even the tiniest bit erotic.

I mean, you try feeling sexy when your knickers are full of plaster dust. Go on, I dare you.

'Did you have a moment to look at the Pinterest board I set up of possible fireplace surrounds, Sloane?' Bianca cut into my gloomy introspection.

'Not yet.' I forced a smile. 'Why don't you make a list of the decisions we need to make over the next week, and Myles and I will be sure to focus on everything, together?'

'Great plan,' my husband said, glancing at the vintage Rolex watch I'd saved and saved to buy him for a wedding present, even going without cigarettes for an entire week and taking in peanut butter sandwiches for my lunch. 'Shit, I must be off. I've got a client meeting in half an hour. I'll leave you ladies to it.'

Never mind that I'd rescheduled three client meetings that morning to fit this in, hoping that, with all three of us there together, we might actually make some decisions.

He kissed Bianca on both cheeks and me on the lips, swung his leather messenger bag over his shoulder and breezed out, apparently oblivious to my simmering annoyance.

'Now,' Bianca said cosily, once the front door had closed, 'how about a nice cup of tea?'

I opened my mouth to point out that the corner of what used to be the kitchen was a no-go zone filled with dirty cups, the floor gritty with rubble and spilled sugar.

But she was way ahead of me.

'I never visit clients without a flask of my special chai latte,' she said, rummaging in her linen tote. 'You never know when you'll need sustenance on site. And disposable mugs – bamboo, of course, and compostable – and some of my special chia brownies. I've trained Charis to make them; even though she's only seven, that child is a *Great British Bake Off* winner in the making, I can tell you. Shall we go upstairs?'

Upstairs. I felt a flicker of panic, remembering that, although I'd asked Myles to dispose of the remains of our Chinese takeaway the previous night, he hadn't, and that it was probably swarming with flies in the makeshift kitchen.

That left our bedroom – the one room that was at least vaguely habitable and serene. I didn't want Bianca in our bedroom, but I had no choice.

'Come on then.'

I led her up the stairs, half-listening to her remarks about how stair runners were ever so fashionable now, of course, but they did attract dust and we might want to consider a fitted carpet, which was a much more practical and classic choice. I gestured for her to go ahead into the bedroom and watched as she arranged napkins and cups, poured the latte and carefully unpacked the brownies her daughter had baked, which she'd brought in a white cardboard box.

'Recyclable, of course,' she assured me. 'There's no plastic waste in our house. There's a wonderful packaging-free shop just down the road from ours, where I go once a month with the car full of used glass jars, to stock up on dry goods like grains and seeds.'

Thank God I didn't take her into the spare bedroom, I thought, where she'd have seen the multiple plastic pots that last night's sweet and sour pork, oyster chicken and egg-fried rice had come in, not to mention the whole box of plastic knives and forks Myles had ordered from Amazon to save us washing up in the bathroom. She'd have decided we were single-handedly responsible for the tonnes of plastic waste polluting the planet's oceans, and she'd actually have had a point.

I could, of course, have pointed out the hypocrisy of using a car to drive to the packaging-free shop. But she hadn't suggested this little sit-down to discuss how to be eco-friendly, I was sure.

Cautiously, I bit into a brownie, trying not to wonder whether Charis had washed her hands before going full *Junior MasterChef*.

'Delicious,' I said. 'Please pass on my compliments to the cook.'

Bianca glowed with pride, as she always did when praise came the way of her precious only child.

'Now,' she said, as we sipped our tea. 'I wanted to have a little catch-up, Sloane, just us girls together. My job involves not only making my clients' homes the best they can be, but also doing what

I can to ease the process – which is not all fun, as I know only too well. Michael and I have renovated five houses and it doesn't get easier, even when you're as organised as I am!'

She glanced round, taking in the crumpled, hastily made bed, overflowing washing basket and inevitable film of dust on everything.

'Our cleaner's away visiting her family,' I said defensively. 'And we thought there wasn't much point getting someone else in, not while things are like this.'

'Quite,' Bianca agreed. 'Far be it from me to judge! But, as I was saying, I see my role not only as an interior designer, but also as a guide through the process – a bit of a mentor, if you like – and, of course, a friend! And even more so in your case, as we're friends anyway. Sloane, I just wanted you to know that I'm here to help, if anything at all is troubling you.'

'Everything's fine,' I muttered, annoyed to realise that if she carried on much longer, there was a risk I might cry. 'Just, you know, it sometimes feels like it's never going to end. And work's always full-on, for both of us, and it's hard not to let it all get on top of you.'

Bianca gave one of her tinkly little laughs, and I felt the surge of annoyance she so easily roused in me. Luckily, that stopped my tears in their tracks.

'Well, that rather brings me on to what I was going to mention next.' She leaned in towards me and put an immaculately manicured hand on my knee. 'As I said, I do know how stressful this whole house renovation malarkey can be. Just a couple of months ago, I heard from a client – a massive project, which turned out far better than I expected, given that their style ran rather to bling – that their house is on the market. Such a shame, as it was decorated entirely to their taste – with a bit of moderation and guidance from my end.'

'I'm sure it's lovely,' I said. 'What a shame, though, after all your hard work.'

'The point is, they're splitting up. Hence the house sale. The strain of it all got too much for them. Lovely couple, been together almost thirty years with barely a cross word. But they simply couldn't agree on things. It was the bathroom tiles that did it. He wanted beige marble; she'd set her heart on grey ceramic. And of course there's no middle ground, is there?'

I opened my mouth to suggest that perhaps they could have gone for white, but there was no saying anything to Bianca right then – she was in full flood.

'It drove a wedge between them. And of course, for a wedge to be driven, there had to be a flaw in the first place. The tiniest chink, maybe you don't even know it's there, but when the pressure is on, the chink becomes a crack and then a rift. And then Sharon came home unexpectedly one day to find Derek in bed with the neighbour's nanny. She'd already done the school run, cleared away the breakfast things and put a wash on, fortunately. But still.'

It was all I could do not to burst out laughing. 'How awful.'

'Awful.' Bianca sighed. 'They had to sack her, of course, and reliable childcare is so hard to find these days. But I digress.'

The entire conversation had been one long digression as far as I was concerned, but I didn't say so – I didn't get the chance, even if I'd wanted to.

'Even the strongest marriage has its flaws. Michael and I couldn't be happier, but we still have our disagreements. And when he suggested downlights rather than pendants in the living room in our last house, it almost turned into an actual spat!'

She paused and gave my knee a tiny squeeze. 'You and Myles haven't been having any spats, have you, Sloane?'

Shit. So that's what this is all about.

'Spats? Haha. No! We're fine. Absolutely great. On the same page, even down to the kitchen tiles.'

Which was true, literally – the two possible variations of glazed tiles were on the same page of the website we'd looked at together. Except the one I liked was a distressed, industrial glass look, Myles wanted matte cream, and when we'd tried to discuss it things had got so heated he'd stormed out to the pub and not come back until the next day.

But it was fine – he'd slept in his office; he'd just needed to decompress – and we'd find a solution we were both happy with, when eventually I was brave enough to say the words 'kitchen tiles' in his presence again. In the meantime, the subject had joined the growing list of things that simply weren't worth talking to him about, because they were sure to lead to a conflict that would make the US–China trade war look like a minor difference of opinion.

But I wasn't about to tell Bianca that. Myles and I were all good – and if we weren't right now, we would be soon. We just needed to get this nightmare over with, be living in a proper home again, have a baby, and then it would all be just hunky-dory. The prospect of it not being was one I couldn't even entertain in my own head, never mind confide in Bianca about – especially as I knew that she would immediately share any marital or financial strife around our wider friendship group.

I wasn't going there. No way.

'Sure, it's all a bit stressful,' I burbled. 'But we'll get through it. We're all good. Shall we take a look at those wallpaper samples?'

'Of course – they're just down in the car,' Bianca said. 'Would you mind giving me a hand?'

She led the way out, but she wasn't done with me.

'I don't mean to intrude, but I know you mentioned a while back that you two were hoping to start a family, and things were taking a little while longer than you hoped. I know how difficult that can be, Sloane. Have you tried acupuncture at all?'

Unless the acupuncturist penetrated me with something a lot larger and blunter than a needle, that was unlikely to make the blindest bit of difference, I thought.

'Ah, not just yet,' I replied. 'We're seeing what happens. Taking each day as it comes. And we've got all the time in the world. Once the house is finished, we can get right back to focusing on that side of things.'

Bianca stepped aside to let me lead the way down our narrow hallway, but before I could get a hand on the door to let myself out into blissful freedom, take my phone out of my bag and fabricate a work emergency that necessitated me getting back to our office in Soho, like, stat, she said, 'Sloane?'

I turned around. With the door behind me and Bianca in front of me, the beady gaze of her brown eyes fixed on my face, there was nowhere to hide.

'I'm saying this as a friend. As your friend, and Myles's. Sex isn't just for making babies. It's the glue that holds a marriage together. And if you neglect the bedroom side of things, it makes it ever so much harder to deal with stress elsewhere in the relationship. Never mind the fact that it leaves a vacancy someone else could fill. For your own sake, don't be that couple. Don't be Sharon and Derek.'

The little wave of annoyance I'd felt earlier returned. I had better things to do. Like my actual job. Or, failing that, dusting.

'Are you saying Myles is cheating on me? Because if he was, and you knew, I hope you'd tell me outright.'

Now it was Bianca who looked cornered.

'No, no,' she stammered. 'Of course I'm not saying that.'

'Good. Because he isn't. I just remembered, I'm due in a conference call in forty-five minutes, so the wallpaper's going to have to wait. Thanks so much for all your time and help; we'll be in touch just as soon as we've reached some decisions.'

I leaned over and gave her a cursory air-kiss, feeling like I was signing off an email to a particularly persistent would-be client with an emoji to soften the 'off you fuck, now' message.

And then I opened the door and let myself out into the sunshine, leaving Bianca to do the same whenever she was ready.

Chapter Three

Myles and I met online. Yeah, I know. Like, duh. Doesn't everyone these days? At the time, I'd been living in Brooklyn for three years, and it wasn't exactly turning out to be the *Sex and the City* lifestyle I'd dreamed of. Well, there was plenty of city. Just not, you know, the other bit.

Up until then, my life had felt like a bit of a series of uprootings. There was the first one, when Dad's work moved us away from Calgary, the Canadian city where I was born, to tiny Sparwood. Then, after the thing with Mom happened when I was eight, we moved again. And then, because Dad was a geologist working in the mining industry, we moved around some more. I went to four different primary schools and then to boarding school when I was twelve, because Dad was working away so much. I learned – I had to learn, fast – how to make friends, how to fit into a crowd, how to be just the right level of funny and sassy and taking-no-shit, without being perceived as a threat. And that skill stood me in good stead when I moved to Toronto for university, then to Vancouver for my first job, because by then I'd got used to moving around all over the place.

And then I uprooted myself again, moving to New York. I didn't even have a job to go to; I wasn't even following a guy. I just wanted a change, and to realise the image I had of myself as this freewheeling, about-to-be-successful career girl, who'd find a close-knit group of buddies, date hot guys and eventually settle down. Maybe. Or maybe not – maybe I'd be the woman who's in her forties and lives in a sublimely chic apartment (maybe even in Paris; I speak decent French, albeit with a Canadian accent, and dreamed of living in Europe one day), cooks gourmet dinners for her closest friends on Friday nights, goes to the theatre a lot and doesn't need a man.

I was prepared for all those scenarios. *Friends*, *Sex and the City*, *Eat, Pray, Love*, whatever. I was ready to embrace what my future held, with a kind of starry-eyed enthusiasm that makes me feel kind of sad for my younger self, looking back.

Because what I wasn't prepared for was the loneliness. Oh my God, the loneliness. The aching emptiness I felt every night when I got home from work and my apartment was empty because my roommates were out somewhere with friends they already had. And on the odd occasion when they did invite me along to something, there was so much talk of mutual acquaintances I didn't know, or work gossip that meant nothing to me, or old rivalries from way back, that my old fitting-in skills deserted me.

But I didn't let that get me down. Not that much, anyway. Oh, twenty-six-year-old Sloane, with your optimism and your confidence, what a gal you were. I decided that if I wasn't going to have my own Joey and Chandler and Monica and the rest of them, I was going to date.

And not just date: I was going to date like a boss.

I got myself onto Tinder when Tinder had only just started to be a thing. I did speed dating, even though that was already becoming not a thing any more. I went to ballroom dancing classes and patisserie workshops and even tried rock climbing.

And – yeah, I'm cringing a bit – I began to fancy myself as a bit of a dating guru. I Instagrammed the fuck out of every aspect of my life. I started a blog and then a podcast called *Sorry Not Sorry*, in which I dispensed pearls of wisdom and shared anecdotes about my dating experiences, bigging up the funny parts and leaving out the bits that made me feel wretched, unloveable and ashamed. I built up quite a following, and – however mortifying most of those old posts seem today – I haven't been able to bring myself to take them down.

Anyways, so, Myles was a Tinder date. I think he was the twentieth I'd been on that month. I was a seasoned online dater by that point: I was basically the Hound out of *Game of Thrones*, if dating was war, which it's not unlike to be honest. I was a battle-scarred veteran. But, of course, it wasn't a throne I was fighting for – it was love. More than anything, I wanted to find myself part of a team of two, heading hand in hand towards the future.

I had quite the system going. I spent five minutes lying in bed in my lonely room every morning, scrolling and swiping, sending witty one-liners to guys I liked the look of. Then, at lunchtime, I'd check my messages and likes, and block, block, block. Any one-word approach got a block. Anyone I'd exchanged messages with more than four times who wasn't ready to meet up: on your way, motherfucker. Any dick pic: forget about it. And oh my word, there were a lot of those. Big ones, small ones, shaved ones, ones so surrounded by hair they looked like some shy woodland animal peering through the undergrowth. Circumcised ones, ones modestly enveloped in foreskins. A cock rainbow in every shade from pink to ebony. Sometimes, I swear, I felt like I'd seen every wang in all New York's five boroughs and then some. I even dreamed about them sometimes – a kind of peen sequence, and not in a good way.

Anyway, in the evenings, once I'd finished what I thought of as the Bonfire of the Manhoods, I'd spend another half-hour replying properly to people whose messages I thought warranted it, engaging in a way that I hoped was eager, open, but never needy. And after three messages, if I thought someone seemed hot and smart and non-creepy, I'd suggest meeting for a coffee.

The response I received to that generally told me all I needed to know. *Really busy with work right now, but I'd love to see some more photos of you.* No chance in hell. *Let me tell you all about my sexual fantasies.* Tell your hand, loser. *Travelling in Antarctica right now, but let's stay in touch.* #byefelicia.

I was ruthless and efficient and, like I say, I'd gotten pretty damn good at it.

And then I saw Myles's pic, thought, *okay, you'll do*, and swiped right almost automatically. But then I stopped and looked again, wondering why that one tiny movement of my finger on the screen had felt different from the others – more significant. His pic was fine – great, even. He had a cute kind of half-smile, revealing teeth that might not have been healthcare-plan perfect but at least hadn't been knocked out in a fight. The clothes he wore were just the right balance between stylish and no-care. The backgrounds of two of his profile pics were recognisably London and Paris. *Paris.* I can still remember the little lurch of excitement I felt at that. Here was a man who'd travelled, who'd want to travel more, who I could explore the world with. *Could this one be special?* I wondered, barely daring to hope. But soon we were chatting, and he was funny and zany and didn't send me even one pic of his junk. And when he responded to my message suggesting a coffee with, *How about a cocktail instead?* I threw caution to the wind and said okay.

One cocktail turned into three. I was as intoxicated by his British accent as I was by the booze, and his looks didn't do any harm at all. I was charmed by the way he pronounced 'water' and 'vermouth', and enchanted by his giddy excitement about being in New York, where I normally felt like an outsider but, in contrast to him, was a native. The way his denim-blue eyes crinkled and narrowed when he laughed made me melt inside.

So when I asked what had brought him to the Big Apple, and how long he was staying, his answer made me feel punched in the gut.

'I'm here on a three-month gig. I'm about to be promoted to partner at the firm I work for in London, and this project is make or break. I want it to succeed because, yeah, I want to do my best for our client and the business, but more than that – I want this to be the springboard that'll let me set up my own practice.'

'Which would be based…?' I asked tentatively.

'Well, in London,' he said. 'But also, the world. There's so much potential everywhere. The firm I work for now has clients in Singapore, Australia, the UAE – as well as here and in Europe, of course. So right now I'm here, and part of being here is meeting people. People like you.'

And he looked right into my eyes and smiled a smile I'll never forget.

But there was the London thing. The three-month thing. The fucking-off-all-over-the-world thing. But I liked that. I loved the idea of being part of a global couple – that Paris apartment still figured largely in my dreams – and when I thought about London, I was like, *well, why not?* I mean, Big Ben, the Queen, fish and chips with mushy peas (whatever those were) – what wasn't to like?

So we went on a second date. And, that time, we slept together. And it was amazing. Blissfully, spontaneously, meltingly amazing. The time after was, too, and the time after that (and the time after that). And before I knew it, we were an item – until we weren't.

'Sloane, sweetheart,' Myles said one night, after we'd shagged (he called it that, so I'd learned to, too, and the word never failed to make me giggle), 'I'm gutted, but I'm not going to be able to see you next week. You know I said how I want to get my own firm off the ground? I've been approached by a potential backer in London, who's asked for a meeting on Wednesday. I feel like such a snake, but I've got to go for it. If things work out, I'll have to jump ship – and fast.'

'So what does that mean?' I asked, my hard-as-nails dating persona slipping away from me as fast as our sweat dried on my skin.

'It means that, after tonight, I might not be back. And you and I should make a plan about what to do if that ends up being the case.'

And so we did. We lay together that night in the tiny, hot room in my apartment, eating take-out noodles, and we talked and talked. And we ended up figuring out that, if things with Myles's job went as he hoped, I'd come out to London. I'd come, and, if that was what it took for me to stay, I'd marry him.

'I mean it, Sloane,' he said, smiling down at me over a bowl of ramen in a way that was as intense as it was tender. 'Will you? Will you marry me, if that means we can be together always?'

Put like that, there was no way I was going to say no – and I didn't. Less than six months later, we were married, quietly, in a registry office in south London. My dad came out from Canada with my stepmother to be one of our witnesses, and Myles's mother was the second. Afterwards, we went for drinks in a local pub, because neither of us could afford a big reception – I hadn't found a job yet and every spare cent Myles had was being ploughed into getting his business off the ground.

It was quite the whirlwind romance. And now, I felt as if I was courting my husband all over again.

Having weekly date nights had been my suggestion, obviously. These things generally were: over the years, we'd fallen into a bit of a pattern, one in which most of the admin, from booking holidays to emptying the dishwasher, fell to me, because otherwise it just wouldn't get done.

I resented it sometimes – okay, I resented it often. But if the choice was between taking a load of laundry out of the washing machine and moving it over to the tumble dryer while I rushed to get ready for work, or doing it when I got home, late and knackered but not as late as Myles or as knackered as he claimed to be, or having a massive row about it – well, what was five minutes of my time versus a happy marriage?

So, yeah, it was me who'd said – spooked, I guess, by Bianca's words of warning – that we needed to make more time for us, and Myles had happily agreed.

And here I was, at eight o'clock on a Thursday night, when to be quite honest I'd rather have been getting into my pyjamas and flopping on the couch to watch *The Handmaid's Tale* on catch-up, stepping out of the shower and going through to the bedroom, still wrapped in my towel, to decide what to wear.

It wasn't a massive date, obviously. It was a work night, Myles had texted apologetically that he was held up at the office after being on site all day and would only be able to meet at nine, and we were only going for pizza up the road.

But still.

I pulled on a pair of lace-topped hold-up stockings, a black and red lace bra and matching pants, a full, knee-length black skirt printed with red poppies, and a tight black T-shirt, then stepped into a pair of pointy kitten-heeled mules. My style had always been a bit retro, a bit rockabilly, and now it was suddenly back in fashion, which I wasn't sure whether to find gratifying or annoying. Though at least it meant I could shop in the high street, rather than relying on thrift stores and Etsy.

I did my face, hurriedly, sweeping on my signature black winged eyeliner and red lipstick, glad that I'd managed to sneak off at lunchtime to get my eyelash extensions topped up, so there was no need to add mascara. It had rained earlier, making my hair frizz like crazy, but I had no time to put it in rollers, so I scraped it back into a knot, securing it with a vintage enamelled clasp.

Then I hurried down the bare wooden staircase and out, ignoring the chaos of the house behind me.

I was ten minutes late but, even so, I arrived at the restaurant before Myles. It was warm enough to sit outside, and still light, so

I settled myself at a table for two in the courtyard garden. I checked my phone but there was no message from him, so I guessed he was on his way. I ordered a carafe of red wine, and the waiter brought it over with two glasses, a bowl of olives and some breadsticks.

I glanced at the menu, sipped my wine and ate three olives, then told myself I'd better stop and leave some for Myles. Sitting there alone at our table for two, I started to feel horribly self-conscious. I imagined people looking at me, feeling sorry for the woman who'd been stood up, whispering to each other, speculating about whether I'd give up and leave or front it out and eat alone.

Don't be ridiculous, Sloane, I told myself. *No one's looking at you. No one's judging.*

But still, it felt as if they were. I twisted my engagement ring on my finger – it was a plain band of nine-carat gold set with a cubic zirconia instead of a real diamond, all Myles had been able to afford at the time. He'd promised me an eternity ring, a full circle of diamonds, but I'd said we should wait and get it when we had the birth of our first child to celebrate.

Remembering that brought the familiar twist of misery to my gut. I gulped more of my drink and checked my phone again, but there was nothing.

I'd finished the wine and the olives and was about to ask for the bill and go home when he arrived.

'My sweetheart, I'm so sorry. Three-quarters of an hour late – that's unforgivable. But I got a call from a client that couldn't wait – he's travelling in the States and I guess he forgot the time difference – and then there were delays on the Jubilee line and I had to wait ages for a train. How are you? You must be starving.'

I wasn't, really, any more. But he'd ordered a bottle of wine and must have been hungry himself, so I scanned the menu and picked out a salad and an aubergine dish that I didn't really want.

'I'll have the mussels, and the quattro formaggio pizza, please,' Myles said.

And then, the business of apologies and orders out of the way, we looked at each other across the red-checked tablecloth. We were as awkward as people on a first date that wasn't going well or – worse – like one of those couples you see in restaurants who clearly had their last meaningful conversation round about Christmas 2012 and now just stare morosely at each other across the table while they shovel spag bol down their necks.

I rummaged around in my mind, trying to think what I could talk about that wasn't the progress of our house renovation (none that I'd been able to see; the builders had turned up first thing, had a coffee and then vanished off on another job), the importance of us having sex that night because of where I was in my menstrual cycle (ace passion-killer right there), or the hints Bianca had dropped that if I didn't keep Myles in a frenzy of erotic desire, I'd only have myself to blame if he looked elsewhere (not even going there).

I tried to remember what we'd talked about when we were dating. Movies we'd seen, books we'd read, our lives before we'd known each other, our hopes and dreams. We must have talked about all that stuff, and more – I could remember us sitting for hours and hours in bars and restaurants long after our plates and glasses had been bussed, until the staff finished clearing up and turned the lights up in a not-so-subtle invitation for us to get the hell out of there.

'So how's work going?' Myles threw me a lifeline, albeit a mundane one. 'How are you coping without Megan?'

'It's all good, so far,' I said. 'I'm going to visit her tomorrow, to meet little Ethan and bring her up to speed on what's been going on at the agency. Which, to be fair, hasn't been very much. It's been business as usual, really. But that's good, right?'

'Better than it all imploding as soon as her back was turned.'

Myles splashed more wine into our glasses. I was drinking fast – way too fast, given the head start I'd had while I waited for him. I was relieved when the waiter brought over our starters and there was the flourishing of pepper grinders, offering of more bread and careful presentation of a finger bowl for the gentleman.

With its old-school décor, service and menu, Tre Amici was about as unfashionable as a restaurant could get, but Myles loved it, saying that it was how Bermondsey used to be before the property developers moved in, and I'd come to love it too, because it reminded me of the small-town trattorias my dad used to take me to when I was little.

I forked up some salad and Myles tweezed out a mussel using the empty shell of another, then passed it over for me to try. He'd always done stuff like that: if I came downstairs when he was up already, he'd make me a coffee and offer me a bite of his toast. If we ordered cocktails, he'd let me have a sip of his before even tasting it himself. When he shopped online, his order would always include some random gift for me – a scarf or a little box of chocolate truffles or a pair of earrings. I loved his generosity.

The taste of that garlicky little morsel, and the awareness of what it represented, made me suddenly feel relaxed and happy. Or, of course, that might have been down to the fact that I'd necked almost an entire bottle's worth of Primitivo. I forked up some salad – a good bit, with lots of shaved Parmesan and salted anchovy – and passed it across to him, brushing his hand with mine as he took it.

The touch of his skin – warm and smooth, but also strong, somehow, like an expensive leather purse – was another, heady reminder of why I fancied him. Now, I found I could look across the table, meet his eyes and smile.

'So I was on the subway today,' I said, 'and there was this guy. Totally normal-looking dude, in jeans and a kind-of smart shirt and normal leather shoes.'

'Right…'

'Except, alongside all the normal, he was wearing a dog collar.'

'What, he was a vicar?'

'No! Not that kind. A literal dog collar. A studded brown leather one round his neck.'

'Like a bondage thing?' Myles looked amused, fascinated and mildly horrified, as I'd known he would. I adored his essential Britishness; how he'd be shocked and intrigued to see such a thing, but would never, ever lean in for a closer look, as I admitted I'd done.

'Yeah, like that. And you could see the way the strap had worn away, when it had been on a looser setting. It was kind of tight, not restricting his breathing or anything, but definitely snug.'

The waiter brought Myles's pizza and my *melanzane*, and I noticed that Myles waited until the guy was well out of earshot before he said, 'So he'd displeased his mistress, maybe? His punishment might have been getting sent out with a reminder of his status, right there round his neck.'

I laughed. 'That's what I figured.'

'So it gave you ideas, did it? Like next time I forget to put the recycling out or I'm late to meet you for dinner or whatever, it'll be on with the leather humiliation kit?'

'Well, now you put it that way, I'm thinking maybe you're on to something.'

Our eyes met, held each other for a long moment, and then we burst out laughing. Even though I knew Myles had no interest in being a sub or wearing a dog collar, and I couldn't think of anything worse than making him, the brief glimpse we'd shared into the sex life of strangers made everything between us charged with an electricity that hadn't been there for the longest time.

We finished the wine, but we didn't make much headway with the food. Myles kept brushing my knee under the tablecloth, gradually moving his hand higher up my thigh until he encountered the top of my stocking and the skin beyond it, and I saw his face go all still and heard his half-gasp of excitement and pleasure.

'Shall we get the bill?' he asked.

And I nodded, knowing I didn't need to say anything at all.

Chapter Four

'You look so well!' I said to Megan, once I'd finished hugging her, handing over a bottle of champagne, a hamper of ripe blue cheese, camembert and brie (which I knew she'd found so hard to resist during her pregnancy) and a bright yellow fluffy dinosaur for Ethan, who I could only peer at and whisper over, because he was fast asleep in his carry cot.

If I'm honest – well, I wasn't being honest. Megs looked exhausted. Her hair was unwashed, scraped back into a ponytail secured with what looked like the ribbon from another gift. She was wearing a towelling bathrobe that smelled of what could have been cheese but was more likely to be baby puke. And her apartment – which usually looked like something straight out of a magazine – was a mess. There were plates, cups and glasses scattered over every surface, a bumper pack of diapers spewing out its contents in a corner, and the open washing machine spewing its contents out in another.

'Sorry about the state of the place,' she said wearily. 'It's all gone to pot since Matt left to go back to China. He could only stay for three days so now I'm flying solo again. Honestly, it's all I can do to get in the shower some days. Most days, actually. I think I just about managed to get wet in there yesterday before His Highness started yelling his head off for a feed.'

'Oh, bless him!' I said. 'He's so little still. He misses his mommy.'

'He does, of course. It's just – well, he needs me all. The. Time.' She flopped down on the couch and gestured for me to sit next to her. 'He feeds and feeds, so my nipples are shredded – don't worry, I won't show you, it's too gross – and he won't sleep unless I'm holding him. And my midwife says my C-section scar is infected so that's a right state too, and I'm taking antibiotics to clear it up, but they make me sick as a dog.'

The baby squeaked and stirred, and Megan sat upright, then gave a little gasp of pain.

'Let me get him, and then I'll stick the kettle on.' I peered down at the little scrunched-up face and whispered, 'It's okay. He's still sleeping. Why don't you grab a quick shower? If he cries I'll bring him to you. In the meantime I'll clear up a bit. And would you like something to eat?'

Megan stood up, which looked like it took some doing. 'I'll be five minutes.'

'Take your time. Seriously, I've got this.'

As soon as I heard water running in the bathroom, I sprang into action. I rounded up all the dirty crockery and loaded the dishwasher. I opened the door to the garden to let in some fresh air. I transferred the tangle of damp laundry – mostly baby clothes; it didn't look like Megs had got as far as washing any of her own stuff – to the dryer and switched it on. I made a pot of tea and six slices of toast, found butter, jam and Marmite, and put it all on the coffee table.

And maybe it was that that woke the baby. He made a couple of little bleating sounds, and then opened his wide, ink-blue eyes and started to bawl properly. The shower was still running and the bathroom door closed, so I guessed she hadn't heard. I knew next to nothing about small babies, but I reckoned waiting five minutes for his lunch wouldn't do him any harm, so I scooped him up, held him close to my chest – *Oh God, if I drop him she'll never, ever forgive me* – and took him out into the warm, sunny garden, shushing and jiggling him in the way I'd seen mothers do. And, to my amazement, he settled down in my arms, gazing up at the sunlight falling through the leaves of the cherry tree with unfocused fascination.

I stared down at him, equally fascinated. He was so tiny, but he looked almost old, like all the secrets of the universe were held right there in his downy head. His skin was rose-petal perfect, so soft and new I worried that even a kiss would leave a mark on it. The weight of him in my arms was unfamiliar, yet it felt as if they'd been waiting, empty, for this moment for the longest time.

'Sloane?' I heard a high note of fear in Megan's voice and hurried back inside.

'Here we are,' I said. 'We're all good. I think he's hungry, but he was fine. He only cried for a minute.'

'Sorry.' She sat back down on the couch and held out her arms for her baby, who was starting to yell in earnest now. He might have been the most adorable thing ever, but his volume control was seriously lacking. 'It's like, when I can't see him – the anxiety's off the fucking scale. My midwife says it's normal, but Jesus, it's hard. I worry about him so much, all the time.'

She opened her robe – a clean one now – and Ethan snuffled his way to her breast and started sucking enthusiastically.

Megan bit hard on her lower lip. 'God, that hurts. No one tells you how fucking much it hurts. It's okay after the first couple of minutes – well, okay-ish – but at the beginning…'

'You poor thing,' I said. 'It must be tough, having to do it all on your own.'

'I don't know if it would be any less tough if Matt was around.' There was a flash of her old spirit in her voice. 'At least, by the time his secondment finishes, I should have got the hang of things a bit more. We'll be okay. At least I think we will. When it gets too brutal, I tell myself we're just taking it one day at a time – or hour, or minute, depending on how much I feel like taking him back to the hospital and asking about their refund policy. And then other times I look at him and I just want to claw my own heart out because loving him hurts so much. Isn't that right, you greedy little monkey?'

She caressed the back of her son's head, and for a second the scene was what I'd hoped I would find – the orderly room; the serene, doting new mother; the quiet, contented infant. And Megan seemed confident that she'd be able to manage, that it would all be okay.

I felt confident, too, on her behalf – after all, this was a woman who'd built up and managed a successful business from nothing, who'd run four marathons, who could work a twelve-hour day, then do an hour of hot yoga before showering and partying until late, and still be at her desk the next morning at eight, having already sent fifteen emails on the train on her way in.

She *would* cope, I was pretty sure about that. Just, right now, it clearly didn't feel that way to her.

I watched her nursing her baby and noticed her eyes closing. Maybe she was nodding off – maybe she'd get a decent bit of shut-eye, right there, while Ethan enjoyed his brunch, or whatever meal babies had at eleven in the morning. Maybe I shouldn't let her, though; I was pretty sure I'd read on one of the parenting websites I hung out in sometimes that falling asleep with a baby like that was dangerous.

So I said, 'Megs, you could get someone in to help, you know. There are, like, night nannies and stuff. The agency could pay for it. Even though you're on maternity leave, you're still our founder, right? Your health matters. *You* matter, just as much as that little bundle you've got there. And I'm his godmother, right? Which means I've got a special interest in looking after him – and that means looking after you, too.'

She gave me a watery smile. 'Thanks, Sloane. But I'll cope. I'll get through it, somehow.'

I passed her the plate of toast – I'd spread butter and Marmite thickly on a couple of slices – and she took one, folded it in half and ate like a starving woman, apparently not noticing or caring that crumbs were dropping down onto the baby's head. I bet he got bathed right on schedule, though, unlike his mother.

'Sure you will. But for now, you need a bit of support. What can I do? How about if I come and sleep in your spare room a couple of nights a week? Just so you can get some rest?'

'It won't help. It's my boobs he wants. All the bloody time, apparently. Don't you?' And the look of tenderness was back on her face as she kissed the tiny hand that was gripping her thumb tight as a vice. 'Honestly, just having a shower has been amazing. Just talking to another adult. I know I need to get out to baby-signing classes or breastfeeding support groups or coffee mornings or whatever, but seriously? I can't even get my shit together enough to file my nails.'

I couldn't help glancing at her hands. Her nails, which had always been perfect, glossy squovals, were bitten and ragged. I mean, they were only nails. Nothing in the grand scheme of things – nothing compared to having brought an actual new life into the world. But it made me think, *what would I be like as a mother? What would Myles be like as a dad?* This looked like hard, hard work, and although those few precious minutes when I'd cradled Ethan in my arms in the garden had filled me with intense longing to hold my own baby, I also felt something that was maybe fear and maybe awe. How did people do this? Do it multiple times, as if it was the most normal thing in the world?

'I bite his nails, too,' Megan was saying. 'I have to. He won't let me near them with an emery board and he scratches his face to pieces while he's asleep if they get too long. But, like I said, I'm feeling practically human again now you're here, I've had tea and some food and I don't ming to high heaven. It's so good to see you. The best thing you could do is just pop in, when you can, for a chat. Remind me there's life outside these four walls.'

'Of course,' I promised. 'And there are going to be all sorts of things I need your advice on. Seriously. Everything's going fine, but you know – it's like you say, you need to bounce ideas around.'

And so, even though everything actually was running perfectly smoothly, I told her how stuff was going at the agency. I told her how Gemma Grey, one of the first clients I'd signed who'd gone on to hit the big time, had been booked to go on the cover of *Cosmopolitan*. I told her that Rosie, who we'd originally employed two years before as an office assistant and had gone on to become our right-hand woman, had received an offer from a rival agency and I'd upped her salary significantly so we could keep her. I told her about the new ramen bar that had opened down the road where the smoothie place used to be.

As I chatted away, I saw Megs relaxing, engaging, starting to look more like her old self and less like the exhausted, frazzled shadow of it she'd been when I arrived.

'Shit, that reminds me,' she said, rummaging in the pocket of her robe – carefully so as not to disturb the baby, whose eyes were beginning to droop in a milk-drunk way that made my ovaries twang – and getting out her phone. 'I've had a couple of calls on my personal number. Well, I've had loads, obviously, but a couple of them are actually work. And I know you made me promise I wouldn't do any work at all for at least the first two months…'

'I did. And I'm holding you to it. Hand over the phone before I get the Feds to take it off you by force.'

She hooted with genuine laughter. 'God, I'm so happy you're here. So, Ruby-Grace Miller's freaking out. You know she auditioned for *Love Island* but didn't get on? Well, now she's throwing a total diva strop and saying her career's over and it's somehow all our fault. I didn't even get to the end of her message because this one started bellowing at me, but she's really upset. Could you get her in for a face-to-face, maybe? Calm her down a bit, come up with some ideas for what she can do next?'

'No problem,' I said. 'I know how high-maintenance she is. I'll give her a call and sort something out. Manage her expectations, if nothing else.'

She reached over and gave my hand a squeeze, carefully checking that the small movement wasn't disturbing the now deeply asleep Ethan.

'And then there's Vivienne Sterling. First client I ever signed, ten years ago. I thought I'd hit the big time with her, but how wrong was I? Anyway, Sloane, I'm really sorry, but you need to go and see her.'

'Of course. No problem at all.'

The look on my friend, partner and former boss's face was all I needed to tell me that it was going to be a very big problem indeed.

Chapter Five

I worked from home the morning I was due to go and meet Vivienne. Normally, of course, our clients came to us. Not for nothing had Megan invested heavily in a swanky Soho address and chic interior design: it was our shopfront, our way of creating the impression of Ripple Effect as a far bigger hitter than it actually was. In reality, the agency was just Megs, me, Rosie and a rotating cast of freelancers and unpaid interns, but if you looked at our website or walked into our office you'd think we were a seriously big deal.

And we weren't going to squander that investment – not to mention our time – by going to see our clients in their homes. Well, the important ones we did, of course – the YouTuber Glen Renton even had a freelancer permanently at his beck and call, doing everything from watering his houseplants to ironing his shirts, as well as managing his diary, writing his blog and Instagram posts and dealing with his regular, epic strops.

I'd offered Gemma Grey – initially a rising star in the YouTube world and now well established, with five million followers and three book deals under her belt – the same, but she'd looked at me with her enormous Bambi eyes and said, 'Don't be daft, Sloane! I can do all that myself. It's not like I'm Meghan Markle or someone.'

Anyway, the fact that Megan had told me I'd have to go to Vivienne Sterling's home in suburban south-east London for our meeting had been a hint in itself that she was something of a special case. Now, I was perched at the tiny table in our second bedroom, which also held the microwave, kettle, coffee machine and toaster, conducting some last-minute research into her background.

Vivienne was an actress, as Megs had told me, and – unsurprisingly – it was hard to figure out her age. For several years in the late nineties, she appeared to have been thirty-nine. That, I guessed, meant that she could be anywhere between sixty and seventy now, and probably nearer the latter.

Her CV early on in her career was fairly standard: she'd been to a well-known performing arts secondary school and then done her drama training at RADA. She'd had several minor roles with the Royal Shakespeare Company before getting her big break as Cordelia in a production of *King Lear*, for which she'd won several awards and a sheaf of glowing reviews. She'd looked, back then, set for stardom.

But at some point it all appeared to have gone wrong. She hadn't worked at all for the past seven years, Megs had told me, which meant she hadn't brought in any revenue for the agency, but Megs had kept her on the books for sentimental reasons, as well as because her name was still well enough known for it to be trotted out to impress a certain type of potential client.

Now, though, Vivienne was looking to reboot her career – a tough ask for anyone in any industry, but for an ageing actress vanishingly unlikely to happen. She must be desperate for money, I thought. If I could only figure out what had gone wrong – what had led to her going from playing Desdemona at the National Theatre to doing pantomimes in Blackpool and being the face of a fabric softener on telly – I might be able to come up with a plan to get her earning again.

I typed her name into Google once more, trying to search for mentions of her that were more than fifteen years old, but as the results flashed up on the screen, I sensed that I was being watched and heard a discreet shuffle of feet behind me.

Shit. It's the builders.

Sure enough, when I turned around, there were Wayne the bricklayer and Shane the carpenter, hovering just outside the room. I'd heard them stop working a few minutes before, I realised – I'd grown so used to the crashes of masonry and whine of power tools that I barely noticed it until it stopped. And now it was ten o'clock.

'Sorry to bother you, Sloane,' Wayne said.

'We can see you're busy,' said Shane.

Well, yes, I was. And I was tempted to say so, but I didn't.

'How are you getting on down there?' I asked.

'Getting there, getting there,' Shane replied. 'Just laying the last of the ply, then they can start pouring the floor tomorrow.'

'We'll need to get another coat of intumescent paint on them steels,' said Wayne. 'Otherwise they'll never get through building control, on account of the fire regulations.'

But they weren't here to talk about fire regulations. There was another reason why they were both loitering there, watching me, shoulder to shoulder in the doorway in their high-vis jackets and steel-toed boots.

I sighed and stood up, stretching the tension out of my shoulders, which were all knotted from hunching over my laptop, but still standing defensively in front of the table. Together, Wayne and Shane took a step over the threshold. They looked hesitant – diffident, even – but they knew they were going to get what they wanted. All three of us knew – after all, they always had before, every single time.

It was inevitable; I just had to get on with it.

'Would you guys like a coffee?'

Shane's face lit up like he'd thought I'd never ask.

'Wonderful! Cappuccino, please, Sloane. Two sugars. If it's not too much trouble.'

'I'd love a peppermint tea, if you have any.' Wayne was practically salivating.

I closed my laptop and switched on the kettle and the coffee machine, trying not to let them see my annoyance. After all, as Myles had pointed out so often, this was my fault entirely. I'd made a rod for my own back.

But it wasn't my fault. I'm Canadian, for God's sake. We've got old-fashioned ideas about courtesy. When the builders arrived on their first day on site I'd offered them a hot drink as soon as they walked in the door and brought it to them on a tray with a plate of home-made choc-chip cookies. They'd acted as if all their Christmases had come at once, and I'd been delighted – I wanted them to like me.

I'd believed, somehow, that by providing baked goods and hot drinks, I'd fuel their endeavours and get the building project finished sooner and more smoothly.

How naïve I'd been. Almost as naïve as thinking I'd find myself up the duff the second I stopped taking the Pill.

'Just give them a kettle downstairs and let them get on with it,' Myles had advised. 'Buy some lump sugar, if you want, otherwise they'll tread it all through the house. Or don't – let them bring their own.'

'But I can't! They're guests in our house!'

'They're working for us, sweetheart. They don't expect it.'

But, of course, once I'd started, they did expect it. Every day, if I was home, I made multiple rounds of teas and coffees. I'd become a dab hand at making chocolate fudge cake in the microwave. On Fridays I made platters of smoked salmon bagels.

But all the home baking and fancy espressos weren't making the blindest bit of difference. The project was still behind schedule. The house was still a chaotic shell. And, to add insult to injury, Wayne and Shane had taken to turning up on Fridays, drinking their tea and coffee and devouring their bagels, thanking me profusely – and then, as soon as I'd left for work, disappearing off to spend the rest of the day working on another project like I was the local Starbucks or Tim fricking Hortons or something.

And when I moaned to Myles about it, he was able to say, quite justifiably, that he'd told me so.

Thanks to Wayne and Shane's complex and ever-escalating requirements ('Oh, I'd love the milk frothed just a bit, if you don't mind', 'I don't suppose you've a spare iPhone charger anywhere, do you, Sloane?'), it was late by the time I left for Vivienne's place.

I'd planned to take the Tube and then a train, or possibly a bus, but that, while being the sensible, environmentally friendly thing to do, would take the best part of an hour. And there, right outside, was my darling, ancient little yellow Mini, which I'd stretched my finances to their limit to buy soon after arriving in London.

Now, I needed to be somewhere my mapping app told me would take twenty minutes by car and forty by public transport and – oh, look – I had a car, and I wasn't afraid to use it.

Three minutes ahead of schedule, I pulled into a suburban street lined with Victorian terraces on one side and sixties low-rise flats on the other, wondering which kind of dwelling was my client's. It was an important distinction: if she lived in a house, chances were Vivienne owned it. If, on the other hand, she was a council tenant in a flat or renting privately, her situation might be more precarious.

I found a parking space, checked the complicated rules on the sign above it to make sure I was allowed to leave my car there (I'd been caught out and clamped more than once in my early days of London driving) and got out.

It was a boiling, sunny day, still high summer with no sign of rain. I could feel my T-shirt clinging to my back where it had been pressed against the car's leather seat, my thighs clammy under my skirt, and I was grateful for the shade of the chestnut tree under which I'd parked my car.

I checked the street numbers, which were made extra confusing by the presence of the block of flats, which seemed, randomly, to be in the hundreds. On my right, though, the Victorian houses went in orderly progression: 36, 38, 40. Vivienne's was number 62. I crossed the street and walked along the sidewalk, the sun beating down.

Unlike most of the other houses on the street, it didn't have a freshly painted door or white shutters in the windows. The front yard was bare and paved, the render coming off the brickwork in parched-looking sheets. The door had once been green, but the paint was faded and flaking, the number two missing one of its screws and leaning drunkenly against the six.

As I approached, the door opened and a middle-aged man emerged. At least Vivienne had other visitors, I thought, and then I noticed the British Gas logo on his turquoise and black polo shirt, and the toolbox in his hand.

'You here for the lady in there?' He gestured back towards the door.

'That's right.'

'You her carer?'

'Her…?' Megan hadn't mentioned anything about a carer. Maybe her problems were greater than I'd realised. 'No, I'm just a friend.'

He put his toolbox down next to his van and folded his arms, lowering his voice as he said, 'It's bad in there. Really bad. I see plenty of places, trust me, but that…'

'What do you mean? Bad how?'

He grimaced. 'You'll see soon enough, love.'

And he opened the van, swung his gear inside and drove off.

Full of trepidation, I approached the house and knocked. The knocker was an iron ring, stiff with lack of use and rusted in places.

I waited for a long minute. If she didn't answer, I'd try calling. I imagined the phone ringing and ringing in the silent house, and wondered what I would do if there was no reply.

But, at last, the door opened and Vivienne Sterling stood there, smiling.

In the flesh, it was impossible to narrow down her age. She was tall and rail-thin, her legs as fragile as twigs where they emerged from her denim mini-skirt. Her hair was dyed almost black, but a good two inches of white roots showed at her hairline. Her skin was lined, but not deeply, and was pearl white – the skin of a woman who'd never succumbed to sun-worship or smoking – and her eyes were remarkable, huge and grey-blue. I could see how beautiful she must have been as a young woman. She was still.

But my impressions of Vivienne herself were drowned out by what I saw beyond her – and what I smelled. In the heat of the day, the reek that came out of that house was overpowering. It wasn't smoke, or cats, or rotting food – it was just dirt. The oppressive stench of a house that hadn't seen bleach or antibacterial wipes or even a hoover for a long, long time.

'Darling! You must be Sloane. Do come in.' Her voice was much younger than her face, clear and actressy, the product of years of training.

'Hello, Vivienne. Lovely to meet you.' I extended my hand for her to shake, but she leaned in instead and kissed me on both cheeks. I was almost knocked sideways by a waft of strong perfume, which couldn't even begin to hide the smell of gin on her breath – a smell that, even now, made me feel frightened and helpless.

She turned and led the way into the house, and it took all my willpower to force myself to take the first step over the threshold. There was a carpet on the hall floor, a long runner extending into the gloom and up the shadowy staircase, but it was almost indistinguishable from the floor on either side of it; everything was thick with dirt. I could see dusty cobwebs festooned in every corner, catching the sunlight from outside. It was impossible to tell what colour the walls had once been. My shoes stuck to the floor as I followed her inside.

It made my own home, dust and all, look like something straight out of *Good Housekeeping* magazine.

'Can I offer you a tea or a coffee? I suppose it's too early for a drop of sherry,' Vivienne said, although it was clear that, for her, it was nothing of the kind.

I could think of nothing I wanted less than to put anything near my mouth that had been in that house. But, when Vivienne made the offer of a hot drink, I saw her eyes rest on my face and a brief flash of awareness cross over her. She knew. She knew exactly what I saw in her and her home, and what I was thinking.

And she was ashamed.

'That would be lovely, thank you,' I said.

I followed her through to the kitchen. The curtains covering a door that presumably led to the garden – I dreaded to think what state that was in – were closed, as was the blind over the window that looked out onto the street. The curtains were dark with grime, the ghost of a geometric pattern barely visible. The metal Venetian blind was so thick with dust and grease I couldn't imagine it ever opening.

Vivienne flicked on the kettle. There was a clean patch on the switch where her thumb must have pressed, over and over. She took a small box of teabags from a cupboard into the depths of which I didn't even want to look – not that I could, because the bare forty-watt bulb hanging from the ceiling would have given out very little light even if it hadn't been filmed with dirt.

Over the reluctant hum of the kettle, there was suddenly another sound, tentative at first, building up to a steady patter and then a roar.

Vivienne looked up from the two mugs she was carefully placing teabags into with a trembling hand. In the angle of her jaw, the tilt of her head, I saw a woman who'd been trained to expect cameras to be always on her face.

'It's raining,' she said.

'Finally! How long has it been now – six weeks with not a drop?' It felt comforting to be able to share a bit of weather-related chit-chat.

But Vivienne looked dismayed. 'I thought we could have our coffee out in the garden. But now we can't.'

'That's okay,' I soothed. 'I'm fine indoors, really.'

Now that I'd been in the house a few minutes, the smell was less of an assault on my senses and more a background horror, which made me breathe shallowly. And, of course, all the time I was keeping a polite, bright, professional smile on my face, even though I felt that the dirt might be sticking to my teeth.

Vivienne handed me a mug, which looked relatively clean, with a teabag soaking in its depths. I thanked her and she said, 'Come through to the front room, then, darling, and let's have a nice chat.'

I followed her through the dining room, where a table that looked like it had once been polished mahogany was now thick with dust and littered with piles and piles of unopened post, newspapers, magazines that should have been glossy but weren't, and unwashed plates and glasses.

The lounge was the same: drifts of paper, empty blue plastic carrier bags and gin bottles, discarded clothing, CDs and DVDs in haphazard piles, many of them toppled over, lay on every surface. Only one couch, facing the television, was clear of junk, and here Vivienne sat, gesturing for me to join her.

She had said nothing about the state of the place. It wasn't because she didn't notice it, I was sure – it was as if, by ignoring the elephant in the room herself, she hoped I would somehow not notice it.

'Tell me all about yourself,' she said brightly. 'And about dear Megan, and the little one. How are they both?'

Her question wasn't asked just out of politeness or curiosity, I realised. It was her way of deflecting me from the obvious things I was going to have to ask: *what had happened to her? How could she be well enough to work? What could I possibly do to help her?*

So I chattered away for a bit about Megs and the baby and answered her questions about myself and how I'd come to move to London.

'So romantic!' she exclaimed. 'You moved halfway across the world for love!'

'I did.' I smiled. 'One of my rasher decisions. But it all seems to be working out okay. I love my job. I love working with such talented people, helping to get their careers off the ground – or to resume them, after a bit of a break.'

This was a business meeting, after all – if I was going to help her, I had to find out when and why things had gone so badly wrong for our client.

'I haven't worked for a few years,' Vivienne said, with what I guessed was meant to be a cheerful laugh but sounded almost hysterical. 'I've been resting, as the saying goes. But I've realised that I'm not quite ready for retirement.'

'Of course, in your business, plenty of people never retire – it's a vocation as much as a career, isn't it?'

'Exactly!' Her poise recovered, she tilted her head and opened her eyes wide. 'I feel I still have so much to give. And besides…'

She paused, and I waited for her to carry on.

'I need the money, Sloane.' Briefly, the mask slipped and I saw naked fear in her face. 'I've been living off savings and investments, and now it's practically all gone. I'm skint.'

'Are there any particular goals you have in mind?' I asked carefully. 'I mean, are you thinking of stage roles, or television commercials, or film?'

If she got her shit together – like, a lot – she might just be able to cope with a few hours' filming for a TV ad, I thought.

'I do appreciate that I'm not the big name I once was,' Vivienne said. 'I'm starting again, in a sense. So I don't mind taking smaller roles at first, just to get my hand back in.'

Which, I supposed, was at least some acknowledgement that she was virtually unemployable.

'Okay. Let me put some feelers out. I'm sure you know as well as I do that it's tough out there, but we'll do what we can. We're totally committed to doing our best for you.'

And that, as I was sure she knew perfectly well, was my way of telling her that there was no way I could make her any promises.

'I'm sure you will, darling,' she said. 'And I'm so grateful to you for coming all this way to see me. Do drop in again. I don't get many visitors.'

The understatement of the century.

We stood up and I carried our mugs through to the kitchen, trying not to wince as the smell of gone-off food assaulted my nostrils again. If Megan's house had needed a bit of a tidy-up, this was in another league entirely. It would take a crack team of cleaners, probably in hazmat suits, to make any impact at all.

I said goodbye, and she kissed me again, and I headed outside, inhaling great gulps of the rain-fresh air. I'd intended to go straight into the office, but there was no way. I drove home – back to the house that had felt so chaotic that morning and now seemed like a haven of peace and order – took a boiling shower and put all my clothes on a hot wash. Even after that – for several days – I kept remembering the smell of that place and imagining Vivienne waking up there, alone, day after day.

And my own dreams were filled with memories I thought I'd put behind me long ago, so I found myself reaching for my sleeping tablets at night, hoping to find oblivion, if not actual peace.

Chapter Six

I've got one photo of me and my mother together. In it, she's wearing denim dungarees and a red and white striped T-shirt. Her hair is done in one of those spiral perms that claimed so many victims at the time. She's wearing giant round spectacles, a fashion statement just for the camera, I suppose, because in my memories her eyes are always bare of everything, even make-up.

She's holding me, in that photo. I must have been almost too big, but she'd held me anyway, hefting me up onto her hip so our faces were touching. I asked Dad once if the picture was taken the day we moved into the white clapboard house you can see behind us, dwarfed by the soaring blue mountains behind it, which in their turn look small against the vast, deeper blue expanse of sky. But Dad says it was taken later, when we'd been there a few months, right before winter fell and things started to go wrong.

I can't blame Mom, really, looking back. When I was six, Dad's job moved us from Calgary, a city I can barely remember, to Sparwood, a tiny town almost two hundred miles away. Mom had quit her job when I was born – I guess she'd had some vague idea of going back to work later on.

But there was no work for her in Sparwood; there wasn't a whole lot of work for any women, unless they were nurses, waitresses or teachers. Oh – or mining engineers. Not that there were many women doing that job, back in the early nineties.

So there Mom was, in the house on Cherrywood Boulevard, alone every day while I was in school. She could have looked for work, I guess – found an admin job with the mining company or something. She could have joined the golf and country club, only she didn't play golf. She could have gone to aerobics classes at the recreation centre, as so many of her contemporaries did, made friends and had coffee or lunch after.

But she did none of those things.

I do remember that, in those first few months at least, she tried to keep things settled, for Dad and me. I'd get home from school and find the house sparkling clean, music playing softly on the stereo, whatever she was making for dinner already filling the kitchen with smells that made me want to know when Dad would be home.

'Not for hours yet, honey,' she'd say. 'Let me fix you a sandwich, if you're hungry.'

And she'd make me something to eat, and maybe we'd do some kind of craft together, or walk round the neighbourhood, or watch a video. And then at around six, while I was having my bath, I'd hear from downstairs a sound I grew to anticipate with the same certainty I waited for the thunk of the car door closing and the key in the lock when Dad got back from work.

It was the rattle of ice cubes in a glass.

When I went back downstairs in my pyjamas, I'd find Mom on the chesterfield, watching whatever was on TV, almost horizontal, a drink in her hand. In the beginning, she'd still be herself at that stage – happy to help me with my homework, let me set the table ready for when Dad arrived.

But after that first winter, that changed.

I don't know why. It snows in Calgary, too, after all. I think Mom's sense of isolation was about far more than the deep drifts that surrounded the house, bleaching the landscape.

Maybe it was the time she skidded on ice driving to the supermarket and hit a tree, leaving her jittery behind the wheel even once the written-off car was replaced. Maybe it was that I was making friends, not coming home right after school to keep her company like I had before. Maybe it was Dad going back to the firm's head office in Calgary for a few days a month, so she didn't even have his arrival to look forward to.

But I do know that by the time I started second grade when I was seven, life had taken on a different rhythm. I never knew, when I walked up to the green-painted door after school, what I was going to find.

Sometimes, Mom was more or less herself. The cheese or turkey sandwich would be made, we'd snuggle together on the couch and it might be a while before she fell asleep, the glass of ice and clear liquid in her hand spilling onto the beige corduroy if I didn't catch it in time.

Sometimes, I'd wait outside and knock and knock, and there would be no response. The first time that happened, I didn't know what to do. I stood, shivering even in my windcheater and winter boots, knocking harder and harder, and calling for her, until Mrs Tremblay next door heard and came and let me into her house. She said Mom must have popped out and I could wait with her until Dad got home before I caught my death of cold, and why didn't she fix some pancakes.

Sometimes – the worst times – Mom would open the door and she'd pull me close against her, the smell in the house of scorched food, vodka and fear. Then, she'd say, over and over, 'What am I going to do, Sloane? What's happening to me? I'm such a bad, bad person. No one will ever forgive me.'

And I'd try to cuddle her, ignoring my rumbling belly, until she fell asleep on the couch or on the rug in front of the fireplace – cold and unlit – and I'd sit there by her until I heard Dad's car in the drive and jumped up, giddy with relief, knowing that he'd get Mom to bed and fix us some food from the freezer.

Dad knew things weren't right. Of course he did. Later, when I was older, he apologised over and over for not doing something sooner, and not doing more later on. I guess he must have thought that it was just the winter, and that when spring came Mom's mood would lift. And then when spring did come and she was just the same, either morose or manic or passed out, cracking open the vodka as soon as she was alone in the house, I guess he must have looked forward to summer, when I'd be home and able to keep her company.

They talked about what was going on, of course. On weekends and in the evenings when I was in bed, on the rare occasions when Mom was in a state to talk at all. I'd hear Dad starting out all calm and reasonable – even pleading – and Mom's cold, one-word answers. And then it would escalate, until they were both shouting at each other, furious, frightened words that I buried my head underneath the pillow so as not to hear.

The summer holidays came eventually, and for a while Mom was better. She and I went for walks together. She talked about getting a bicycle so we could explore further afield, but that never happened. Dad took us camping and Mom cooked bacon and eggs for breakfast over the Primus stove and swam in the lake with us, and got a tan, and seemed happier.

But then the leaves started to turn colour, and Mom's mood turned too. When I said goodbye to her in the mornings, I saw an unfamiliar expression on her face that I realise now must have been fear. Fear of the long day stretching ahead of her, fear of her own weakness that she'd fight and fight against, until she couldn't any more.

And, I expect, fear of how it would all end.

Dad grew more desperate. He checked Mom into a hospital for a while, and for a month I went to Mrs Tremblay's every afternoon after school until Dad collected me. I remember those weeks as being strangely happy and serene, and when Mom came home, she was better – for a while. The house was clean again; comforting smells of cooking greeted me when I walked in the door. I'd lie in the bathtub and wait and wait for the rattle of ice cubes, my fist squeezed around my washcloth so tight it hurt to release my fingers – but the sound didn't come.

For a month or so, over Christmas and into the next year, everything seemed like it would be all right again.

And then it wasn't. I don't know what tipped Mom back over into that dark, lonely place. But one day, I arrived home and she opened the door in her bathrobe, a glass in her hand. I knew, somehow, that this wasn't just a blip, and when Dad got home I could see from his face that he knew, too.

The row they had that night was the worst one ever. I lay under my quilt, shivering with horror, too afraid to cry, until eventually, in the early hours of the morning, I fell asleep.

And when I got in from school the next day, Mom wasn't there. Her car was gone and so was she. She hadn't packed any clothes apart from her winter coat, I heard Dad tell the police officers who came round much later. She'd only taken a few hundred dollars in cash – no passport, no driving licence. Nothing that could have identified her but the registration plates on the car and the clothes she was wearing.

Chapter Seven

'Would anyone like some more salad?' Bianca asked, passing a wooden bowl around the table. 'Or a little more of the tempeh bake?'

'It was all delicious,' I lied. 'But I'm absolutely stuffed. I couldn't eat another thing.'

'I'll make us all a pot of fresh mint tea, then,' Bianca said. 'So good for the digestion, after a heavy meal like that.'

I looked longingly at my empty wine glass, but clearly no more booze was going to be forthcoming – or indeed any dessert. Bianca had added a total ban on sugar to her new healthy-eating regimen. Dairy products had been first to face the axe, followed by wheat, red meat, all animal products – and now, not so much as an organic date or a spoonful of honey was allowed to sully the temple of purity that was her body.

I glanced across the table at Myles and wondered if he was thinking, as I was, that stopping off at the pub on the way home and necking a stiff drink and sharing a portion of fries was on the cards. Like Bianca's diet, her home had also recently undergone a makeover. Just a few months back, her kitchen had been all countrified, with a scrubbed pine table, a quarry-tiled floor and even bunches of herbs and lavender hanging from the ceiling.

Now, she'd redone it in an urban, industrial style, with exposed brickwork on the walls, stainless-steel worktops and open steel shelves holding the chunky white plates and recycled glassware she'd purchased.

I sometimes wondered what her husband, Michael, who was presumably footing the bill for these constant transformations, made of it all, but I'd never asked. Michael, Bianca had told me, ran his own company 'in logistics'. Myles had subsequently informed me that his business was actually Bettabogs, which supplied chemical toilets for large-scale events like festivals and which Bianca clearly considered beneath her.

Sometimes I caught myself wondering whether she considered Michael himself beneath her, too.

'And how's your work going, Sloane?' Michael asked, as his wife poured fragrant hot water into retro glass cups with steel handles.

'Not bad. I met a new client the other day. Well, new to me. Vivienne Sterling. I'd never heard of her, but I believe she was quite well known here a good few years back.'

'Oh my God,' Bianca breathed. 'Vivienne Sterling! She was amazing. My parents took me to see her in *Macbeth* – ever such a long time ago now – and I totally idolised her for a while. But then she seemed to completely drop off the radar. There was some sort of scandal, I recall, but I can't remember any of the details now. I had no idea she was even still alive. What's she like?'

'Very beautiful, still. But…' I hesitated. It felt wrong to share the details of what Vivienne and her life had become. 'I think she's quite troubled. I guess she's had a difficult life.'

'Wasn't she married to Max Sterling?' Myles said. 'The director? Didn't he win an Oscar for something, back in the day?'

'*Dark Rhapsody*,' Michael replied. 'It was a kind of noir art-house thing. I've got it on DVD somewhere, I think.'

'I do keep saying, sweetheart, that you need to get rid of all those old CDs and DVDs of yours. It's so pointless and such a waste of space, when we can stream everything online now. And it makes that study of yours look like such a man cave.'

Michael ignored his wife's reproach – if he'd even heard it. I reckoned the ability to tune Bianca out would be an essential survival skill for him. 'Want to come up with me, Sloane? I'll see if I can dig it out.'

'Sure! That would be great.'

I followed Michael upstairs. The new industrial décor had been extended to there, too, with a series of framed prints of photographs taken in disused factories lining the stairs, hung against a wall painted battleship grey. Bare filament light bulbs in tarnished copper holders that looked like they were made from upcycled pipes illuminated the landing.

'In here.' Michael opened a door and led me in. 'This is my study. Or rather, as her indoors puts it, my man cave.'

To be fair, I could see where Bianca was coming from. The room was lined with shelves groaning with books, magazines, vinyl records and even plastic cases of VHS tapes. A huge TV was mounted on one wall. In a corner was a desk holding a computer and an Xbox, and a giant leather gaming chair filled almost all the remaining space.

'Sometimes you just need to get away from it all, right?' Michael said, sounding slightly defensive.

'Of course you do. And that chair's seriously cool.'

He brightened. 'It's designed for pro gamers. It's got 4D-adjustable armrests and memory-foam cushioning, and it offers a full ninety-degree recline. It was my Father's Day present to myself earlier in the year. Well, it was from Charis officially, of course. We took a special trip out together to buy it.'

It felt kind of sad, I thought, that Bianca's disapproval of Michael's man cave – and presumably his hobby – was so stringent that he had to use his daughter as an excuse to treat himself. But then, maybe Michael's hobby meant that he holed himself up in that room for hours and hours, neglecting his duties as a husband and father, and Bianca's resentment was entirely understandable.

I had no way of knowing; Bianca had never hinted to me that things in her marriage were anything other than rainbows and roses, all the way.

Michael cleared his throat and looked, slightly guiltily, towards the closed door.

'Can I offer you a drop of something? Bourbon, maybe?'

'You know what, I'd love a bourbon. Thank you.'

He nodded approvingly and moved a stack of magazines off a shelf. Concealed behind it was a tiny fridge, the kind hotels use for their minibars. He took out an ice tray and threw a couple of cubes into two glasses, then added whiskey. After a moment's hesitation, he produced a box of Ferrero Rocher from the fridge, too, and offered them to me.

Accepting that chocolate and Jack Daniel's felt seriously weird. Like I was being inducted into some kind of secret society. Or maybe like I was enabling a dangerous, destructive habit that his wife would be appalled by. But how was Michael having the odd treat in the privacy of his study really all that different from the wine and fries Myles and I would no doubt indulge in on our way home?

I knew Bianca's ways: if she said their home would be an alcohol-free, sugar-free zone, there'd be no point Michael objecting. Well, he could, of course, but Bianca would end up getting her own way. The only question would be whether it happened before or after World War Three.

So I sat in the absurdly comfortable chair and watched while he rummaged through shelf after shelf, running his finger along the spines of his movie collection proudly and lovingly, occasionally taking one out to show me, saying, 'Now this – this – is a great film.'

Soon, we found ourselves deep in conversation. I couldn't persuade him that Scorsese was a much better director than Tarantino, but I learned that he shared my unashamed fandom of *Buffy the Vampire Slayer*, *Star Wars* and *Game of Thrones*.

While we chatted, he splashed more whiskey into our glasses and we finished all the chocolates.

At last he said, 'Aha, here it is! *Dark Rhapsody*, directed by Max Sterling and starring his wife, Vivienne. I saw it in the cinema when it came out and bought it on VHS, then when we got rid of the player I just had to own it on DVD too.'

He passed the plastic box over to me. The cover art was in shades of navy blue, silver grey and black, and it was dominated by a woman's face – a face I instantly recognised as Vivienne's. God, she was stunning. Cheekbones you could use to open an envelope, lashes so long they cast shadows, lips so full and pouting you'd think she'd been at the filler, although I wasn't sure that was a thing back then.

'We could start watching it now, if you like,' Michael suggested. 'The opening scene's a cracker. I guarantee you'll love it.'

I glanced at my watch, briefly tempted, then realised we'd been up there for almost an hour. Bianca would be furious – even though she had no reason to be; I was just socialising with her husband.

'Myles and I should probably be heading home…' I said.

'Sure.' Reluctantly, Michael stood up. He was a big bear of a man, well over six foot tall, with the build of a rugby player and a prominent nose that looked like it had been broken at some point in the past, and a pair of thick-framed spectacles. He was also a good ten years older than Bianca – pushing fifty, I reckoned, albeit in good shape for a man of his – or indeed any – age.

I wondered, not for the first time, what had attracted Bianca to him – she was so image-conscious, the kind of woman you'd expect to marry a banker or a lawyer who wore thousand-pound suits and visited his barber every other week for a trim and a wet shave. Michael's money must be part of it, I guessed, but tonight he'd revealed another side of his character – he had a passion.

'I'll just pop to the gents,' he said. 'See you down there in a second.'

'Cool,' I replied. 'And thanks for the movie. I'll watch it over the weekend and let you know what I think.'

I padded downstairs. Bianca's was a shoes-off house, and there was a basket of felt slippers by the front door which she suggested

– or insisted – her guests slip on. I'd obeyed, trying not to think of the athlete's foot their previous wearer might have had – although I'd reassured myself that it would take a seriously determined fungus to survive in Bianca's spotless home.

The kitchen was empty, everything tidied away and the lights turned down low. I could hear the hum of the dishwasher, and saw the red digital display projected onto the floor saying it had two hours to go. From the front of the house, I could hear music playing – some sort of modern jazz, which I hated but Myles adored.

The lights in the living room had been turned down low, too. I could smell whatever room fragrance Bianca used – something clean and sophisticated, like freshly ironed linen.

Myles and Bianca were on the couch, next to each other, very close. They were talking intently but quietly, and I couldn't make out their words over the music. But, as I watched, Bianca stretched out a hand and touched my husband's thigh, quite near the top, and gave it a little squeeze.

'Uh, hi there,' I said. 'Sorry we disappeared for such ages.'

When they heard my voice, they sprang apart like two magnets suddenly turned the wrong way around.

'We should get going,' Myles said. 'It's late.'

In that moment, everything changed. I went from thinking that everything in my marriage was more or less okay – and if it wasn't, it would be, just as soon as the house was finished and I'd got a double line on a pregnancy test. My dad always used to say that if you believe in yourself and work hard for your goals, nothing can stop you.

I'd believed in myself. I'd put in the hard yards. I grafted at my job and my marriage and my friendships and – well, everything. And, mostly, I achieved what I set out to. I won't say I'd led a charmed life – of course I hadn't. Plenty of things had gone wrong for me, but when I got knocked down or knocked back, I picked myself right up again and carried on.

But this – this I wasn't sure I could handle.

Myles and I didn't talk on the way home. We got into an Uber and he stared at his phone, not tapping on the screen like he was messaging someone, just staring and scrolling and staring and scrolling. And I gazed out of the window, trying to get my thoughts into some kind of order.

Bianca had hinted that Myles might be playing away – or at least considering it. I'd dismissed her warning out of hand, thinking that she was just trying to meddle, or seem like some kind of oracle of wisdom.

At the time, I'd genuinely believed I was right. If Myles was being unfaithful, I'd know. Don't ask me how, but I would. Some deep-rooted spider sense would tell me, and I'd confront him, and if I was right I'd leave. Maybe. Or maybe, if leaving didn't seem like the right thing to do – if his transgression had been relatively minor, like a drunken snog on a night out, or something – we'd talk things through and see a counsellor and fix things so that it would never, ever happen again.

But now, there'd been evidence, right there in front of my eyes, that something wasn't right. It wasn't just the way they'd been sitting together, oh so close, and the way Bianca had touched – okay, stroked – my husband's long, denim-clad thigh. That by itself I could have put down to her habitual boundary-pushing; her assumption of an intimacy that wasn't actually there.

It was the way they'd behaved when they heard my voice; when, in my Scandi-chic felt slippers, I'd padded silently up behind them and abruptly announced my presence, and they'd reacted like they'd both just had a thousand volts zapped through them.

But if my new-found suspicion – which was rapidly crystallising into certainty – was correct, why the hell would Bianca have alerted me to the possibility that my husband was fooling around? Why wouldn't she have wanted me to remain oblivious, the stereotypical wife who's always the last to know?

Watching the rows of dark houses and lit-up shop-fronts flash past the cab's windows, trying to take deep, steadying breaths of the cloyingly pine-scented air, listening to the meant-to-be-soothing sound of Smooth Radio and the driver occasionally taking a call, I struggled to figure it out.

And then it hit me.

What would I do, if I was married to a man I no longer found sexually desirable but who offered me the financial stability, security and status (so long as you were able to look past the chemical toilet thing) I craved? Well, if that were me, I'd have a long hard think, beyond the present to the next forty or however many years of my life, and I'd make a decision based on my long-term happiness.

But what if I had a daughter to think about? And, more to the point, what if I was Bianca, a woman who seemed to thrive on drama and intrigue and secrets? What if I was Bianca, in that marriage that seemed happy enough on the surface but might be riven with problems beneath it? And what if, in her position, I met someone else?

Someone like Myles.

Someone who was, by any measure, infinitely desirable. Handsome, successful, polished and groomed like an expensive car. Charming, sparky, funny, sexy. But taken.

What if I fell for him, and he for me? And what if the situation was further complicated by me being friends with his wife?

Well, if that were me, I'd walk away. No question about it. I wouldn't even acknowledge the chemistry that was there, the growing closeness. I'd put my feelings back where they belonged, in a secret no-go zone deep inside me, and I'd carry on. Either I'd work to make my marriage better, or I'd check out of it in a sensible, sensitive way.

But if I was Bianca?

I tried to put myself inside her head, feel her emotions, share her insecurities. But it was so hard – even though I'd known her, and seemingly been her friend for a couple of years now, I didn't really understand her. She was like a Teflon pan with an impermeable surface off which everything from a drop of water to a burned omelette would glide without trace.

And, thinking about that, I figured I had my answer. If I was Bianca, I'd want to get my man. But I wouldn't want to do it with a load of mess and carnage and fallout, like chucking a hand grenade into my own life. I'd want to do it by stealth. I'd want my result, but for it not to have been instigated by me.

So I'd find fault-lines I could exploit, and I'd gently chip away at them, widening them gradually and imperceptibly, until suddenly everything fell apart, leaving a clear field for me – or at any rate, for me if I was Bianca.

She'd begun that process already, I thought, by insinuating herself into our marriage by offering to design our home. And she'd built on it further by sowing seeds of doubt in my mind that would make me cantankerous towards my husband, and make him more likely to contrast his needy, scrappy wife with the smiling, accommodating, admiring presence of her rival.

If that was how it was, it was going to be all-out war. And I was in it to win it.

Chapter Eight

In it to win it. The words reverberated through my hung-over brain the next morning, when I pinged awake next to Myles's snoring form at five thirty in the morning. At first, I wasn't sure what they meant. Instinctively, as I always did, I ran through my checklist of things I needed to do that day.

Spruce up Vivienne's résumé and sound out a few directors who I knew had massively tight budgets and could be attracted by the lure of a big name, even if that name hadn't been big for twenty years. Meet with Ruby-Grace Miller to talk about her career aspirations now *Love Island* was off the table. Tell Wayne and Shane that the delivery of our new kitchen had been delayed by a week or possibly more. Make appointments to get my eyebrows and lashes done, legs and bikini line waxed and gel nails in-filled. Pick up Myles's suit from the tailor who'd been taking up the legs.

Oh. Myles.

Thinking of my husband instantly brought back what I'd seen the previous night. Myles and Bianca. My husband and my so-called friend. The reminder was like a bucket of cold water being chucked over my head and, with it, all prospect of further sleep vanished.

I swung my feet onto the floor and stood up. God, I felt like seven shades of shit. Michael and I must have got through more whiskey than I'd realised. My head hurt, my eyes were scratchy and dry and my mouth tasted foul.

But all that was nothing compared with the deep, sick weight of dread that filled my stomach. *I think my husband's having an affair.* Saying the words, even silently inside my own head, made them feel more real.

I glanced over at Myles. He was deeply asleep, his face still and relaxed, one arm thrown up behind his head. He looked just the same as he did every morning. There was no hint in his peaceful face of anything wrong.

I wondered if he was dreaming about her.

Next to him, on the nightstand, I could see his phone, plugged into the charger as it always was. I walked carefully around the bed and reached for it, but just as I touched it, it vibrated and beeped softly. An incoming email from a client abroad, maybe. Or maybe something else. It was face down, so I couldn't see, and the sound had disturbed Myles's sleep; he turned over, before pulling the duvet back over himself.

This is not a smart idea, Sloane. If I took the phone into the other room and it rang, Myles would wake up for sure. And he'd want to know what I was doing. And I'd have to tell him. I wasn't ready for that yet. If there was going to be a confrontation – and I wasn't sure I wanted one, not yet – I needed to be prepared and in possession of far more information than just a hand on a thigh, a start of guilty surprise.

I needed proof. And I needed a plan.

I went through to the bathroom – the one part of the house that was actually, properly finished. With its freestanding copper tub, walk-in shower, expanse of marble surrounding the washbasin and piles of carefully folded, fluffy towels, it was just how I'd wanted it to be: a haven for pampering and relaxation.

Only I didn't feel relaxed now.

I peeled off Myles's old T-shirt I'd worn in bed and squeezed toothpaste onto the brush, catching sight of my reflection in the mirror. *Jesus.* I didn't just feel like shit, I looked like I'd been dug up after several days. My hair was a tangled snarl, there were clumps of yesterday's mascara still clinging to my eyelashes and black smudges under them that were either also make-up, or just the legacy of a crappy night's sleep. The pillow had left a deep crease in my cheek.

In it to win it.

One thing was certain: I wasn't going to win anything unless I upped my game.

I cleaned my teeth, even though the feeling of the brush in my mouth made me want to gag, switched the shower on to boiling and got in.

An hour later, I was ready to face whatever the day had in store for me. I'd got myself ready for work far more painstakingly than usual, ironing every last bit of frizz out of my hair, smoothing on scented body lotion and using industrial amounts of concealer to cover up the dark circles under my eyes and the angry red spot that had erupted on my chin.

I'd put on a navy blue wiggle dress with tiny red dots that I knew Myles loved – the first time I wore it, he'd literally whistled and said,

'One of the things I love about you, sweetheart, is that you've not only got curves, you're not afraid to use them.' The memory gave me a small, much-needed confidence boost – as did the matching navy satin bra and pants I slipped on underneath. He did fancy me – or he had, at any rate.

I slipped my feet into ballet flats for my commute to the office, tucking my mid-heeled red peep-toe shoes into my bag to change into later, and checked that I had everything else I needed. Only then did I allow myself to switch on the coffee machine. It was still not yet seven, so I had time for a leisurely breakfast. I microwaved some oatmeal, added cream and maple syrup, and perched at my makeshift desk to eat, trying to gather my thoughts.

It might well be that nothing was happening with Myles and Bianca – or, at any rate, nothing from which there was no turning back – yet. I knew that there was an element of truth in what she'd said to me: that, when a marriage was under strain from external factors, infidelity was more likely to happen.

I knew I'd been cranky and snappy with Myles, annoyed that the ambition of the building project had thrown our treasured home into chaos and worried that the end result would be more about winning awards and appearing all over people's Pinterest boards than about creating a home for us to raise our family in.

I knew that my anxiety about conceiving a baby had made sex feel functional and lacking in the spontaneity and passion we'd both revelled in so much before.

So, I figured, sipping the last of my double espresso and spooning a final mouthful from the bowl, I needed to do two things. First off, I needed to find out what, if anything, was going on. I needed to get hold of Myles's phone at the earliest opportunity and have a look at what was on there. It would feel wrong, and horrible, and intrusive. It *was* all those things. But, at the same time, it was necessary. I needed to be in full possession of whatever facts I could gather before I had a serious conversation with him about what – if anything – was going on.

And anyway, it wasn't like we had some sort of strict confidentiality thing going on between us. My own phone was often lying around, Myles knew the passcode, and if a text came in when I was having a bath or painting my nails, I'd often ask him to check it. I knew his passcode too: one zero eight zero, because the football team he supported had last won the FA Cup by one goal to nil in 1980.

I knew it, but I'd never needed to use it. Until now.

I'd have to wait for the right opportunity. I'd need a good half-hour to have a proper look through his email, text messages, WhatsApp and photographs. If I found nothing, I'd be reassured. If I found anomalies – messages that seemed to have been replied to, for instance, but the reply was missing, or a contact saved under a name that looked false – I might have to investigate further. Though God only knew how.

But the important thing, I decided, was to bide my time, wait for the right moment and do my investigation – okay, my snooping, because that's what it would be – discreetly.

In the meantime, my strategy had a second prong. It was based on the assumption – which I hoped with all my heart was the correct one – that nothing was actually going on. That, at most, Myles had looked at Bianca and compared her with me, and the grass had appeared greener on the other side of the fence. That he'd noticed how she pandered to him, thought how much of an asset someone like her could be to his architecture business and then seen other things about her too: her pearly skin, her pert breasts, her slender ankles, her tiny ass.

Which was all fair enough, I thought, trying to force down a wave of sick envy. Married people had crushes too. Just because you had a ring on your finger didn't mean you'd never look at anyone else that way again, ever. Hell, I'd had my moments too, like when Ripple Effect signed David Albright, a former footballer, to launch him into an exciting new career as the face of a well-known brand of low-fat ready meals. For a few months, I'd caught myself getting all giddy with excitement when I had a meeting with him in my diary, dashing into the ladies to spray on scent before he came into the office, and even having the most cringe-making dreams in which we declared our mutual passion for each other and lamented that we could never be together.

And then David asked us to manage the publicity for his wedding to his partner, Phillipe, and my crush died an easy, painless death right there.

So, yeah, I got it. Myles might have a crush on Bianca. And the way to counter that was to remind him about all the things that first attracted him to me. Hence the trouble I'd taken with my appearance that morning. And until I had evidence that there was actually anything untoward going on, I was going to double right down on my efforts to be the perfect wife.

I fired up the coffee machine again and made a cappuccino for Myles, extra hot, the way he liked it. I rummaged in the tiny freezer compartment of the temporary fridge that currently served as part of my desk, found a pack of crumpets and stuck them in the toaster. Then I slipped off my ballet flats, retrieved my high heels from my bag and stepped into them and, a couple of minutes later, I was bringing my husband breakfast in bed, just as his alarm went off.

'Hey, you,' I said. 'I brought you a coffee.'

'What?' Myles sat up, blearily pushing his hair off his face. 'Coffee? Oh. Thanks.'

'And crumpets. Because we never got to stop off for fries last night.'

He reached out for the plate and bit hungrily into a crumpet.

'God, darling. You're an angel. Just what I needed.'

'All part of the service.'

'And look at you, in that foxy frock. Come here.'

I sat on the bed next to him, carefully weighing up my options. On the one hand, I wanted him to want me, and I wanted him. But, on the other, I was freshly made-up and dressed and could hopefully get out of the door before the builders arrived.

But there wasn't much of a contest. Myles won.

I leaned over and kissed him on the mouth, tasting oily saltiness on his lips. I slid my hand down underneath the duvet, caressing his chest and belly, and running my fingers teasingly close to – but not quite where – I knew he wanted them to be. I felt his own hand reach for the hem of my dress and try to ease it up over my hips.

The dress was fitted snugly over my thighs, and it was quite the challenge. In the end, he had to abandon his breakfast and use two hands. I kept kissing and stroking him while he grappled with it, then, after a few minutes, we broke away from each other and started to laugh.

'Get me – Mr Smooth,' he said. 'I know how to undress a woman.'

I stood, quickly rucked the skirt up to my waist, stepped out of my knickers, and then got back onto the bed, this time straddling him, the duvet pushed aside. He was naked, the way he always slept, and I buried my face in his chest, inhaling the musky, sleepy man-smell of him.

Slipping lower, I kissed my way down his abdomen, running my tongue over the line of fine hair that began at his belly button. He was hard already, eagerly waiting for my lips, and I heard his gasp of pleasure as I took him in my mouth.

We'd been together a long time. I knew what he liked, and I did it, slowly at first, teasing him with my lips, hands and tongue, not caring about the state of my lipstick, then gradually building up speed as I heard his breathing turn fast and ragged.

'Sloane. Oh God, darling, I'm going to…'

'Wait.'

I shuffled up the bed and slipped myself down onto the hot hardness of him, taking him deep inside me. There was a moment of pressure, then I felt him filling me, the pressure giving way to pleasure. He gripped my hips and moved me in the rhythm of his thrusts, closer and closer, until I broke off our kiss so I could see his face when he came inside me.

'Sloane. Oh my God. I love you.'

His breathing was fast and ragged, and mine was, too.

'I love you too.' In spite of everything – all my doubts and suspicions – it was true. Surely, surely, he couldn't have said the same words to Bianca? Not last night on the couch in that softly lit room – not ever. If I wanted enough for it to be true, it must be.

I rolled over and lay next to him, waiting for my heartbeat to slow.

'Sweetheart, was that okay for you... Did you...?'

'It doesn't matter.' And in that moment, it didn't. It might have been just for him in one way, but in another, it had been all for me.

Normally, I'd have waited, lying there still for as long as I could, waiting and hoping that, somewhere inside me, two gametes would meet and fuse: a moment of biology so fundamental, yet so tiny and subtle there was no way of knowing when it happened, or if it happened at all.

But today there was no time. I needed to get to work, and anyway, my period was due in a couple of days – there was very little point even hoping for a miracle today.

Myles had picked up his phone. 'Shit. I'm due to meet a client on site in forty-five minutes. You've made me late, you temptress.'

He sat up and swung his legs off the bed, bending to retrieve my pants from the floor and chucking them over to me.

'Let me run to the bathroom first,' I said. 'I just need to get cleaned up and fix my face, then it's all yours.'

I stepped back into my high-heeled shoes, forgetting my practical flats, and picked up my handbag in one hand and my knickers in the other, hurrying out onto the landing, my skirt still rucked up around my waist.

And then I stopped dead. Because there, halfway up the stairs, face to face with me – or rather, mortifyingly, face to vag – were Wayne and Shane in their high-vis jackets. They must have come into the house when we were too caught up in passion to even notice.

We all froze. Wayne turned around to hurry back downstairs, no doubt hoping that if he got out of there fast enough we could all style it out. But Shane was blocking his descent, standing there gawping at me like he'd never seen a landing strip before.

'Uh, good morning, Sloane,' he said. 'Any chance of a coffee?'

Chapter Nine

All the way to work, I kept remembering what had happened and cringing so hard I practically turned inside out, in between full-body blushes. I remembered standing there for a second, unable to move, before whipping my knickers in front of me like an inadequate blue fig leaf. Which, of course, if anything made matters worse. I was torn. Did I sprint back to the bedroom, or forwards to the bathroom?

The bathroom won. I locked myself in and texted Myles, telling him that he'd better bloody well make the builders their coffee and take them downstairs, and keep them there, right at the far end of the house, for as long as it took for me to escape, because I never wanted to see either of them again in my life, ever.

But I'm desperate for a piss, he texted back, *and I need to shower and leave for work.*

I DON'T CARE! I just gave them an eyeful of my muff.

You what? And he added a whole load of emojis, clearly indicating that at least someone found the situation funny.

I hastily cleaned myself up, stepping into my stupid underwear at last and easing my dress back down. I waited, literally shifting from foot to foot with impatience, while I heard Myles switch off the coffee machine and exchange pleasantries with Wayne and Shane as if they hadn't just seen his wife practically in the buff. I heard their awkward, monosyllabic replies; clearly they weren't as good at fronting this out as he was.

'Now, I've just got a question about the angle downstairs where the steel's fitting into the party wall,' he said. 'Can you spare a second?'

I heard their three sets of footsteps on the stairs and peered out of the window until I could see them through the skylight below.

Then I made a run for it.

And now, I was in the lift going up to the sixth floor and the Ripple Effect office, having stopped on the way to pick up a coffee.

As always, stepping through the door made me happy. Whatever curveballs life threw at me, however riven with doubt I was about my marriage, my home and my uncooperative reproductive system, here at least I felt calm and in charge.

Rosie was already in, sitting behind the desk in the reception area, which was lined with glossy headshots of our most famous clients. Isla and Sam, our latest two interns, were there too, leaning against the high counter of the reception desk, chatting to her.

When they saw me, they both sprang to attention as if they'd been caught doing something wrong. Bless their cotton socks, I thought. If only they knew that the agency would more or less grind to a halt without the benefit of their low-paid labour. I felt bad about the fact that they worked for no more than their Tube fare, an allowance for lunch and a payment that was little better than pocket money. I felt worse about the fact that being able to do so was considered a massive opportunity, a lucky break into a competitive industry, and that the nature of the work meant it was open only to those with comfortably off parents who could afford to keep their twenty-something kids at home while they forged a career.

'Hey, guys,' I said. 'How's everyone this morning?'

'Oh my God, Sloane, I am so hung-over,' lamented Rosie, pushing a strand of silky dark blonde hair back off her face. Even if she was feeling like death, her skin looked fresh and dewy and her eyes were bright and clear. It was yet another reminder that I was ten years older. 'That function I went to last night at Alcotraz was amazing. Phoebe Waller-Bridge was there, but I managed not to go full fangirl. We ended up staying until they chucked us out, and then we went on to a dive bar and then for a kebab. I legit thought I was going to die this morning.'

'Well, kudos for getting in early,' I said. 'Can you face eating? Sam, why don't you pop out and get a round of bacon sandwiches – or whatever you fancy, Rosie – and some full-fat Coke or orange juice or whatever? Grab some money from petty cash. And then I'd like you to join me in the meeting with Ruby-Grace Miller. She's coming in at eleven. Isla, you're off to Reading later, right?'

'Right,' she said. 'To do that book signing with Gemma Grey. Oh my God, I'm so excited to meet her! Do you think she'd sign a book for my little sister?'

'Of course she will,' I said. 'And make sure you keep back a goodie bag for her, too. Just make sure the venue's got proper checks on the door – it's confirmed guests only, and keep an eye on social media in case some smart-ass decides to leak details of the location. Order yourself a cab, and make sure you tell them it needs to have plenty of room for all the merch and stuff.'

'Great!' Isla said.

'And please give Gemma my love.'

Isla hustled off to her desk, and Sam headed for the lift.

Once they were out of earshot, Rosie said, 'Vivienne Sterling rang for you. Really early – the phone was ringing when I got in just after eight.'

'What did she want? I know she's looking for work but it's only a couple weeks since we met. I'm good, but I can't work miracles.'

'She didn't exactly say. Sloane, if I'm honest, she didn't sound great.'

Shit. 'Not great how?'

'Well, to be totally honest, she sounded a bit… what my dad calls tired and emotional,' Rosie said. I admired her diplomacy: we all knew that Ripple Effect's clients could sometimes be total nightmares – Glen Renton's reaction when his hairstylist gave him an all-over number one buzz cut instead of the low fade he'd requested was still talked about in hushed tones – but there was an unspoken company policy to try to keep slagging them off to a minimum.

'Right. Did you manage to catch anything at all?'

'Not really. She asked for you, and I said you weren't in yet, and she said something about maxed. I thought maybe a credit card or something. She was like, "Maxed it, maxed it, maxededed," but I couldn't really make it out, because then she started to cry. I tried to talk to her but she just said to let you know she called. At least I think that's what she said.'

I heard the lift ping behind me, and Sam emerged laden with paper bags from the hipster deli down the road, which masqueraded as an old-school greasy spoon but charged three times the price.

'Okay, thanks, Rosie,' I said. 'Leave it with me.'

'Bacon buttie, Sloane?'

'Thanks, Sam, but I already…' I caught a waft of savoury goodness coming out of the bag. Breakfast had basically only been porridge, after all, and a long time ago. 'Oh, go on then. Good man.'

Ten minutes later, second breakfast demolished, I'd tried Vivienne's landline twice and listened to it ring out, imagining the persistent trill sounding through that squalid house. I wasn't sure what to do. I couldn't cancel my eleven o'clock, and I couldn't leave Sam to do it on his own – he was keen, but he was inexperienced and there was no way he'd be able to deal with a potentially pushy client. Even Rosie, who I trusted implicitly, might be out of her depth, given what Megs had told me about Ruby-Grace.

And that wasn't the only item demanding my attention. There was an approach from *The Coolector* magazine for an interview with Charlie Berry. I had an inbox full of emails I needed to respond to, including one from the fashion retailer luxeforless.com wanting to book one of our up-and-coming influencers for a shoot. And Liz, the blindingly competent retiree who did our books, was coming in the next day and I had a mountain of paperwork to get ready for her.

I tried Vivienne's number one more time, listened to it ring and ring, and eventually hung up. I realised I was gripping my phone so hard my hand hurt, the familiar sense of guilt and helplessness washing over me. *She's not your mom, Sloane – she's a client.* But still, I'd have to go and see her. I checked my calendar: I had two hours free tomorrow, round about the middle of the day. Last time I'd met her at that time, she'd been sober. Or sober-ish. I'd have to come into the office in the morning, sack off my lunchtime hair appointment, then get the train to Hither Green and work from home in the afternoon.

Which would mean seeing Wayne and Shane again. *Oh God. Dying.* Once more, the blood rushed to my face as I remembered what had happened that morning.

'Um, excuse me, Sloane.' Sam appeared by my side. 'I've written up some bullet points on Ruby-Grace Miller. Can we run through them together before our eleven o'clock?'

I pushed back my chair. 'Sure. It's ten thirty now, so why don't we head through to the meeting room? Will you sort some tea and coffee, and water, and I guess some biscuits or whatever?'

The Ripple Effect meeting room was my favourite thing about the office. I remembered when I'd come to meet Megs the first time, to be interviewed for the job I desperately wanted, looking around at its three stark white walls and one scarlet one; taking in the elliptical white table, surrounded by sculptural white chairs; admiring the framed portraits on the walls, and thinking, *This woman is a pro.*

It was typical of Megs: she understood that, in our business, image was everything. And now, even though the portraits of our clients were more numerous than they had been back then, and there were the additions of a floating shelf on which a host of award trophies jostled for position and a squashy white velvet chaise longue (on which we had to warn clients not to sit if they were wearing new jeans), I still felt the same sense of excitement when I walked in.

I saw Sam pause and smile when he came in with the coffee tray, and I knew he felt the same.

'So,' he said. 'Ruby-Grace. She's twenty years old, from Exeter originally but lives in London now. Her mum's Kelly Burke –

apparently she was a Page Three girl, back when that was a thing. And she did various nude shoots for lads' mags, back when those were a thing.'

I nodded, remembering that Sam was only twenty-two – for him, the pre-#MeToo era must feel like ancient history.

'Her dad's a footballer. Kyle Roberts – played for a few Championship teams but never really hit the big time. He's retired now, obviously, and so's Kelly, but they're not together any more.'

'Okay. Nice background intel there.' He hadn't told me anything I didn't already know, but it was good to see he'd done his homework.

'Anyway, so I guess Ruby-Grace always wanted to be famous. She was on *Britain's Got Talent* a few years back, with a teen girl band, but they didn't get very far. She already had an Instagram account though, and a YouTube channel, and she got a bunch of followers from there. And after Ripple Effect signed her last year, that scaled quite fast and she got a few influencer-type deals through us. And then she auditioned for *Love Island*.'

'But she didn't get on.'

'Nope. I'm not sure why – she totally looks the part. I guess maybe there was another girl who was similar who they liked better.'

Another girl they liked better. So far, since arriving at the office, I'd managed to engross myself in work and push my thoughts about Myles and Bianca out of my mind, but Sam's words brought the horrible reality rushing back. Once again, I remembered Myles and Bianca next to each other on the couch. Like a high-definition camera, my memory zoomed in on her hand on his thigh; that intimate, caressing touch.

'Don't you think, Sloane?'

My mind jerked back to the present, and I realised I'd missed a load of what Sam had been saying.

'Well, let's see what she has to say for herself,' I replied lamely.

'Ruby-Grace is here.' Isla opened the door and ushered our client in.

Obviously, I'd seen Ruby-Grace's Instagram feed and YouTube channel. Her portrait was right there on the wall of the meeting room. But still, nothing could have prepared me for the reality of her in the flesh.

Ruby-Grace wasn't tall, but her six-inch Perspex heels made her the same height as Sam, and she towered over me. She was wearing a neon-pink vest top that ended just below her nipples but had a layer of fringing below hanging down to the bottom of her tiny white hot pants. Her body was – well, let's just say it must have taken an enormous amount of work in the gym and a fairly extensive amount of work in a private cosmetic-surgery clinic to achieve curves like that. She had platinum-blonde hair that fell in glossy waves halfway down her back. Her eyelash extensions were so long they almost reached her perfectly microbladed brows, and her lips were plumped with filler and painted the same colour as her top. She had a see-through plastic handbag in one hand and a miniature dachshund in the other. In spite – or perhaps because – of all the various enhancements, she was mind-blowingly pretty.

Sam was gazing at her, transfixed, like a man who'd seen a vision.

'Hello, Ruby-Grace,' I said. 'Thanks for coming in. It's lovely to meet you. And who's this?'

'This is Minou.' She carefully deposited the dog on the floor, and it settled down with a weary sigh. 'She's my baby – she comes everywhere with me. Could she have a drink of water, please?'

'Of course.' I bent down to stroke the smooth nut-brown head. 'Are you thirsty, Minou? Sam, would you mind…'

'Sure.' But Sam didn't get up. Instead, he picked up the phone on the table and I heard him ask Isla to bring a bowl of water. It wasn't like him to pull rank on a colleague like that – especially not a female one – and it took me a second to work out that he was both trying to impress Ruby-Grace with his seniority and also reluctant to waste a second he could spend gazing at her.

'Now,' I said, once Minou was lapping happily away, Sam and I had coffees and Ruby-Grace had a glass of filtered water and was looking at the plate of biscuits the way I imagined her little dog would look at a cheeseburger. 'As you know, Megan's off on maternity leave, so I'll be looking after you in her absence, with some help from Sam. Megs mentioned that you had a bit of a knock-back from *Love Island*. You must have been disappointed about that.'

'I was gutted, if I'm honest. I mean, like, they approached me and asked me to audition. And I went through the whole process. I worked so hard for it, and I really wanted to experience that journey, Sloane. I really feel that I have something to offer to viewers. And it would have been so great for my career.'

'Yes, of course, I quite—'

'And I, like, really wanted to find love in the villa,' Ruby-Grace interrupted me, presumably realising she'd gone off message. 'I've been single for a year and a half now and I just know there's someone special out there for me.'

'*Love Island* is a very pressured experience, though,' I said, choosing my words with care. 'Of course, we do our very best to help our clients achieve their goals, but if it's a long-term relationship you're after I'm not convinced that's the place to find one. Look at all the couples who break up straight after the show – the island's not like real life, and then you come out of there into this media frenzy, and there's no time for your relationship to grow. But, of course, we're a talent agency, not a dating agency. Much as we'd like to, we can't always help with life goals as well as career goals.'

'But you didn't help with my career goal,' Ruby-Grace pointed out. 'It's been my dream for three years to get into the villa and I feel like I've been mugged off before I even started. You know what I mean?'

She took a tissue out of her transparent bag and carefully dabbed it under her eye.

'You could apply again next year,' Sam said. 'A few people have done that and been accepted second time round.'

Then he blushed furiously, as if amazed at having found the courage to speak.

'But I don't want to go on next year! I want to be on now! They'll be flying out there literally this weekend, and I'm here in pissy London.'

'I know it's disappointing,' I replied. 'But it is what it is. There are so many opportunities for you here – there's all sorts of exciting stuff going on with our partner brands that I know they'd just love you to be involved in. Cuticle Inc., you know, the nail enamel, are looking for a brand ambassador, and you'd be absolutely perfect for them.'

I glanced at Ruby-Grace's nails. They were a perfect coffin shape, protruding almost a centimetre beyond her fingertips, and painted in alternating hot pink and white, except for the index finger on her right hand, which was gold glitter.

'I don't do my own nails,' she said petulantly. 'God! Where would I find time for that?'

I wondered how making the journey to a nail salon and sitting there while someone applied a full set of acrylics then painted and cured them was less time-consuming than slapping on a coat of enamel at home, but what did I know? Clearly my standards were not the same as Ruby-Grace's.

'Okay, I take your point. How about activewear? We've just got a new brand on board, Lulu and Luther. They're really edgy and fun – all about bringing a bit of glamour to your workout. Sam, shall we let Ruby-Grace have a little look?'

Sam fired up his iPad, which was connected to the big screen at the end of the room. He tapped onto a website, then scrolled through a few screens of images of fit, smiling models wearing leggings with mesh inserts, sports bras with skinny criss-cross straps and Lycra in animal, marble and psychedelic prints. Their stuff was seriously cool – almost cool enough to make me want to visit the gym for the first time in months.

'Yeah, that's all right.' Ruby-Grace inspected a fingernail. 'But do they want me to, like, wear it in the gym? And post pics on Insta? Because when I work out I look manky as fuck.'

I felt a flash of admiration for her honesty. The body I'd clocked with awe when she walked into the room couldn't have been achieved by doing some gentle stretches and lifting the occasional dumb-bell while wearing a full face of make-up, that was for sure.

'You could do selfies and stories before your workout, maybe? Or after, once you've showered?'

Ruby-Grace looked shocked. 'But I believe in showing my followers my true self.'

I almost laughed out loud. Bless the woman – her true self, breast implants, hair extensions, nail art and all. There was a kind of internal consistency going on there. Probably.

'I see, right,' I said. 'So maybe something a bit more glam would work best for you. We've already got you working on the MissMinx fashion brand, and they totally love you. That top you're wearing is from there, right?'

'Yeah, they're all right,' she said. 'I mean, I deeply value my partnership with them. But if I'm going to grow my career, Sloane, I need more opportunities, more exposure. I want to reach out to more people, connect with them on a deeper level. Like, Gemma Grey, she's got a make-up collection coming out. Can't I do that?'

Quite what was deep about putting your name to a range of highlighters and lip stains, I wasn't sure. But it was pretty clear that Ruby-Grace wanted to hit the big time, with all the money and recognition that came with it, and wasn't too bothered about how she did it.

'Have you thought about doing some charity collaborations? A few of our clients are involved in that side of things, and it's great for building your personal brand, while also, of course, making a positive difference to people's lives.'

'Yeah.' Ruby-Grace inspected her fingernails. 'That or, like, *Celebs Go Dating*, or *Ex on the Beach*.'

Once again, I had to suppress a giggle.

'Okay, Ruby-Grace,' I said. 'It's clear you want us to explore more opportunities for you. I get that. You're fantastically talented, you've got a great, engaged following, and we're really proud to be working with you. And with Minou, of course – the camera just adores her!'

The little dog opened one eye and sighed as if to say she didn't adore the camera one bit.

'I really hope you'll have some good news for me soon, Sloane,' Ruby-Grace replied, standing and scooping up her dog and handbag, 'because let me tell you, I've been approached by other agents and it's just because I'm so loyal that I've stuck with Ripple Effect. For now.'

Oh no. Not the ideal note on which to end a meeting with a client who – while not exactly A-list – was still an asset to the agency. And I knew Megan would want to hear how the morning had gone, and would worry if I told her the truth.

Then inspiration struck me.

'Just one thing before you head off, Ruby-Grace. I'm sure you're aware that we like to offer our clients one-on-one support when they're exceptionally busy or at crucial times in their careers. Sam is one of my most talented colleagues, and he'll be available to curate your social media, assist you with any life admin you need help with and just generally be on hand for you. Of course I'll be overseeing any new partnership arrangements we propose for you, as usual. How does that sound?'

Ruby-Grace stopped mid-flounce, one hand already on the door. 'Oh. That's… Thank you. Thank you very much. I appreciate it.'

'It's our pleasure. Sam will reach out and set up a face-to-face to discuss what he can do to support you initially.' We said our goodbyes and our client clacked off to the lift, fringes swishing.

'So that went okay in the end,' I said.

Sam nodded mutely. He looked, I thought, like a man who'd been handed the keys to a Ferrari and didn't want to admit he hadn't passed his driving test.

Chapter Ten

When I went to see Vivienne the next day, I knew what to expect – kind of. But the anticipation of that squalor, that smell, the flies buzzing around the overflowing kitchen waste, actually made it worse, not better. And added to my dread of going back was concern about Vivienne herself.

I'd called, several more times, but still there had been no answer. *Maxed it* – what the hell had that been about? Could she have reached her overdraft limit and been evicted from her house, hence her not answering the phone? Could she have been trying to tell Rosie that she'd gone beyond whatever her no doubt formidable alcohol consumption limit was and had been hospitalised – or worse?

The thoughts that had haunted me for more than a decade – *I should have done more; I should have been there for her* – swirled around my brain like cloudy water in a washing machine. But had I been negligent in whatever duty of care I had to Vivienne? As her agent, I had no idea whether I had any at all. But should I have gone round sooner, not waited thirty-six whole hours before going to check on her? Should I have called the emergency services? I didn't know, and as I approached her street, I found myself feeling sicker and sicker with anxiety.

Before I reached the house, I noticed a black taxi pulling up outside. Probably the driver arriving home after a shift, I thought; this was the sort of area where cab drivers lived, rather than one where they dropped off fares. And, as I expected, the driver swung open the door and got out. But before I could hurry towards him, ask if he was a neighbour and knew Vivienne, he hurried round the back of his car and opened the passenger door with a flourish.

Vivienne stepped out.

She was dressed all in black. A slim-fitting shift dress, a little jacket with sparkly threads through it – I could see them glinting in the brilliant afternoon sunshine – sheer black tights with seams down the back, high-heeled patent leather shoes and a black pillbox hat on her head.

I was close enough to hear her say, 'Darling, you've been ever so kind. Here, keep the change.'

And his reply, with a gesture that was almost a bow: 'Thank you, madam.'

He got back in the driving seat and started the engine. Vivienne walked, quite steadily, up the path to the front door and fitted her key in the lock.

'Hello,' I said. 'I just dropped by, to see how you're doing.'

I decided not to mention her call to the office; not yet, anyway. Maybe she wouldn't even remember making it.

'Sloane! Darling girl! How lovely to see you. Do come in.'

She remembered me, at least. If I'd had to go through the rigmarole of explaining who I was, that would have been awkward to the max.

'How are you, Vivienne?' I followed her into the shadowy, chaotic house, trying to breathe through my mouth and wondering for how long it would be possible to not breathe at all before I keeled over in a dead faint.

But Vivienne said, 'It's a beautiful day, thank goodness, so we can go outside. Follow me.'

Bewildered, I obeyed, barely noticing the grime that lay thick on the floorboards and the dusty cobwebs draped from the chandelier over the dining table until she pushed apart the heavy velvet curtains that covered the French door leading to the garden. Light flooded the room, dazzling me and illuminating the squalor in which she lived so that, suddenly, I understood why she chose to keep the house in that state of twilight gloom.

'Come straight out. Mind your step, darling. And have a seat over here.'

'Here' was a little marble bench underneath a bower of roses, with an elegant white wrought-iron table in front of it. I sat down. I had to. My legs literally wouldn't hold me up, I was so completely baffled by what I saw around me.

'Now, I know it's early but I do feel a breakfast Martini is called for. May I get you one, darling?'

I was as bemused as if I'd already necked several, too bemused even to feel guilty about enabling – even encouraging – her to drink alcohol. All I could do was nod and say, 'Thank you, yes please.'

Vivienne stepped back inside the house, and I took a deep breath and looked around. I must be hallucinating. But everything – the dappled sunlight falling on my face, the solid marble under my thighs, the heady scent of flowers everywhere – was real. But also surreal.

I looked around, disbelieving. The garden was exquisite. Long and narrow, it extended quite far beyond where I was sitting. There was a winding path, paved with round, pale-gold flagstones with vivid foliage surrounding them like a kind of living mortar. Bees hummed industriously through the bank of lavender opposite me. Two olive trees in stoneware pots, trimmed into perfect spheres, flanked a pathway that led onwards to an area I couldn't quite see, but from which I heard the splash of a fountain. Hanging baskets over my head trailed flowers whose names I didn't know, but whose colours were lilac, cream and deepest pink.

How is this possible? My mind whirred. *How can someone so incapable of keeping her home habitable have a garden that would nail it in every flower show going?*

But I didn't have time to frame all my questions, never mind consider what the answers to them might be, because Vivienne reappeared from the gloom of the house, carrying two brim-full cocktail glasses, one in each hand, quite steadily. They looked perfectly clean, I noted, and were filled with clear liquid, each garnished with a sliver of lemon peel.

Vivienne placed them carefully on the table and then sat down next to me. Her hands, which had seemed perfectly steady when she carried the glasses out, were trembling now as she raised one to me. I picked up my own glass and touched it to hers.

'Chin chin, darling,' she said. 'Thank you so much for dropping by. I needed the company. You see, I've just come from a funeral.'

Right. That explained her formal, all-black outfit. But it didn't begin to explain anything else at all. Not the state of the garden and its stark contrast to the sordid interior of the house. Not her distressed call to the office. And most of all, not why she seemed so poised now, so chipper, almost radiating confidence.

Or was she?

'I'm very sorry for your loss.' I took a careful sip of my drink and tried not to wince – it was lethally strong. 'Do you mind me asking who…?'

Vivienne picked up her own glass, regarded the contents, then downed the whole thing in one go, like necking four units of alcohol in seconds was as normal as having a drink of water.

'Max,' she said. 'My husband. Max is dead. Max is dead – Max. Dead, dead, dead.'

And she broke into hoarse, rasping sobs.

I didn't even think, or hesitate. I wrapped my arms around her and held her close while she cried. I stroked her heaving back and made the best soothing noises I could come up with, feeling her hair tickle my face and breathing in the smells of her face powder and perfume and something a bit musty that might have been the feathers on her hat.

She cried for a long, long time. It was like there was a huge reservoir of tears inside her that had been waiting to come out for years, and now a dam wall had broken and there was no stopping the flood. I held her tight and stroked her back and waited it out, smelling the scents of her and the garden, hearing a blackbird singing over the sound of her sobs, watching the shadows the climbing roses cast over us moving almost imperceptibly with the breeze and the sun's high arc.

I didn't say anything much, and she said nothing at all – I don't think she could have done if she'd wanted to. I just made soothing noises like, 'There, there,' and, 'I'm here,' until as last, when my shoulders were screaming with tension from holding her close and the front of my dress was soaked through with her tears, she gave a final, hiccupping sob, sniffed and moved away from me.

I pulled a pack of tissues from my bag, extracted one and handed it to her and then, after a second's hesitation, passed her the rest of the pack and my drink as well. I felt torn about it – tempted to tip it out into a flowerbed or something – but I knew I couldn't make that decision for her, any more than eight-year-old me had been able to make it for Mom. Besides, if ever there was a woman who could be forgiven for wanting a large gin, it was Vivienne.

'Do you want to tell me about it?' I asked, once she'd blown her nose and mopped her eyes. Her carefully made-up face was a ruin now, eye make-up and lipstick smeared everywhere and all her face powder washed away.

I could have kicked myself for not researching Vivienne's marriage more thoroughly. Presumably, when she'd said 'husband', she must have meant ex-husband. There was no way, surely, that a woman living the way she did lived with someone else. And Megan, when she'd first told me about Vivienne, hadn't mentioned there being a husband on the scene. Of course, I knew he existed, from the conversation I'd had with Bianca and Michael and their names together on that midnight-coloured DVD box, the contents of which I still hadn't got around to watching.

'I'm so sorry, darling. What a state I'm in. You must think I'm quite mad.'

'Of course not. You've suffered a bereavement, you poor thing. I'm just glad I came.'

She took a gulp of my cocktail and grimaced. The drink must have been warm by now, and pretty unappetising, but she sipped again, undeterred, then took a shuddering breath, her shoulders trembling.

'The worst thing is, no one told me,' she said in a small voice. 'I read about in *The Telegraph* on Saturday. No one thought to contact me, or tell me about the funeral. I just turned up, like a wicked fairy in a children's story.'

She managed a laugh – a harsh, unsteady sound.

'I'm sure he would have wanted you to be there,' I assured her, although of course I had no idea whether that was true.

'Hardly anyone even recognised me. It was like being a ghost. I could hear people whispering behind my back, and Sarah, who was our PA way back in the day, came over and said hello, but I could tell she didn't want to. She was embarrassed to see me, clearly. I didn't go on to the wake – it would have been too humiliating, even though I could have murdered a drink. But that wouldn't have been wise, would it?'

She looked down at my glass, then lifted it and drained it.

'I only stayed until his coffin was in the ground,' she said. 'I'd had some vague plan about throwing my wedding and engagement rings into the grave, so at least something of our marriage would have been with him forever, but I couldn't do it. I couldn't cause a scene like that.'

She pulled off one of her long, skintight black gloves – she must have been sweltering in the summer heat – and looked at her hand. Sure enough, a huge solitaire diamond and its partner, a simple platinum band, still sparkled on her finger. She hadn't been wearing them the first time I met her – or had she? I'd been too appalled by what I'd found in the house to notice.

'I only take them off for gardening,' she said. 'I have a horror of losing them in a flowerbed somehow. But there I was today, quite eager for them to be buried in the ground. Isn't that silly?'

'Not at all. It's normal to want to mark a loss in a symbolic way.'

There were so many questions jostling for position in my mind, but I knew better than to ask them. I knew that Vivienne would tell me all she wanted me to know, in her own time.

'So I waited until the vicar had said his piece – "Earth to earth, ashes to ashes, dust to dust", such beautiful words, although what they mean is so grim. Max was always a traditionalist – he would've had no truck with the cosy modern version. Someone must have told them what to do, and someone must have chosen the hymns and the readings. A man I've never met gave the eulogy, and to be honest it was like he was talking about someone I didn't know, either. I tuned it out. And as soon as he was in the ground I realised there were going to be no grand gestures from me, so I left and got a taxi home.'

She gave another choking sob and pressed a soggy tissue to her eyes.

'I'm so very sorry,' I said. 'It sounds like it was awfully difficult for you.'

Vivienne twisted the tissue in her hands like she was trying to wring it dry of her tears.

'Darling, I'm going to have another cocktail. And I drank yours, so will you keep me company?'

You should stop now, Vivienne. Why don't we have a nice cup of tea?

But I didn't say that. I wasn't her mother – and, more to the point, she wasn't mine.

'Thank you, that would be great. Do you need a hand?'

'Of course not. You stay out here and enjoy the garden.'

Once again, I had a flash of awareness of Vivienne's own knowledge of what her life must look like through my eyes. I thought of the rolls of rubbish bags in my handbag, which I'd bought at a corner shop on the way, and how I'd been going to suggest diplomatically that we might as well have a bit of a clear-up. But this wasn't the time for subtle hints about her housekeeping standards. At least there'd been enough gin in that drink to destroy all the disease-bearing microorganisms in south-east London. Who needed anti-bac wipes when you had Tanqueray Ten? Presumably that had been Vivienne's approach over the past however many years, and if she was going to change it, it wouldn't be today, that was for sure.

While I waited for her to return, I strolled along the pathway between the stone pots to explore the rest of the garden. There was a huge ash tree shadowing a circle of emerald-green lawn. There were raised stone flowerbeds crammed with blooms in all shades from white to pink, pink to crimson, crimson to violet. There were taller shrubs, too, one still bearing lush, fleshy flowers that I thought might be magnolias.

There was a cascading water feature like a miniature waterfall, which was making the soothing sound I'd noticed earlier. Looking up, I saw birds' nests in the tree above, and butterflies flitted through the plants, sharing the work of the bees. Tucked away behind an immaculately trimmed hedge were a small, green-painted shed and a tiny greenhouse, empty now, because anything left there would have wilted and died in the heat.

I thought of the minimalist, low-maintenance garden Myles and I were planning and felt suddenly sad, contrasting it with this lovingly tended, life-filled work of love. Myles. Myles and Bianca.

Saying his name in my mind didn't fill me with happiness like it used to; now, I felt only a cold, sick churn of dread. Had he betrayed me? Him and Bianca both?

'Are you there, darling?'

'Sorry.' I hurried back to the stone bench, trying to leave thoughts of Myles behind me. 'I was just admiring your garden. It's spectacular.'

'Well, one does need to keep busy,' Vivienne said, sitting back down and crossing her slender calves. 'When you've been alone as long as I have, something has to fill the space where people would be. The robins keep me company out here. Britain's favourite bird, officially. There was a poll. "Art thou the bird whom man loves best / The pious bird with the scarlet breast." Wordsworth. But they're nasty little bastards, really.'

Whether it was having had a good old cry or being two cocktails down I wasn't sure, but my client seemed to have recovered her poise. I joined her on the bench and we clinked glasses again.

'Now, darling, you must tell me all about yourself. Who is Sloane Cassidy – such a fabulous name; were you lucky enough to have been born with it? – and what makes her tick?'

'I guess I kind of did luck out on the name front. My husband's last name is Taylor.' Saying those words brought a fresh surge of pain. 'When we got married I think he expected I'd take his name, but I stuck to my feminist principles and, when that wasn't enough, I pointed out that Sloane Taylor sounds like Lone Ranger and was pretty ridiculous, so I won.'

Vivienne laughed. 'Good girl. And you and Mr Taylor – are you happy? Children?'

'No kids yet. We started trying a few months back but it's not happening, so far. I worry…' I took a sip of my drink. Vivienne might have been literally crying on my shoulder just minutes before, but she was still my client. 'I guess we all have our ups and downs.'

'Do you trust him?' Vivienne asked, reaching over and wrapping her left hand around my wrist. Her grip was tight, and surprisingly strong, and the two rings dug uncomfortably into my flesh.

'Do I…'

'Do you trust him to hold your heart in his hands and keep it safe?'

Suddenly, I felt tears welling up in my own eyes.

'I don't know. I hope so.'

'When I met Max,' Vivienne said, leaning in close to me so I could almost count the false lashes she'd glued – only slightly askew – above her remarkable eyes, 'I thought he was The One. And he was, in a sense. I mean, the only one for me. My whole life, there's only been him.'

'Oh.' I had no idea how to react to this. I could just about believe that Vivienne – if she'd met Max in her early twenties – might have been a virgin. Even in the late seventies. Maybe. But that she'd had a long and varied career as an actress and there'd never been another man in her life, not one? God.

'I gave him my heart to hold in his hand,' she went on, 'and he held it carelessly. He didn't care if he dropped it, or crushed it, or if it got squashed up against one of the other hearts women gave him to carry. He had so many, you see.'

'Oh, Vivienne. I'm sorry.'

I put my hand over hers, where it pressed against my arm, and she placed her right hand over it and squeezed down hard.

'He was never faithful to me. Not ever. Not even before we got married and certainly not after. I didn't know, at first. And then I knew, but I preferred to pretend I didn't. And then I got confronted by it, over and over again, so I couldn't pretend any more.'

'I understand,' I said, although I didn't really. 'It must have been horrible.'

'He kept saying I was the only one who mattered. That the others were just… nothing. Just a bit of fun. Just playthings. I should have realised that I was a plaything, too. But I didn't. I buried my head in the sand. Ostriches don't really do that, of course. Did you know? It's just a myth. And why would they, anyway, poor birds? Like they don't have enough problems, being made into hats and feather dusters. But I did. For thirty years, I just carried on, like everything was fine, like eventually it would stop and he'd come back to me properly, and stay.'

'And did he?' I asked, although I already knew what the answer would be.

But she carried on as if I hadn't spoken. 'I kept busy, with whatever work I could get. And Max was travelling a lot, of course. He was over in the States a lot of the time – most of the time, even. It made it easier for me to pretend that he wasn't being unfaithful to me, or that if he was, it was because I wasn't there and he was lonely. As if Max would ever be lonely! That man was surrounded by people from the moment he woke up in the morning until last thing at night. And after that, too, of course.'

She gave a mirthless little laugh that reminded me a bit of Bianca's. It made me flinch, and I hoped she didn't notice.

'And then he stopped coming home. Stopped calling, stopped everything. I suppose he'd seen what I'd become, the state of me, and it disgusted him. I was what he'd made me, and he couldn't bear it.'

Vivienne paused for a moment. She was gazing off into the distance, towards the wisteria plant that covered the garden wall in a haze of lilac flowers, but I wondered if she even saw them, or if she was just looking back, far into the past.

'It was ten years ago when I last saw him. I didn't know it was the last time, but I must've had some kind of premonition, because I gave up the lease on our flat in Covent Garden. I wasn't earning enough to pay the rent, but I had some savings and I used them to buy this place. And I suppose, since then, I've just been hoping that he'd come back – find me here somehow. Just walk through the door like he used to. But he never will now.'

I said again, 'I'm so sorry, Vivienne.'

She turned and fixed me with her enormous eyes. 'Don't be sorry. Just don't let this be you. Don't waste the best years of your life on a man who'll only ever love himself. Don't let it destroy you like it has me.'

There was not a lot more I could say, except come up with a few bracing platitudes about how this could be her chance for a new start, and she should rest and take care of herself and get over her grief and shock, and give me a call when she was ready to have a talk about working again, and in the meantime I'd stay in touch.

And then I kissed her and left, passing through the dusty gloom of the house and back out into the sunlight as quickly as I could.

Chapter Eleven

Vivienne's words made me more focused than ever on my plan to make my marriage work, whatever it took. If – and it was still a huge if, one that played on my mind all the time – my husband had been unfaithful, I'd need to find concrete evidence before I decided what to do about it. And if he hadn't, I was resolved to make sure he never was. I'd be the perfect wife: attentive, loving and available.

So, for the next couple of weeks, I tried to create a kind of honeymoon for Myles and me. Well, if instead of a luxury suite in the Bahamas you'd decided to spend your romantic break on the top floor of a building site, that was. Wayne and Shane had disappeared off to Tenerife and Ibiza, respectively, for their summer holiday, so the work downstairs had ground to a halt. Even though the house was still in a state of chaos, a brief respite from constant noise and dust felt almost like a vacation for us, too. In fact, it felt as if the whole of London had gone into a kind of giddy holiday mode. Almost every email I sent came back with an auto-reply saying that the person I was trying to contact was away with limited access to emails.

Rosie and Sam and most of our clients were on vacation too, and Isla and I took long lunch breaks during which she went to the gym and I wandered round the shops, not finding anything I wanted to buy. We knocked off early most days, and I felt no guilt about allowing my intern to slack off.

Myles's work was similarly quiet. The building trade had more or less shut down for the summer and his major projects were on ice, and as far as I could tell he was spending most of his time polishing the presentation he was due to give at a conference in the Middle East. He went into the office every day but was home by five and seemed happy to hang out with me. So we did: we went out to the pub together and ate fish and chips. We watched Vivienne's movie in bed, our shoulders close together so we could see my laptop screen, and we agreed that she was breathtakingly talented. We went to museums and art galleries on the weekend, and strolled along the river hand in hand.

We had sex, like, a lot. Almost every night. And to my relief, it felt like it had before trying to conceive had stopped it being joyful and spontaneous and turned it into something loaded with hope, disappointment and fear.

I remembered what Vivienne had told me – of course I did. Her words of warning cast a shadow over my happiness, but it was one I was able to ignore, for the most part: a cloud passing over the sun on an otherwise perfect summer day.

I wanted my marriage to work, and last. I wanted people to think, *Look at Sloane and Myles – they're so successful as individuals but so united as a couple.* And I wanted that to be true.

But, despite my optimism, I had to be sure that there was nothing untoward going on – nothing for me to worry about. I waited, patiently, for my chance to do just a little bit of digging, a few minutes' research – okay, to have a massive snoop. It was surprisingly difficult. Even though he wasn't busy, Myles's phone was always by his side. Had it always been like that? I couldn't remember, because I'd never felt the need – the compulsive, niggling urge – to check it. Until now.

At last, one Thursday evening, an opportunity came. Myles announced that he was going to have a bath, a palaver that involved scented candles, bubbles, jazz playing on the portable bathroom speaker, a wet shave with a cut-throat razor and hot towels, and even a face mask. My husband, the original metrosexual.

Normally, he'd have taken his phone into the bathroom with him – he'd destroyed more than one handset by dropping it into the bath. But this time, the battery was low and he'd left it to charge in the makeshift kitchen, plugged into my laptop. I waited, seething with impatience, until I heard him lower himself into the water and tell Alexa to open Spotify and play Scott Joplin.

And then I reached for his phone and tapped in the passcode.

It was horrible. I felt furtive, guilty and ashamed. There was no excitement, no thrill of the chase. I felt only hollow dread at what I might find, and a kind of grim resolve: the sooner I got this over with, the sooner I could put my suspicions behind me and move on – on to a future that would be like this week had been: relaxed, united, happy.

I looked at the screen, memorising what was there: an article from the *Independent* newspaper talking about a shake-up in building regulations. I'd make sure to restore it when I was done, like a guerrilla fighter covering his tracks. I pressed the home button.

Myles had eight unread text messages. I touched that icon first, my finger trembling slightly. One was from his mother, one was a notification that he had new voicemails, one was from his mobile provider telling him there were great new deals on the latest handsets, one was an appointment confirmation from his barber, one a notification that a delivery had arrived safely at his office… The others were equally innocuous. I scrolled quickly down through the messages he'd already read, but there was nothing to see there, either.

Okay. What next?

I tapped through to his personal email. Here, there were many, many more unread messages. Unlike me, Myles didn't religiously check and clear his promotional items folder, or file away the stuff he wanted to read and reply to. His inbox was chaos – just looking at it made me anxious, and not just for fear of who might have been emailing him. It would take me ages to go through all of them, especially if I accidentally opened some and then had to go back and mark them as unread, covering my tracks.

So I returned to the home screen again and opened WhatsApp. It showed me a group chat between Myles and the friends he went to football with – message after message of banter, arrangements to meet in a pub before the next game, links to articles analysing the team's performance. Nothing to concern me.

Apart from the fact that I was actually doing this. I could feel sweat trickling down my back, and my hands were slick and hot. Even my face was burning – whether with heat, shame or a mixture of the two, I wasn't sure. I paused for a second and listened. Scott Joplin was still playing from the bathroom, and occasionally I could hear Myles singing tunelessly along, or a whoosh and splash of water.

The bathroom would look like a tidal wave had hit it once he was done, I knew, and he'd leave a ring of scum and stubble around the tub, and if I asked him to clean it he'd say he didn't want to harsh his mellow and he'd do it later. 'Later', of course, meaning never, because I'd sit twitching with frustration, imagining the crud drying and hardening until it had to be scrubbed away with bathroom cleaner and a sponge, and eventually I'd snap and do it myself.

Emboldened by anticipation of my own annoyance, I tapped back to the main list of all his conversations in WhatsApp and scrolled swiftly down the list. There were chats with his brother and sister, who lived in Manchester and Geneva, respectively; with his old uni mates; with former and current colleagues. There were chats with mutual friends, which I was signed up to as well – the four couples we occasionally went to wine tastings with; Al and Sunita, who we'd met on holiday and still sometimes met for drinks; our neighbours Rafe and Devlin, who we kept up to date with the progress of our building project and supplied with regular bottles of wine by way of apology for all the noise.

And, of course, the group that included Myles, Bianca, Michael and me, on which our get-togethers were arranged. I was up to date with all the messages on it. I knew there was nothing there that Michael or I weren't totally at liberty to see.

I'd drawn a blank with WhatsApp, too.

I should have felt reassured. Everything I'd seen in fifteen minutes of combing through Myles's phone had been totally innocuous. No alarm bells rang, no red flags waved. So why did I still feel this sick, churning sense that there was something I needed to find?

Returning to the home screen, I swiped right, on to the apps Myles used less often. He didn't have them grouped into folders, like I did. His MyFitnessPal icon was right next to the YouTube one. The CAD app that he must use all the time for work was three screens over next to BBC Weather, as was the Slack app Bianca had made us install to track the progress of our own house renovation.

Shit. Slack.

I tapped the icon and up came the familiar screen: 'Sloane and Myles Project', with discussions about the delay to the kitchen being delivered, paint swatches, the list of contractors, and all the rest.

But Slack had another function, too. You could send direct, private messages to anyone in the group.

And there it was, with one easy inch-long movement of my finger: a series of messages between my husband and my friend. The most recent ones were displayed first.

12 August

Bianca: Ignoring me like this is not on. You know how I feel.

Bianca: Look, Myles, please. Let's talk about this like adults and stop pretending nothing happened. Come on. We could talk to her together, if that would make it easier for you? xxxx

Myles: I'm just not comfortable doing that right now, okay? Can't you trust me to deal with this in my own way, in my own time?

11 August

Bianca: Have you had a chance to think about what I said when we met today? I'm sorry if I came across a bit intense. But I *feel* intense.

Myles: I understand that, you know I do. I have feelings too. I just don't want to rush into anything that could hurt us both and end two relationships.

Bianca: Don't you think that's a risk we have to take? Because I do. I've had enough of hiding it. It's tearing me apart.

Myles: What do you think it's doing to me? I can't discuss this any more, sorry. Not now. X

9 August

Myles: I never loved her. It was just sexual attraction.

Bianca: That's not relevant, really, is it? The point is, Sloane needs to know. We can't carry on hiding this from her.

Myles: Do you really want to do that? Do you really want to tell her, and break her heart? Because I don't. She's my wife.

Bianca: And she's my friend. That makes this even worse.

*

I felt a churning surge of nausea reading their words: an overwhelming sense of loss and misery and – absurdly – shame. This had been going on behind my back – never mind that, practically under my nose – for how long, without me having a clue? It had taken Bianca's own heavy-handed hints to shake me out of my oblivious, false security. I thought Myles loved me. He said he did. Okay, we had our ups and downs – recently, rather more downs than I'd have liked – but I'd never stopped believing in his love.

And there it was: that cold statement of fact. *I never loved her.*

Who, besides my husband and… that bitch, who I'd thought was my friend, knew about this? Did Michael know? Did Myles's football mates know, and promise to cover for him when he sneaked off to see her? Imagining that, imagining the pity and contempt they'd feel for me, imagining them saying, 'Poor Sloane. The wife's always the last to find out,' felt like a dagger sliding under my ribs and straight into my heart. There was a huge, choking lump in my throat and my eyes stung with tears, but I didn't let them fall. I'd never been much of a crier – I thought I was too tough for that, tough enough to deal with whatever life threw at me, pick myself up, dust myself off and carry on, stronger and wiser. But I felt like I could never recover from reading those words. I felt like the entire foundation of my life had been torn away. I felt hollow, bereft, the pain so intense it was almost like numbness – almost too huge to comprehend.

It was like the pain I'd felt all those years ago, when Dad had sat me down next to him at the kitchen table in the house in Sparwood and explained gently to me that the police had done what they could, but they hadn't traced Mom. That she was an adult, and if there was no sign that anything bad had happened to her, we would have to accept that she'd made a choice to leave – to disappear. And we'd have to accept that she might never come back.

Then, I'd still been a little girl, without much concept of what 'never' really meant. Mom was gone – that itself was too big, too devastating, for me to grasp properly. But now its meaning was all too clear.

I looked down at the screen again, but it had turned itself off and I had to enter the password again to torture myself with those words once more. *I never loved her.*

Which must mean he loved Bianca.

It wasn't just a flirtation, a passing crush, even a reckless drunken snog after too many tequilas. I could have dealt with those things (not that the last would happen, not with Bianca, who was virtually teetotal). It was serious. So serious that they were having in-depth discussions about how to tell me.

I looked down at the phone again. My hands had started to shake violently. And I was sweating, too, I realised – I could literally smell the panic coming off my own body.

I transferred the phone to my left hand to wipe my right one on my skirt, but it slipped right through my clumsy fingers and fell to the wooden floor with a hollow crash. My head was full of a sound that wasn't there – a kind of roaring, like waves on a beach. I wondered if I was going to have a stroke or something, and drop dead right there.

I almost wished I would.

And then Myles walked in, naked except for a white towel around his hips. He smelled wonderful – of the Tom Ford cologne I'd bought him for Christmas.

He must have finished his bath, had his shave, filed his nails – done all of that stuff, while I was sitting there, reading those messages, feeling our marriage come crashing down around me.

'Hey, darling, that feels better. Bathroom's all yours if you want it. We could go out later, maybe, try that new Peruvian place that's opened up the road.' He stopped and looked down at the floor by my feet, his expression suddenly guarded. 'Did you knock over my phone?'

I didn't say anything. I felt like a tight band was constricting my ribs.

'Sloane? Are you okay?'

Maybe the sensible thing to do would have been to wait. To prepare myself for confrontation, rather than rushing headlong into it. I could have said I was fine, only I had the beginnings of a migraine, or bad period pains, or hay fever or something – anything – and I should have got up and walked out and gone to bed. I could have taken a sleeping pill and then, in the morning, assessed my situation rationally and calmly. Maybe that would have meant talking to Bianca. Maybe it would have meant seeing a solicitor. Maybe it would have meant going round to see Megan and pouring my heart out to my friend.

But I didn't do any of that. I couldn't. The new knowledge I had was so huge and horrifying there was no way in hell I could keep it bottled up inside of me for even a second longer. The feeling of compression around my chest was so strong now it was like I might burst with the agony of it, and there was only one way to let it out.

'How long have you and Bianca been fucking?'

'What? Bianca and me… What? Are you mad?'

'You heard me. Answer the question.'

'Sloane, I have absolutely no idea what the fuck you're talking about.'

'Yes, you do. I'm talking about you sleeping with Bianca. I want to know how long it's been going on for.'

He stepped towards me, and the towel sagged to half mast and then slithered to the floor, releasing a further waft of clean fragrance. His penis was just about level with my chin. For a brief, deranged moment, I thought about hurting him – grabbing his balls in my hand and squeezing the truth out of him, making him feel some of the white-hot pain I was experiencing.

But the idea vanished from my mind as quickly as it had appeared, and anyway I wouldn't have had the chance, because he said, 'Hold on,' turned around and went into the bedroom, reappearing seconds later in boxer shorts and a T-shirt.

'Come on,' he said. 'Let's sit down together in the bedroom and talk this through calmly.'

I stood up. 'I. Am. Not. Calm. And I'm not going anywhere near a fucking bed with you ever again, you cheating shit.'

He reached out and wrapped his arms around me, holding me tight. My entire body was rigid, my hands clenched into fists by my sides, so tight I could feel my nails digging painfully into my palms. But at the same time, the proximity of his body, the scent of him, the hardness of his chest pressing against my cheek, the warmth of his embracing arms, almost made me weaken. Almost, but not quite.

'Let go of me.'

He did. He took a step back but kept one hand on my shoulder. I shrugged it off.

'Sweetheart. Please, let's talk about this. I don't know where you've got this idea from, but I do know you've been under so much stress lately. You need to calm down. I promise you, absolutely faithfully, that I'm not sleeping with Bianca. I'm not. Never have and never will. Scout's honour.'

'Right. Then how exactly do you explain those messages on your phone? On Slack?'

I was looking right into his face, even though meeting the eyes of the man who, just an hour earlier, I'd believed loved me – held my heart in his hands – was just about the hardest thing I'd ever done. And I saw his expression change from concern to panic, like a black cloud passing over the sun, and then to total blank impassiveness.

'You looked at my phone.'

One of us here was lying, and it wasn't going to be me. 'Correct.'

'What the fuck? Why would you even do that? I thought we trusted each other.'

'So did I. Until I read those messages. I guess at least one of us doesn't trust the other one any more.'

'Jesus, Sloane. What were you thinking? What's happened to you? I can't believe you'd invade my privacy like that.'

'Fuck your fucking privacy! What about our marriage?'

'Our marriage isn't worth the shit on my shoe if my wife thinks it's okay to snoop around like some bunny-boiling psychopath. I thought you were better than that. I thought you were a fucking adult.'

His sudden rage shocked me. I don't know what I'd expected from him, but I guess I'd been hoping for a totally plausible explanation at best, or abject contrition at worst. But what I'd got was my husband managing to make me feel like this whole ugly scene was my fault.

'What can I have that's private from you? Huh? The accounts for my business? Me taking a shit? Having a wank? What, you want one-hundred-per-cent, twenty-four-seven access to every last aspect of my life? If that's how you see our marriage I suggest you tell me now, because I'll be out so fast you won't see me for dust.'

Maybe there are some women who'd have responded to that with, 'Off you go then, and don't let the door hit your ass on your way out.'

Up until that day, I'd have said I was one of them.

But I was so blindsided, so reeling with shock at what I'd seen and how he'd reacted, that there was no fight left in me at all.

'Myles, this isn't my fault. I can't help what I saw.'

'You could. You could have respected my privacy and not gone grubbing through my personal business.'

'But our marriage *is* my business.'

'Right now, I'm not sure we even have a marriage.'

He gave me a brief, cold stare, then turned and went into the bedroom, closing the door firmly behind him. I stood there, alone and appalled, totally unequipped to deal with what had just happened, for a few seconds, until my legs lost the ability to hold me upright and I flopped back down into my chair. That was it. I wasn't going anywhere. I couldn't even lift a hand to brush my hair off my face.

I could hear Myles's footsteps in the next-door room, brisk and purposeful, moving back and forth. Soon, their sound changed and I knew he'd put shoes on. Then the door opened again and he stepped out, dressed in jeans with a cream linen shirt over his T-shirt, carrying his leather overnight bag.

'You need to think about what you've done. I'll be spending the night in a hotel,' he said, each word like a cube of ice dropping into an empty glass.

Chapter Twelve

The persistent bleeping of my alarm dragged me out of a deep, chemical-induced sleep. My head was pounding and my throat felt raw and sore. My whole body ached, like I'd been run over by a bus. I rolled over, instinctively reaching for Myles, but there was only emptiness where his body should have been.

My eyes snapped open and, with the blinding sunlight, my memory of the previous night rushed back. The messages I'd seen. The horrible row we'd had. His cold words as he left the house, slamming the door behind him. I closed my eyes, as if that would shut out the memory, but of course it didn't.

And anyway, even though I felt like I was dying – worse, like my life was already over, and I was just trapped in a kind of limbo waiting to be released – I had to work.

Any other job, I might have considered calling in sick. But Ripple Effect wasn't just a job – the business was half mine and the other half was off on maternity leave. It was my livelihood, my future. And now, with my marriage in crisis, I needed it more than ever.

I pushed the duvet aside. The sheets were damp with sweat; I must have gone out like a light after the two sleeping pills I'd taken, not noticing that the night had been far too hot for our bedcovers.

Since long before I met Myles, I'd been plagued by insomnia, and while I'd learned to live with it for the most part, I still kept the big guns in reserve: the sleeping tablets I persuaded my reluctant GP to prescribe or stocked up on for trips abroad. I couldn't remember how long I cried for, after Myles had left. I remembered wanting desperately, more than anything, to turn back the clock, to make what had happened unhappen, but I knew it never would. It was like when the builders started work on our house, and I'd watched in horror as they swung a mallet repeatedly at one of the walls until it collapsed in a pile of rubble. I felt like I'd done that, only to our marriage, and all that remained to be seen was what, if anything, could be salvaged from the wreckage.

Well, I needed to make sure that Megan's and my business would survive, at any rate. And that meant hauling my ass out of bed and getting ready to face the day.

Just walking to the bathroom felt like an arduous challenge. I had to force myself to pick up each foot in turn and place it down again. When I made it, I flopped down on the toilet like I needed a rest as well as a pee. My toothbrush felt like it weighed a ton. The water in the shower was like needles on my body, either boiling hot or freezing cold, but never soothing or cleansing.

When I was twenty, I thought I'd experienced the worst grief I ever would – enough loss and shock and trauma to last a lifetime. And since then, I'd survived all the usual brickbats that life throws at us all. But this physical pain – this leaden exhaustion – was new. I wondered if I was coming down with flu, but I was pretty sure that wasn't it. It was as if my brain was so soaked in misery, it had forgotten how to make my body work.

Well, it was going to have to remember pretty damn quick.

'Pull yourself together, Sloane,' I told my reflection in the mirror. 'Get through today and you can come home and cry.'

And I did. I went through my skincare routine on autopilot, and made up my face, slathering on illuminating concealer to hide the black rings under my eyes and tipping in eye drops to try to erase their angry redness. I tapped liquid blush onto my cheeks, hoping to achieve a healthy glow. I used waterproof eyeliner and mascara, because the choking tightness in my throat warned me that I could cry again at any second.

My hair had frizzed horribly in the heat and I couldn't summon up the energy to style it properly, so I ran my straighteners ruthlessly over it on too high a setting, even though I knew I'd pay for it later in rebound frizz and split ends.

After fifteen minutes in front of the mirror, I reckoned things weren't going to get any better. I needed to put some clothes on, drink some coffee, and get the hell out, or I'd be late.

But I couldn't. I sat down on our bed and put my head in my hands, a numbing tiredness overwhelming me. More than anything else in the world, at that moment, I wished my dad was there to give me a hug, instead of being thousands of miles away.

When I was at boarding school, Dad sent me a letter once a week, regular as clockwork, however busy he was, wherever in the country work had taken him. Back then, email had only just become a widely used thing and, although I knew Dad had it at work, when he wrote to me it was the old-fashioned way, on textured pale-blue paper with almost invisible white lines on it, in his scribbly, scientist's handwriting.

I rarely wrote back. Maybe I averaged one short, scribbled note to every four of his painstakingly detailed letters – more if I wanted something, like money to buy the new Shania Twain album or tickets to a hockey game. I told him school was fine, I was studying hard, a friend had asked if I could spend Labour Day weekend with her family and was that okay. At the time, I barely thought about the effort those letters must have taken him to write, the weight of guilt the necessity of sending them must have brought down on him, because I was his only child and I was so far away.

And it was only much later, when I went back home for a visit a couple of months before I met Myles, that I told him how much I'd treasured each one, reading it over and over, even pressing my nose to the page in case there might be a whiff of Dad on it, a ghostly memory of home.

'Of course you did, honey,' he'd said. 'I did the same, when I was away at school. Why do you think I wrote them?'

And we'd had one of those massive, squeezy hugs you sometimes have that transcend time and silence and distance, his beard tickling my face. I'd told him he was the best dad in the world and he'd got too teared up to reply.

Anyway, I looked forward to Dad's letters far, far more than I could ever admit to anyone – not my classmates, not him, not even myself.

It was a Friday in October – Halloween fast approaching, the leaves long turned into their autumn colours, cladding the playing fields in amber and gold – when I received a letter from Dad that must have been incredibly hard for him to write. I'd planned to save it until after my friends and I had been out to town for a burger and a movie, so I could savour it in bed, alone, reading it over and over until the gentle timbre of his remembered voice soothed me to sleep.

But just as the bus was pulling up to take us off for our Friday treat and Janine was saying, 'Come on, Sloane, if you put on any more lip gloss you'll stick your mouth together!' I saw the envelope lying there on my pillow and for some reason it felt really important for me to read it right then.

I said, 'Actually, I'm staying in tonight. I don't feel great. You guys have fun.'

And in spite of my friends' protests – Carla even brought out the big guns and reminded me that hot Pierre might be working in the burger bar that night, and he'd come *this* close to asking me out last time we went there – I held firm. As soon as they were gone, I pulled off my sequinned combat trousers and Nirvana T-shirt, put on my pyjamas, got under the bedcovers and opened Dad's letter.

Hi, Sloane honey,

I'm writing this in a motel room in Red Lake – they sent me up at short notice last week and I reckon I'll be here for another month. It's pretty cold already, but the sunsets are sensational and some of the guys have invited me to go fishing on the weekend, so it's not all bad! I hope your chemistry test went okay – I was thinking about you on Thursday and hoping to channel everything I know about the periodic table directly into your brain! Maybe it got there – or maybe you aced it on your own.

There's a slightly complicated reason why I'm writing this letter – as well as wanting to touch base with my girl as usual. Yesterday I got a call from your mom.

I know this is going to come as a shock to you. It's been seven years now and we've heard nothing – the police did what they could to trace her in the beginning, but when there was no sign that anything bad had happened, they came round to the view that she'd decided to take off on her own. As she was an adult, they couldn't really pursue her and make her come home to us if she didn't want to.

I'm sure you remember me suggesting a counsellor, and the sessions we had with Erin, when we went through how troubled Mom was, and how none of this was your fault. I recall at the time holding you on my lap and telling you over and over how much Mom loved you, and how dark a place she must have been in to leave you, her baby girl – even though you were all of eight years old at the time and almost too big for me to hold on my knees. But now I've spoken to her and she's told me herself how heartbreaking that decision was for her to make.

I guess it wasn't even a decision, as such. Now that you're older, I think you can probably understand some of what the move to Sparwood was like for her – the isolation, the boredom, and how that made her behave. I think – and this is pretty much what she told me when we spoke – she just couldn't see a way forward other than to run away.

I blame myself. Not just for making the move in the first place, although saying no to it would have meant quitting my job and finding another livelihood for us all – but for not realizing how hard it all was for her.

And the years in between were hard too. She's been to some pretty bad places – practically and emotionally – and had harder times than I like to think about. But one thing your mom told me when we spoke on the phone was that through it all, she held close to her love of you and hoped that sometime she would be able to see you again and be a part of your life. She just didn't want it to be when she was so messed up, knowing that seeing her would hurt you and confuse you even more. She told me she understood how hurt and angry you would be about what she did.

Honey, I'm going to cut to the chase. She'd like to see you. She's well now, much more like herself, and she's living back in Calgary, where you were born. I want this to be your decision, Sloane. If you want to meet up with Linda, I'll do whatever I can to support you – I can be there, or I can talk to Mrs Klingmann and ask her to have you meet right there at school in her office. Or, if you'd rather not, I'll understand completely and I'll pass on the message.

There's no pressure from me either way, honey. I respect you and I trust your judgment. When you can, give me a call and we can have a talk about it before you decide what to do.

I love you,
Dad

I read the letter through again, but I didn't need to – not really. I knew what I was going to do. I left our room and hurried to the bank of payphones by the gym, and dialled Dad's cellphone number. As usual, he answered straight away.

'Hey, honey. Everything okay?'

'Sure. Dad, I got your letter. I'll see her. You don't need to be there.'

And so, the next Saturday afternoon, I got the bus into town on my own. I'd spent the past few days veering between fear, anger and wild hope, while determinedly concealing that I was feeling anything at all. I'd dressed carefully, in my new low-rise flared jeans, platform sneakers, a skinny vest top and an outsize baseball jacket. I'd plucked my eyebrows to careful arches, except I'd been a bit overenthusiastic and was worried I looked permanently surprised. My hair was in bunches behind my ears.

I was aiming for no-care cool, and fifteen-year-old me reckoned I'd nailed it.

The main street was home to an array of places where my schoolmates clamoured to be taken by our visiting parents: a McDonald's, a Burger Baron, a Taco Bell and all the rest of them. But I was meeting Mom in Starbucks.

She was already there when I arrived, but I didn't recognise her. Why would I have? It had been more than seven years since I last saw her, and my memory of her was as dim as half a lifetime would have made it.

I paused on the threshold, holding open the door, looking around for an empty table, until the woman sitting nearest me tutted at me for letting in a draught. And then a woman in the far corner half-stood and gave an uncertain wave.

I realised it was her, and simultaneously understood that she'd barely recognised me, either. The thought gave me a stab of painful, angry pleasure. *She missed me growing up. Her loss.*

She looked much, much older. Not just the ageing you'd expect through the passing of time, but way older than a woman in her late thirties should have looked. Her hair was cropped short, greying at the temples. There were deep grooves under her eyes and furrows on either side of her mouth. When she smiled in greeting, I saw that her teeth were stained and one of them was chipped. But she was dressed smartly, in tailored wool pants and a knitted sweater, and her face was carefully made-up.

I approached the table slowly, still unsure.

'Mom?'

'Sloane.' Her voice sounded older, too – a smoker's rasp. There was a pack of Camels on the table in front of her, but the ashtray was clean and unused.

She held out her arms towards me and, after a second's hesitation, I let myself be hugged. She didn't smell familiar at all – she could have been anyone.

She had a cup of coffee in front of her. I hesitated again for a second and then said, 'I'm just going to order. Do you want anything?'

She shook her head and I made my way to the counter. Clearly, she didn't understand this crucial ritual of boarding-school life: that visiting parents always couldn't wait to treat their kids to burgers, doughnuts, ice cream – whatever we wanted, and often stuff we didn't.

But how was she to know? It wasn't like she'd ever done this before – another reminder of the huge chunk of my life she'd missed.

Aware that my dwindling allowance had to last me another week, I bought a small cappuccino and looked longingly at the blueberry muffins, but said, 'No, thanks,' when the barista asked if I wanted anything else.

Mug in hand, I returned to the table, sat down opposite my mother, and waited.

'You look great,' she said uncertainly. 'You're a proper teenager. I can hardly believe it.'

I didn't smile or return the compliment.

'Thank you for meeting me,' she went on. 'I know this must have been a shock for you.'

I shook my head. All the things I wanted to say – I'd even practised saying them, in the shower at school and, silently, on the bus on the way here – seemed to have been wiped out of my brain.

'Sloane, I owe you an explanation. I don't expect you to understand, but maybe you could just listen?'

I nodded, stirring four sugars into my coffee.

'Sparwood… It was awful for me. It was like being buried alive. I know I was a terrible mother. I know it must have been terrifying living with me. I'm so very sorry. I can only imagine what it must have been like for you. But I just felt like I had to get out of there – I had to run away. Because if I'd stayed it would have destroyed me, and damaged you. I'm very lucky to be here at all. I was fucked up. I was in a terrible place for a long, long time. But now I'm better.'

I said, 'You never called.'

'I wanted to. Believe me, I did. But my life – everything was just so chaotic. For a while I didn't have a home, never mind a phone. And I felt so guilty about what I'd done, every single day. I wanted to say sorry but I didn't have the words.'

'And I didn't have a mother.'

'I know.' Her face fell, the lines deepening. 'Honey, I know. It's the worst, worst thing of all the bad things I've done. But now I've been sober for almost a year. I'm working through the twelve steps. You know what those are?'

I nodded. The previous quarter, a lady from Alcoholics Anonymous had come to give a talk in assembly. At the end, she made us all join her in saying the Serenity Prayer, and I'd never felt less serene in my life.

'So one of them – the eighth one – is to make a list of people we've hurt and be willing to make amends to them. Sloane, you and your dad were right there at the top of the list. I know I hurt you. I know what I did was unforgivable. I just wanted you to know that I know that, and that I'm sorry. And maybe one day I'll be able to make amends somehow.'

Suddenly, all the words I'd practised were right there in my head, ready to come out.

'You left me when I was just a little girl. I loved you and you just disappeared. I had no mom any more. Kids at school bullied me because my mom was a drunk and I had to go and see a shrink. Dad had to send me away to boarding school because you weren't there to look after me. You ruined my entire life, and you think you can make amends? You didn't even pay for my coffee!'

I stood up so quickly I almost tipped over the table, knocking over my mug so it smashed on the floor, sending hot liquid splashing over the frayed hems of my jeans. Blinded by tears, I hurried out of there as fast as I could, ran across the street and threw myself into a bus that was just pulling away, before I could change my mind and before Mom could see that I was crying.

Chapter Thirteen

I didn't hear from Myles for two days. I'd like to say that I maintained an icy, dignified silence, but I didn't. I knew I was being needy and stupid and desperate, but I couldn't help myself. I texted him and WhatsApped him and called him more times than I could count, but he didn't respond, and after a bit he turned off his phone. Or possibly the battery gave up, exhausted from ringing and ringing and being ignored.

I didn't go to work on Friday. I called Rosie and told her I had a throat infection and would work from home. In reality, what this meant was doing almost no work but instead staring blankly at my phone, which returned my gaze just as blankly, and obsessively dialling Myles's number in between making cups of coffee for the builders, who'd returned from their holidays tanned and apparently bursting with fresh enthusiasm.

I fired off emails to several of the companies Ripple Effect regularly worked with, asking if they'd be interested in Ruby-Grace Miller representing their brands. I contacted a handful of casting directors to find out if they had any opportunities that might be right for Vivienne Sterling, and called Vivienne herself to check that she was okay and to let her know I was thinking of her and putting out more feelers on her behalf. I called a bunch of potential venues for Ripple Effect's annual Halloween party. And then, weary and sad, I went back to thinking about Myles.

The strangest thing – the worst thing – was not knowing where my husband was. I don't want to give the impression that I was some kind of helicopter wife, a jealous psycho who rings hotel reception desks when her husband is away with work to check that he's where he said he'd be, and with who he said he was with.

I wasn't – at least, I never had been. I'd never had reason to be. Now, though, with no idea whether Myles was in fact in a hotel or staying with a friend or even at his mother's house or – the thought made me cold inside with horror – even somewhere with Bianca, I wished I was. I wished I'd covertly installed Find my iPhone on his mobile so I could track him down. I wished I'd made him tell me where he was going. I wished I'd reminded him that he was walking away not only from me, but from the life we'd built together, the hope of having a family together. I wished I'd begged him to stay.

I wished, over and over again throughout that long Friday, that Wayne and Shane would knock off early as usual so that I could crawl into bed and cry in peace. But they were unusually industrious, sawing and drilling relentlessly until my head ached so much it was like they'd taken an angle grinder to my skull.

I couldn't even leave the house, because what if Myles came home while I was out, picked up some clean clothes and left again? What if I didn't have the chance to speak to him, to say how sorry I was for snooping, to beg for an explanation of his and Bianca's messages that would set my mind at ease and allow me to trust him again?

As I veered from sadness to anger and back again, one thought never left me: *what if this is my fault?* I remembered the first time Myles and I had had sex after he'd got back from Lisbon. Physically, it had been the same as always, but in another way it had felt entirely different, more significant. I'd had the sense that this wasn't just expressing my love for my husband; it had a different purpose.

I wondered if he'd known that – if it had changed his feelings for me. And over the months that had followed, as I started to try harder, reading articles and books about how to increase my fertility, taking so many vitamins I practically rattled when I walked, charting my cycle and taking my temperature and, when it was the right time, jumping on Myles with a passion that he must have known was about desire for something more than just him.

I remembered one time when he'd said, 'Do we have to?'

It was the first time ever he'd said no to me. The first time I'd sensed that this had become a duty for him – a chore.

Was that what had driven him into Bianca's arms? Into her bed?

But even if it was – even if he'd felt unhappy, sought comfort with another woman – why her? How could either of them – one my husband, the other my friend – conspire to betray me like that? How could Bianca come into our home, waft around with her paint swatches and mood boards, knowing that she was working like a double agent to ruin my life?

Over and over, in between dialling Myles's number, I scrolled through my contacts to Bianca's. But I never pressed the call button. Even stronger than the hurt and fury I felt towards her was a deep, sickening sense of own failure. I'd failed to prevent my husband from straying. I'd failed to spot the signs. I'd let my own friend make a fool of me. And calling her, accusing her, would be laying bare that sense of inadequacy to her as well as to myself.

I played the contents of those messages through my head on an endless loop, trying to think of an innocent interpretation of them. But nothing came to mind at all, and I found myself struggling to remember what the words had actually been. At the time, I'd been so furtive and guilty, and then so appalled by what I found, that it hadn't occurred to me to take screenshots, or write down what I'd seen, or even commit the words properly to memory. And the more I replayed them to myself, the more confused I became about what I had actually seen.

Only one line remained clear, as if it had been burned into my brain.

I never loved her.

It could only mean one thing: that the past five years, the whole of my marriage, had been a sham.

I looked at the ring on my finger, the gold-plated band with its outsize cubic zirconia. I'd known all along that the stone was ersatz and valueless, but I'd thought that what it symbolised was real. Now, faced with the truth, I thought about ripping it off and flinging it out of the window, or flushing it down the toilet, or at least throwing it in a drawer somewhere.

But I couldn't. I couldn't bear to. It felt too final, too much of an admission that there hadn't been some sort of stupid, easily explained mistake.

At last, when it was gone five, Wayne and Shane came upstairs to say that they were done for the day and would see me on Monday. I'd been sitting still for so long, hunched over my laptop and my phone, that it hurt to move. I hadn't eaten all day – the thought of food made me feel sick.

Stiffly, weary as if I'd run a long, long way, I forced myself to my feet. I made it as far as the bedroom, where I lay on the hot, unmade bed and closed my eyes. Images of Myles and Bianca flashed in front of me, as clearly as if I was still staring at a screen. My husband's pewter hair; his eyes the dark indigo of a pair of new jeans. Bianca's perfect, porcelain skin with its dusting of freckles, her pert little ski-jump nose, her razor-sharp red bob.

I remembered seeing the two of them together on the couch in Bianca's living room, her hand on Myles's thigh. I knew what I'd seen, and their messages had confirmed it. But I couldn't imagine them kissing, or naked together; my mind wouldn't let me.

It wouldn't let me sleep, either, even though I was aching with tiredness. My brain was in overdrive, jumping from one horrible emotion to the next: grief, fear, jealousy, anger and, above all, shame. I was ashamed of myself for snooping. I was ashamed of myself for having been cheated on. I was ashamed of myself for not realising sooner what was going on.

I was ashamed of myself for wanting more to torture myself with: more evidence, more proof, dates and times and places where they might have met.

My eyes snapped open and I sat up, looking around our bedroom. One wall was floor-to-ceiling wardrobes, about a third of which held Myles's clothes. There was a chest of drawers under the window, in which three drawers were his. Under the bed was the suitcase he used for longer trips away, and in the other room were three boxes of files and papers. I'd go through it all if I had to. One way or another, I'd find it.

Whatever 'it' was. I had no idea. Still, galvanised, I got up. I was filled with something that most definitely wasn't enthusiasm, but for the first time that day, the sense of life-sapping despair had left me. I had a purpose. A horrible, furtive sense of urgency filling me, I went to Myles's side of the wardrobe and opened it.

An avalanche of wire coat hangers fell on top of me with a clatter.

What the... For fuck's sake! Hadn't I asked Myles to take those to the charity shop, or the dry cleaner, or chuck them in the bin even if it would destroy the planet, like a million times?

But he hadn't. Instead, he'd shoved them up on the highest shelf, out of sight and out of mind, waiting for them to fall on someone's head. On my head. Because he knew that, in the end, he could outlast me. He could put those hangers – there must have been fifty or more of the bastards – back up there as many times as it took, until eventually I would get so annoyed that I'd take them to the charity shop, or back to the dry cleaner, or bin them.

Because, deep down, he believed that dealing with things like coat hangers – his fucking coat hangers – was my job, not his.

Well, I wasn't dealing with them now, that was for sure. I had bigger fish to fry. I kicked them under the bed and turned, energised by my anger, to the rail of shirts and suits. Steadily and methodically, I went through every pocket. Myles never emptied his pockets – it was another bone of contention, one that had made me rant furiously at him when, for instance, my favourite velvet dress had emerged from the washing machine covered in a zillion tiny fragments of shredded tissue that even an hour of lint-rolling hadn't been able to remove.

In his winter overcoat, I found an empty plastic box that had contained mints, a handful of crumpled receipts from bars, his barber, black cabs and the corner shop, along with three business cards, bent and creased, all with men's names on them. His dinner jacket yielded the crushed cage from a champagne bottle, more business cards and a couple of wrapped strips of chewing gum. In the tweed jacket with leather patches on the elbows were more receipts, a handful of loose change and an empty crisp packet.

On and on I searched, steadily and methodically, but I found nothing of significance. I returned every last scrap of paper, every twist of foil, back where it had come from. I was operating in deep cover, gathering evidence, but leaving none behind myself. At last, the wardrobe was done – there was nothing left to go through but the piles of neatly folded trousers and underwear, and the clean shirts on their hangers, all of which I'd put in their places myself. If there'd been anything there, I would have found it days or weeks before.

Hangers. In order to get to Myles's suitcases, wheelie bags and garment carriers, which were stored under our bed until a permanent home could be found for them once the house renovation was finished, I'd have to move the forest of wire hangers I'd kicked under there in a fury half an hour before.

Seething with resentment and flagging, now, because it was roasting hot and I was becoming dizzy with hunger, I got down on my hands and knees and collected them all up. A fresh surge of annoyance tempted me to pile the lot under the duvet on his side of the bed, but there was no point – I'd be sleeping there alone tonight, and for the next God only knew how many nights. Instead, I shoved them back up on the high shelf where he'd left them and slammed the wardrobe closed before they could slither out again.

Then I bent once more to the space under our king-size bed, which was thick with dust and balls of nameless fluff. The overnight bag Myles used most frequently was with him, so there was nothing to see there. His gym bag contained an empty plastic water bottle, an unwashed, stiff, smelly sock, a can of deodorant and a tube of athlete's foot cream, squeezed almost empty. His small cabin bag was empty apart from a crumpled boarding pass from a long-ago flight. The battered old leather briefcase he never used any more but refused to part with because it had been a gift from his father was empty too, except for, tucked away in one of the pockets, a photograph of Myles as a baby with his parents. I looked at that for a long moment, a pang of sadness washing over me as I wondered who had put it there – Myles's late father, his mother or Myles himself? – and then I closed the bag and put it on the bed with the others I'd been through.

The white duvet cover was grimed with dirt now, but I'd deal with that in the morning. I was almost done, the sky outside turning from violet to deep blue, and the energy I'd started out with on this horrible, self-destructive task was almost spent. There was just one thing left in this room.

Myles's big suitcase. The one I'd given him as a present the Christmas after Megan had made me a partner at Ripple Effect – a serious, grown-up piece of luggage with a designer label, gunmetal grey in colour, sleek as a sports car. I pulled it out and put it on the bed; it was lighter than it looked, and I remembered trawling the web for ages deciding which one to get him, and opting for the model that boasted it was made from premium quality anodised aluminium and had silent 360-degree spinning double wheels.

I popped the catches and let the lid drop back onto our bed. The last time he'd used that bag was when he'd spent those two weeks in Lisbon, when I'd gone out to see him, filled with love and eagerness. When, as I remembered, Bianca had also been in the Portuguese capital, hen do-ing away with her friends. Had it happened then? Had he stayed there that weekend to see her? I remembered his shock when I'd turned up unexpectedly, the unmade-up hotel room, and I felt sick. And there, at the bottom of the case, as if I needed reminding, was my Zippo lighter, my untouched pack of contraceptive pills, the book about becoming a father and the card I'd handwritten.

Had my desire for a baby, my longing for Myles and me to have a family, been the killer blow that would end our marriage? Surely that was too cruel, too ironic.

There was one more thing in the bottom of that suitcase. An empty condom wrapper.

I was woken the next morning by the familiar sound of a key turning in the lock downstairs, the heavy thud and crash of the front door closing and the knocker crashing back on itself. I sat up, immediately awake. Had the builders arrived? That must mean I was late for work. Feeling a surge of panic, I groped for my phone, before remembering that it was Saturday.

Wayne and Shane would sooner chisel their own fingernails off than work on a Saturday.

That meant it had to be Myles. The only other person who had a key to the house was Bianca, and she always knocked before using it. Myles. Bianca. Those first few moments of wakefulness before I remembered what had happened – was happening – in my marriage were over, and the horrible dread of what would happen next descended on me.

If Bianca's turned up here and let herself in, she's going to regret it.

I sprang out of bed and pulled on a bathrobe. The room was as I'd left it the previous night, Myles's suitcase tipped over onto the floor, its dusty imprint still clear on the sheet. I closed the case and shoved it back into its place under the bed, turning the duvet upside down to hide the mark. Then, slipping my feet into slippers to protect them from the dust and discarded nails that littered the floor downstairs, I descended to find my husband.

He was standing in the new extension on the bare plywood floor, looking up at the skylight, his overnight bag at his feet. He was wearing the same jeans he'd had on when he left two days before, but his baggy purple T-shirt was unfamiliar – he must have run out of clean clothes and had to go shopping. I wondered with hollow sadness if there'd come a time when everything he wore was new to me, acquired after the end of our marriage, never washed or folded by me.

'They'll need to tidy up that lead flashing around the glass,' he said. 'Tell Wayne to take a look at it on Monday, will you? And they're coming to pour the concrete floor on Tuesday, so you'll need to wait in. It'll take a couple of days. Shane won't be able to work in here while that's happening, but he can get on with the decorating in the front room.'

I stood there in silence, not knowing how to respond. We were in crisis – everything was falling apart, spiralling away from the centre of what had been us, and he was talking about building work as if nothing had happened.

'I'm off to that conference in Doha, remember?' he went on. 'My flight's at eleven fifty-five.'

I did remember, of course. The event had been in our shared calendar for weeks. But still, his words might as well have been gibberish. It was like we were standing in a burning house and he was talking about whose turn it was to cook dinner.

'B-But…' I stammered. 'But what about…?'

'What about what? I can't cancel work arrangements just because you've got some paranoid idea in your head about some non-existent affair. And anyway, some space will be good for both of us. I'm going to shower and pack.'

He slung his bag over his shoulder, heading upstairs, and I trailed after him.

'Aren't you at least going to talk to me? About what happened? Where you've been? You owe me an explanation, Myles. If we talk, maybe we can sort things out.'

He turned to face me, his blue eyes cold and steady. 'I've been staying in a hotel. The Travelodge down the road, if you must know. I needed to think, and I've thought. I'm not sure I want to "sort things out". I'm not sure a marriage to a woman who's so neurotic, so suspicious, who doesn't respect my privacy or trust my integrity, is even a marriage I want. Or even a marriage, full stop.'

'But you… you told Bianca…' His unexpected arrival at the house, his cold dismissiveness, had left me so shocked that all the words I'd prepared, all the carefully phrased requests for him to explain it all away, were forgotten. Even the contents of his messages to her, which I'd thought were burned indelibly into my brain, had slipped away from me now.

'I told Bianca I was having doubts.' He walked past me into the bedroom, dumped his bag on the bed and pulled his T-shirt off over his head. His body was so familiar: the lean, strong arms that had held me so many times; the chest I'd pressed my face against; the curve of his spine as he bent to unlace his shoes. It was the words he was saying that made him feel like a stranger.

'I confided in her. I don't know why – I guess I figured a woman, someone who knew us both, might be able to give me some good advice. I told her I've been having doubts about you – about us – for some time now. That I'm not sure whether this marriage is working.'

'What do you mean, not sure whether our marriage is working?' I could hear a high-pitched note of panic in my voice. 'Our marriage was fine! We were trying for a baby!'

'Maybe that just brought everything into focus.' He unzipped his jeans and stepped out of them. 'I don't know if I'm ready for that. I've felt trapped by you, Sloane. Stifled. You're quite high-maintenance, you know. You need me to support you the whole time, but you don't support me back.'

'What? Myles, I literally don't know what you're talking about. Of course I support you.'

'You see? This is the reaction I expected from you. This is why, when Bianca said I should discuss it with you, I held off. I needed some time to clear my head and think about things, and I'm hoping these few days at the conference will give me that. Although I highly doubt I'll get much downtime. It's going to be frantic.'

He walked through to the bathroom. I heard the click of the lock, the hum of his electric toothbrush and the patter of water in the shower tray.

I sat on the bed, frozen with shock and fear, my mind racing as frantically and fruitlessly as an animal caught in a trap. All my energy had been focused on finding out what he'd been doing, knowing the truth. But, confronted with what seemed like incontrovertible evidence, I had no idea what I was going to do next.

What do you want to happen? I asked myself.

I want none of this to be real.

Try as I might, I couldn't shift my thoughts out of that endless, circular loop of despair. If he'd admitted what he'd done, begged for forgiveness, told me he loved me, I might have weakened. If he'd provided some kind of proof that I was mistaken, that I was imagining things, I'd have grasped his explanation with eager relief.

But he'd done neither of those things. He'd leapt from defensiveness straight to attack.

I heard the shower shut off, and Myles came back into the room, a towel around his waist, damp and fragrant. He pulled his smaller cabin bag from under the bed and I watched helplessly as he packed. He didn't say a word; it was as if I wasn't there.

At last, he finished, snapped the case shut, dropped the towel on the floor and pulled on jeans and a T-shirt. Even when he sat next to me on the bed to put on his shoes and socks, so close I could feel the mattress move under the weight of his body, he ignored me completely.

Then he picked up his bag, turned and walked downstairs.

Somehow, I made my numb lips move. 'Aren't you going to say goodbye?'

He turned and glanced back at me. 'Goodbye, Sloane.'

Chapter Fourteen

In the meeting room at Ripple Effect, Vivienne was practically vibrating with tension next to me. She'd been to the hairdresser, I noticed; the jet-black hair with its white roots that had been hidden beneath her hat when I saw her the day of Max's funeral was lighter now, a cool dark chestnut with ashy streaks through it. Her face was flawlessly – although heavily – made-up, and she smelled of expensive perfume that all but concealed the whiff of gin that had made me shudder involuntarily when she kissed me.

Apart from that, she couldn't have appeared more appropriate for the occasion. She was wearing a silk shift dress in a colour somewhere between peach and apricot, with a little cream jacket over it. Her shoes were stylish tan leather ballet flats, and there was a string of pearls round her neck that I was pretty sure were real.

The whole look was almost – but not quite – mother-of-the-bride at a posh wedding. Not a full-on, hat-requiring affair. Maybe a second marriage of a son to a much younger woman of dubious suitability. She'd planned this meticulously, I realised. When Isla had come in to offer tea or coffee a few minutes back, Vivienne had asked for Earl Grey, black with a slice of lemon. She was playing a part, carefully and precisely. She was method acting.

I imagined her in her bedroom (I'd never been in there so I could only guess how cluttered and oppressive it must be, going by the rest of the house) taking one item after another out of her closet, turning to angle herself in front of the dusty, foxed mirror, scrutinising her look from every angle.

Is this okay? Will I do?

'Vivienne.' I reached over and touched her hand. Her skin felt icy cold. 'You really mustn't worry too much about this. I put out some feelers for you, following the gardening angle, to see if there was an opportunity for any interview slots or features, just to raise your profile a tiny bit. These kinds of stories – in Sunday supplements or glossy magazines – take months and months to plan. You won't have to do anything for ages.'

Her eyes were wide with anxiety as she looked back at me. 'Thank you, darling. Thank you for understanding. I just don't want to waste anyone's time.'

'Seriously, you won't. This woman we're meeting – the editor of *Gardens Today* – was thrilled to bits when I approached her. I reckon she thinks you'd be a massive scoop for them. Normally they're lucky if they get the local mayoress showing them her veg patch. She'll love you, I promise.'

Again, she gave me that frightened stare. 'Really? Promise?'

'I'm occasionally wrong.' I smiled. 'But I don't think I will be this time. Trust me.'

Vivienne managed a smile that was almost genuine and squeezed my hand back. 'Thank you, Sloane.'

Isla's head popped round the door. 'Louisa Pettigrew-Rowse is here. And so are the cakes we ordered from Pat Val. Are we good to go?'

'Sure we are.' I glanced at Vivienne, who nodded. 'Show Louisa in, please.'

Mrs Pettigrew-Rowse – it was even in her email signature: Louisa Pettigrew-Rowse (Mrs), Editor in Chief, *Gardens Today*, followed by an address in a Cotswold village so chocolate-box perfect that when I googled it I could imagine people carefully applying paint effects to the apples in their orchards – swept into the room.

She was a tall woman and solidly built, the buttons of what I was willing to bet she called a 'blouse' straining slightly over what I was equally willing to bet she called a 'bosom'. Her trousers ('slacks'?) were a shape and style that hadn't been in fashion for years, if ever, and her hair was highlighted salt-and-pepper blonde, and cut in an actual mullet. She looked like a heftier Jon Bon Jovi in drag.

But her smile when I greeted her was warm as sunshine.

'How do you do, Sloane,' she said. 'And Vivienne! The actual Vivienne Sterling! I'm quite overcome.'

'As am I, darling,' Vivienne cooed, leaning in for a double-mwah whammy, her nerves apparently forgotten. 'I adore *Gardens Today*. It's been my bible for years. That feature you did on agapanthus was quite seminal.'

I waited for Louisa to call my client's bluff, but clearly Vivienne's research had been thorough.

'We are rather proud of that,' Louisa preened. 'So many gardeners feel the African lily should be brought indoors over winter, but of course if you select the right variety, they can thrive outdoors all year round.'

Isla reappeared with tea and cakes, and Louisa – surprise, surprise – asked for Earl Grey with lemon, while Vivienne requested a top-up. I was deeply impressed by how thoroughly my client seemed to have immersed herself in the role she expected to have to play.

'Just look at those eclairs!' Louisa breathed. 'I really shouldn't.'

'I will if you will,' Vivienne said, with a sidelong wink.

Seconds later, the two of them were stuck in, hoovering up cream, ganache and pastry in between sips of tea, nattering away about trellising sweet peas and mulching spring bulbs like they'd been BFFs 4 EVA, as my younger clients would have put it.

There wasn't really a role for me to play. I sat there in silence, sipping my coffee, letting them get on with it. The more they bonded, the better the chance was of Louisa featuring Vivienne in the pages of her magazine, which would give my client the small publicity boost she so badly needed. So I nodded and smiled, and waited until the last crumb had been appreciatively devoured, the discussion about the war on aphids concluded, before I chipped in.

'So, as I understand it, Louisa, you're looking for well-known faces to feature in *Gardens Today*, people who are not only inspiring gardeners, but who also really resonate with your readership.'

'That's right,' Louisa agreed. 'We recently conducted an extensive survey of our readership. We found that the *GT* lady – our readers are seventy-eight per cent women – is not only passionate about gardening, but has wider cultural interests too. Music, art, ballet, opera and, of course, theatre were all listed as interests. And although seventy-one per cent of our readers live outside the M25, many of them do also have a London home. So a well-known actress who has a thriving urban garden was a real box-ticker for us.'

I wondered if Vivienne had ever been described as a box-ticker before. She certainly looked pleased about it.

'Great!' I said. 'So we'd be looking at an interview and photo shoot, presumably?'

'That's correct. We'd provide a stylist and hair and make-up artist, but of course we expect our interviewees to express their own signature look – we're not prescriptive at all. And the story would include little nuggets that offer an insight into your personal life and career, as well as your top tips for keeping a garden thriving during those tricky autumn months.'

Autumn? My positive frame of mind was disturbed by an alarm bell. I knew how magazines worked – features were planned months ahead of publication. But over a year ahead? That would be unusual.

'When you say autumn…' I began tentatively.

'Well, yes.' Louisa spread out her hands in a 'what can I say?' gesture. 'You know how it is in publishing. We had Petronella Dawson lined up for the October issue. The interview and shoot were all done, copy approval secured, the pages laid out, all exactly on schedule. And then that story appeared in the *Telegraph* – you know.'

I didn't, but Vivienne came to my rescue.

'About her affair with the MP? Too fascinating. I know one shouldn't, but I do love a good scandal. Fancy him having a thing for cuddly toys in the bedroom. Honestly, the richness of human life!'

'Quite,' Louisa said. 'All that we could have possibly overlooked, but the fact that he is a *Labour* Member of Parliament – well, we felt we had no option but to pull the story. And it's left us in a bit of a hole.'

'So just to be clear – you've got a gap in your October issue?' I said, my head spinning. 'October this year? And it's the first of September tomorrow.'

'Correct. We're due to land on shelf two weeks from today. So in order to get the interview and shoot done, the pages laid out and passed through our internal checks, and go to press just a day or two behind schedule – well, let's just say we need to get our skates on. We'd need the interview done in the next couple of days.'

I heard Vivienne give a little gasp, but Louisa carried on, undaunted. 'Of course, I'm sure your garden is absolutely on point. But we'd be delighted to provide a small team to do any small jobs – the odd bit of pruning and so on – if you find it's not quite as you'd like it to appear.'

I had no doubt at all that Vivienne's garden was exactly as she'd like it to appear. But her house? That was another matter entirely. I imagined Louisa, her journalist, photographer, stylist and all the rest of them stepping through that front door, into that scene of chaos. I imagined the journalist telling a friend, and the friend telling her editor, and a story appearing in a tabloid, complete with some pictures sneakily shot by the photographer.

Actress's hoarding shame, the headline might read. Or *Former Oscar winner's life of squalor*. It would put the kibosh on my hopes of reviving Vivienne's career and – more importantly – the personal humiliation for her would be awful. Next to me, I could feel her starting to tremble again.

'What a pity,' I said. 'Isn't it tomorrow that you're off to France, Vivienne?'

'To… Yes, that's right.' After a slight pause, Vivienne's words came out in a rush. 'To stay with my dear friend Marion in Cannes for a fortnight. Her pet parrot passed away recently and she's devastated, poor lamb. I couldn't possibly let her down.'

'So you see, Louisa, on this occasion I'm afraid we won't be able to help. But it does sound as if Vivienne would be such a brilliant fit for *Gardens Today*, I know you'll consider her for future issues.'

The meeting limped to a close, and Louisa headed off, presumably to spend the rest of the day doing the rounds of other agencies, frantically trying to fill her last-minute celebrity gardener slot.

Vivienne didn't get up to say goodbye – I'm not sure she could have done. She stayed in her chair, immobile apart from her shaking hands.

I poured her a fresh cup of tea, and although I knew she must be longing for something much stronger, drinking it seemed to comfort her a little.

'Don't worry, Vivienne,' I said. 'I know that wasn't ideal, but there will be other opportunities. We'll keep working our hardest to find them for you.'

'Thank you, Sloane. Thank you for rescuing me.'

I shook my head and patted her hand. I hadn't rescued her – I'd just come up with a half-plausible lie in a tricky situation. Rescuing Vivienne would mean doing far more than that, and I wasn't sure I was capable of it. All I could do was be there for her – in a way I hadn't been for my mother, all those years ago.

After I saw Mom that day in Starbucks, I fled back to school like a mouse into a hole. I knew I'd done something bad, something I'd regret, but I had no idea how to fix it. My anger and hurt had been so carefully concealed for so long – from Dad, from Erin the therapist, from Mrs Klingmann and my teachers and friends, even from myself – that the explosion of it terrified me.

The school corridors had been almost deserted that Saturday afternoon. Some girls were out seeing their parents or bowling together; others had joined an excursion to a new museum of indigenous Canadian art; and a rebellious handful had sneaked out to watch the nearby boys' school's hockey team play and go for beers afterwards.

My shared room was empty. I got onto the bed and sat there, rigid, my hands clenched between my knees. But the need to move, to do something, was too strong to resist. I got up and ran to the bank of payphones, dialling Dad's cellphone number.

'Honey? Are you okay?'

'I saw Mom.'

'Right. That's good.' His voice sounded uncertain over the crackly line. 'How did it go?'

'I told her I can't forgive her and I don't want to see her again.'

I heard Dad's voice exhale in a long sigh.

'Okay, honey. That's your decision, and I respect it. I understand how you feel, and I'm sure your mother does, too. But if you ever change your mind, that's fine, too. You just keep talking to me, hey? Because if you don't, I can't support you.'

That was Dad, through and through. A man so kind, so measured and reasonable, that he was a model parent in many ways. But he'd never parented a teenage girl before – or been one. He wasn't to know that what I wanted – what I needed – him to do was to encourage me to change my mind, to point out that this was a decision I'd come to regret deeply.

Hell, I was already deeply regretting it.

But I never said that to Dad. He stayed in touch with Mom over the years – first to get their divorce finalised and make sure she had enough money to support herself, and, later, out of what I suppose was genuine concern for a woman he'd loved deeply, alongside a sense of guilt that he may have been partly responsible for her falling apart.

And even after he'd met and married sweet, motherly Maura, who wasn't able to have kids of her own, he'd mention every now and then to me that he'd seen Mom.

I'd say, 'I don't want to hear about it.'

And he'd give that weary sigh and reply, 'Okay, honey.'

Until one time he didn't. I was at university in Toronto, in my second year, and by then I had a cellphone of my own. I was just coming out of an English Lit lecture when I heard Avril Lavigne's Sk8er Boi trilling from my satchel. My friends and I were all broke – we SMSed one another rather than calling. A call meant something serious – and a call from Dad, when he knew I'd be in and out of classes and when we'd spoken just the previous evening, meant something definitely serious.

'Dad? What's up?'

'Are you able to talk for a second, honey?'

I glanced at my watch. I wasn't due in another lecture for an hour, but I'd promised to meet a friend for a coffee.

'Sure,' I said reluctantly.

'It's your mother, Sloane. I think you need to see her.'

'Dad, you know how I feel. We've had this discussion.'

'I know how you feel.' Again, that sigh. 'But this is different. She's not well, honey. She's dying. She wants to see you, and I think you ought to see her.'

Chapter Fifteen

'Oh my God, Sloane, it's so amazing to see you!' Megs jumped up from the teal-coloured leather cocktail chair and hugged me. 'I got us a bottle of prosecc— What's happened? What's the matter?'

It was three days since Myles had left for Qatar and a day since Megs had texted me in a state of high excitement to say that Matt was home and she was primed and ready to go '*out* out'.

He's totally besotted with Ethan and he's been amazing the whole past week, I'm so glad he's home. He's figured out how to make him take a bottle – total baby whisperer. And I've expressed shedloads of breastmilk and Matt says he's really looking forward to spending a night on the sofa with Ethan bingeing box sets and eating pizza. So we are GO! Let's get shitfaced and dance around our handbags! Let's order a whole fishbowl full of cocktails!

I'd replied saying that sounded like a fabulous idea but maybe a slightly more sedate night was in order, and Megs had said, *Sheesh, I guess you're right. Especially since as soon as I show you pics of Ethan on my phone my boobs will start leaking everywhere. But it will be amazing to see you.*

We'd settled on a super-trendy new restaurant in Soho, just down the road from the Ripple Effect office, and Megs had called in a favour with the publicist to get us a table, and here we were. Or here Megs was, sitting underneath a blossoming cherry tree that I was pretty certain couldn't be real, wearing a button-through chambray midi dress and nude leather sneakers, her hair so on fleek you'd swear she'd just spent hours in a salon rather than having had no time to do anything more than rake a comb through it, her skin managing to glow in spite of the smudges of tiredness under her eyes.

And here I was, having rushed from the office after spending half an hour at my desk with my hand mirror trying to make myself look like I hadn't been dug up after being dead for a week. Since Myles's departure, I hadn't been able to face proper food, and my diet of cornflakes – eaten out of the box, flake by flake, nervously waiting to see which would be the rogue one that would send me dashing to the bathroom just in time to spew – with the occasional cinnamon Danish thrown in by way of a balanced diet, had taken its toll on my appearance.

My skin had broken out, my hair was frizzing so badly no amount of serum could tame it, and the new rust-coloured velvet bodysuit I'd ordered online was cutting into my crotch and had dark stains of perspiration under the arms.

I felt like shit, and I looked it, too. And Megs knew me well enough not to be fooled by all the slap I'd applied, or even my new eyelash extensions.

I flopped down into the chair opposite hers, feeling one of the poppers at my crotch ping adrift, as Megs splashed fizzy wine into a glass for me. She'd filed and painted her nails, I noticed, relieved that she'd been able to make some time for herself. She was getting to grips with this motherhood business, I thought with affection.

'What's up, Sloane?' she asked. 'Tell me. Is everything okay in the office? Are *you* okay? I feel so bad, leaving you holding it all together on your own.'

'I'm not on my own. I've got Rosie, and Sam and Isla. It's fine. We're busy, but we're all good. Ruby-Grace threatened to flounce but I've got Sam ready to hold her hand if she gets stressy again. I've put out some feelers for work for Vivienne. Everything's under control, Megs – you really don't need to worry.'

She looked at me astutely. 'I wasn't worried. I don't have time to worry. I barely have time to drink a cup of tea, never mind worry. But I am now. Something's up. I can tell.'

I took a big gulp of prosecco, the bubbles tickling my nose and reminding me of the ever-present threat of tears and the wide rim of the champagne coupe making some of it trickle down my chin.

Then I took a deep breath. I hadn't spent all that time applying make-up only to cry it all off again. Besides, this was a public place. I knew full well how quickly news spread. I wasn't anywhere close to being a celebrity, but would-be clients of ours hung out in places like this in the hope of being seen and wouldn't hesitate to garner attention by sharing the fact that they'd seen Sloane Cassidy having a meltdown in Fifty-One Wardour all over social media. And, besides, it was Megan's longed-for night out, and I didn't want to ruin it for her.

I said, 'Things with Myles are kind of weird. Kind of shit.'

'Right. Go on.'

Megs topped up our glasses and leaned in close, and I edged my chair nearer to hers, and I told her everything that I'd seen, and read, and the horrible, bewildering conversations I'd had with my husband.

'And now he says we need a break, and he's making out like it's all my fault, and he's in the Middle East at a conference and I have no bloody idea what to do.'

'He says you need a break?'

'Yes! When five minutes ago we were talking about having a baby. I thought we were in a good place. Well, good-ish. Given everything. And now I'm stuck alone in a building site, I think my husband's cheating on me, he's fucked off abroad, and what the fuck do I do?'

We both drank more fizz. I could see Megan's mind working at speed. In a similar situation, I knew I'd be just as conflicted. I mean, you come out and say what you really think ('Kick the cheating bastard to the kerb, woman!'), and six months later you find they've patched things up and you're persona non grata. Or you say, 'Are you sure it wasn't just a drunken mistake? Not worth ending an otherwise happy marriage over, surely?' and then you find out things are actually terminal and you've had to watch your friend being torn apart for months when she could have been moving on.

Megs said, 'Okay, we need to deal with this one issue at a time. First off, how do you know he's cheating on you?'

'I don't *know*! I mean, I'm about as sure as I can be but I haven't caught them in bed together or anything like that. I saw him and Bianca together at her house and they were – not canoodling, exactly. But she touched his leg.'

'I'm not sure one touch on the leg is exactly the smoking gun, is it?'

'Well, no. But then I saw those messages they sent each other on his phone and I was completely sure. But he says he was just asking her for advice because he's not sure he wants to be with me any more. And I can't remember exactly what the messages even said, but I think they could have meant that. I mean, they weren't exactly, "You're the most amazing fuck ever and I want to be with you." But it was something about what they were doing being wrong. And how could Bianca even do that to me? She's supposed to be my friend.' My voice had risen to a trembling almost-wail.

'Oh, Sloane. You poor love.' Megs reached over and squeezed my hand. 'I don't know Bianca. I don't know what she could've been thinking. But I know one thing: if they were sleeping together, he wouldn't come out and admit it, would he? They never do.'

'But why not? If it was me, I wouldn't want someone to stay married to me because they thought I hadn't been unfaithful when I had. That seems like the worst kind of false pretences.'

'In my experience – which is thankfully limited – men in these situations want to see themselves as the good guy, the wronged party. And if they fess up and say their head was turned by someone else and they gave in to temptation, they can't do that any more. It would present them with an image of themselves that they don't want to see.'

'That makes sense. I guess. But what do I do, though? Do I keep digging until I find proof? And if it turns out it's true and they are shagging, what do I do then?'

Megan sighed and topped up our glasses. The bottle was almost empty. 'I think you're looking at this the wrong way round. Don't go around playing Sloane Cassidy, Girl Detective. You'll just cause yourself more grief and give him more ammo to paint you as a jealous, paranoid bunny boiler.'

'But what if he's not doing anything wrong? What if I am a jealous, paranoid bunny boiler?'

'Honestly? I think that's unlikely. I've known you for a long time, Sloane, and you're not an insecure person. You're not a jealous wife and you're not a fantasist. I reckon women whose partners are being unfaithful are far more likely to delude themselves into thinking everything's okay, to not trust their gut, to hide from the truth until it's literally staring them in the face, than to imagine there's something going on when there isn't.'

'So you're saying he is shagging her?'

'I don't know. I can't possibly know for sure. But I think his reaction speaks volumes.'

'How do you mean?'

'Let's say he was fully committed to your marriage. Let's say he'd never so much as looked at another woman, and suddenly you turned around and started flinging accusations at him. What would he do then?'

'Deny them?'

'Well, yes. But he'd show you his phone, wouldn't he? He'd be like, "Here, read the full exchange between me and Bianca and you can see that it's entirely innocent, and put your mind at rest." And he didn't do that, did he?'

'No. He went ballistic at me for snooping.'

'And then, two days later, he came up with the story about asking her for advice because he was thinking of checking out of your marriage?'

I nodded miserably.

'That's kind of significant. So he had a chance to have a good think, and he thought that if he came up with a plausible – or plausible-ish – explanation, he could do two things.'

'Which are?'

Megan took another sip of wine and extended a finger.

'One, he averts the initial suspicion. He's given himself a cover story, basically. And two – and this is more significant to me – he makes you think you're at fault. Not only are you imagining things that aren't there, you're also vulnerable because he's not sure about your marriage. So you doubt yourself on both levels, you try desperately to patch things up, you become a pushover and he gets to crack on and do whatever he wants. It's gaslighting, Sloane, and it's not something I'd be happy to have done to me if I were you.'

'But what can I do?' I asked pathetically.

Megs thought for a moment, taking another glug of prosecco. 'You know what I'd do? I'd talk to Bianca.'

'What? But I'd basically be accusing her of boffing my husband behind my back. That would go down like a bucket of cold sick, right?'

'Wait, just hear me out. If – and I know it's a big if – you can manage to stay calm and reasonable, tell her you saw some messages on Myles's phone that freaked you out, and ask her, as your friend, to tell you the truth about what's going on, what do you reckon she'd do?'

'Honestly, I have no idea. I guess it depends on whether it's true or not.'

'Exactly!' Megs said triumphantly. 'If it's not true, she'll be like, "Oh my God, Sloane, I can't believe you were freaking out when we were just talking about the surprise birthday gift we got you," and she'll show you the messages, and then all you have to do is make things right with Myles, after you've given him a massive bollocking for being so manipulative.'

'And if it is true?'

'If it's true, I bet you a fiver she'll fess up. Seriously, I've read a lot of the agony-aunt columns in trashy magazines over the past few months – I know, right, but my attention span is totally shot and I don't have head space for anything else – and loads of them are women sleeping with married men basically begging the agony aunt for permission to come clean to the wife. They all want to. Either it's because they feel guilty, or it's because they want the whole thing to blow up in the hope the bloke will land in their lap.'

She tipped the bottle over her glass, but it was empty. I was about to signal to the waitress but noticed her coming over with a fresh bottle in an ice bucket – not prosecco this time, but proper decent champagne.

'Sorry to bother you, ladies, but the gentleman over there in the corner said to offer you this, if you'd like it.'

And she handed me a business card – a fancy number on see-through acetate, with the name Edward Reeves printed on it in frosted letters and the logo of a company called Clear Future.

Astonished, Megs and I looked over to the corner of the room, where a group of late-twenties men were drinking cocktails. All of them were wearing sharp suits, except one who was in jeans and a T-shirt. He was tall and dark-haired, with a chiselled jawline any male model would be proud of – and he caught my eye and raised his glass.

Megan and I both started to laugh.

'I tell you what, Sloane,' my friend said, 'no matter what happens with Myles, at least you know you've still got it.'

We didn't talk much more about Myles after that. I wasn't sure how to respond to the generous gift of the champagne – it was so long since either Megan or I had been in the dating game that neither of us had a clue. I thought with a pang of nostalgia how the old, single me would have got up, gone marching right over there and thanked Edward Reeves in person, joining him and his friends for a drink.

Although, of course, it was a total no-brainer where it would have gone from there. Right back to his flat, or mine, for a night of slightly drunken sex that would have left me feeling either wildly elated at the prospect that he might call me the next day and turn out to be The One, or sunk in depths of despair and self-disgust, wondering how I'd turned into someone who'd put out in exchange for a bottle of Taittinger.

That wasn't going to happen tonight, obviously. So I found a notepad in my bag (after trying and failing to write on the slippery surface of Edward's business card), and scribbled a few words: *Thank you for the generous gesture! I'm just catching up with my friend, but I hope you have a great night.* And I signed it with my first name and asked our waitress to deliver it.

Then we ordered poké bowls and edamame and kimchi and seaweed salad and pickles and debated splitting a miso brownie for dessert before deciding to hell with it – we'd have one each.

While we ate, Megs told me – in between telling me how wonderful it was to be talking about something other than mastitis and shitty nappies – how adorable Ethan was and what a relief it was to finally be getting some sleep for the first time in two months. I told her how things were going at the agency, and how shocked I'd been to meet Vivienne, and she said yes, she'd suspected that her client wasn't in a good place, and we chatted about the best way to deal with that. I told her that I was determined to do everything I could to help Vivienne find work and get back on her feet again, although I didn't yet know whether I'd be successful. But I didn't tell her about the horrible, dark memories Vivienne had brought back for me, about my own childhood and about Mom.

And soon we'd finished the bottle and all the food, and Megs looked regretfully at the time and said she really needed to get an Uber home or her tits would start leaking everywhere, and I said I was ready to call it a night, too.

As we paid our bill, I glanced over to the corner where Edward Reeves and his crew had been hanging out, but they'd gone – presumably moved on to more fertile pulling pastures. Once more, I felt that pang of nostalgia – but this time it was tainted with a hint of terror.

I'd played the dating game, and played it well. At the time, I reckoned I'd got every dating app nailed and known whether to swipe right or left within seconds of seeing a profile. I'd done the analogue thing, too, mastering the art of striking up conversations with strangers in gyms and bars and on the subway. I'd forced myself to assume a veneer of confidence and, having faked it, I'd found myself eventually making it.

But now, the idea of returning to that world filled me with hollow dread. I wasn't twenty-something any more. I had a mortgage and a business and lines round my eyes that definitely hadn't been there when I met Myles. I had a wedding ring on my finger. I'd thought that once you had those things, it was game over – and the game was one you'd won.

Now, the glaring naïvety of that assumption was staring me right in the face.

'Sloane, my love, call me, okay?' Megs said, tumbling tipsily into her Uber. 'We'll have coffee, or do this again. It's been amazing. I feel human for the first time in ages. I'm sorry if my advice was crap. I feel so bad for you. I love you.'

And I told her I loved her, too, and asked her to give Ethan a big smooch from his not-so-fairy godmother, and told her to text me when she was home safe.

I waited for my own cab, my head spinning, all sorts of ways of interpreting Megan's advice jostling in my thoughts like dodgem cars at a fairground. Maybe, I figured, once I'd had some sleep, it would all become clear.

And, amazingly, the hungover morning provided not clarity but a determined resolve to take matters into my own hands.

Chapter Sixteen

What does a girl wear, I pondered bitterly, to confront the woman she suspects of having an affair with her husband?

It was Saturday, and I'd tried to ring Bianca several times, but my calls had gone unanswered, my messages ignored. Myles was incommunicado, too, which made me mostly furious, but also a bit anxious. He was thousands of miles away in a foreign country where anything could happen. A pile-up on a motorway in a rental car, an arrest for breaking some law he didn't know about, a mugging in the street. I tried to tell myself not to worry, but it was no good – the niggling fear wouldn't die down; it just crystallised into anger.

With Myles returning home the next day, I needed to take control. I needed to make some decisions – or, if I couldn't do that, to at least have a clear plan of action, a set of if-then scenarios in my head that would hopefully help me to make them in future.

And so, since Bianca was blanking me, I was going to go and find her.

I'd put my hair up in a twist on the back on my head, secured with a clip. I'd done my make-up, focusing on a strong red lip but not putting on any mascara, in case I cried. In my wardrobe, I found a black shift dress I'd bought in a charity shop a few years back – it was older than me, but it was Chanel, I knew, even though the labels had been cut out by a previous owner. I slipped it on and did up the zip, contorting myself to get it all the way up, remembering how I always used to get Myles to do it for me.

Would I ever walk up to him again, casually turn my back and feel one of his hands on my waist as the other pulled the zipper tab to the top, his warm kiss on the nape of my neck? Would I ever hear him say, 'Turn around and let me look at you' and see the desire in his eyes?

Had he ever zipped up the back of Bianca's fucking dresses? That at least was unlikely, I told myself – Bianca favoured unstructured cocoon-like garments in natural fibres and earth, oatmeal and sludge tones.

Bianca. If I was going to do this thing, I needed to do it now, before my courage deserted me. I stepped into a pair of taupe heels, perched a pair of outsize Jackie O-style shades on my head and left the house, picking up my car keys on the way.

Fifty minutes later, I found a space and parked my car. This was one of those parts of south-east London where, from the endless terraces of drab suburbia, sudden little enclaves of wealth and prestige emerged. There were leafy streets lined with grand detached houses, many designed to look like half-timbered cottages or Gothic mansions. There was a sign pointing to a golf and country club. The chichi high street where I'd parked boasted an organic juice bar, a women's boutique, a hipster barber shop, a place selling hand-painted wooden toys for children and a French restaurant.

And, of course, Casa Bianca. The shop window was crowded with broderie anglaise bedding, twiggy things in tall vases, rag dolls in Victorian-style dresses and bits of upcycled furniture that seemed to serve no purpose except to hold the various knick-knacks that jostled for space on every surface.

Bianca's home might have recently been upgraded to industrial-style minimalism, but clearly her interiors emporium hadn't got the memo.

I pushed open the door and a bell pinged. Two voices said in unison: 'Good morning, how may we help you today?'

Neither of them was Bianca's. Behind the little table that served as a counter were a teenage girl, hastily screwing the cap back onto a bottle of nail enamel, and Charis.

'Oh, hello, Sloane,' Charis said. 'We've got some French porcelain, just in. Would you like to see it?'

If things between Bianca and me escalated into a proper bitch fight, the French porcelain would be the first casualty, I thought.

'Actually, I'm here to see your mummy,' I said. 'Has she popped out?'

'Bianca's not working today,' the girl said. 'Have you tried calling her?'

It was absolutely typical, I thought, that Bianca would leave her – presumably underpaid – Saturday helper to mind not only her shop but also her daughter.

'I haven't been able to get hold of her,' I said. 'Is she at home, do you know?'

The girl shook her head indifferently. 'No idea, sorry. I guess not, otherwise…' And she glanced down at Charis, with a hint of entirely justifiable resentment.

'Mummy said I should ask you about promoting my YouTube channel,' Charis said. 'She said you can get me free stuff to do unboxings of, and find me celebrities to interview. Is that right? She says I've got a real presence in front of the camera.'

'I'm sure she's right,' I said. 'But let's have a chat about it another time.'

I'd dealt with some nightmare clients in my time, but it was hard to imagine one who'd be more demanding than Bianca's daughter. She'd make Ruby-Grace – stripper heels, designer dog and all – look like Influencer Management for Dummies.

'Mummy said you don't know that Myles has been playing away,' Charis went on. 'Why not? And what game's he playing? Are you going to go and watch?'

The girl's eyes widened and her jaw literally dropped.

I forced out what was meant to be a casual laugh, but came out more like a strangled croak. 'I think you mean working away. Working, not playing. He's in Qatar this week, in a town in the middle of the desert. So I thought I'd swing by and see if Bianca was free for lunch. But I guess she's not.'

'Nah,' the girl said, unscrewing her nail varnish again.

'Can you do nail art, Shawna?' Charis asked. 'Can you do my nails? I want them ombre blue, with gold tips.'

I hovered for a second, considering asking Shawna if she could try calling Bianca from her own mobile, thinking up some pretext to get her back here, and then ambushing her. But I was nowhere near ready to embrace that level of humiliation, and I'd clearly outstayed my welcome. Not that I'd had a welcome in the first place.

'Right, I'll head off then. Don't bother telling Bianca I came round; I'm sure we'll catch up soon.'

The girl didn't look up from her nails as I left, the bell pinging again as the door closed behind me.

Back in the safe haven of my car, I realised I was shaking all over. My teeth were chattering so hard I had to clench my jaw to stop them, and the ache I felt deep down in muscles I'd barely known were there made me realise I must have been clenching them a lot. My hands on the steering wheel were trembling and slick with sweat.

I was in no state to drive, but I didn't care. Like some frightened animal – a cat, maybe, racing across a busy road in panic – I was desperate to get home. I put my Mini into gear and reversed jerkily out of the parking space, turning back onto the A road towards home, grateful that I had the satnav to guide me, because I was certain I wouldn't have made it on my own.

But I did make it, more or less safely, apart from a narrow miss with a cyclist that earned me a mouthful of deserved abuse. My usual space outside our house had been occupied for several months by the builders' skip, and the one around the corner that I'd been using was taken too, by a powder-blue soft-top Mazda with a vanity plate that could, if you squinted a bit and substituted Is for ones and Bs for eights, read BIANCA.

Fuck. Surely I must have been imagining it?

I got out of my car, my legs so unsteady I could barely balance in my high heels, and walked around the corner. Bianca was standing on our doorstep, tapping in exasperation at her phone. As I approached, I heard my own phone begin trilling in my handbag.

Bianca heard it too. She turned around, the look of annoyance on her face segueing into relief.

'Sloane! There you are! I'm so sorry I haven't returned your calls. Everything's been frantic, and to be quite honest with you I've had nothing to report. But the wallpaper samples arrived just this morning, so I rushed straight round to share them with you, and we can make some proper decisions at last!'

She brandished a document carrier at me in a way that I guessed was meant to be inviting.

'Bianca, what the…?'

'I've updated all your mood boards. I didn't even go into the boutique this morning, I was so excited to get all this ready to show you! Shall we go inside?'

'Yes. I think we'd better.'

I unlocked the door and she followed me in, still gushing on about foil embossing and the resurgence of flock. Like I gave even a fraction of a shit about wallpaper at that point.

'Any chance of a glass of water, Sloane? It's baking out there, isn't it? And I did ninety minutes of hot yoga this morning – I think I'm still dehydrated.'

I thought, *I think you know where the tap is. Feel free to use it.* But I said, 'Of course, give me a second.'

And I went upstairs, grabbed the only two pint glasses we had that weren't packed in boxes, filled them from the bathroom tap and carried them downstairs.

I handed one to Bianca. My determination to remain calm and diplomatic forgotten, I said, 'What's going on with Myles? I need you to tell me right now. I've had enough of the bullshit. You know what's going on, he knows, even your daughter knows. So come on. Out with it.'

Bianca flinched like I'd threatened to slap her. 'What do you mean?'

'You know what I mean. Seriously, Bianca. Are you sleeping with my husband?'

The glass slipped out of her hand and fell to the ground. If the polished concrete floor had been laid, it would have shattered into a million pieces for sure. But as it was, it bounced off the bare boards, showering both of our feet with water that felt shockingly cold in the heat of the day.

'Oh, God, I'm so sorry. Here, let me…'

'I've got it. It's fine.'

We both squatted down, reaching out together for the glass. Our hands bumped together and I recoiled as if she'd given me an electric shock, leaving her to pick up the glass. I grabbed the roll of blue paper towel the builders had left and chucked some of it onto the spilled water.

'There. Now, explain what's going on.'

'Sloane, I genuinely have no idea what you're talking about.' But her eyes were wide and anxious, and didn't quite meet mine. She clutched her folder to her chest like a shield, looking like a tiny, red-headed Brienne of Tarth.

'I think you do, Bianca. I went to your shop earlier, because I thought you'd be there. Charis said you said Myles is playing away. What's going on? If you're sleeping together, you owe it to me to be honest about it.'

'I really think you should be discussing this with Myles.' Bianca sipped her water, her eyes darting from one corner of the room to the next, like she was looking for an escape route.

Well, I wasn't giving her one. 'Do you think I haven't discussed it with him? For Christ's sake. Are you stupid or just acting like it? Of course I've fucking discussed it with him. And he's denied it. He says he just sought your caring advice as a friend, about our marriage, and I presume you gave it – as a friend. Possibly in a horizontal position.'

'There's no need to take that tone of voice with me,' Bianca said.

'Oh, right. What tone of voice, exactly, am I supposed to take with someone who's meant to be my friend, who's been lying to me and going behind my back with my husband?'

Once again, she glanced around. 'I didn't… I… Look, Sloane, please, please believe me. There's nothing going on between Myles and me. Nothing at all. And Myles never asked me for advice about you. I don't have the faintest idea where you got this idea from.'

'I saw!' My voice rose to a shout. 'I saw the messages you sent, on Slack, saying he needed to tell me – something.'

'I really don't think my private correspondence with Myles is any of your business, frankly. I'm sorry things are difficult between you. I did try to warn you. And clearly I was right. But to suggest that I'd betray my own husband, put my family at risk, is just insulting, Sloane, and I'm actually quite disgusted that you can even think of me in that way.'

Her defensiveness completely wrong-footed me. I wasn't sure what I'd expected – denial, certainly, but followed by something – a confession, an explanation, something I could work with. Not this cold, outraged offence. I didn't know what to say; not that it mattered, because Bianca wasn't giving me a chance to say anything.

'I tried to help you, and what do I get? Baseless accusations. I love my husband. We trust each other. I've never – and will never – do anything to jeopardise that. And that includes having relationships – business or personal – that call that trust into question. So I think it's best if we terminate the arrangement we have here. I wish you every success in sorting out your personal life, Sloane. But I'm out.'

And she handed me her empty water glass, then rummaged in her bag and passed me the set of keys Myles had given her, before turning around and walking out, closing the front door behind her with a precise click.

I stood there, in the centre of the space that was going to be our kitchen, where I'd imagined cooking dinners and pureeing baby food and icing cakes. The room I'd imagined – eventually – being the heart of our home. And I looked around and saw it as it was: the pile of paint pots and power tools and ripped-up floorboards and ladders and buckets and chaos, and I thought, *how did this happen? How exactly did my life come to this?* It wasn't just the house that was a mess – it was everything.

It was me. And I needed to fix it. Obviously, I couldn't pour the concrete floor or fit the kitchen or even paint the walls. But I needed to fix things in other ways. I needed to take back control. I couldn't control what Myles was thinking, or feeling, or doing. But I could control my reaction to it.

I sat down on the floor, not caring that I'd get sawdust all over my Chanel dress, and I tried to order my thoughts. I'd gone round to see Bianca that morning, determined to confront her, even if it meant doing so in front of her employee and her customers. Thinking about it now, it seemed crazy, reckless, the behaviour of a madwoman. I wasn't mad. I was rational. I remembered what

Vivienne had said – how her suspicions about her husband had chipped away at her sense of self until there was nothing left.

I wasn't going to let that happen to me. I was worth more than that. And besides, unlike Vivienne, I wouldn't be able to find solace in gardening – even houseplants carked it on me after a couple of weeks. I'd only had one plant thrive on me, staying green and lush for weeks as I watered it faithfully – until I realised it was plastic.

I took out my phone and clicked through to my message history with Myles. In the past twenty-four hours, I'd sent him an increasingly desperate, needy series.

What aren't you answering your phone?
We need to talk. I want to make things right. I love you.
Myles, please just answer me.
I can't deal with this.

Well, I could deal with it. I had to.
Choosing my words carefully, I typed another, longer message.

Myles, clearly you're not sure about things. I'm not, either. I think we need to have some time apart. I don't want to live with you right now and I think you feel the same. Please can you make other arrangements for a couple of months. S.

It wasn't much; it was barely anything at all. But, having sent it, I felt like, finally, I'd clawed back a tiny piece of my self-esteem.

Chapter Seventeen

I got through the next two weeks. Somehow. It was a bit like when I was first at boarding school, after Mom left. I can barely remember the detail of those days, but I remember how every morning I woke up, thinking for a second that things were normal before reality snapped shut on me like a trap, and I knew I had the whole day to get through: the horrible food, the lessons I couldn't focus on, the other girls in their little cliques, the humiliation of track and hockey and basketball, all of which I sucked equally at. And, worst of all, the free time, when we were supposed to enjoy ourselves but all I could do was plug into my Sony Walkman and play The Doors at full volume on the tapes Dad had given me to remind me of home.

And I remember how the thing that got me through it – the only thing, really – was the prospect of that brief moment in between sleep and waking when I forgot I was there: when I thought I was at home, waking up to go downstairs and somehow Mom would be there in the kitchen cooking eggs on the hob, dressed and smiling and coming over to fold me into a hug.

Hardly ideal, I know, but it was familiar. I'd had a degree of freedom then, an independence that boarding school had stripped me of. And now, as an adult, I had it again. I didn't have to consider anyone's needs but my own – well, not Myles's, at any rate.

The discussion we'd had when he returned from Doha was awful. Literally every bit of me was longing to tell him I'd changed my mind, I wanted him to stay, I needed us to work through this. But I'd made my decision and, somehow, I managed to stay firm.

'Where the hell do you want me to go, Sloane?' he'd said. 'This is my home. I live here, remember? This was your idea. If anyone moves out, it should be you.'

'It was not my idea. It's the only way I can see of finding a way forward. You said you need time to think – that's what I'm proposing.'

'I can think here.'

'Maybe you can. But I can't. And there are two of us in this situation, so something has to give.'

'This is my home,' he'd said again, stubbornly.

'And that's not going to change. If you decide you want us to give this our best shot – have counselling, whatever – we might live happily ever after here. And if we split permanently, we'll work out the finances like adults and decide what to do. But, for now, we need some space, like you said.'

'I can sleep in the spare room.'

'That doesn't work for me, Myles. Two of us in two rooms, sharing a bathroom, with downstairs a building site? We might as well be camping together.'

'What do you want me to do, sleep on the street?'

'Of course not. I'm sure you can find a solution. Stay with your mother for a bit. Rent an Airbnb.'

But, magically, a solution presented itself. I suspect it was the prospect of crashing on the sofa in his mother's one-bedroom flat but, the next day, Myles proudly announced that an unsold flat in a luxury development designed by a business acquaintance of his could be made available for the time being.

'I hope you appreciate the sacrifice I'm making here, Sloane. It's going to be highly inconvenient.'

I opened my mouth to say I was sorry, this wasn't what I wanted, either, and couldn't we please just try again. But I was amazed to hear my voice say, quite calmly, 'I'm sure you'll cope just fine.'

Coping myself was a whole different ballgame. In a way, I was grateful for those long-ago schooldays, and the lessons I'd learned about shutting down my feelings, going through the motions, faking it until I could make it.

Every morning, I found myself wide awake at five o'clock. I'd never been an early riser but, without Myles there next to me, there was no reason to stay in bed, no warm body to curl up to. With only my thoughts for company, the time until I could legitimately get ready to go to work felt like an impassable chasm of dead loneliness. So I forced myself to get up, pull on yoga pants and a T-shirt, and go out for a walk. It was summer, at least – not like those icy mornings when I was a child. And after a few days, I began to recognise the rhythm of early morning in the streets around our house: the sinewy woman I saw each day on her morning run, presumably getting the miles in before work. The young dude on his bicycle delivering unpasteurised milk in glass bottles, presumably for a start-up of some kind. The guy feeding frozen peas to the birds on the pond, who explained to me that bread was bad for them and provided unasked-for snippets of intel about the life cycle of swans.

And, obviously, the homeless guys who hadn't made it into a shelter the night before, the bedraggled working girl making her way home unsteadily on her wobbling high heels, the old bearded man drinking coffee outside the betting shop, anxious before it was due to open.

It sounds kind of crazy, I know, but it all made me feel connected to our neighbourhood in a way that I never had before. Home had always been a place to come after work, a bolthole where Myles and I had our lives together, and the world outside was just a sort of hinterland I passed through.

I found myself returning from those long, aimless walks feeling strangely serene, reminded that I was just another cog in the huge, whirring machine that was London, which would carry on whether I was happy or sad, married or not married, there or not there. My problems didn't go away – far from it – but they felt less overwhelming than they did inside the four walls of our house.

Back at home, I showered and was dressed and ready for work by the time Wayne and Shane arrived. I found myself offering them tea or coffee quite cheerfully, and I realised that it wasn't making their hot drinks that I'd resented – it was *me* making them, when Myles could just as easily have been the one to do it.

And once I stepped through the door of the Ripple Effect office, there was no time for navel-gazing. My to-do list ran to several pages, and it never seemed to get any shorter – for every item I ticked off, I seemed to add another three.

I'd signed two new clients: an Instagram influencer for whom I'd got a great deal as the face of a new electric smoothie maker, and a fitness YouTuber who brought the entire office to a standstill when he came in to meet me, such was the sizzling hotness of his ripped physique. Only Sam was unmoved, saying, 'Bloke's a plonker – anyone can see that,' while Rosie and Isla practically got into a handbags-at-dawn stand-off for the privilege of making his Redbush tea.

Preparations for the Halloween party were well under way, and a venue had finally been booked. But the invitations still needed to be sent out, and in order for that to happen I had to sign off the guest list – a daunting spreadsheet that seemed to change every day. I remembered with horror the year an intern had accidentally deleted Glen Renton's name from it, and we'd had to have an invitation couriered to him three days before the event, together with a cooked-up story about the original having been lost in the post.

Meanwhile, Charlie Berry was about to embark on a trip to South Korea, Singapore and Japan to promote his new skincare line. It would mean Rosie being out of the office for a week babysitting him – a job that would normally have been mine but, with Megan off, there was no way I could take such a chunk of time out of the office.

Somehow, I got through that week. I'd have been dreading the weekend, but work came to my rescue in the form of VlogCon, a two-day conference that kept me rushed off my feet all day and showing my face at various drinks parties long into the evening.

As was customary on Monday mornings, I gathered the Ripple Effect team around the meeting-room table over coffee. It was a ritual Megan and I had started back when I joined, when we were the only two members of staff; not a formal meeting – more a chance to bond, touch base, and sketch out a general plan for the week ahead.

I filled them in on the goings-on at VlogCon, then asked how my team's weekends had gone.

'I went to a festival,' Isla said. 'I thought it was going to be really chilled – it's just a little local thing near where I live, but I ended up spending both days there and getting totally hammered, and look how sunburned I am. And I ate all the junk food. There were these pimped hot dogs that were off the scale. I thought I'd try one for lunch on Saturday and they were so good I legit had about six more. I didn't eat anything else all weekend. And I'm really sorry guys, I'm going to be sweating tequila all over you all day.'

'I was at a hen do,' Rosie said. 'It was so brilliant. We went for brunch at Shack-Fuyu and then we had spa treatments and then we did a cake-decorating class and then we went for cocktails and had dinner and went clubbing afterwards. I brought us cupcakes.'

She opened the shiny white cardboard box in front of her, and there were more oohs of appreciation at her frosting and sprinkle-arranging skills.

'That one there's chocolate fudge, the middle one's red velvet, that one's lemon, the violet one's – well, violet, obviously – and the other one's salted caramel. I'll have that if no one else wants it – it's a bit Marmite, to be honest. Literally. I overdid the salt a bit.'

Even though it was only nine thirty in the morning, we all launched enthusiastically into the cupcakes and agreed to split the remaining one between whoever was still in the office in the afternoon.

'It won't be me,' Sam said, with a hint of pride. 'Ruby-Grace wants me.'

'Fnar, fnar,' Rosie said. 'Lucky boy.'

Sam turned absolutely scarlet. 'Not like that! But seriously –
she's dead high-maintenance. On Saturday I had to go shopping
at Westfield with her. We must have visited every single store in
the whole mall and she bought an absolute fuck-ton of stuff and
I had to wait outside the fitting rooms while she tried on, like, a
million things and tell her if she looked good in them – she did,
obviously; she'd look amazing in a spud sack – and carry all her
bags. I thought my arms were going to fall off and my feet were
legit killing by the end. And she did it all in heels, she's hardcore.'

'So what does she want you to do this afternoon, then?' I asked.

'Go with her to have her lip fillers done. Apparently she's scared
of needles and she needs someone to hold her hand.'

'Wow, Sam, isn't that above your pay grade?' Isla teased.

'I wish it was. I'm shit scared of needles, too. I'll probably faint
or something, and make a total arse of myself. But, you know, I'll
get to hold her hand.'

I wondered briefly whether I ought to remind Sam about not
getting too close to our clients, but until we had some more work
for Ruby-Grace, it was probably best to keep her sweet. And
besides, I had a client of my own whose hand needed holding. I
said, 'Vivienne Sterling got a callback for that TV commercial she
auditioned for, so I'm going to go along and give her some moral
support. In fact, I should head off in, like, five minutes. They always
keep you waiting around for ages.'

Sure enough, two hours later, I was sitting in an under-air-
conditioned reception area next to Vivienne, who was growing
increasingly jittery.

'My God, I'm absolutely sweltering,' she whispered to me, pulling her jumper away from her body. 'And the itching!'

'I know,' I soothed. 'Just endure it for a few more minutes, okay? I'm sure they'll call you in soon. And they clearly loved your look in the first casting call, otherwise they wouldn't have called you back.'

'Glamorous granny.' Vivienne sighed. 'Is that what my life has come to? Still, I suppose it's marginally better than auditioning to play some frumpy old dear in support stockings and a perm that makes your head look like a cauliflower.'

'You look fabulous,' I reassured her, and it was true. She was wearing black leather trousers, a scarlet woollen jumper, and over-the-knee suede boots – which, while totally inappropriate for a hot London afternoon in September, clearly chimed exactly with what the advertising agency had had in mind when they'd decided that their client, Timpson's Turkeys, should feature an older woman in its Christmas advertising campaign.

In her first casting call, all Vivienne had had to do was smile to camera, say her name, turn around so they could see her from all angles (I hoped they hadn't noticed the moth-eaten patch on her jumper) and tell the director that she loved gardening. She'd managed it with an impressive mix of calm and sparkle. But now that she'd been summoned back for a second audition, the nerves were clearly getting to her.

I could see her glancing around at the other women, patiently waiting their turn on hard plastic chairs. One was wearing a full-on evening dress in sage-green velvet, teamed with gold stilettos, which I thought was taking the 'glamorous' idea a bit further than necessary. Another was wearing ripped jeans and a jumper with Rudolf the

Red-Nosed Reindeer on it, surrounded by flashing LEDs. I imagined her looking in the mirror, saying to herself, 'Festive? Certainly. Too much? Oh God, it is, isn't it?' and then thinking, 'Fuck it, it'll be worth it if I get the gig,' and determinedly covering the jumper with her coat. I noticed Vivienne glance at her, then glance away again, suppressing a smile, and wondered if she was imagining the same.

The door at the opposite end of the room opened and another middle-aged actress appeared, accompanied by a woman who might have been her daughter or might have been her agent. Wearing a cream jumper dress in a chunky knit and caramel-coloured suede boots, her hair an edgy silver pixie crop, she looked every inch the part. Again, Vivienne stole a glance at her then looked away, ducking her face to rummage in her handbag.

'That's Sheila Andrews,' she whispered as soon as the two had left the room. 'She was at drama school with me. An absolute bitch. I suppose it's comforting in a way to know I'm not the only one to have fallen on hard times.'

'This isn't the end, you know,' I said. 'Think of it as a beginning – just a way of getting your performance and audition head back on, okay? It doesn't matter if you don't get it. There'll be other opportunities. It's only an ad for turkeys, right?'

'Vile meat it is, anyway,' Vivienne said, with a brief show of animation. 'Always as dry as cardboard no matter how much you brine and baste the buggers. Goose is far tastier.'

I smiled. 'Mind you don't say that to the team in there.'

Vivienne turned her head towards the door, and I swear she paled under her carefully applied, natural-looking make-up.

'God, I'd forgotten how terrifying this always is. I wish I'd brought a hip flask.'

I'm bloody glad you didn't, I thought, pain twisting my heart again as I thought of Mom. Besides, going into a callback and wafting gin all over the assembled decision-makers would have been an absolutely terrible look.

'You'll be fine. Deep breaths, remember? Right down into your diaphragm.'

Vivienne nodded, then closed her eyes. I could see her chest rising and falling, and hoped that she was willing herself into her happy place, wherever that was. Hopefully, in her mind, she was in her glorious garden, looking at the sunlight filtering through the leaves overhead, hearing birdsong.

'Vivienne Sterling?' A young girl with indigo hair, clutching an iPad, had opened the door to the audition studio. 'We're ready for you now.'

Vivienne's eyes snapped open and she sprang to her feet, forgetting her handbag on her lap. Keys, wallet, mobile phone, tubes of lipsticks, stray tissues and a plastic box of mints all spilled out onto the floor, and for a second I thought she was going to cry.

'I've got this.' I knelt down and scooped everything hastily together. 'You go on in. I'm right behind you.'

Seconds later, I followed Vivienne into the studio and took a seat in a corner, cradling her bag and mine. She was on her own now – there was nothing more I could do.

'I'm Lucy,' the purple-haired girl said, shaking Vivienne's hand. 'And this is…' And she quickly rattled through the names of the art director, the casting director, the camera and sound crew, and the head of marketing for Timpson's Turkeys.

Casting by committee, I thought gloomily. Everyone in the room would have come with their own preconceived ideas of what made a granny glamorous and what was right for their brand – it could go any way at all. The CEO's mother-in-law could decide she wanted a crack at acting and get the gig, and the ad agency wouldn't be able to do a thing about it.

'If I could just ask you to stand over here,' Lucy said, and Vivienne followed her obediently to a spot on the floor marked by an X of masking tape, surrounded by a forest of lights, mics and cameras.

In the glare of the lights, she looked small and terrified, her skin as white as snow against her red jumper.

'You've seen the script, of course,' Lucy said, 'but here's an extra copy if you like.'

'That's all…' Vivienne began croakily, then tried again. 'That's all right, thank you, darling – I can manage perfectly without it. But could I possibly trouble you for a glass of water?'

There were a few minutes of faffing about while water was fetched, a battery pack on one of the cameras changed, and the head of marketing decided he needed a bathroom break.

The delay could go either way, I reckoned: either it would give her a chance to compose herself, or it would rattle her further. Looking at her face, so still under the lights it almost looked frozen, it was impossible to tell which.

At last, Vivienne had said her name for the camera – twice, because the first time the sound guy sneezed right in the middle – and we were ready for the main event.

'Whenever you're ready,' Lucy said encouragingly.

Vivienne paused for a second, and then said, 'Having all my family around me makes Christmas the most special time of the year. That's why I choose tasty, juicy Timpson's Turkeys.'

She was amazing. She managed to pack cosiness, foodieness and even sexiness into those few words. Her voice was slightly husky, not too posh, warm and welcoming. She looked like Nigella Lawson's equally glamorous aunt.

'Once again, with a bit more oomph,' requested the casting director, and my heart leaped with excitement. If he hadn't been impressed, he would have thanked Vivienne and let her go – by asking for more, he was seeing how she took direction, assessing what it would be like to work with her.

Vivienne said her lines again, with more oomph. Then the casting guy asked her to try in a Northern accent, and she pulled it off perfectly. He asked for 'more Mary Berry' and she nailed that too.

'Let's have a go with the baby, shall we, Luce?' said the marketing guy, and I noticed a slight grimace on the casting director's face and an exchange of eye-rolls between two of the creatives. Whatever this was, it was controversial. And it wasn't in the script.

I wondered if Vivienne had picked up on the vibe too – she looked suddenly afraid again, immobile like she was pinned to that taped X on the floor.

Lucy hurried off to the back of the room and returned with a plastic doll, dressed up in a Santa babygrow.

'We'll have a real one for filming, obviously,' she said, handing it to Vivienne.

'Just a bit of a snuggle, and a "coochie coochie coo".' The marketing guy spoke for the first time. 'Our customers love a sprog. First Christmas as a nana, that's what we're after.'

Vivienne was holding the doll like it was made of ice, as far from her body as possible, barely touching it with her fingertips.

'Take your time, Vivienne.' There was a note of respect in the casting director's voice, but some apprehension, too. He'd seen what I'd seen – that Vivienne wasn't comfortable with this at all.

She tried. I could see her steeling herself, taking the bundle of fabric, fake fur and plastic close to her breasts, struggling not to recoil from it.

'Who's Nana's little princess then?' she began. 'Who's a little Christmas mirac—'

She stopped abruptly and dropped the doll to the floor. Lucy scurried over and picked it up, holding it out encouragingly to Vivienne.

'Just one more time?' the casting guy suggested gently.

Reluctantly, Vivienne took the doll. This time, it was worse.

'Who's Nana's little princess?' Her words were wooden, utterly without feeling. Then she bent down and placed the doll on the floor by her feet, almost tenderly. 'I'm sorry, I can't do this. I'm sorry to have wasted your time.'

She turned and rushed towards the door like she was leaving a burning building. I stood and hurried after her, taking her arm and guiding her out onto the street and into a café. She'd probably rather we'd gone to the pub, but I figured what she needed right then was sweet tea, so I ordered two cups.

'I honestly wouldn't worry about what happened there,' I heard myself jabbering. 'They loved you, they really did. The thing with the baby – I bet the agency will persuade the client to drop it. Never work with animals or children, right? And even if they decide to go with another actress, at least you know you can do it. You totally smashed it – you were great.'

Vivienne looked at me, her eyes hollow in her pale face.

'You're very kind, Sloane. But I fucked that up.'

I'd never heard her swear before. In her beautiful, resonant voice, the word sounded shocking.

'What happened, Vivienne? Do you want to tell me about it?'

She shook her head. 'It was a long time ago. Water under the bridge.'

But I was fairly sure she did want to talk, so I just waited, sipping my tea.

'Max and I never thought we wanted a family,' Vivienne said. 'At first it seemed like it would be an interruption to my career, one I didn't want. And then Max... well, I realised our marriage was in big trouble. But I kept trying to make things right with him, and then, after one of his visits home, I found out I was pregnant. I was forty-three – the doctors called me an elderly primigravida because I was having my first so late. Isn't that awful?'

'Awful,' I agreed.

'But once I knew I was having the baby, everything changed. I suddenly realised I didn't mind so much about Max and his other women. He was thrilled about being a father – I suppose he thought it was proof of his virility. But for me it was as if there was something of him – some piece of what we'd felt about each other in the beginning – that could be salvaged. Something precious.'

'I can see why you'd feel that way.' I felt a stab of sadness for her – because clearly, nothing had been salvaged.

'I loved being pregnant,' Vivienne went on. 'I was never sick or anything. I felt marvellous, right until six months. And then I started to bleed.'

I reached across the table and held her hand, but I didn't say anything.

'They told me afterwards that the placenta had come away. Quite often babies survive when that happens, but Juliet didn't. She died before she was born. She was so small, but so perfect. My beautiful daughter. Max never saw her – he wasn't there. He wasn't there very much at all, after that.'

I imagined Vivienne bearing the burden of her grief alone for all those years, hoping in vain that Max might eventually come back to share it with her, and then losing him, too. No wonder she'd been trapped in that kind of limbo all this time, unable to cope with daily life but tending her garden with the same loving, nurturing care she'd have lavished on her daughter.

'Vivienne, I'm so sorry. That's the most terrible loss. I feel awful that you had to go through what happened today – it must have brought it all back.'

'Oh, darling,' she said. 'It didn't bring it back, not really. I think about her every single day.'

Her voice overflowed with sadness, but her eyes were dry – I sensed that all her tears for Juliet had been shed long ago.

Chapter Eighteen

As well as adjusting my morning routine to keep my mind off the yawning gap left by Myles's absence, I'd changed my habits after work, too. I was busy enough to keep me in the office until after seven most evenings, and after that I didn't hurry home. Months before, I'd joined a fitness studio down the road from work and been to about half a dozen classes in my first frenzy of enthusiasm, imagining myself becoming fit, toned and limber and eventually sailing through childbirth thanks to yoga breathing.

But, obviously, that hadn't happened. I hadn't got pregnant, for one thing. And also, life had got in the way. As the house renovation lurched from crisis to stasis and then back to crisis, I'd had to spend more days working from home, and my preoccupation with the meltdown of my marriage had left little space in my head for the calm and stillness I so badly needed.

But I'd convinced myself that it was just a blip. I'd get back to it next week, or as soon as the extension was weathertight, or once I wasn't getting home as early as I could to shower and cook dinner and be a perfect wife.

And all the while, the direct debit for the frankly extortionate monthly membership had kept winging its way out of my bank account each month.

Now, though, I had time. I had mental space that was all too ready to be filled with anxiety, regret and shame, if I didn't fill it with something else instead. So, after work on Mondays, Wednesdays and Fridays – Fridays being the evening I most desperately needed to fill, without the ritual of a takeaway, a bottle of wine and, most likely, sex with my husband – I left the office, walked the short distance to The Space, as it was rather pretentiously named, changed into my Lycra kit in the sumptuous locker room and joined whatever class there was a space in.

I sweated and groaned my way through hot yoga. I tried a HIIT spin class and literally thought I was going to throw up afterwards. I gave Thai boxing a go, imaging that the unfortunate woman I was partnered with was Myles as I pummelled her with my padded gloves. I tried Zumba one time, but when I caught a glimpse of myself in the mirror, I literally saw my dad dancing to Gloria Estefan in our living room in 1997 and was so mortified I couldn't bring myself to go again.

At first, it was the promise of a luxurious shower, using copious amounts of free aromatherapy shower gel, shampoo, conditioner and body lotion, as well as vast fluffy white towels that I didn't have to wash, that kept me coming back. Then I discovered the on-site café, which offered a pay-by weight buffet of organic wholefoods. I was always starving after a workout, and I soon learned to game the system by choosing the highest-value, most delicious options. Marinated tofu and hard-boiled eggs could go to hell – I was all about the flame-grilled free-range chicken, garlicky puy lentil salads and tuna sashimi. Oh, and of course the vegan chocolate brownies.

After a week or two, I was well into it. I found that it wasn't just the prospect of a fragrant shower and meal I hadn't had to cook that kept me coming back – I was actually relishing the challenge of the classes themselves and the endorphin-induced euphoria I felt afterwards.

It was in this supremely chilled-out state that I arrived home on the last day of September, almost three weeks since I'd last seen Myles. Okay, it was Friday. Friday was hard. Saturday was harder and Sunday was purgatory. I'd been through two weekends alone so far. On the first one, I'd spent Friday night crying, Saturday pacing up and down the stairs, taking occasional rest breaks during which I flung myself down on our bed and cried some more.

Then I'd bought a bottle of bourbon on Amazon Prime Now and drunk almost half of it, ordered a Domino's meal for two (large Pepperoni Passion, wedges and a bottle of Coke) and troughed most of that before passing out and waking the next morning with the worst, puking, meat-sweating hangover I'd ever had in my life. So Sunday, obviously, had been spent ricocheting between my bed and the toilet, hoping I might die soon and end this self-inflicted agony.

The following weekend, lesson learned, I'd gone to visit Megan, trawled the shops on Bond Street and bought stuff I didn't particularly like or need (but at least returning it would fill some time, I guessed), and slept. A lot. And in between, I binge-watched the whole of *Jane the Virgin* on Netflix, desperately filling in every spare moment that I might otherwise have spent thinking.

And this weekend, I had a plan in place. When I got home on Friday, I was going to go straight to bed and sleep for as long as I could. On Saturday I'd have a healthy breakfast, go for a long walk, clear out my closet and take a bunch of clothes to the charity shop, grab some sort of street food for lunch, go and see a movie… And so on. Literally every hour was accounted for. I was not – repeat, not – going to think about Myles even once. Or about Bianca and her betrayal of our friendship. Or about my dreams of becoming a mother, now torn to pieces. Or about that empty condom wrapper.

But when I got home, I saw with a jolt of surprise that the lights were on, both upstairs and downstairs. None of the blinds were closed, and the boards the builders put over the downstairs windows, so passers-by wouldn't see their power tools lying about and break in and steal the lot, weren't in place.

What the…? Wayne and Shane weren't still there, surely? It was gone ten on a Friday night. They'd have been in the George and Dragon pub for hours.

I fitted my key into the lock, turned it and stepped cautiously in. In the blaze of light cast by the bare one-hundred-watt bulb strung from the ceiling, I could see the new part of the house clearly for the first time in days. The floorboards were mostly covered by dust sheets, but round the edges I could see smooth, golden, newly varnished wood. The concrete floor had been poured and polished, and it glowed with a deep sheen like frosted glass in the harsh light. Around the walls were the carcasses of the kitchen we'd agonised over planning and ordering months before.

It was all beginning to look a bit like a home. Instead of heading straight upstairs, I found myself wanting to linger, explore and admire.

Then I heard a voice. 'What d'you reckon, Sloane? Looking pretty good, isn't it?'

Myles was standing on the stairs, about halfway down, his hand resting on the balustrade, which I noticed had been freshly painted a smooth, deep charcoal colour. He was still in the suit he must have worn to work, but he'd taken off his tie – I could see the end of it dangling out of his jacket pocket. It was the silk one with owls on it that I'd bought him on a work trip to Milan a couple of years back.

'It looks amazing.' *And so do you.* My happiness at seeing him made me furious, but I couldn't help it. He was there. He'd come back.

'Shane texted me with a few questions about the kitchen cabinets, so I thought I'd better drop in and check things out. I tried to ring you, but your phone was off.'

Of course. I'd turned it off for my yoga class in accordance with The Space's strict rules and forgotten to turn it back on, so I couldn't even tell Myles off for turning up at the house without notice. Although it wasn't that I resented so much as his entirely casual demeanour, as if seeing me for the first time in almost a month was nothing remarkable at all.

'Come and have a look.' He stepped down the last few stairs and paused in front of me in the hallway. For a second I wondered whether he might be about to kiss me, or hug me, or say he'd missed me, but he didn't. My arms were almost aching to reach out to him, but I didn't either.

He lifted a corner of the dust sheet and said approvingly that the floorboards had come up great, inspected a new piece of cornicing that had been fitted below the ceiling and said that looked a bit neater now, didn't it, then strolled through to the new part of the house with me following him, my heart racing in my chest like I'd just done a spin class rather than restorative Yin Yoga.

'I reckon another month, and we'll be done,' he said. 'Now they've started the kitchen, it'll all go really quickly. And then the worktops and the appliances will go in, last bit of decorating in the front room – and voila.'

Voila indeed. The house being finished would surely have to bring to a close this strange limbo of 'some time apart'. A decision would have to be made about whether we'd sell it or if one of us would buy the other out, or something else.

Stay together. Try again. Make a new start.

'It's looking great,' I agreed, without enthusiasm.

Myles glanced at his watch. 'God, I'm starving. I had a conference call with New York that only wrapped up an hour ago, and I came straight here. Shall we see what's still open on Deliveroo?'

'I've already eaten.' Let him wonder who with – there was no need for him to know about the solitary chicken salad I'd eaten while flicking through *Philosophies* magazine.

'Pity,' he said. 'I picked this up on my way home – fancy a glass?'

He took a bottle of cold Pol Roger champagne out of an Oddbins carrier bag. I felt fresh annoyance at his presumption – turning up here on a Friday night, assuming I'd be home, assuming I'd want to sit down with him for a glass of expensive champagne and a chat.

Only problem was, he was right. I did want to.

'Why don't I go and grab a blanket and a couple of glasses from upstairs? It's not exactly habitable down here but it's better than it's been for months.'

I should have said no. I should have told him to take his champagne and get lost. But I didn't.

'Sure,' I said.

And so, a couple of minutes later, we were sitting on an old faux-fur throw in the front room, glasses in our hands.

Myles looked at me and said, 'Well, cheers.'

'Cheers, I guess.'

We clinked and sipped. Myles stretched his long legs out in front of him and let his head tip back against the wall. Part of me hoped the paint was dry; another part hoped it wasn't, and he'd spend the next two days walking around with a smear of Manor House Gray on the back of his head, and not know why people were staring at him. I was sitting cross-legged, next to him, still in my yoga gear. The throw wasn't large, but there were still a couple of inches between my knee and his thigh.

'The ceiling in here's a decent height,' he remarked. 'You really notice it now the partition wall's come down. And we're lucky that those original fireplaces didn't get ripped out by some vandal doing the place up in the seventies.'

'It's a lovely house,' I agreed, with a pang of sadness.

'A piece of decent art on the chimney breast, or maybe a mirror to make it all feel bigger, open up the space,' he went on, 'a statement light fitting, and it'll be spectacular. Maybe a chaise longue in a bold colour between here and the dining room, to define the spaces.'

I felt uncomfortably aware that we were discussing the decisions we'd hired Bianca to help us make, and wondered if Myles was also thinking about why she'd taken herself off the case. It was quite the elephant in the room – just as well we had those high ceilings. But I wasn't going to mention Bianca and, evidently, neither was my husband.

'Listen to you,' I said. 'You sound like a right design wanker. Remember that thing we watched on telly. "It's all about the yin and yang," they kept saying.'

'"It's all about the expression of the client's personality,"' he countered.

'"It's all about textures and the tension between them."' Saying those words reminded me uncomfortably of the tension between Myles and me, so I quickly changed the subject. 'It's lucky that birch tree in the garden's still there. Lots of people would've chopped it down to make it sunnier out.'

'And probably slapped down decking over the whole thing.'

'There were a load of those green parakeets in the tree this morning. They woke me up, screeching away, at about six o'clock.'

I'd already been awake when I heard the birds, but I wasn't going to mention that to him, either.

'There could be a water feature out there, just something small, to help drown out the traffic noise,' Myles mused. 'And maybe a built-in barbecue or a pizza oven or something. Make the garden a real outside room.'

'And herbs in pots. Right outside the French doors, so when you were cooking you could literally just step out and grab stuff.'

'Herbs, yes, definitely. Vegetables, no. I mean, tomatoes picked five minutes before you eat them might taste great, but they look bloody terrible. It's a garden, not a fucking allotment.'

It was a conversation we'd had before – almost, but not quite, an argument – when I'd suggested planting the living salad we'd bought from the farmers' market outside to see what happened, and he'd looked at me like I'd suggested parking a tractor in the street outside. We'd bickered for some time about what constituted a crop, and what a plant, half-annoyed, but mostly just being dumb, exaggerating our positions on the subject to absurd levels. When I suggested the world's tiniest wheat field in a corner, we'd collapsed in giggles and gone to bed.

Remembering that now, I smiled and said teasingly, 'What about some potatoes? Just a few plants. They grow well in pots, I'm told.'

Myles filled up our glasses. 'I reckon it would make more sense to rip everything up and put down artificial lawn. It might be plastic, but you'd never know. It gets hot underfoot and you have to hose it down if you spill ketchup on it when you're having a barbecue, but apart from that, what's not to like?'

'I'm not convinced. Wouldn't it get in the way of the compost heap I was thinking might fit in that back corner by the laurel tree? Apparently if you do it right they hardly smell, and the flies are minimal.'

'Or of course there's the Japanese approach. Gravel over it all, with just one small maple tree in the centre.'

'Now that's a great idea! Especially for cats. Imagine, a whole garden that was basically one giant litter tray? Way to encourage the local wildlife, right there.'

I turned my head to look at him and discovered that he was already looking at me. Whatever tension there had been was gone, and we both started to laugh.

'God, Sloane, I've missed you.'

I didn't mean to say it, but I did. 'I've missed you too.'

He reached across the short distance to my knee and touched it. And that touch was everything. All the anguish I'd felt, all the fear and loneliness, the pizza and the bourbon and the yoga and the mindfulness – it was like none of it had ever happened, or like the memory of it was washed away by my need for him.

I didn't move, but he must have sensed my total, instant capitulation; the way the reserves of strength and resolve I'd been carefully building, grain by grain like the world's slowest sandcastle, was demolished in a wave of longing for the past to be the present again.

He said, 'It's actually kind of uncomfortable down here. Shall we finish the bottle upstairs?'

I couldn't say a word; I just nodded and stood, and he took the fizz and our glasses and we went up to the bedroom, but we didn't even have another sip. We fell on each other like teenagers who'd been waiting months for an empty house so they could fuck.

I fell asleep straight after, and I didn't wake until long into the morning. When I did, I felt blissfully happy, totally at peace for the first time in months. I stretched luxuriantly, loving the warmth of the sun spilling through the window, savouring the moment before I opened my eyes and saw my husband there next to me. But there was no one else in the bed; my foot encountered a brief resistance, a weight on the duvet that I hadn't expected to be there, and then I heard something thud to the floor.

I sat up, startled, and looked over to the other side of the bed. There, upended on the carpet, was an empty KFC box, and a few leftover nuggets had tumbled onto the carpet, smearing it with ketchup. Myles's suit was in a crumpled heap in the corner; his wheeled suitcase was lying open in the doorway, unwashed clothes spreading out across the landing. Clearly, in the time he'd been away, Myles had reconnected with his inner student – and now he'd brought that same inner student back home with him. But he himself was nowhere to be seen.

I straightened up, pulling the pillows up against my back, and listened. I could hear traffic from outside the open window, and a breeze rustling the leaves of the tree outside. The air blowing into the bedroom carried the chill of early autumn onto my naked skin, and I reached over my shoulder to tug the window closed. That shut out most of the sounds from outside, so I could listen to the silence in the house more intently.

No one was moving. I couldn't hear pipes humming in the bathroom, footsteps on the floor downstairs, or even the creaky wheels of the old Ikea chair that stood in front of my makeshift desk in the room next door.

I called out, 'Myles?' but, as I expected, there was no response at all. My phone told me it was half past ten – at least I could be thankful that I'd had a fantastic night's sleep, exhausted by work, yoga, sex and – I supposed – sheer relief.

But now I felt none of the joy I'd experienced the night before, the thrill of seeing our house taking shape, the overwhelming ecstasy of being in my husband's arms again.

I was alert and calm, and – in a sudden rush of awareness – I knew what was going on.

West Ham United, the team Myles supported, were playing Tottenham Hotspur at home. The fixture had been on our shared calendar for months. Myles, I knew, would have been making plans with his mates arranging which pub to meet in, exchanging banter about the various players and generally gearing up for a massive day out, as usual.

And, as usual, he'd expect to come home to an orderly house, his washing done and sorted, a home-cooked meal waiting for him, or at least a wife who'd patiently indulge his slightly lairy ranting if West Ham lost, or celebration if they won, order in a takeaway, and not mind when he capsized into bed, smelling of beer, sweat and fried onions, and snored the night away.

Myles, I realised, expected that because we'd slept together again, everything was now going to go back to normal.

My calm had evaporated, and I was furious. Partly with him, for choosing a football match over the chance to talk about what was going on between us, maybe even find a way to make things right – or at least talk about what might happen next. But mostly with myself.

Why the hell had I let myself weaken like that? Why had I melted at his familiar touch, let my defences be stripped away by his unerring ability to make me laugh?

'That muggy fucker!' I fumed aloud, swinging my feet out of bed and storming through to the bathroom. 'And you're no better, Sloane.'

Brushing my teeth, the electric thrum of the bristles was grazing my gums in a way that was pleasantly almost-painful, I thought. It was like I was hoping the vibrations would somehow make their way to my brain and kick the stupid, feeble thing into gear.

I didn't know, not for definite, whether Myles and Bianca had been having an affair. But I knew, with total, one-hundred-per-cent certainty, that he'd treated me badly. Not just recently, I realised, energetically spitting white, minty foam into the basin, but for a while. Why was it that I waited in for the builders? Why was I in charge of everything from the laundry to our social calendar (football excepted) to his family's birthday cards? How had I let this happen?

I thought again of that condom wrapper, lying there in his suitcase with the tokens that showed I was willing to make the ultimate commitment, far more lasting and profound even than marriage, of bringing his child into the world. If I asked him about it, I knew he'd come up with any number of excuses.

It must've slipped under the lining somehow, sweetheart.

But the suitcase had been new eighteen months before, and Myles and I hadn't used condoms for at least three years before that.

The housekeeping in that hotel was atrocious – I found it in the bed sheets.

Then why didn't you throw it in the bin?

I was missing you. I had a posh wank, into a condom instead of my hand.

Bullshit.

I don't fucking know how it got there, Sloane. Why are you so paranoid?

Because I know you've been cheating.

That was it. I knew.

I didn't need the kind of evidence that would convince a jury, beyond reasonable doubt. I didn't need Myles or Bianca to confess to having done anything. All I needed was the deep, iron-hard certainty in my own head and heart, which I realised I'd been ignoring in favour of chasing after what-ifs and maybes.

I didn't need any evidence beyond what I'd seen that morning. With our marriage in crisis, Myles had chosen to go and watch a football game. Sure, it was important to him. But how important, exactly? Clearly, more important than waiting for me to wake up, holding me, reassuring me, explaining what was wrong with us, what it meant and what we might do to fix or finally fracture our marriage.

I emerged from a hot shower and went through to my makeshift desk, swung open my laptop and sat down, still wrapped in my damp towel. I had time now – Myles wouldn't be back for hours – and I was going to make a plan. However much it cost in money, inconvenience and heartache, I needed to take charge.

First of all, I needed to call Dad and tell him what was happening. He'd be devastated, I knew, sad and worried for me. But he needed to know – and I needed to hear his voice, hear him say, 'It'll be okay, honey,' even though it felt like nothing would ever be okay again.

Over the next few days, weeks and months, I knew I'd have hard, awful decisions to make. Now, though, I'd only needed to make one.

When my husband came home, I wasn't going to be there.

Chapter Nineteen

'Ross and Angela Granger are here to see you, Sloane,' Rosie said.

'Oh, right. I thought they weren't going to show up – it's almost twelve and they were due to be here at half eleven.'

'Yeah, well… they're here.' She looked at me with a half-raised eyebrow that told me that I was in for an interesting meeting. 'I've shown them into the boardroom, but I have to dash out now to that meeting with Glen Renton.'

Again, we exchanged glances. However challenging the Grangers might prove to be, they were nothing compared to Glen Renton, Ripple Effect's biggest influencer client, who had an ego as large as his YouTube following.

'Sam, do you mind sorting some coffee out, please? And then you may as well sit in on this.'

I grabbed my iPad and a notebook and hurried through to the meeting room, preparing my best professional smile, hoping that I didn't look like someone who'd lain awake the previous two nights, unable to sleep in the unfamiliar surroundings of the Airbnb apartment I'd found to rent for a few weeks while its owner was working away in Johannesburg. I'd packed my belongings in a massive rush and my mind kept returning to my precious stash of sleeping pills, forgotten in my nightstand at home.

I was so tired that, when I first saw Ross and Angela, I thought I might be hallucinating. They were a forty-something couple, seated at adjoining chairs, holding hands. Both of them were dressed from head to toe in black leather. Ross's head was shaved and Angela's hair was dyed bright pink. Between them, I counted at least a dozen piercings, and I was willing to bet there were loads more in places I couldn't see and hopefully never would. Both of them were wearing heavy black eyeliner. Angela's wet-look stiletto-heeled boots came about six inches up her thighs, and there was a good four-inch, fishnet-stocking-clad gap between their tops and the bottom of her zipper-embellished skirt.

For a Monday morning, even in Soho, it was a pretty strong look.

'Sorry we're late,' Angela said, extending a hand heavy with chunky silver jewellery for me to shake. 'We had a meeting with our daughter's head teacher.'

For a chat at your kid's school, theirs was a *seriously* strong look. I imagined some poor, harried woman trying desperately to focus on little Chloe's literacy or the contents of little Lily's packed lunch while thinking, 'Okay, but does he have a Prince Albert piercing? Does he?'

I introduced myself and took a seat.

'So, you're looking for marketing opportunities for your clothing line?'

'That's right,' Ross said. 'Own the Night. We design clubwear, with a slightly edgy aesthetic.'

'Strongly influenced by the bondage scene,' Angela explained unnecessarily. 'We like to think we're our own best brand ambassadors, but we're looking to reach out to a younger market.'

'Especially now there's this whole post-punk trend going on,' said Ross.

They talked a bit more about their brand and their marketing strategy, and I began to realise that, outlandish appearance or no, the two of them knew their stuff. In turn, to show that I knew mine, I rattled off some statistics about the benefits of influencer marketing and the reach of the people we represented.

'We were thinking someone like Gemma Grey…' Angela began.

Imagining Gemma's face if I told her she was henceforth going to be expected to fall out of nightclubs dressed like Mistress Whiplash, I hastily intervened and explained that Gemma's focus was primarily on beauty products and her own make-up range.

'But there are numerous other, fantastically talented people who'd be a great fit for your brand and would love to work with you,' I said. 'Take Ruby-Grace Miller, for example.'

I passed over my iPad with Ruby-Grace's résumé on it.

'A bit vanilla,' Angela sniffed.

'Oh, no,' argued Ross, looking so closely at the screen he was practically misting it up. 'I can totally see her look working for us. A bit "dark angel", you know. A bit girl-next-door-gone-bad.'

Next to me, I heard Sam's sharp intake of breath. Whether he was excited or appalled at the idea of Ruby-Grace got up in studs and leather, I didn't know – and I wasn't sure I wanted to.

'I suppose you might be right, munchkin,' Angela admitted, and Ross leaned over and did a sort of snuggly thing with his head into her shoulder – okay, almost her highly cantilevered cleavage – that made me feel both tender and a bit weird.

I said, 'Great! Sam's the main point of contact with our client, so he'll reach out to her and discuss this opportunity, and one of us will feed back on whether Ruby-Grace is keen to get on board with you guys.'

The meeting ended with warm handshakes all round, and Sam and I escorted the Grangers to the lift. But instead of heading back to his desk, Sam hovered by my side.

'Sloane, I was thinking… Have you got a second?'

'Sure.' I headed back into the meeting room, closely followed by my intern.

'I was thinking,' he said again. 'Remember we mentioned the charity angle when we met Ruby-Grace originally. Why don't I do some research, see if there are any organisations that might benefit from being represented by someone like her?'

'Like what, though? I mean, you have to admit, Own the Night is pretty much perfect for her.'

'Yeah but… There's more to her than just that, Sloane. I mean, she's really passionate about things.'

'What things?'

'Animals, for instance. She loves dogs.'

'What, like little Minou? Poor thing, she's just another accessory.'

'No, she genuinely does. She volunteers at Battersea on weekends and everything.'

'What? How do you know?'

'I went there with her last weekend. They were short-staffed and she rang me on my mobile and asked me to help out. So I did. She was cleaning the dogs' crates and feeding them and everything. Minou was a rescue dog, you know.'

I tried to imagine Ruby-Grace, in her six-inch heels and barely-there shorts, weighing dog biscuits and scooping poop, and failed totally. But if Sam said so, it must be true.

'And she loves kids, too,' he went on. 'I really think there's an opportunity to reveal more of her true personality through her social media, show her giving something back.'

'Okay,' I said. 'Go ahead and put out some feelers to charities. But talk to her about the Own the Night opportunity too, right?'

'Yes, of course.'

He stood up and headed towards the door. But before he got there, I said, 'Sam? One more thing.'

'Yes, Sloane?'

'Remember when you started here, Megs and I spoke to you about our company policy regarding relationships with our clients.' He ducked his head, but I could see a tide of colour rising up his neck. Cringing for him, I carried on. 'When we work so closely with people, getting involved in every aspect of their lives, it's very easy to overstep the boundaries. But... Just don't, okay?'

'No, Sloane.'

'Right. Now, why don't you go and get some lunch? I'm going to – I'm starving.'

*

I hadn't had dinner the previous night and, still unaccustomed to my new commute from the rented apartment, I'd got to the office too late that morning even to grab my usual coffee on my way in.

Fortunately, I was in Soho. The food options within just a few streets of the office were almost limitless, from sandwich shops to greasy spoons to salad bars to burger joints. But I knew where I was going. I grabbed my bag and headed out, my steps quickening as I hurried towards the street where there had always been a market. When I first came to the city, it had been a traditional London market, with a fishmonger and fruit and veg stalls where Cockney voices shouted, 'Get your ripe peaches here! Sweet juicy peaches, three for a pound!'

Gentrification had taken its toll, the fishmonger was gone and only one veg stall remained now, though, and the rest had been taken over by street-food vendors. My mouth watered as I considered my options. I could have a giant hot dog, a burger laden with fried onions, a burrito encased in a giant Yorkshire pudding instead of a tortilla… Choice paralysis threatened to grip me, so I decided to opt for my favourite falafel wrap, which had the significant advantage of delivering about a thousand calories for a fiver.

I joined the long line and watched, impressed as always by the efficiency with which the three guys manning the stall took orders, assembled the wraps and salad boxes, and finally handed them over to their customers, managing somehow to keep turning out freshly made chickpea patties and freshly cooked flatbreads in between.

'A large wrap, please,' I said when at last my turn came to order. 'With no tomato, but extra aubergine and lots of chilli sauce.'

Behind me, I heard a man's voice say, 'Large wrap, hold the tomato, extra aubergine, heavy on the chilli, please, mate.'

I glanced around, smiling. 'I guess there's an echo in here.'

The young guy behind me laughed. 'Guess there is.'

'The food's great here, isn't it? It's one of my favourites.'

'And a guaranteed hangover cure,' he agreed.

Then I looked at him more closely. He was hot – hot and kind of familiar. 'Hey, do I know you from somewhere?'

'I believe you do.' He smiled, but there was a hint of embarrassment in his face. 'From Fifty-One Wardour, a few weeks back.'

'Oh my God! You bought me and my friend a bottle of champagne!'

'I did. It seemed like a great idea at the time, but I guess you were too busy catching up to want to talk to a random stranger.'

I remembered his glossy see-through business card, doubtless languishing now in the bottom of my handbag, or possibly thrown away with a load of used tissues and old receipts. Suddenly I felt bad for him.

'I'm sorry. Yes, we were, but it was such a cute gesture. Let me buy you lunch. It's the least I can do.'

'I've already paid for it,' he pointed out.

'Oh! Of course you have.' I considered handing him five pounds by way of repayment, but thought how pointless that would be, given he'd spunked north of a hundred pounds on a bottle of fizz for Megs and me. Instead, I pulled one of my own business cards out of my purse and handed it to him, saying, 'I'll buy you a drink in return, then. Give me a call sometime.'

He looked at my card like I'd just handed him a winning Lotto ticket and said, 'Cool. Yes, I will.'

We looked at each other, smiling, for a second, and then he turned and went one way to wherever his office was, and I went the other.

Chapter Twenty

Despite my warning to Sam, my relationship with the client I was meeting that evening had definitely progressed beyond the professional. Over the years, Gemma Grey had become a friend, and I looked forward to our regular meetings at the Daily Grind, the café near Gemma's home, which she had a fondness for not only because it was convenient and did great cocktails and bottomless brunches, but because it was where she'd met her boyfriend, Raffy.

We were perched at Gemma's usual table, in a corner with a view of the room, and we were both drinking breakfast Martinis, even though it was evening. The drink made me think with a pang of guilt of Vivienne – even though I'd been calling her every week to check she was okay, I was no closer to finding that breakthrough acting role for her.

'So the photo shoot went great,' Gemma said, smoothing a lock of hair back from her exquisitely pretty heart-shaped face. It was dyed a colour she'd told me was called mushroom blonde, and I'd have laid money on it being a massive trend in a few months. Hair salons were constantly getting in touch with me wanting to do Gemma's hair for free in return for a mention on her vlog, but she steadfastly refused, insisting that she'd always go to her mum's salon in Nottingham.

'Brilliant! How was Isla – did she look after you okay?'

'Of course she did. She's really nice.'

'Good on her. She's a keeper, Isla, and so's the other intern, Sam, who you haven't met. I'm hoping we can offer them both jobs – I've had my hands full with Megs off, and Rosie's rushed off her feet.'

Gemma grimaced sympathetically. 'How's Megan getting on? I sent her some flowers ages ago, to congratulate her on the baby.'

'She loved them. And she sends her love. She's got the whole mommy thing nailed now – she's already talking about coming into the office one day a week and bringing Ethan with her.'

'Adorable! You won't be able to keep your clients away if she does that.'

'So we've had the first packaging samples in for your new make-up collection,' I said, forcing my mind back to business. 'They look amazing – you'll love them. Here.'

I pulled a silver and coral box out of my bag and spread out the contents for Gemma to see, and she oohed and aahed appreciatively.

'Fab! I'm so excited about it all. Colours by Gemma Grey – OMG, I can't believe it's actually happening.'

Then Gemma said, quite casually, but with a note of tension that made me think she wasn't feeling casual at all, 'Oh, Sloane, there's something I meant to ask you. I got a DM through Insta from a PR who works with a clinic that does Botox and fillers and stuff. She wanted to talk about a brand-ambassador-type relationship. So I told her to get in touch with you, obviously.'

'Quite right,' I began, but it was like Gemma hadn't heard me.

'Sloane, do you think I need to start with that stuff? Like, already? I mean, prevention's better than cure, right? I'll be twenty-seven in a few months. And I look at the girls on *Love Island* and I'm like, they look so amazing. And I reckon they've all had bits of work done here and there. Should I?'

I thought, *If you ever let a needle near that beautiful face of yours I'll kill you.*

'Gemma, honey, you know I'll support you in whatever you do, always. It's your life and your face. I'm not going to be the buzz-killer here and tell you that you need to grow older gracefully. Because the reality is that in our business, the playing field isn't level. And some people give nature a helping hand here and there, because they can, and because it matters to them.'

Gemma nodded, listening carefully to me. 'So should I…'

'Seriously? No fucking way. Not now. You're a way off thirty yet, Gemma. Don't even go there. You're beautiful, stunning, perfect, just as you are. Wear sunscreen every day and just enjoy every second of being you. But if you decide, in fifteen years' time, you want to tweak things here and there, do it for you. Not because you feel pressure to look a certain way.'

I was reminded again of Vivienne, whose beauty had been preserved, as far as I could tell, by sheer freakish good luck but whose life was in all kinds of turmoil in every other way. And I thought, if I was the fairy godmother at the feast, bestowing my blessings on Gemma, who I loved – or on the daughter I might have, who I'd love orders of magnitude more – what would I wish for her? Beauty, or happiness? And what if being happy were dependent on being beautiful?

But Gemma was oblivious to my complicated internal analysis.

'I'm so glad you think that. Seriously, I was panicking that you might say I should go for it. And the idea gives me the right heebie-jeebies, if I'm honest.' She glanced at her phone and pushed back her chair. 'Shit, I'm so sorry, Sloane, but I have to dash. Raffy's cooking and I said I'd be back by eight. We've got some friends coming over and he's doing this smoky jackfruit thing. Kind of like carnitas, only vegan. He says. Who knows?'

I stood up and reached over to hug her, intending to pick up my own things and make my way to the Tube station and on to home. But then I heard my phone humming on the table, and I said, 'I'll just take this call and then head off. Take care, love you, bye.'

Of course, my phone stopped ringing the second I picked it up. Impatiently, I glanced at the screen, thinking it might be Dad, who, since I'd broken the news about Myles and me separating, had taken to ringing every few days to make sure I was okay. But it was Myles. Now that I'd moved into my temporary rental apartment, he'd been calling me more often than he had for weeks, always with some trivial request that he presented as desperately urgent. Had I sent his mother a birthday card? Had I packed and taken with me his favourite green and white striped shirt by mistake? Did I know what the flashing red light on the washing machine meant?

To which my answers had been *No*, *No* and *Read the fucking manual*.

Well, he could leave a message and I'd call him back in the morning. However annoying and trivial his calls were, I couldn't help, every time I saw his name on my phone's screen, feeling a leap of hope that maybe, this time, he was going to say sorry. Maybe finally he was going to explain that it had all been a mistake. Maybe, after all, there was some way to make things right. But he never had, and I was beginning to realise that in order to protect my own sanity, I'd have to keep our calls short and to the point, or avoid them if I possibly could.

So I'd ring him back tomorrow. If I felt like it. In the meantime, I was going to have another cocktail, putting off the moment when I'd have to leave the bright, cosy room and the company of other people, even if I wasn't actually talking to any of them, and return to the soulless one-bedroom flat.

The waitress brought my negroni and I sipped absently, glancing around me. The bar was filling up. There was a table of bearded men next to me drinking craft beer; a group of women excitedly ordering cocktails, who looked like they were having a rare night off from their families; a few couples on dates. Soon I'd have to ask for the bill and leave – it seemed selfish to be hogging a table for two when I was just drinking. But the thought of the lonely Airbnb apartment, of filling another evening with only my confused thoughts for company, was too bleak to face.

My eye was drawn to the far side of the room, where a group of two women and three men were settling down, chatting excitedly. I watched them, distracting myself by trying to figure out how they fitted together, who was with who, or whether they were just friends. One of the women looked familiar, and I tried to place where I recognised her from, but I couldn't.

She was pretty – the kind of pretty that creates the impression at first glance of generic blue-eyed, blonde English-rose good looks, but then when you look a bit harder you see a lot more. She was average height with an average build – unlike her friend, who was model-tall and slender – but she exuded something special. Confidence, charisma, comfort in her own skin, happiness – whatever it was, it glowed from her like she'd swallowed a garland of fairy lights.

Also, she looked a tiny bit like Ivanka Trump, the POTUS's daughter. That must be why she seemed familiar – Ivanka's face had been all over the web recently.

I'd been staring, I realised, and hastily looked away – but not hastily enough. As if she knew she was being watched, she glanced in my direction and our eyes met for an awkward moment. I saw her see me, freeze, look away and then look back again with a flash of recognition before turning to whisper to her friend.

The room was crowded and buzzing by now, so there was no way I could hear what she was saying and I'm no lip-reader, but I didn't need to be – it was all right there in her face and her body language.

I know that woman.

I saw her friend glance my way, too, and the two of them whispered intently for a few seconds. Then the Ivanka-a-like looked towards me again and stood up.

I'm going over to talk to her.

Damn it. The last thing I needed right now was an awkward encounter with someone who knew me, but who I had no recollection of ever having met. Could she be a client contact from way back? Someone who'd come to Ripple Effect wanting us to represent her and been knocked back? A random acquaintance from the gym? I had no idea.

But I was about to find out.

'Hello. I'm so sorry to bother you. You're Sloane Cassidy, aren't you?'

'That's me.'

'Do you mind if I join you for a second?'

Yes. 'Not at all.'

She put her glass of white wine down on the table and sat opposite me, where Gemma had been. She didn't look happy about it, though, I realised. She didn't look like someone who was popping over to have a nice cosy gossip.

She looked like a woman sitting down in the dentist's chair.

'My name's Charlotte Bell.'

So she didn't expect me to know her, at least. But she paused, in a kind of anticipatory way, as if she thought I would recognise her name.

'Nice to meet you, Charlotte.' *Could she be a YouTuber?* Unlikely – I didn't spend hours and hours of my life on the site for nothing. I knew just about every style, beauty and wellness vlogger there was.

I took a sip of my cocktail and saw her eyes flicker towards my left hand and stay there for a moment, widening in surprise.

'I used to work at Colton Capital.' Again, there was that questioning inflection in her voice, like she expected me to make some connection.

Colton Capital. That name was familiar. And then I remembered – the massive workplace renovation project Myles's firm had been engaged to do the previous year. Something had gone wrong with it, and the contract was terminated. Myles had been mortified, then furious, threatening to sue, but as far as I knew nothing had ever come of that – aside from his decision to focus more heavily on residential projects.

'If this is related to Taylor + Associates, I'm sorry but I can't really help you.'

The woman – Charlotte – blushed, a dark tide of crimson that rushed up from her neck and over her face. She took a big gulp of her wine.

'This is really awkward,' she said. 'Please bear with me. I just wanted to explain, and to apologise to you in person.'

'Apologise for what?'

'I… it was me who Myles… I'm so sorry, there's just no easy way to say this.'

Had she somehow been instrumental in getting the firm removed from the project?

'Look, these things happen in business,' I said. 'If you feel bad about the contract, by all means discuss it with Myles. It's really nothing to do with me.'

'No! It's not that. I thought you knew. He said he'd told you.'

She flushed again and downed more wine. She was literally squirming in her seat, and her obvious distress made me feel sorry for her.

'I think you should explain,' I said gently, 'because I genuinely have no idea what you're talking about.'

She brushed a thumb under her eye, leaving a smear of mascara, and leaned close across the table. I could smell her perfume, subtle and fresh like spring flowers.

'Myles and I had an affair.' Her words came out in a rush. 'I'm sorry, there's just no other way to say it. It didn't last very long. I didn't know he was married – he told me he was separated and I believed him. I'd honestly never, ever, ever have let it happen if I'd known. Not that that makes it any better. I'm really sorry. I just… I'm sorry.'

My whole face felt numb, and my lips didn't want to move. 'You what?'

'I thought he'd moved out,' she babbled. 'He told me he had, and that your marriage was over, and I – well, I'd fallen for him and I guess I wanted that to be true. I should have known it wasn't, but I didn't. I only found out when Bianca told me.'

'*Bianca* told you? Bianca Cole? How?' Of all the details I wanted – or didn't want – to know, for some reason this seemed the single thing I most needed to understand.

'She… My friend Maddy's married to her brother,' Charlotte said. 'So she knows me through them. And I'd been going on about this man I'd met and she told me he was married to you and you were trying for a baby. And then I ended it with him straight away. I told him that if he didn't tell you, I would, and he said he had so I didn't, but now I see that wasn't true. But even if you'd known already, I wanted to apologise and ask if you were okay.'

'When did this happen?'

'Last year.' Again, that painful blush, that gulp of wine like it was medicine. The glow of happiness and confidence that had illuminated her was all gone. 'It didn't last long, honestly. Like, four months? It was over by Christmas.'

Four months. Over by Christmas. I tried to piece together the events of last autumn, but my thoughts were too disordered. Later, I knew, I'd open my calendar and I'd check every day, torturing myself with analysing when, and where, and what, and how. Now, I could barely hear her words over the roaring of blood in my head.

'And Bianca knew?'

'Yes. Well, I guess not at first. But she must have figured it out somehow. Maybe she asked him. I don't know. Sloane, I'm so terribly sorry.'

Bianca had known. She'd known, and not said anything to me. Not one word, not when we went shopping together and when she came over for dinner and we went round to theirs and we went out to a swanky restaurant for Michael's birthday and when she planned the décor of our fucking house. And Michael must have known, too, and this Maddy girl and Bianca's brother and no doubt all of Charlotte's friends. That happy group over in the corner, chatting to each other and carefully not looking our way. They'd known. I was the only one who hadn't.

The wife's always the last to find out.

And, more to the point, when Bianca had delivered that veiled warning to me months before, it had been this girl she was talking about. Not some theoretical infidelity that might happen in the future. And, more importantly, not a relationship between Myles and Bianca herself.

A wave of sick, churning shame engulfed me. I'd been a fool. I'd been made a fool of, by this pretty young woman, by my supposed friend, by my own husband. By the way I'd behaved towards Bianca, which, I now realised, had been unforgivable. And most of all, by my own inability to see what had been going on in my own sorry life.

'I can see this has been the most horrible shock,' Charlotte was saying. 'I didn't realise – I wouldn't have come over if I didn't think you knew. But now I have, and I… I mean, is there anything I can do? Could I get you a glass of water, or another drink or something?'

She'd finished her wine. She looked so abjectly miserable sitting there, I almost wanted to say something to comfort her. But I couldn't, not quite. *He told you he was married.* Maybe she was lying. Maybe Myles hadn't told her we were separating. Maybe she just didn't care who she slept with, whose life she ruined.

I managed to say in a croak, 'No, thank you.'

'I'll send you an email, with my contact details. Nothing else. Just in case you want to talk. And, Sloane, I really am so awfully sorry.'

I nodded. I didn't know what I wanted, beyond a sudden, desperate urge to get out of there, away from her concern and the eyes of her friends. If she got up and went back to their table and I saw them leaning over to her and imagined them saying, 'Oh my God, Charlotte, what did she say? Are you okay?' I thought I'd die of humiliation.

And then I thought, *No. It's not for me to be ashamed, or humiliated. None of what happened was my fault. I'm not going to run away. I've got this.*

I said, 'Don't be sorry. You weren't to know. Hell, *I* didn't know. Well, I kind of did but I got it all wrong. I thought Bianca might have been hiding something but I didn't realise exactly what it was. Thank you for coming over and talking to me. It must have been a bloody hard thing to do.'

Relief washed over her face. 'Not as hard as what you're going through. I had a part in that, and I wish I didn't.'

'No point in wishing. It's done now. I hope you've moved on, and you're happy.'

She smiled, and again I saw the radiantly pretty girl who'd caught my eye across the room. 'I am, you know. Thank you for asking.'

'I'm glad,' I said. 'And you know what? I'm going to be, again, too. I'm already getting there.'

And I said goodbye, got my stuff together and watched as she went back to her table. Her friends all leaned in, and I saw her talking softly to them, but instead of looking remorseful and pitying, she looked relieved, lightened, full of hope.

I'd done that for her, and I was glad I had. And I was glad to be able to walk out of there, my head held high.

Chapter Twenty-One

'So how long were you married for?' Vanessa Pinkrah asked, her pen poised over her spiral-bound notebook.

'Five years. Well, almost six now.'

'And the house is in your joint names?'

'Yes. The house and the mortgage. Although Myles paid the deposit, because he had savings and I didn't.'

'And you paid how much for it?'

I told her, and when she asked how much the deposit had been, I told her that, too. I was glad I'd done my homework – all the details I needed were in a plastic folder in front of me, literally at my fingertips.

'And how much would you say it's worth now?'

'I don't know, exactly. We're just finishing off a massive renovation and extension. But a lot more than we paid for it, although we bought when the market was at a bit of a peak. We'll get proper valuations, obviously.'

'And are there any other assets you hold, jointly or separately? Any other properties, investments, pensions, that kind of thing?'

'Myles has his business, and I'm a partner in the company I help to run. We both have pensions, but no other properties or anything like that. I've got some savings, but not much.'

I told her the amount, feeling a great wave of weariness wash over me. Since I left New York to move here with Myles, back when I'd had literally nothing except a heart full of love and a suitcase full of clothes, I'd hoped that our lives would knit together over the years, growing more complex and entangled as we accumulated possessions, memories, children. All but the last had happened, and now it never would.

But back then, it had never crossed my mind that it might one day be necessary to unpick the tapestry of our life, separate the threads that were mine from those that were his, and try to roll them up again into tidy skeins, ready to be crafted into something new.

Now I'd begun the process, the complexity of it overwhelmed me.

Vanessa was speaking again, outlining all the steps we'd need to take: the disclosure of every minute detail of our finances, the forms that would need to be exchanged between her and Myles's solicitor and submitted to a court, the lengthy delay before, finally, a judge somewhere put a stamp on a piece of paper that told us we weren't married any more.

'I know it seems daunting,' she said. 'But we take it one step at a time. If he doesn't decide to be awkward, the process can proceed quite smoothly and amicably. I'll put everything we've discussed in an email, and you can confirm whether you want me to act for you, and then we get the ball rolling. Okay?'

'Okay.'

'And I'll email over my invoice.'

'Thanks, Vanessa.'

'Do you have any more questions?'

I shook my head.

'Nice to meet you, then, Sloane. And don't worry, we'll get through this.'

I suppose we'll have to, I thought, barely able to feel the grey carpet tiles under my feet as I walked back out through the tastefully, blandly decorated office in a nondescript mid-rise block in the City, and into the lift.

Megan had asked around on my behalf, and a friend of hers who'd recently taken her financially abusive husband 'to the cleaners', as Megs reported, had recommended Vanessa Pinkrah. Another contact had recommended an independent financial adviser, who'd hopefully be able to help me scrape my own affairs into some sort of sensible order, once I knew how much money I'd get when the house was sold. If, of course, anyone wanted to buy it.

Wearily, I emerged into the street. It was a blustery October day, sunshine occasionally bursting through the clouds and then being blotted out by squalls of rain. One of them was squalling away right now, threatening to soak my too-light denim jacket, so I ducked into a coffee shop, bought a hot chocolate and sat at one of the little circular tables to gather my thoughts.

The house was on its way to being finished. Eventually, someone would buy it, live in it, make it their home. I hoped it wouldn't be haunted by the echoes of my unhappiness, the shattered pieces of our marriage littering the floor like grit underfoot, no matter how often its new occupants swept or their robot hoover trundled around.

For now, at least I had a roof over my head. Jared, who owned the Airbnb apartment I was renting, was going to be away for another three weeks and had been relieved to accept a long-term tenant rather than renting his place out to tourists on an ad hoc basis. But once he came back, I was going to need another plan – and I had no idea what that might be. With the mortgage on our house still eating away more than half of my take-home pay, renting a flat was out of the question for now unless I dug deep into my meagre savings.

I thought longingly of my apartment in Brooklyn: its white walls and white bed linen; the one wall I'd painted bright, sunshine yellow because the room was dark; the fresh flowers I bought from the market and arranged in thrift-store vases. Okay, there'd also been the battalions of roaches that had marched across the kitchen floor at night; the downstairs neighbour's weed smoke drifting in whenever I opened a window; the choking traffic on the busy road below, leading out of town. But it had been home – it had been mine. The first place that had felt like home since I was a little girl in Sparwood, when Mom was still truly a mother.

But I could never go back. Even if the flat was the same – which it wouldn't be; it would have rocketed far out of my reach in price, apart from anything else – *I* wouldn't be the same, and I'd feel like I was trying to wear clothes I'd last put on when I was twenty-five.

I couldn't go back to Canada, either. Dad and Maura, my stepmom, would be thrilled to have me, I knew – they'd say I was welcome to stay, rent-free, for as long as I wanted. But no matter how strong the longing was to flee back to their warm house and their waiting arms, it was no good as a long-term prospect; there wasn't exactly much call for new media agents in small, remote Ontario mining towns.

I could, I supposed, sell my car. That would cover a deposit on a flat and a couple of months' rent. But I thought of my beloved little Mini, the independence and freedom it represented, and how loyal a friend it had been to me over the years – never once breaking down, always there for me when I saw its friendly face waiting in the street, as if it was saying, 'Are we going anywhere nice today?' – and I knew I couldn't do that. I had enough sadness to deal with without adding one more loss to the pile that weighed down on my heart.

I sipped the last of my hot chocolate – the chalky, bitter dregs of it – and took my phone out of my bag. I'd written a long checklist of things I needed to do, and the first visit with the solicitor could, at least, be checked off.

Way down at the bottom of that list, below 'Find a place to live' and 'Get quotes from removal companies', was 'Talk to Bianca'. I was going to have to do it – I knew I was. I was going to have to apologise to her for the hurtful conclusion I'd jumped to, and explain how I'd got things so wrong. But whenever I thought about picking up the phone and calling her, I felt so flooded with hurt and rage – *She knew. She knew all along about Charlotte, and she didn't tell me* – that I couldn't do it. I knew that in order to tell Bianca sincerely that I was sorry, I'd have to get past that first, and I was nowhere near that yet.

I looked out at the grey, rain-swept street, already beginning to fill with commuters hurrying, umbrellas held rigidly over their heads against the rain, towards the Tube. I'd be joining them soon, cramming myself onto the Central line, which would be uncomfortably hot even on this chilly day. I imagined edging myself to a free square foot of space, the damp bodies pressed closely around me in the fug.

I loved my job. Ripple Effect was far more than just a workplace; it was half mine. I'd helped Megan build up the business over the past five years, so we'd gone from a scrappy newcomer to a respected force in the world of influencer marketing. I loved most of my clients, too – even the high-maintenance ones, whose diva ways often hid deep insecurity, and who needed the most handholding and ego-boosting of all. Ruby-Grace, I was beginning to suspect, fell firmly into this category, and I was glad that Sam had her back – or at any rate that she had his strong arms to carry her shopping hauls. Vivienne, on the other hand – well, finding some proper work for her was a challenge I hadn't yet cracked.

But still, at that moment, I wanted nothing more than to turn my back on it all and walk away. Not that I would, of course – I had responsibilities to Megan, my clients, the partner companies who we'd brokered sponsorship deals with, my team – all of them. But the germ of a thought had been planted in my brain: I might not do this for ever.

Maybe the end of my marriage would mean other changes, too – not just to where I lived, but to my life more generally. In the meantime, however, I had no option but to keep on keeping on, taking it one day at a time, even though just opening my eyes in the morning sometimes felt like a task so huge I might not be able to achieve it.

With a twist of pain, I remembered the last time I'd seen Myles. In a coffee shop like this one, which I'd chosen on the basis that it was best to meet on neutral territory. It was a decision I'd regretted straight away when I realised that the tables were so close together we had to lean over so our noses were practically touching, and conduct the entire meeting in whispers so the woman working at her laptop on one side of us and the teenage boy eating cake with his granny on the other couldn't overhear.

I'd started off by saying, 'I think I owe you an apology.'

Hope flashed in his eyes and he said cautiously, 'Why's that?'

'I accused you of having an affair with Bianca. I was wrong about that.'

'Thank God you've realised that at last, sweetheart. Look, I want to put this behind us just as much as you do. But before we can do that, you really do need to address these trust issues you have. I never thought you were the jealous type, until—'

I held up one hand for him to stop and, to my surprise, he did. 'You weren't cheating on me with Bianca. But you were cheating on me.'

'Oh come on, Sloane. Not this again. You're paranoid; you're making shit up. It's got to stop.'

I leaned in slightly closer. The woman at the next table glanced curiously at us, then turned determinedly back to her work. I was willing to bet she was listening as hard as she could, though – I knew I would have been, if I'd been her.

I said, 'A couple of days ago I was approached by a woman in the Daily Grind, after I'd had a meeting there with Gemma. Her name's Charlotte Bell.'

Myles flinched. That movement, almost imperceptible, told me everything I needed to know.

But he wasn't going to give up that easily. 'Charlotte who?'

'Charlotte Bell,' I repeated, with exaggerated patience. 'She was an admin assistant at Colton Capital. I presume you remember that name? Or shall I repeat it as well?'

'Don't be absurd. Actually, I do remember the name now. Blonde girl?'

'Yes, an attractive blonde woman in her twenties. About ten years younger than you, I'd say.'

I meant that to sting, but I realised that it hadn't – what man ever feels ashamed of sleeping with an adult woman significantly younger than he is?

Myles said, 'She had a bit of a thing for me. Bit of a crush. I never mentioned it at the time – it was pretty awkward but I didn't have anything to do with her on a day-to-day basis, so I just let it go. And it's just as well I never mentioned it to you, Sloane, given how irrational you're being. Clearly not only can I never look at another woman again, but if one looks at me I'm in trouble too.'

He'd moved from being angry to being dismissive – and now he was giving jocular a try. It was like trying to nail jelly to a wall, I thought with hindsight. But at the time, I had been almost overwhelmed with frustrated despair.

'Myles, I don't believe you. I believe her. I think that what she said was true.'

'You'd take the word of some woman you'd never met before – some lying fantasist – over your own husband's?'

'Yes, I think I do. Why would she make something like that up? Why would she accost me in a coffee shop and tell me some made-up story? She thought I already knew it had happened. She said you'd said you told me.'

Myles glanced around. Laptop woman was still there. The boy at the next table was still determinedly eating his carrot cake, but his granny had given up on her scone and was sitting, agog, drinking in our words while her tea grew cold in front of her, occasionally casting what I guess she thought were discreet sideways glances at us.

Who needs EastEnders *when you've got a couple airing their dirty laundry eighteen inches away from you in Caffè Nero?* It would have been funny if it hadn't been so mortifying.

Myles said, 'Oh, for God's sake. Okay, there might have been a thing, a bit of a flirtation. But there was nothing more than that. Honest to God, I never laid a hand on her.'

'I don't believe you, Myles. I've been through it over and over in my mind, and I just don't.'

'You said that about Bianca!' he burst out, like it was some kind of 'gotcha'. 'You said you knew something was going on, but you were wrong, weren't you, Sloane? Deluded and wrong. You were wrong then and you're wrong now.'

I leaned in even closer to him, getting a waft of his coffee and his cologne. The scent was almost cloying, I realised for the first time. I'd always thought I liked it, but now I reckoned I'd hold my breath if he got in a lift with me.

'I wasn't wrong, though,' I hissed. 'I just got the wrong person. I suspected something was going on. Bianca tried to warn me, and after that I knew. And I wasn't wrong. I was right. Myles, this can't go on. What do you think you're going to gain by lying to me? You're not going to keep me in this marriage under false pretences. You're not going to keep me in it at all. I've made an appointment to see a solicitor. That's why I wanted to meet you today. To tell you that. Not to have some massive argument where you try and convince me I'm imagining things.'

Myles took a final sip of his coffee and put the mug down.

'Okay,' he said. 'So I slept with Charlotte. There, I said it. That's what you wanted to hear, right? I had a thing with her. It lasted maybe four months in total. Just four. During that time I probably saw her a dozen times, if that. She didn't know about you. I did it because I was lonely. Lonely in our marriage. I did it because you don't support me, you don't appreciate me. You're so busy organising your own life. I felt like you didn't give a shit about me, and Charlotte did.'

Next to me, the grey-haired lady gave a little gasp. I'd have gasped myself, only I could barely draw breath. I felt like I'd been punched in the gut. Sure, I'd had suspicions. Sure, Charlotte had confessed to me what had happened, and I'd believed her. But still, a tiny, stupid part of me had been hoping that, somehow, it might all turn out to be a mistake.

'But we were trying to have a baby.' My voice sounded thin and desperate.

To my left, the woman with the laptop stopped typing, her hands suspended motionless over the keyboard.

'You were. It consumed you, Sloane. You couldn't talk about anything else, half the time. And when it didn't happen – how do you think that made me feel? Like shit, is how. Men want to be wanted, Sloane. Wanted for themselves, not as some kind of glorified sperm donor. Charlotte wanted me for myself.'

'Right.' I managed to get the word out even though my lips felt numb and my tongue too large for my mouth. 'So you felt like you were entitled to some kind of last hurrah? Like a dude sleeping with a hooker on his stag night? Is that it?'

There was another sharp intake of breath from the elderly woman.

'For God's sake,' Myles said. 'I'm not continuing this conversation with you. You're not rational; you're not listening to me – unlike the rest of this bloody coffee shop.'

There was a brief pause. Laptop woman started frantically typing again.

Then the elderly lady put her knife and spoon together on her plate, very correctly, next to her half-eaten scone, and said, 'Actually, yes, I have been listening. And I have to tell you, Myles, I'm not on your side.'

'Nan!' her grandson protested.

'You know what, I agree with her,' said laptop woman. 'It sounds like you've behaved disgracefully and your wife's had a lucky escape.'

'What they said,' muttered the boy.

Myles turned absolutely scarlet. 'My solicitor will be in touch,' he said, and stood up and did what I guess he intended to be a flounce out the door.

But, with the eyes of everyone around us following him, it was more like a furtive skulk.

Chapter Twenty-Two

It was Thursday and I was alone in the office. Sam was out looking after Carly Matthews, one of our mumfluencer clients, at the launch of her new book. Because Carly insisted on taking her Fruit-Shoot-fuelled four-year-old twins, Richie and Ralphie, absolutely everywhere with her to bolster her perfect-mother credentials, I knew that his role would largely consist of charging around Waterstones after them, trying to stop them eating all the cupcakes and tripping up old ladies.

Isla was off on holiday, having headed to Croatia with a bunch of mates the previous weekend, and Rosie had taken the afternoon off to go to her nan's seventieth birthday afternoon tea.

Which meant that I could take my time getting ready to go and meet Edward Reeves for what I firmly told myself was definitely, categorically not a date.

I looked at myself in the full-length mirror we kept in the corner of the office for our obsessively image-conscious clients to check that they looked the part before braving the legions of fans they imagined were waiting for them on every street corner. I was wearing a full-skirted red dress with a sweetheart neckline and a white ditsy print of daisies on it, and bright yellow high-heeled shoes. My hair was up in a French twist on the back of my head, and I was wearing my usual bright-red lipstick.

It was my look, I supposed. It was the way I dressed, and had been for years. Myles liked it, it felt like me, and I'd never really bothered to change it. But it had become more than a habit – it had become a burden. Like how when we first slept together I'd been wearing lace-topped hold-up stockings and Myles had been so overcome with lust when he saw them, I felt obliged to wear them all the time. And of course the Brazilian wax I'd had before that first time, which I'd felt obliged to maintain throughout our marriage, telling him that honestly, having hot wax applied to my bits and then ripped off barely hurt at all.

Now, though, my outfit felt frumpy, almost self-consciously kooky. I felt like I needed a change.

It was half past four, and I was meeting Edward at seven. The day had been quiet, the phones silent and my email inbox obligingly allowing me to clear it without filling up again straight away. No harm would be done if, just this once, I snuck out of the office to start the weekend early.

Feeling like a kid on the last day of term, I switched off my computer, picked up my bag, set the alarm and headed out into the street. I'd just see, I told myself, if anything caught my eye. If it didn't, I was fine as I was. After all, this really wasn't a date, or anything to get excited about at all.

So why was my stomach suddenly full of an absolute swarm of butterflies?

An hour and a half later, I found myself standing in front of a different mirror, looking at my reflection with something that was almost bemusement. I'd taken my hair down and brushed it out, so it fell in natural, beachy waves down past my shoulders. The lovely girl in the Charlotte Tilbury store had applied a full face of natural, neutral make-up that made me look fresh and glowy and about five years younger. I was wearing silky wide-legged trousers and a cropped top that showed off an inch of skin around my waist.

In the mirror, the person looking back at me could have been one of the cool older girls I'd looked up to with such awe when I was just starting high school in the late nineties. I could hardly believe that she was me.

To be fair, earlier I'd tried on a white button-through dress that had made me look like a nurse in a porno movie. But still, now I felt transformed, as if I'd shed a skin I hadn't known I'd grown out of. Still gazing at my reflection, I took my wedding and engagement rings off my left hand and tucked them carefully away in my wallet. My hand felt strangely light without them, as if a weight far greater than the two small bands of metal had been removed.

I happily handed over my credit card to pay for my new outfit, got changed back into it in the fitting room, and stuffed my old clothes into a carrier bag. For a second I considered ditching the lot in a rubbish bin on the street, but then I remembered the state of the planet and decided to do a charity-shop run instead, at some point over the weekend. There were plenty of other garments that would be joining these ones, after all.

The cool breeze tickled my skin. My flat shoes made me feel like I was walking on a beach. I practically skipped to the Tube station and couldn't help noticing heads turning to look at me, people catching my eyes and smiling.

I remembered Megan's words: 'You've still got it.'

Maybe I did. But I'd almost lost it, somewhere along the way.

Edward was already in the bar where we'd arranged to meet. And it wasn't just any bar – it was the glass-walled space at the top of the Shard, London's tallest building. I'd never been there before, and I couldn't suppress a little gasp at the amazing panorama of the city spread out below us, vast and beautiful in the evening.

Edward himself didn't look too shabby either. He was wearing a suit, a sort of silvery grey that made his eyes look very blue, and a dark green shirt. His hair was brushed back from his face, dark brown and glossy like expensive chocolate. He was drinking a Manhattan, and when he saw me he put the glass down, stood up from his chair and kissed me on both cheeks.

'Hello,' he said. 'I got here early, so I could nab a table by the window, and I've been sitting here on my own checking my phone every five minutes like a total prat. I was worried you'd change your mind.'

'Why would I do a thing like that? I wouldn't pass up the chance to look at this view.'

But when I said it, I was looking right at him, not out through the window.

'I'm glad you like it. I wanted to impress you.'

He smiled. For such a hot guy, he was quite touchingly eager to please.

'Consider me impressed.'

I ordered a drink for myself – a dry Martini, which I wouldn't normally have chosen. It was a glamorous drink – Vivienne's drink – and I'd never felt glamorous before. Edward wasn't the only one trying to make an impression, I supposed. If I was going to play the part of the sophisticated older woman, I wanted to nail it right from the beginning. And the drink surprised me with its icy, bone-dry hit of alcohol, just as my own appearance had. Maybe, I thought, the Sloane Cassidy who wore flats and bared her waist to the world would be a dry Martini woman.

I wasn't sure. I didn't know who the new, single Sloane was going to turn out to be. But, I realised, I was starting to look forward to finding out.

We drank our cocktails and Edward ordered a plate of salami, and we ate that and then ordered another round, and I asked him about his job.

'I used to work in the City,' he said. 'But I left a year ago. I'd had enough of the corporate world, of being a suit.'

'But you've still got great taste in suits,' I said, and he smiled that sweet, almost shy smile again, like my mild compliment was the best thing that had happened to him all day. I wondered if his slightly puppyish eagerness was an act – if it was, I bet it worked like a charm on every woman he dated. I could feel myself relaxing, becoming a bit flirtatious, starting to enjoy the evening.

'And how about you? Tell me all about yourself,' he invited.

I wasn't about to do that. But I did tell him about Ripple Effect, and living in New York, and that I was newly single, although I didn't mention that I'd been married. I thought about my wedding ring, carefully tucked away in my wallet. The empty place on my finger where it had been for so long still felt strange; I wondered if he could see the indentation it had left on my finger.

Then we moved on to more general conversation, telling each other about places we'd travelled to and places we hoped to go. I heard all about his gap year travelling around South America, and I wondered exactly how much younger than me he was. Three years? Five, maybe?

I wondered, but I didn't particularly care, because it was so obvious that he didn't and a few years wasn't exactly cradle-snatching.

'Another drink?'

I opened my mouth to make the sensible suggestion that we call it a night, but instead I heard myself saying, 'How about that bottle of fizz I owe you?'

A feeling of giddy irresponsibility washed over me, and it wasn't just down to the two large cocktails I'd drunk. There was no way I was going to have a relationship with this man. There was no point pretending that we were going to be friends, or be useful to each other professionally.

And that meant we were there for one thing. I knew it now and so did he, and thanks to the booze, the spectacular panorama of London spread out below us, the lights gleaming along the river like a necklace of precious stones thrown casually down, and Edward himself, with his sharp suit and his perfect teeth and his compliments, it suddenly seemed like a totally great idea.

Before ten o'clock, we were in a cab together, snogging each other's faces off like teenagers. Half an hour later, we'd arrived at his flat in Clapham and he was fumbling to get the key in the lock with one hand, the other firmly gripping mine. His skin was warm and dry, he kissed like an expert, and so far I was feeling entirely happy with my life choices at that moment.

He got the door open and led me in, closed it, then turned and kissed me again, his hands on the bare skin of my waist, his mouth eager yet somehow also tender. It had been more than five years since I'd kissed anyone other than Myles and it should have felt like some kind of massive watershed moment, but it didn't. I'd forgotten the thrill of anticipation, the knowing but not knowing what was going to happen, what we would be like together, and the excitement of it was intoxicating.

At that moment, it was like Myles had never existed.

The kiss ended, we looked at each other in the dark of the hallway, and he said, 'Can I get you anything? A drink or something? I'm being a crap host.'

'I'm not here for your hospitality,' I replied, and he laughed.

'Come on then.'

I followed him the few steps to his bedroom, which was pleasingly neat, everything squared away, not like the room of a single guy at all. I wondered if he'd made the effort to clear things up in anticipation of me coming home with him. I figured he probably had, but I didn't mind if he'd taken the outcome of the evening for granted.

After all, I'd done the same myself, pretty much from the moment I'd seen him sitting there at the table with his Manhattan.

He reached out for me again, and this time he took my face between the palms of his hands and looked intently at me, before lowering his mouth to mine. His kiss was intense and hungry, but also tender and almost reverent. I slid my hands up his back and felt his body beneath his suit jacket – he had the lean frame of a man who ran or cycled rather than someone who worked out in the gym. I slid the jacket off his shoulders and let it fall to the floor, broke off our kiss and stepped back to undo the buttons of his shirt, slowly, one by one.

As my fingers brushed his bare skin for the first time, I heard him gasp with pleasure and the anticipation of pleasure to come, and I felt an answering surge of excitement in my own body, hearing my breath come faster. His hands reached for the buttons of my top, too. He had it easy – there were only three, and he undid them quickly and expertly, before dropping the garment to join his on the floor. I stepped out of my shoes and felt his hands on my waist again, fumbling to find how to get my trousers off.

'There's a zipper on the side,' I whispered, and we both laughed.

'Of course there is. I knew that.'

His own trousers came off with less difficulty, and we stood there, lit only by the glow from the light in the hallway, looking at each other, delighted by what we saw.

He cupped my breasts through my bra, and I felt my nipples spring to attention, loving the way his strong hands looked on the lacy fabric. His own chest was hard and smooth, a thin band of soft hair running down over his flat abdomen.

Our bodies came together again and we kissed, more eagerly this time, moving towards the bed and lying down together before kissing again, on and on. Involuntarily, I found myself twisting one leg over his, pulling him close, feeling the hardness and size of him against me. He unhooked my bra, with no fumbling this time, and it fell to the bed between us. I felt his lips move against mine as he murmured, 'Oh my God.'

There was no slowness after that, no more tentativeness. I hooked a thumb into the waistband of my panties and pulled them off, and he did the same with his boxer shorts. My hands reached for his cock and I stroked it, then gripped the hot, pulsing length of it. I kneeled above him, looking down and seeing the desire on his face, along with something like adoration.

In that moment, I could have sworn undying love to that sweet boy. I had no intention of doing so, of course – if I had, he would probably have legged it out of there screaming in horror, and rightly so. But everything about it – his tidy bedroom, his smooth, lean body, the dark hair that spilled over his pillow like a tangle of silk – was perfect. And the way he looked at me, I felt perfect, too. I felt desirable and desired, turned on as much by the knowledge that this was okay, I could do this with no fear and no consequences, as I was by his hands, now gently exploring me and discovering how eager I was for him, how ready.

There were a few seconds of awkwardness while he slipped on a condom, and then he was inside me, our bodies moving together, slowly at first then faster and faster until I flung back my head, arching my back and letting pleasure fill every atom of me. Seconds later, I felt him shudder to stillness inside of me, and I flopped down on top of him like a puppet with the strings cut.

'My God, Sloane. I can't – that was amazing. You're a goddess.'

I laughed in pure, easy happiness, getting a mouthful of his soft hair. 'You're not so bad yourself. I should pick men up in the queue at Jerusalem Falafel more often.'

'I should send bottles of fizz to hot women in bars more often.'

'You mean you don't do that all the time?'

'I've never done it before in my life. I just saw you and I was like, "I fancy that woman rotten."'

'Well,' I said, surprised, 'for a beginner, you certainly managed to style it out.'

I rolled over and lay next to him, my breathing steadying, and he took my hand and held it, and we lay there together in the half-light, both of us smiling.

I remembered the podcast I'd recorded all those years back, which I'd billed as a bad girl's guide to love and sex. I'd been a bad girl tonight, I guessed. I'd rediscovered that part of me, that bold, sassy girl who went after what she wanted without fear or embarrassment, and as often as not got it.

And I realised that whoever the new, reinvented Sloane Cassidy might turn out to be, there'd be a good bit of the old me in her.

'I should go,' I said.

'Really? Can't you stay?'

'Better not.'

I knew what mornings in strange men's beds were like. I knew how, with a hangover and no toothbrush, the most magical night could break into an awkward morning. This night had been perfect, and I wasn't going to do anything to tarnish it.

I kissed Edward one final time, and he said, 'I'll call you,' and although I didn't believe a word of it, I still left feeling a serene and optimistic glow.

The taxi journey home was a more civilised version of the walk of shame I'd done so often back in my single days in New York – but now, I didn't feel any shame at all.

Chapter Twenty-Three

When I woke the next morning, I wasn't sure at first where I was. I was conscious of a mild hangover, offset by a deep glow of well-being. I might not have been fully awake, I might not have been sure where I was, but my body was telling me it had recently enjoyed truly off-the-scale sex. I looked around me and saw soft autumn light streaming through the gaps round the edges of the ill-fitting blackout blinds; the ugly black crystal chandelier suspended from the damp-stained ceiling; the drab passageway stretching beyond the bedroom door to the travertine-tiled bathroom, a world of beige that made my skin look like old newspaper when I put my make-up on in front of the tiny, ill-lit mirror.

Right. It was my rental Airbnb apartment, in which I'd only booked to stay another week. After that, I had nowhere to go – and I was running seriously low on cash, so low that moving to a similar place, even one sketchier than this, would be beyond my means.

I was in the last-chance saloon. So why did I feel so replete with contentment?

Then I thought about the events of the previous night. Edward. Edward and me. I closed my eyes again and let myself slip back into the memory of it: the intoxicating newness of him, the way it had gone to my head even more than the alcohol we'd drunk. The joyful, puppyish enthusiasm of sex with him. The way I'd felt young, unfettered, free and happy.

It hadn't meant anything. Edward – I'd checked his profile on LinkedIn, of course I had; I wasn't some kind of amateur – was four years younger than me. Hot, kind and funny as he was, he was no kind of prospect as a life partner, and I wasn't sure I was ready to enter into some time-limited, casual thing that would inevitably end up with one or both of us getting emotionally entangled and subsequently hurt.

That would just be dumb, I told myself firmly. That would be like going for a spa day when you're super stressed, and deciding all your problems will be solved if you move somewhere with a sauna, steam room and massage therapists forever. It would be like going on holiday to Bali and deliberately missing your return flight, imagining a life of endless sunshine and piña coladas, then realising there's a monsoon season and fuck-all affordable healthcare. It would be like…

But I was jerked out of my musings by the determined trill of my phone.

I swiped my mobile to life and glanced at the forest of notifications on my screen. I had sixteen missed calls, eight new voice messages, eighty-five unread emails, and a host of Twitter mentions and Google alerts.

Also, I had a cheery message from my cycle-tracking app.

Did your period start?

Shit. Why, no, Eve, now that you mention it, my period has not started. I'm two days late and my period is AWOL. I didn't even remember that it was due, on account of my life disintegrating around me.

With trembling hands, I rummaged in my bag. Before – before what had happened with Myles – I'd gone through truckloads of pregnancy tests, ordering them in bulk on Amazon, testing two days before the app even told me I needed to and then again and again until I came on and had to give up hope for another month. The little plastic wands, hygienically wrapped in yet more plastic (the fertility industry clearly hadn't much time for saving the planet, which I suppose oughtn't to surprise me, since it was predicated on getting more babies born to live on it) had been everywhere: in all my handbags, in our bathroom cabinet, in my desk drawer at work.

But now, there were none in my bag and I knew there weren't any in the bathroom, either. When I moved myself out of the house, I remembered now, I'd chucked a handful of them in the waste bin next to my desk in the spare room, feeling a kind of burning triumph at leaving them there for Myles to see, a reminder of the future he'd thrown away.

It hadn't even occurred to me, on that frantic morning, that when Myles and I had slept together the night before, I might have got pregnant. Even at the time, with him inside me, holding me, my mind had only been on him – on the possibility that everything might, after all, turn out okay.

And since then, I'd been so consumed with the need to keep on keeping on, to bury my feelings deep in work and yoga and the practicalities of us splitting up, that it hadn't even crossed my mind that I could be having a baby. Myles's baby. But it was possible – more than possible. I hadn't considered at the time whether I might be ovulating, only whether this could be the glue that would hold our marriage together. I checked the app and my calendar, panic rising inside me.

And then another thought flitted across my mind: *what if it's Edward's?* What if it was last night when that mysterious biological fusion happened, silently and invisibly? No. Surely that couldn't be possible. We'd used protection – once we'd eventually got the condom onto his overeager penis – and even if we hadn't, it was far too recent for pregnancy even to be a thing. If, by some weird freak of nature, my always-regular cycle had taken matters into its own hands and delayed my ovulation until Edward was around and Myles wasn't, even if the condom had split without either of us noticing, it would have been barely twelve hours earlier.

It just wasn't possible. I almost wished it was, because then I could simply trot off to my local pharmacy and ask for the morning-after pill. But if I was pregnant, I was too far along for that. Properly pregnant. Even though strictly speaking it would be dated from when my next period – the one that hadn't shown up – was due, I could pinpoint to the day, almost to the hour, the moment when Myles's small gamete would have met my large gamete, the union of the two tiny cells setting off a chain of events that would blow my world apart all over again.

That, and result in a whole new person.

I was so not ready for this.

I realised, with a rush of queasy-making fear, that for all my longing for a child, I hadn't the faintest idea how to be a mother. I hadn't even known how to be a daughter.

I remembered Dad's words, all those years ago. 'She's dying.'

And remembering them, I was instantly transported back to university, to Toronto, to being twenty years old and terrified, standing there with my satchel and my phone in my hand, my mouth dry, my heart pounding. All the guilt I'd packed away over the years came flooding to the surface, making me feel like I was drowning.

'Sloane? Are you there?'

I tried to answer, but all that came out was a kind of croak.

'I'm sorry. It's a shock for me, too. I'll buy you a ticket for Saturday, okay, and text to let you know what time the flight is. I'll be right there at the airport to pick you up.'

'Okay.' I paused a beat and then said in a rush, 'Thanks, Dad. I love you.'

And so, two days later, in the short-term airport parking, I climbed into Dad's Chevrolet Tahoe SUV. The car was new and I knew Dad was proud of it, so I listened patiently while he explained about its enhanced four-wheel drive and cruise control.

He was just filling in time, waiting for the moment when he would have to explain to me what was going on.

At last, swinging off the motorway, he said, 'So Linda relapsed. She was sober for almost seven years, then she split up with the guy she was seeing and I guess she didn't deal with it well.'

'It wasn't because of me?' I gripped the strap of my satchel, pleating the leather so hard my fingers ached. 'Because I wouldn't see her?'

'Oh, honey,' Dad said. 'I'm sure it wasn't. Who knows what pushes a person off the edge? And you're seeing her now, right?'

As we drove, he explained how Mom had lost her job, fallen into arrears on the rent on her apartment and gradually spiralled back into the dark, chaotic place she'd been before.

'Some of her friends from the programme stayed in contact with her,' he said. 'I tried to, also, but it was hard. She had no phone; she was moving around all the time. Then I heard she was in hospital, in casualty. She gave my name as her next of kin and they tracked me down. And here we are.'

Carefully, he manoeuvred the big car into a parking space. Ahead of us was the sprawling white hospital building, its windows glinting in the early spring sunshine.

I wondered which of them Mom was behind, and felt sick.

'All set?' Dad asked.

I clutched my bag to my chest. Even if I had a hundred years, I wouldn't be ready for this.

'I'll come in with you,' Dad said. 'I won't leave unless you tell me it's okay.'

I nodded mutely, swung open the car door and trailed behind Dad to the entrance.

Hospitals are bizarre places, if you think about it. You walk in and it's all flower kiosks and coffee shops and pleasant-faced receptionists, and it's almost like being in a normal building. Then you walk through a door and – bam – suddenly you're in a place where people die.

That's how it seemed to me that day, as I followed Dad along what seemed like miles of corridors, past signs with words on them I didn't understand: rheumatology, electroencephalography, computed tomography. Then we came to a door with a sign on it that told me all I needed to know.

Critical care.

Dad spoke briefly to a nurse, and I followed them both to a bed at the end of the room. I'd never have recognised the woman lying there as Mom. Her face was so thin that her yellowish skin looked like paper stretched over a skull. Her hair was almost all gone – just a few coarse grey strands were draped over the pillow. Even under the covers, I could see the bloated dome of her belly.

'She's very confused,' the nurse murmured. 'But if you stay a while, you may find she has a lucid period.'

Dad nodded, pulled two plastic chairs forward to the bedside, sat down and took Mom's hand.

'Linda, it's Dean. I've brought Sloane with me to see you.'

I sat in the other chair. I couldn't bear to touch that skin, marked all over with livid red bruises. But I reached over and brushed a tendril of hair away from my mother's face.

'Hi Mom. I'm sorry you're not feeling so great.'

Her eyelids flickered and her free hand plucked at the covers.

'Sloane?'

'Yes, Mom. I'm right here.'

This time, her eyes opened fully and she smiled. 'Look at you. My grown-up girl. Dean says you're at university now.'

The pride on her face made me feel like I was being ripped apart by guilt. But I managed to steady my voice, and I started talking.

I told her about my courses, about my roommate, about my boyfriend, about trying out for the dodgeball team. I told her about waitressing at Mandarin on weekends, and how I was learning to play guitar. It was like I was trying to catch up on all the trivial details about my life that she'd missed since I was a little girl, which she shouldn't have needed to be told all in one go. *All those years I wasted hating you,* I thought – and then I understood how bitterly she must regret wasting them, too.

After a while, Dad squeezed my shoulder and mouthed, 'Okay?' and when I nodded, he stood and softly left the room. I stayed there with Mom, talking on and on, telling her I loved her and I hoped she'd get better soon, even though I knew she wouldn't.

'I love you, too, Sloane,' she whispered. Her eyes closed and her breathing slowed. I stayed there for a few minutes, until a nurse told me that she'd sleep all night now. Then I said goodbye, kissed her and went to find Dad.

I didn't need to visit again, because she died that same night.

Chapter Twenty-Four

It wasn't like me to be in denial, but there's no other way to describe the state in which I spent the next couple of days. I went to work, where we were consumed with planning the annual Halloween party. I read two texts from Edward and replied with one-word answers and emojis; if he was after another hook-up, there was no way it was happening now. I opened my desk drawer again and again, looked at the pregnancy tests rattling around with my pens and business cards, then closed it once more, unable to find the courage to use one. I didn't know which result I dreaded more, so I put off the moment when I would have to know. It was early days, I told myself – whatever the outcome was, I'd have several weeks in which to make a decision.

But, wish as I might that it would stand still, time kept passing and, with it, the period of relative stability I'd had in my rental Airbnb apartment was coming to an end. And, the day before I was due to leave, my failure to make alternative arrangements came back to bite me right in the ass.

Thanks to my wilful blindness to the reality of my situation, I hadn't found somewhere else to go. There wasn't much point, anyway, I told myself – I was rapidly running out of money and the thought of spending yet more on yet another grotty apartment was downright galling.

So, like I say, it wasn't like me, but I left making a decision until the last possible minute. To be exact, I left it until two nights before I was due to leave, when I was in bed, at about quarter to eleven. And when I flicked reluctantly through to the app, I saw I had a new message from Jared, my host and the owner of the apartment.

Hiya Sloane

Hope you're well and enjoying your stay. I'm really sorry but I'm getting back from Johannesburg a day early. The project here finished ahead of schedule and there's an urgent meeting happening tomorrow that my line manager wants me there for, so I'll be getting in on Tuesday rather than Wednesday. I know you're booked to stay Tuesday night – sorry if this is inconvenient. I don't mind sleeping on the sofa!

Best,

Jared

PS – my flight lands at 5 a.m., so I should be at the flat by seven. Hopefully I won't wake you!

Shit. No, Jared, you won't wake me, because I won't be here.

I had no reason to be pissed off, but I was. It was Jared's home; he was perfectly entitled to return to it earlier than we'd agreed. He was even being apologetic, and offering to spend a night on the couch so I could have his bedroom for the additional night I'd paid for. But there was no way I was doing that. Pleasant as he was, the idea of settling down for my last night in this temporary home with a stranger sleeping next door – a stranger who'd be exhausted from an overnight flight and a day of full-on meetings, and quite rightly wanting to sleep in his own bed on his first night back after a month working away – was unthinkable.

Almost as bad was the prospect of seeing him in the morning, surrounded by my half-packed things, responding to his solicitous questions about whether I'd found an alternative place to stay, whether I was sure I didn't need an extra night? Really? Was I sure? I couldn't face it. I was getting out of there, right now.

All thought of sleep forgotten, I jumped out of bed, stripped the sheets and threw them in the washing machine, packed my stuff at warp speed, and carried everything down to my car, which took two journeys.

Then, before I could change my mind or even think things through properly, I slammed the door shut and posted the keys through the letter box like we'd agreed. I tapped out a quick message to Jared saying it was fine, I'd made other arrangements, I hoped he'd have a safe flight and I was hugely grateful for his hospitality.

And then I stood in the dark street at half past midnight, next to my patiently waiting car, and I realised I'd made myself home-less, again.

I could go to a hotel, I supposed. It might seem a bit dodgy turning up at a Premier Inn at one in the morning, but I expected they saw worse all the time – at least I wouldn't be bringing a punter back with me for an hour-long booking. I'd have somewhere safe to sleep, and in the morning I could wait until Myles left for work, go back to the house, shower and pick up some clean clothes.

Or I could get an Uber to Megan's place and throw myself on her mercy. But, putting myself in her shoes, I dismissed that idea straight away. I knew she'd say it was fine, she'd welcome me even if I woke the baby – she'd want to help. But I also knew exactly what she'd be thinking.

How long is this going to go on?

She'd be too kind to tell me that she could only put me up for a couple of nights, but I knew that would be exactly what she'd be thinking.

I could sleep in my car. No, I couldn't. I'm not exactly tall, but there was no way I'd be able to lie down in the back seat of my tiny Mini. And besides, the prospect of someone seeing me there, some concerned passer-by or even a police officer tapping on the window some time in the small hours and asking if I was okay was too mortifying to contemplate.

I could go to Bianca's. No, I couldn't. There was no way – no fucking way, even if there'd been a zombie apocalypse and hers was the last safe refuge in London – I was going to ask my former friend for help. I'd take the zombies, no problem. Shambling around, undead, with sightless eyes and my insides hanging out of a gaping wound was a small price to pay for not having to do that.

The Premier Inn it was, then. I took out my phone and swiped the map app to life. But just as I did so, it began to vibrate and trill in my hand. Fearing that it might be Myles, calling me when I was at such a weak point that it would take just a few kind words to make me drive straight back to the house and say I was sorry, I almost flung the phone away from me.

But then I saw that it wasn't Myles's number – it was an unfamiliar landline. We didn't have a landline in the house and never had.

'Hello? Sloane Cassidy speaking.'

'Sloane? It's Vivienne Sterling. I'm most awfully sorry to bother you at this time of night, but I'm in rather a fix and I didn't know who else to ask for help.'

'Vivienne? Are you all right? Where are you?'

Horrible images flashed through my mind, and I felt my mouth go dry with fear. Was she drunk, lost somewhere, not knowing how to get home? Had she had some kind of medical emergency – fallen down the stairs or had a seizure or something? Had she been mugged or burgled or worse?

'I've been awfully stupid,' she said. She didn't sound drunk – not paralytic, anyway. But it was hard to tell; her voice was honed by years of coaching and even when she was utterly hammered, she managed to speak quite clearly.

'What's happened? It's okay, you can tell me, and I'll do whatever I can to help.'

What exactly that would be, I had no idea. Of all the problems that faced Vivienne, I was possibly the least well-placed person in the world to help her deal with them. However, it looked like I was the only one awake in London on that Monday night, so I guessed I would have to do whatever I could.

'It's just… I've locked myself out of my house.'

'You what?'

The absurdity of the situation wasn't lost on me. Here were Vivienne and I both, out on the street with nowhere to go. Of course, I was there through my own choice and she apparently wasn't, but still – there it was. In spite of myself, I realised I was on the verge of giggling.

'I went to put the milk bottles out. I keep forgetting when the milkman's coming, and I've started to accumulate a bit of a mountain of them. So I put my watch on the wrong wrist, like my mother always used to when she needed to remember something, and it worked. But I forgot to pick up my keys. I'm such a fool, darling, but here I am. I'm in a call box down the road in my nightie, and I don't know what to do.'

'Okay. Hang in there, Vivienne – I'll be right there.'

I wasn't right there, of course. I drove carefully but quickly, and all the same it took me the best part of an hour to get there. But at last, I arrived in the dark, silent street, parked and got out. A fox trotted across the road and disappeared into a garden. A freight train clattered along the railway tracks, the sound carrying in the cold air. There was no other sound, and no sign of Vivienne.

'Hello?' I called softly.

'Sloane! Oh my God, darling, I'm so glad you're here.'

Vivienne emerged from behind the magnolia tree in her front garden. She'd been hiding there, I realised, and I could see why. She was wearing a skimpy, thigh-length, lacy garment that I guess you'd describe as a negligee, or possibly a peignoir. It was bright, flamingo pink. On her feet were feathered mules.

She was shivering violently. Typical Vivienne, glamorous even when she's putting out milk bottles, I thought, once more fighting the urge to break into giggles, knowing that if I did I wouldn't be able to stop. I realised I was very, very tired.

'I came as fast as I could,' I said. 'Are you okay?'

'Just utterly mortified. And terribly cold. Did I get you out of bed? I'm ever, ever so sorry.'

'It's okay. I was up anyway. Late night.'

She raised her eyebrows. 'I see.'

She had it all wrong, of course; I hadn't been having a wild night out on the tiles. But I wasn't about to explain that – I needed to find a way to get Vivienne into her house.

Together, we approached the front door. Pointlessly, I reached out and gave it a push with my hand, but it didn't budge.

'It's a Yale lock,' Vivienne said. 'I don't suppose you know how to open it using a credit card? Isn't that what burglars do in books?'

'I haven't got a clue. But I'll give it a go. Come, wait in the car, I'll turn the engine on so the heater works.'

I installed her in the passenger seat then hurried back to the house. I rummaged in my purse and found my Amex card. I suspected that this attempt would be futile, and I was right. After five minutes of poking at the latch with the sliver of plastic, I'd achieved the sum total of fuck all.

'This isn't going to work. We should call a locksmith,' I reported back to Vivienne after a few fruitless minutes.

Vivienne looked alarmed. 'At this time of night? It'll cost hundreds of pounds.'

I nodded. 'Yeah, it will. They see you're desperate and they charge whatever the hell they feel like, unfortunately.'

'Surely there's another way.'

'We could break a window, I guess. But that'll cost even more, getting a glazier in tomorrow to repair it. And you don't want to spend the night with a smashed-in window, do you?'

Vivienne shook her head. 'The bedroom window's open, though.'

I looked up. Sure enough, the sash window on the first floor was open a good eighteen inches – there was plenty of room to climb through it. Only problem was, it was ten feet above my head, and my rock-climbing skills were even more lacking than my ability to break into a house using a credit card.

'We'd need a ladder,' I pointed out unnecessarily. 'I don't suppose you've got one?'

'I've got a small one that I use to prune high branches in the garden. But I have no idea whether it's tall enough, and anyway it's in the shed.'

And the shed was in the back garden, which was behind the high fences of at least four neighbouring houses. I looked down at my pencil skirt and high-heeled court shoes. There was no way I was going to go scrambling over walls dressed like this.

'I honestly don't know what to do. We can't get to your ladder; we can't get to your window. I reckon a locksmith is the only answer.'

'Oh, darling.' Vivienne looked like she was about to cry. 'Are you sure? I'm so sorry, this is entirely my own stupid fault and I feel so bad for dragging you all the way here when I could have called someone myself. But if there's any possible way…'

I sighed. 'Let me go round and have a look. You wait here.'

I walked to the end of the row of terraced houses and around the corner. The end house had a high brick wall around its garden, and, looking over, I could just see the equally high fences of the adjoining properties in the darkness. There was no way in hell, pencil skirt or no pencil skirt, that I'd be able to climb them without risking a broken ankle.

I retraced my steps and met Vivienne's hopeful gaze with a shake of my head. 'I'm sorry, but it's just not going to happen.'

I took out my phone and began googling.

'Locks R Us. Twenty-four-seven service, covers the whole of London. Shall I give them a call?'

Vivienne nodded reluctantly. I tapped the link on my phone and heard the number ringing and ringing. Finally, it stopped and a recorded message informed me that there was no one available to take my call right now but that if I left a message they would get back to me as soon as they could.

'Fucking useless,' I muttered. 'Twenty-four-seven my arse. I'll try the next one down.'

But just as I was tapping on the number, we heard a sound in the still night. It started off as a soft mewling, but soon became a full-on shriek.

'That's next door's baby,' Vivienne said. 'Poor Carlos. They say she's having a growth spurt, and with Melanie working night-shifts it's a nightmare for him.'

Above us, a light came on and I looked up to see a young man standing in the window, holding a baby. He was shirtless and handsome, with pecs to die for and even a six-pack. He looked like the cover of one of those hot dad romance novels. But right now, it wasn't his body I was interested in, ripped or not.

'If he's awake anyway, we can ask him to let us in and go through the back of their house. I can probably climb over one fence. There's just no way I could do a whole load of them.'

'Could you, darling?' Vivienne brightened. 'In fact, the back door may well be open. I was sitting out in the garden earlier and I always forget to lock it. You could just walk in – there'd be no need for the ladder at all.'

But, in fact, there was no need for me to climb over the fence at all. As soon as Carlos opened the door to our tentative knock and we explained the situation, he sprang into full-on hero mode, barely even registering a flicker of surprise at Vivienne's choice of nightwear. He passed me the baby, now contentedly sucking at her bottle, disappeared into his house and, seconds later, Vivienne's front door swung open. Carlos was made of strong stuff – he didn't even look as if the state of the house had jolted him.

'Oh thank you, darling, thank you ever so much. You're so kind.'

'Don't mention it.' He took his daughter back from me and dropped a kiss on her head, and I felt myself go a bit melty inside. *Oh my God. In a few months, that could be me.*

'I don't suppose a drop of sherry would quite be appropriate,' Vivienne said. 'But if I pop the kettle on, would either of you like a cup of tea?'

'I need to get this little one back to bed,' Carlos said. We thanked him a few more times and he disappeared back into his own house.

I thought about summoning a cab and finding somewhere to spend the night, and a fresh wave of exhaustion washed over me.

Sitting in Vivienne's house drinking tea was preferable to that – practically anything was.

'I'd love a cup of tea, Vivienne, if it's not too much trouble.'

'It's no trouble at all.'

I followed her through the front door and stopped dead, as shocked and bewildered as I'd been the first time I saw the house, but for entirely different reasons.

The hallway was spotless. The cobwebs were gone; the floorboards had been cleaned and possibly freshly sanded – they were a rich shade of honey. A smell of some sort of aromatherapy room fragrance filled the air, like when you walk into a swanky spa for a treatment. Vivienne carried on through to the kitchen, like all this was perfectly normal, and I followed her, gazing around in amazement.

Everything was immaculate. All the papers had been cleaned off the dining table, and its mahogany top had been polished to a rich sheen. The kitchen floor tiles sparkled; someone must have got down on hands and knees and scrubbed the grout with bleach and a toothbrush. The walls had been freshly painted a shade of pale mint green. There was a jug of peonies on the table and a row of herbs in brightly glazed clay pots on the windowsill.

I said nothing about the transformation – I couldn't think of a way to do so without seeming to judge the state of squalor the house had been in before. And Vivienne didn't mention it, either – she just flicked on the kettle and reached up to a shelf for a gleaming copper tin labelled 'Tea'.

'Well, that was quite a drama,' she said. 'As it's so late, may I offer you a bed for the night? I mean, of course, if you'd rather get home…'

She couldn't have known it, but she was offering me an absolute lifeline.

'Are you sure? That would be really helpful, actually. You see, I… Well, to be perfectly honest with you…'

I stood there, grasping for the right words to explain what I'd done. But I felt the threat of tears looming larger and larger, and I felt something else, too.

I said, 'Sorry, do you mind if I use your bathroom?' And before she could reply, I dashed upstairs as fast as I could, clutching my handbag.

I just made it to the toilet in time. Cramps were gripping my abdomen like hot pincers, and as I sat down I felt a hot gush from inside me. Blood started to flow like a tap had been turned on inside me.

My period had only been a week or so late. I hadn't even taken a pregnancy test. I couldn't put a name to what was happening to me – if it had been a pregnancy, it had been the merest flicker of one, so small and fragile it could have ended at any time. Or maybe it wasn't even that; maybe it was just a late period, delayed by all the stress and turmoil of my life. But none of that really mattered.

It was still a death.

Right there in that sparkling-clean bathroom, my dream of having a child with Myles died, and with it, the last remaining flicker of hope or desire to save my marriage died, too.

Chapter Twenty-Five

The first thing I noticed when I woke up in Vivienne's spare bedroom was the smell of roses. There were five of them, overblown blooms in shades of pink and coral, in a little cut-glass vase on the table next to the bed, and their scent had passed into my dreams, in which I'd been walking through a garden in summer, the sun hot on my back, searching for something or someone I couldn't find.

Sitting up, pushing the marshmallow-soft pillows up behind me, I tried to gather my thoughts, but the dream, the almost hungover feeling that came from having had eight hours of uninterrupted sleep, and my total uncertainty about what on earth I was going to do next had left me feeling dazed and bewildered.

First things first. I called the office and told Rosie that I wasn't feeling great but would be in as soon as I could. I checked my calendar and confirmed that I had no meetings that needed to be cancelled – or that I'd missed, thanks to my shameless lie-in. And then I turned to my missed calls.

Eight of them were from Myles.

The time had come, I realised, for me to return to the house. I had nowhere else to go; I'd literally run out of road. I'd go home, shower and change my clothes. Next, in my makeshift office in our spare bedroom, I'd deal with whatever work issues were most urgent. And then… Actually, I had no idea what I'd do then. I felt as if my life had shifted into a different gear, or like some kind of autopilot had been switched on, like I wasn't in control any more, and even if I was, whatever system navigated me through my days had failed and I was drifting on a course whose destination I didn't know.

There was a tap on the door and Vivienne came in with a tray.

'Good morning, darling. How are you feeling? I brought you some coffee and a glass of water, and I can get some breakfast on the go as soon as you like, if you're hungry. I hope you don't mind but I popped your clothes in the washing machine – they're just in the dryer now so they'll be ready for you to put on once you're up. I did everything on a delicates cycle, don't worry.'

She reached over and touched my shoulder, just lightly, and I knew that she was thinking about something other than whether my tights might shrink. I felt again the closeness we'd shared when she told me about the daughter she had lost, and it brought a massive lump to my throat. Looking down, I realised I was wearing a pair of mushroom-coloured silk pyjamas that she'd lent me, and I remembered how she'd sat with me on the couch for a couple of hours the previous night, pouring endless cups of tea while I told her the whole story of what had happened with Myles, and the baby we weren't going to have.

'Thank you. Honestly, I can't thank you enough. You've been so kind.'

She waved a hand. Her nails had been manicured, I noticed, and were painted a bang-on-trend shade of lime green. Her feet were bare, and I could see her toes had had the same treatment. She was wearing skinny jeans and a white linen shirt. Even her face looked different – softer, somehow, like she'd put on a bit of weight or maybe had some work done by someone with a seriously subtle hand.

All our talk the previous night had been about my woes, so I hadn't asked her what had brought about the transformation of her house and herself; no doubt she would tell me when she was good and ready.

'I'll just leave this here.' She moved the flowers and slid the tray onto the table next to me. 'There's a new toothbrush for you in the bathroom, and clean towels on the rail. Take your time – I'll be out in the garden potting up my gazanias. The poor things need a bit of TLC or they won't survive the winter.'

She swished out, and I pushed myself up on the pillows and tasted my coffee. It was good stuff – one of the changes Vivienne had made to her house had evidently been investing in a top-end espresso machine. There was even a little jug of milk and a bowl of sugar lumps on the tray.

While I sipped, I turned back to my phone and listened to the message Myles had left – just the one, in spite of all the times he'd called me.

'*Sloane, it's me. I just wanted to let you know I've got an estate agent coming to value the house this afternoon. He'll be there at twelve. I thought you'd want to know and possibly be there if you can. Right, I'll see you later, I hope. Hope you're okay.*'

I swung my feet out of bed, onto the deep pile of the carpet, which looked like it had been newly laid. It was ten o'clock now – if I hurried, I'd make it home in time.

Home. Except it wasn't, really, not any more. Nowhere was.

But if I was to move on to the next stage of my life – whatever that would be – I had to confront this situation, deal with it like a grown-up and try to find solutions.

Just before eleven, having showered, dressed, refused Vivienne's offer of breakfast and thanked her profusely for her hospitality, I pulled up outside the house. My usual parking spot was occupied by a bright blue Beetle emblazoned with a logo: 'Walkerson's – Your local property specialist'.

Our local property specialist clearly wasn't a parking specialist, I thought, noting that one of the car's wheels had mounted the sidewalk. I found a space round the corner for my own car and stepped out, leaving my bags in the trunk for now.

I paused outside the front door, composing myself in readiness for what I might find inside. The door itself had been freshly painted with a smooth black skin, and the knocker, letter box and door number were new, a matte stainless steel. The lock was new, too, I realised, which meant my keys would no longer open it.

If I needed a reminder that this was no longer my home, I thought with a wrench of sadness as I reached for the knocker, here it was.

A guy in a cheap shiny suit and a pink shirt and tie answered my knock, reaching out straight away to shake my hand with a too-firm grip.

'You must be Sloane. Oliver Bridges. But everyone calls me Ollie. Come on in – we're just taking an initial look around this very exciting property.'

I forced a smile, suppressing a surge of sadness that our house had become, in the mind of this chirpy young man with his carefully styled quiff of brown hair and the remains of a shaving rash on his neck, just another asset to be marketed.

I followed him down the hallway and into the centre of the house. Light streamed in through the expanse of glass leading to the garden, and through the roof light I could see a rectangle of blue sky. The steel worktop on the kitchen island reflected the light, making it almost too bright to look at. The new appliances stood in their places, spotless and unused.

I turned to the living room and saw two new, pale grey chesterfields. There was a new rug on the floor, also in tones of grey and silver. The walls were painted grey too, and a white-framed mirror hung over the fireplace.

'It's a perfect blank canvas,' Ollie enthused. 'Just waiting for a new owner to stamp their personality on it. But of course, it's ready to move right in to. The purchaser will be able to do as much or as little as they like. You've created quite a gem here, Sloane.'

'I left most of the decisions to my husband,' I said. Even to me, my voice sounded wooden.

Ollie looked uncomfortable. 'Of course. It must be useful to have a professional in the family, haha.'

'Very useful.'

I looked around again, remembering with a pang all Bianca's talk about a shared vision, French-navy walls and pink velvet upholstery. At the time, I'd been far from convinced by her ideas, but now they seemed infinitely preferable to this austere, characterless space.

'Shall I show you upstairs?' I asked. I hadn't seen it myself, not since the loft extension had been finished and a hole bashed through what had been our landing ceiling.

'Absolutely!'

Clutching his iPad, Ollie followed me up the stairs.

Our bedroom looked more lived-in, at least: one of Myles's suits was hanging from the door handle in a plastic dry cleaner's bag, a pair of trainers was half-kicked under the bed and I could smell my husband's cologne hanging in the air. The spicy, cedarwood smell was like a punch in the stomach, a searingly painful reminder of how much I'd loved him.

But even more painful was the realisation that to do what he had done to me, he couldn't have felt the same way.

'I'm just up here,' Myles's voice called from the new staircase that wound up into what used to be the roof, a space where I'd been too scared of mice and spiders to ever go.

For the first time, and I supposed the last, I climbed the stairs. Myles was standing by the new window that overlooked the garden. The room had been arranged as an office, with a desk holding a computer and printer. On one wall was a door leading the new en-suite bathroom; against the other stood my lovingly restored vintage armoire.

Myles turned away from the window and looked at me. Neither of us smiled.

'A delightful space,' Ollie enthused. 'Perfect for guests, older children, or as you've arranged it, as a work-from-home haven.'

Children. The word transported me back to Vivienne's bathroom, where, the previous night, I'd felt life literally drain out of me. I wondered how Myles would feel if I told him, but it was pointless to speculate – I knew that I never would. Ollie had joined Myles by the window, and they were both looking down into the garden.

'Of course, there's a huge amount of uncertainty in the market right now. Some agents will tell you property like this is always in demand, and they're right. But I'm not going to lie – not like some others – and tell you that you'll achieve top dollar for this home. Not in today's market. My recommendation – assuming you're after a quick sale – would be to price realistically and be flexible. We'll throw all our efforts into marketing the property for you…'

I couldn't help myself tuning him out as he explained about the websites where the house would be listed, the glossy brochures that would be printed, the number of people on Walkerson's books who'd expressed interest in a home just like this, in this highly desirable area, close as it was to parks, schools, nightlife and, of course, central London.

'All things being equal,' he finished, 'assuming you want to have accepted a decent offer by Christmas, I'd suggest we market the property initially at…'

And he named a figure so dizzyingly high that, for a second, I felt my heart leap with wild hope in my chest. It was way more than double what we'd paid for the house, five years before when we'd seen it and fallen in love with it as recklessly and joyfully as we'd fallen for each other. It was more money than I'd ever dreamed of having in my life.

And then the practical part of my brain kicked in. I remembered the huge mortgage we'd taken out back then, and the huge additional mortgage that had been intended to pay for the renovation.

'It doesn't matter, sweetheart,' Myles had said. 'It's only numbers. It doesn't mean anything until we decide to sell, and we're not going to, are we? Because we're building our dream home right here, and we're going to stay for another twenty years at least.'

At the time, I'd agreed willingly, even though the numbers spun through my head at night in a terrifying blur. He was right, I'd told myself – it was only numbers. If we ever wanted to move, it would be ages down the track. The house would, inexorably, increase in value, and the money we'd poured into making it bigger and more modern would recoup itself over and over in the quality of our and our children's lives.

But we had no children, and now we never would. There was no Myles and Sloane any more; no marriage. Just this empty shell waiting for someone else to make their life in it. That, and hundreds of thousands of pounds we owed to the bank – a debt that was the last thing we'd ever have together.

'We'll give it some thought,' Myles was saying. 'I'll ring you in a couple of days. Of course we'll be getting other valuations too. Thanks for your time, Ollie – it was good to meet you.'

He pulled his phone from his pocket and glanced at the screen. 'I've a meeting in twenty minutes, so I'd better get my skates on. Sloane will show you the garden and anything else you'd like to look at, and see you out.'

He shook Ollie's hand, wincing at the vice-like grip, and turned to leave, then paused as if he was noticing me for the first time. But he didn't say anything; he just patted my shoulder briefly and hurried away down the stairs.

I followed more slowly, Ollie trailing behind me taking photographs and making notes, occasionally making a flattering remark about the quality of the workmanship, the light, the space, the enviable location.

I couldn't speak – I felt like my mouth was filled with cold marbles, or blocks of ice, which were rising up from the choking lump in my throat.

I'm not going to cry until he's gone, I promised myself. I'm not going to make a fool of myself, or embarrass this poor guy who's only doing his job.

I managed to hold it together, producing one-word responses to his questions, inhaling the strange newness of the house, the smell of paint that was everywhere.

At last, Ollie said, 'Right, I think I'm done here, Sloane. Lovely to meet you. I'll look forward to hearing from you or your other half once you've made a decision. Don't hesitate to give me a bell if you've got any questions.'

And he swung open the front door and strutted off towards his waiting Beetle, already making a call on his phone, off to his next appointment.

I waited by the door for as long as I could endure, until I was completely sure he wasn't going to come bustling back to ask me a question or pick up something he'd forgotten. And then I returned to the living room, that grey space washed with winter light. The tree in the garden was bare of leaves; the few pots of herbs I'd grown held only blackened sticks now. As I watched, a magpie alighted on the ground and began to hop purposefully around.

'One for sorrow,' I said aloud, and then I turned and subsided, limp with despair, onto one of the grey sofas, my head in my hands.

I'd thought earlier that I was running out of road; now, I felt like I was falling off a cliff. I had nowhere to go. I had almost no money, at least until the house was sold and the mortgage paid off. I'd have to look for a flat to rent. But in the meantime? The prospect of moving back in here, with or without Myles in the house, was unthinkable.

It was him – his careless cruelty, his self-indulgence, his belief that he was entitled to one final fling with that pretty blonde girl who'd believed she was in love – that had brought us to this situation. If the pregnancy that hadn't even properly begun had been real, had carried on, it would have been his actions that would have led to his child growing up without ever knowing what it was like to have two parents who loved each other.

I couldn't bear to breathe the same air as him, never mind live with him, even temporarily.

Up until now, I realised, I'd been existing in a kind of limbo, waiting for something to happen that would set my life back on track – or on a different course altogether. Now, I supposed, Ollie had provided a kind of closure – a kind of impetus that would force me to properly move on. But where to?

Hearing the sound of keys in the front door, I leaped to my feet, heart pounding in alarm, and hurried to the hallway.

But it was only Wayne and Shane.

'Hiya, Sloane,' Wayne said cheerily. 'We're all done here, as you can see. We just dropped in to collect the last of our gear and leave the keys. What do you think? Looks all right, doesn't it?'

'That's a cracking kitchen you've got,' Shane said. 'Just right. You'll be able to have your mates there, drinking cocktails by the island while you cook up a storm, right?'

Then there was a moment of silence, and I saw in their faces that they'd remembered the situation with Myles and me, and that we'd never be hosting a cosy evening with friends in that kitchen.

Wayne cleared his throat. 'I was sorry to hear you and him indoors were having problems.'

'It's a difficult time,' Shane said, looking down at his work boots. 'I hope you're all right.'

It was pathetic, but their kindness completely did for me. I heard a wailing sound, realised it was coming from me, and a second later I'd collapsed to the floor, hugging my knees to my chest, sobbing my heart out.

'Here, Sloane, love,' Wayne said. 'Don't cry. It'll be okay.'

'Why don't I make you a nice cup of tea?' Shane said.

Chapter Twenty-Six

I spent that night in the house with Myles. I had to – I'd nowhere else to go. Like two goldfish in a bowl, we circled around each other, not communicating. Politely, he said he was going to order a takeaway and asked whether I was hungry. Equally formally, I said yes, thank you, I was. Would I prefer Chinese or Indian, he asked, like he was talking to a stranger. I said I didn't mind and would be happy with whatever he preferred.

It turned out that what he preferred was chilli paneer, chilli mushrooms and lamb vindaloo, all served with a side order of passive aggression – he knew perfectly well I couldn't stand spicy food. But I refused to get into an argument, put some rice and naan bread on my plate and ate in the kitchen with my laptop, while he watched football on TV with the sound turned up loud.

As soon as I'd finished, I went upstairs and spent the night lying in the spare bedroom, sleepless, all my senses on high alert as I heard Myles moving about the house, using the bathroom and at last going to sleep himself, in what had been our bedroom, where he snored thunderously all night.

As soon as the square of darkness that filled the window began to lighten almost imperceptibly to grey, I got up. I showered and dressed silently, not because I gave a single fuck about disturbing Myles's beauty sleep, but because I couldn't face another minute of the leaden, toxic atmosphere, which was lightened slightly by him being asleep.

I went downstairs, grateful for the carpet that deadened the sound of my footsteps, and opened the front door. It was cold; the sky was a bleached non-colour somewhere between grey and blue and a brisk wind sent dead leaves scudding along the sidewalk.

It was too early to go to work. I pulled on trainers and a coat, put my work things in my car and started walking. Instead of heading north as I usually did, through the park and towards the river, I found myself making my way south, through unfamiliar streets lined with blocks of flats and rows of unprepossessing modern houses. I passed rows of shops: fried chicken takeaways, bookmakers and vape shops, mostly – signs of an area that had fallen on hard times. Or perhaps times here had always been hard.

I turned off the main road, into another residential street. Apart from the occasional runner and a handful of commuters waiting gloomily at a bus stop, the roads were deserted – it was not yet seven. I imagined the scenes behind all those closed doors – parents hustling their children out of bed and into their school uniforms; lovers snatching a precious last few minutes under their duvet together; dogs padding around behind their owners, eager for breakfast. One of the doors, I noticed as I passed, was open. I paused, curious, wondering if I was about to catch a glimpse of the lives of the people inside.

And then I heard a woman's voice. 'Oh, holy Jesus, come on, you bastard fecking thing!'

In the doorway, a couch appeared – or what had once been a couch. The fabric was ripped away from its sides and I could see springs poking out at odd angles. Pushing it towards the open door was a woman in her fifties.

'Can I give you a hand?' I asked. 'Sorry to intrude – I was just passing and you look like you're struggling there.'

She looked at me for a second, suspicious, and then said, 'Oh go on then. If you don't mind. Thank you.'

I grabbed the other end of the ungainly piece of furniture and, together, we wrestled it out onto the sidewalk.

'The council are coming this morning to pick this up, and a load of other stuff,' the woman said, panting from her exertions. 'My tenants did a midnight flit without paying their rent and left a load of junk behind. I'm trying to clear it all out so I can get the house back on the market.'

'Well, let me help you. It's not a job for one person. My name's Sloane Cassidy, by the way.'

'Eileen Murphy. And you're some kind of guardian angel, you know that?'

Together, we trudged back into the house and got to work.

'I used to live here myself,' Eileen explained as we carted broken bookshelves, a chair with one leg snapped off, a hoover with its entrails spilling out and boxes full of old newspapers out of the house. 'But then my daughter had a baby, so I moved back to Dublin to help her out. I thought renting the house out would be easy, but I've had one nightmare after another. I'm done with it now – I'm selling it and I don't care if I make a loss. It's not worth the hassle.'

In my mind, a small spark of hope ignited, but I kept quiet and kept lifting and moving.

'There we go,' I said at last. 'Job done.'

'Really, I can't thank you enough. I'd offer you a cup of tea, but the kettle's broken and the gas has been cut off, so…'

'That's all right,' I replied. 'I should probably head off to work any— What was that noise?'

We both turned and looked into the house.

'What noise? I didn't hear anything.'

'I'm sure I did.'

I stepped into the hallway and stood, listening. There was silence, then that sound again, a muffled wail. It came again, louder, and I heard a rhythmic thudding sound on the stairs.

'Oh my God,' Eileen said. 'Those gobshites have only gone and left their bloody cat behind, too.'

A silver tabby cat, eyes wide and alarmed, had appeared at the top of the stairs. It paused for a second when it saw us, then came dashing down towards us, meowing at the top of its voice, and started twining itself around our legs.

'Hello.' I squatted down and caressed the silken head. 'Are you hungry? Is that what's the matter?'

'Poor wee mite,' Eileen said. 'That's all I need! Now I'll have to get the cat to a shelter today, on top of everything else.'

All in a rush, I heard myself say, 'Look, I've got an idea. You need a tenant; I need somewhere to live. My husband and I are splitting up, and I was going to start looking for a place this week. But if I move in here, the cat could stay. I'll pay what they were paying. We can get an agent to draw up a proper contract. I won't trash the place, I promise.'

Eileen and the cat both gave me almost identical, hard stares.

'No,' Eileen said. 'I don't reckon you would.'

Three hours later, I was sitting at my desk as if this was just another normal day. But instead of getting on with work, I was staring blankly at the estate agent's contract in front of me, in between staring blankly at my online banking.

Oh my fucking days, what have I gone and done?

I'd only gone and signed a six-month lease on a ramshackle two-bedroom house in a sketchy area. One that came with a free cat. Who would need – in addition to the food and water bowls, litter tray and blanket I'd bought for her in a smash-and-grab raid on the local high street – to be taken to the vet, fed twice a day and generally taken care of to an extent that I wasn't even sure I was capable of taking care of myself.

You wanted a baby, for Pete's sake. Why are you freaking out about a cat?

Because a baby was an abstract idea. And I'd have had Myles to help.

Or maybe not so much.

Thinking about it, I remembered how, when I'd gone away to visit my dad in Canada for ten days the previous summer, I'd come home to find all our houseplants parched and gasping, the bins overflowing with trash and an almost biblical plague of fruit flies feasting on a blackened banana left inexplicably under the couch.

Maybe, I realised, the vision I'd cherished of me, Myles and our child, or children, had been light years away from what the reality would have been. I thought of Megan, struggling alone at first, then finding her feet, getting her mummy hand in, and Matt pitching in and not just helping her but being a proper father to his own child. Not reluctantly or half-heartedly. Not just doing the fun bits like tickling Ethan's tummy to make him giggle and then walking away when shit got real – literally, in the form of the poo-nami nappies Megs had told me about until I clapped my hands over my ears and begged her to stop – but properly. Taking the rough with the smooth.

Would Myles have been like that? Thinking about it now, I simply couldn't see it.

Suddenly, like a ray of light in my brain, a thought came.

Sloane, you dodged a bullet there.

And now – sure, I had a rented house that would need a whole shedload of sorting out. Yes, I had a cat who'd need… whatever cats needed. I made a mental note to google exactly what that was. I'd need to start doing proper crazy cat lady things like talking to her about my day, asking her about hers and cluttering up my social media with pictures of her, so she'd know I loved her. But I was flying solo. I was in charge. I wouldn't have to wash anyone else's clothes, or cook anyone else's dinner or pick up anyone else's dry cleaning or write birthday cards for any fucker who wasn't my own family.

Or, more to the point, deal with the fallout from anyone's self-indulgent shagging around.

I looked again at the contract I'd signed, and this time it looked like a reprieve – a passport to a place where I made the rules. I'd be able to tell Dad I'd found a new home. I'd tell him about the cat, too, so he wouldn't worry so much about me being lonely.

'Sloane?' Sam's voice startled me out of my contemplation. 'Remember, we've got that meeting with the guy from that charity for disadvantaged kids, who might want to work with Ruby-Grace. He'll be here in fifteen.'

'Right. Right, yes, of course. Sorry, I was a bit distracted. Good on you for getting that set up. What does Ruby-Grace make of it – have you discussed it with her at all?'

'Yep, she's on board. So let's see what this Edward Reeves has to say for himself.'

'Edward *who?*'

'Reeves. Apparently he was some big shot at an investment bank, then he jacked it in to give something back. He's from a disadvantaged background himself, apparently, but got into Oxford and then had this high-flying City career.'

Never mind his career. I've slept with the bloke.

'Are you okay, Sloane?'

'Yes, fine. It's just – I think I've met him, socially, somewhere. The name's familiar.'

'Well, let's see if he recognises you.'

Edward did, of course. But, unlike me, he'd been forewarned and knew that the person he was coming to meet was the same Sloane Cassidy he'd last seen pulling on her clothes after multiple orgasms in his bed.

But when he walked into the meeting room and greeted us both, he gave nothing away. His demeanour was purely friendly and professional. I, on the other hand, couldn't help a massive, telltale blush creeping up my neck and flooding my face.

God, you're hot, I thought, admiring his strong, square jaw, the dimple in his chin, the smooth skin of his neck between his dark hair and his dark blue jumper, the length of his legs in his faded jeans.

'Good morning,' I said, trying to keep my voice cool and friendly. 'It's lovely to meet you, Edward.'

'Likewise.' He extended a hand and I shook it, feeling something like an electric shock as our palms connected. He held on maybe just a second longer than he needed to.

'I'd like you to meet my colleague, Sam, who you've spoken to on email. Sam's been working on opportunities for our clients to partner with companies like yours in the charitable sex – the charitable sector – to facilitate hooking them up – I mean partnering them – with organisations where there are synergies.'

I sat down, blushing furiously, my knees feeling like jelly. I was going to have to pull myself together, and fast – that, or shut the fuck up and let Sam run the meeting.

'Perhaps you'd like to tell us more about what Clear Future does.' Sam came to my rescue. 'A bit more of the charity's background, and why you believe influencer marketing could be right for you.'

'Sure.' Edward leaned back in his chair and sipped his coffee. I could see the muscles moving in his lean, strong arms as he raised the cup, and remembered how it had felt to have those arms around my naked body. 'I founded the organisation in 2017, with backing from some of my former colleagues in the finance industry, but also using my own funds. I'm conscious that the gaps within our society, of wealth and opportunity, are only getting wider, and I had a vision to help kids from difficult and deprived backgrounds access chances that might otherwise have been closed to them.'

He carried on for a bit, talking about workshops in schools, placements in corporations up and down the country, meetings with think-tanks and politicians, and I found myself not only admiring his looks but genuinely respecting the values he represented.

I found myself thinking, *I'm not nearly ready for a relationship.* And then silently telling myself off, because Edward had given no sign whatsoever that he was interested in any sort of relationship with me beyond the few hours we'd spent together and the couple of brief texts we'd exchanged. We were cool with that. It was what it was. No regrets, and no repeat performance.

So why was I now regretting that there hadn't been one?

I don't think I'd ever paid less attention in a business meeting in all my life. When, at last, Sam said he'd arrange a face-to-face with Ruby-Grace, and Edward said that would be great, I felt giddy with relief that it was over – but also punched in the gut with disappointment that he'd given no sign that there was anything between us.

We all stood up, my knees feeling more or less normal now.

'It was great to meet you,' I said. 'We're always excited to connect with partners where there's genuine passion.'

Shit. Blushing like an idiot again, I followed Sam and Edward out of the meeting room.

'Angela Granger is on the phone for you, Sam,' Isla said from behind the reception desk, and Sam hurried off, leaving me and Edward standing by the lift.

'It was good to see you again, Sloane,' he said.

'And you.'

The elevator pinged and the doors slid open. Edward stepped in, and my heart cried out, *Noooo!*

I said, 'There's just one thing. About Ruby-Grace.'

'What's that?'

'She's signed with another of our partner brands. Own the Night. You may not have heard of it.'

Edward shook his head. But he'd stepped out of the elevator.

'They're a clothing company. Clubwear. Some of their stuff is pretty out there, and Ruby-Grace posts pics of herself wearing it on her social media feeds.'

Edward said, 'I'll take a look. But in all honesty, Sloane, the kids we work with are exposed to all sorts. I doubt some young woman in scanty clothes will make them even turn a hair.'

'Makes you feel kind of old, doesn't it?'

He shrugged ruefully and nodded, turning back to the elevator door. Then he paused, turned around and said, 'Any chance you're free for a drink this evening?'

It felt like someone had strung fairy lights all over the Ripple Effect office and suddenly switched them on.

'I can't,' I said. 'Not tonight. I've just moved into a new place, and it turns out it came with an unexpected bonus cat. I need to get back and check she's okay.'

'As it happens,' Edward said, 'I love cats.'

Chapter Twenty-Seven

The Ripple Effect Halloween party had started life as a semi-ironic event – a way of getting our clients, partners and staff together for a few drinks to socialise and get to know one another outside of work. Over the years, though, it kind of became a victim of its own success, and now social media was abuzz with gossip and preparations about it for weeks before.

For the minor celebs we represented, it was the chance to get dressed up in the most Instagrammable outfits they could find, get drunk at the agency's expense and, more often than I was entirely comfortable with, hook up with each other. For the big companies we worked with on endorsements and advertising deals, it was a chance to network. And for me and the rest of the team, it meant running ourselves ragged preparing for the party, spending the entire night trying to curb the worst excesses of our clients' behaviour and then cleaning up the mess they left on social media afterwards.

It was exhausting, and I wasn't looking forward to it one bit.

As always, though, I planned my outfit with care.

In the past, I'd done sexy witch, sexy vampire, sexy Day of the Dead carnival attendee and sexy devil. This year, though, I wasn't feeling up to being sexy anything. Instead, I was going for a pared-down, serious, even slightly threatening vibe. My Morticia Addams dress had a high neck and long sleeves, and the skirt trailed all the way to the ground. I was planning on teaming it with bone-white foundation and red lipstick so dark it was almost black, and channelling my best 'don't fuck with me' vibe.

First, though, Rosie, Sam, Isla and I had to spend Friday morning at the venue, a Soho bar so on-trend and popular we'd had to reserve it months in advance. The company we'd hired to do the decorations were on site, draping fake cobwebs in every corner, brushing fake dust on surfaces, arranging green and red lights to faintly illuminate the ghouls and skeletons that lurked in unexpected places.

The bar staff were putting the finishing touches to the cocktail list, which featured a Banana Banshee, Nightmare Negroni, Dark and Shadowy and Vampire Vesper. In the kitchen, trays of creepy canapés were being laboured over by the catering team. A dressing area had been prepared for the immersive theatre performers we'd booked to frighten the life out of our guests in their roles as Dracula and his brides.

It was all completely over the top, and under normal circumstances I'd have been hitting peak excitement about it all. Now, though, I wanted nothing more than a nice, quiet lie-down in a darkened room – ideally one that didn't have zombies lurking in the corners ready to jump out at me.

At three o'clock, my team and I gathered in the centre of the room, surveying the handiwork that was nearing completion.

'I think we're just about all set here, Sloane,' Rosie said.

'I've got my Voldemort outfit here in my bag. I can stick around and get ready here, so I'll be on hand in case there's a crisis,' offered Sam.

'I would too,' Isla said apologetically, 'only I'm coming as a sexy cat, and my outfit's so tight I'm going to have to get my mum to help me get into it. It's the absolute bomb though – just wait till you see it. Or, more to the point, just wait till Charlie Berry sees it.'

I shot her a warning glance. 'Now, Isla, you know clients are off—'

'Off limits, I know, Sloane. Sheesh, you're no fun. But I can at least make him look at me. Can't I?'

I laughed. 'Look, maybe. I can hardly stop him doing that. But no touching.'

And, wearily but cheerfully, the three of us went off home to get changed, leaving Sam in charge.

Home. It had only been two weeks, but already the little house felt like a haven – a refuge. As soon as I opened the door, Beatrice – as I'd christened the silver-grey tabby cat – came running to meet me, mewing for fuss and food. Already, she'd made it quite clear how our relationship was going to play out: she was the boss, and I was her staff. From the moment she woke me in the mornings, tapping my face with her paw to let me know it was long past her breakfast time, to when she curled up at night in the crook of my knees, so I was forced to spend the night in one position for fear of disturbing her, she'd made her wants and needs my top priority.

The house itself was a work in progress – it needed painting, furnishing, probably a full rewire and God only knew what else. But in the meantime, it was a roof over my head – a place of my own. I had a couch, a fridge and a microwave – everything else could wait. Oh, and I had a bed, of course.

I looked at it with fondness. It was nothing special. There were no designer touches here, no artfully arranged scatter cushions that would have made Ollie Bridges nod with approval. There was just a wooden frame, mattress and bedding that I'd ordered in a panic from the only place I could find that offered same-day delivery, when I knew that Edward was coming round. We'd assembled it together, laughing as we got confused by the instructions and fumbled with the Allen key, and Beatrice batted stray screws along the floor with her paws.

As soon as the bed was made, we'd fallen onto it, pulling off each other's clothes, not caring that we were dishevelled and dusty, and it had been just as amazing as the first night. And the next morning, waking up in that strange house with a man I barely knew and a cat I'd just randomly acquired had felt entirely comfortable and familiar.

But once Edward had left, I'd felt a sudden plummeting panic, like I'd been at the top of a rollercoaster, filled with elation, and now I was hurtling towards the bottom. All the security and stability I'd built up over five years with Myles was gone – just like that. I was on my own. I was thirty-five. I wasn't going to have a baby any time soon. If I locked myself out of my house at midnight like Vivienne had, who would I call?

It had taken a massive effort of will, that morning, not to throw myself onto the bed and howl. But I was worried that would upset Beatrice, so I didn't. I went to work, I carried on, and with each day that passed, the little house felt more normal, more like mine.

But there was no time for mooning. I had to get Morticia-ed up ready for the party – just as soon as I'd brushed the cat hair off my black dress.

By six thirty, the bar was buzzing. People in costumes of various degrees of extravagance were mingling everywhere, drinking, talking and laughing. Glen Renton was standing in a corner alone, as usual – the personality that sparkled in his gaming reviews on YouTube totally deserted him in real life. I knew that, as I'd done for the past five years, I'd have to spend a good chunk of the evening finding people I could persuade to speak to him, and then replace them when, after listening to Glen talk about himself for ten minutes, they made their escape.

Isla was looking impossibly pretty, her black latex cat outfit more suited to a furries' bondage dungeon than anything else, and was being chatted up by Craig McLeod, a theatre director contact of Megan's. Across the room, I could see Charlie Berry gazing at her, transfixed. I was going to have to keep an eye on that situation – although, realistically, if they did end up going home together, there wouldn't be a lot I could do about it.

Rosie, dressed as a wicked fairy in flowing purple and black chiffon, was circulating like the pro she was, making sure everyone got introduced to the right people. Megan was working the room, warm and sparkling as always, wearing a glittery red devil costume that showed off the incredible cleavage she'd got thanks to Ethan.

Gemma Grey, wearing a dress that appeared to be made of fake cobwebs, but in which she still looked beyond stunning, was surrounded by a group of admiring, less successful YouTubers, and I knew she'd be dispensing kind, helpful advice and making a point of mentioning vlogs of theirs she'd watched and liked.

Ruby-Grace had come dressed as a sexy… I wasn't sure what, to be honest. If I looked too hard at her, I was worried my eyes might literally pop out. She had on a barely-there black latex bodysuit, thigh-high wet-look boots and… sweet Jesus, was that a vibrator she was holding? No, it must be a truncheon. Sexy police officer, then, I decided with relief. And she was rocking the Own the Night brand, so Ross and Angela would be delighted.

I noticed that Sam, across the room, hadn't managed to tear his eyes away from her, looking at her with a starved intensity that reminded me of Beatrice watching me open a tin of tuna.

Everything, I thought, surveying the room, looked under control. Perhaps I could go in and mingle a bit myself. And perhaps, since we'd learned from experience that the best strategy was to start our annual party unfashionably early, it would be wrapped up by midnight, and I could go back home to Beatrice and sleep for ten hours solid.

But I was jerked out of my gloomy thoughts by a voice saying, 'Darling! I'm late to the party, as usual. Don't you look glamorous? Black is totally your colour.'

For a moment, I thought Vivienne had literally got up and into a taxi, turning up wearing what she'd had on in bed. Then I looked a little more closely and realised that her white, floor-length silk nightdress, worn with a matching robe over it, was a costume – her hands were coloured dark red up to the wrists with some sort of stage make-up, and she was holding a tea light in a brass holder and a cake of soap.

'Oh my God! You're Lady Macbeth! Vivienne, that is total genius. So glad you could make it. Come on in! Let's get you a drink and I'll introduce you to people.'

I ushered her into the bar, found her a glass of fizz and looked around, wondering who would be interested in talking to an actress who they might vaguely remember having heard of, years before. But before I could find a group in which to insert her, Ruby-Grace came hurrying over.

'Oh my God, you're like, totally Vivienne Sterling. I can't actually believe it! My mum made me watch all your films when I was a kid and you were total life goals for me. I was going to go to acting school and learn Shakespeare and everything. Only I couldn't, because I'm dyslexic, so I do modelling and stuff instead.'

Vivienne looked delighted and tried to reach out a hand to shake Ruby-Grace's, but realised that, juggling her drink and her sleepwalking props, she couldn't. Instead, she kissed her on both cheeks, and Ruby-Grace looked as starstruck as if she'd just been snogged by Madonna.

'Do you remember that panto you did in Exeter?' she asked, almost stumbling over her words. 'You were the fairy godmother in *Cinderella*. OMG, that dress you wore! I made Mum sew sequins onto our old voile curtains so I could dance round the house in them pretending to be you. Are you retired now? It would be so awesome if you made another film.'

'That's so awfully kind. I remember that panto well. Paul, who was Buttons, was the most awful letch and was constantly pinching everyone's bottoms – the girls and the boys. No one had heard of hashtag MeToo back then of course – we all just had to put up with it.' Vivienne chattered on, draining her glass, and a waitress immediately appeared, topped it up, and asked if Vivienne could possibly sign her order pad. Ruby-Grace's presence, like a bedside lamp to moths, brought a whole crowd of other guests over, and soon Vivienne was surrounded by an admiring throng, happily holding court and looking like she was having the time of her life.

Since she appeared to be being looked after – or looking after herself – quite well, I found myself free to circulate. I delivered Gemma over to talk to Glen, relieving Sam, who immediately made a beeline for the crowd around Vivienne and Ruby-Grace, and went to the kitchen to tell the caterers to bring out some food before everyone got too drunk. And then I grabbed a much-needed Vampire Vesper for myself and prepared to play hostess for the evening.

By about nine o'clock, the party was in full swing. Charlie was dancing with Isla; Glen had left to drive back to Brighton in his latest supercar; the performers had done their thing to rapturous applause – though I couldn't help but notice how the guy who was playing Dracula made his entrance, clocked Vivienne and almost spat out his fake fangs in amazed surprise. Vivienne might have vanished into obscurity for years, but she still had far more fans than I'd realised.

I found myself beginning to relax and enjoy myself. The middle of the evening, after everyone had had a few drinks and the initial awkwardness was over, but before things got too messy towards chucking-out time, was the most enjoyable part. I was making my way over to the trays of canapés – bloody Mary syringes, miniature pizzas with ghost-shaped melted cheese, meatballs wrapped like mummies in strips of pastry, chocolate cupcakes with pumpkin frosting – when Gemma appeared by my side.

'I'm really sorry to bother you, Sloane. I know you're crazy-busy. But I'm a bit worried about Vivienne. She's had loads and loads to drink and she—'

'Damn it. Okay, honey, thanks. I'll be right there.'

I turned and saw Vivienne standing by the door, swaying gently. Craig McLeod, the theatre director, was next to her, puffing furiously on an e-cigarette. As I approached, I could hear Vivienne talking. Well, not so much talking as declaiming, her voice carrying resonantly, even though her words were slurred.

'"Here's the smell of blood still. Wash your hands. All the perfumes of…" No, that's not right, is it, darling? "Wash your hands, put on your nightgown, look not so pale…" Now, what's the next bit? I used to know it all backwards.'

'Hey, Vivienne. Are you having a good time?'

'Marvellous, darling. I can't remember the last time I went to a party! I was just regaling Craig with my favourite soliloquy. "Come, come, give me your hand. What's done is done and cannot be undone. To bed, to bed, to bed."'

I caught Craig's eye and he smiled sympathetically.

'Would you like to go home, Vivienne?' I asked. 'To bed?'

'Well, now you mention it,' she looked at me, her violet eyes unfocused, mascara smeared down her face. 'I am rather tired. I'm not used to late nights any more, you see.'

'That's okay. Let's get you in a cab. Give me two seconds.'

Cursing the Morticia Addams dress's lack of pockets, I hurried back into the throng and retrieved my bag from the cloakroom. Probably, Vivienne would be perfectly okay getting home in an Uber on her own and putting herself to bed. But, possibly, she wouldn't. I was going to have to see that she got back safely.

I fought my way through the throng of people and eventually found Rosie and told her where I was going, but before I could get back to Vivienne, I was interrupted by Ruby-Grace.

'Sloane? Is she okay?'

'Vivienne? She's fine. Just a bit… You know. She doesn't get out much.'

'Would you like me to give you a hand? I'm… I mean, my dad likes a drink. I'm used to it. I can help.'

I looked at her scanty outfit and her absurd shoes. She wasn't exactly dressed for giving a pissed person a fireman's lift. But then I noticed the impressive muscles in her gym-honed arms and – more importantly – the kindness in her eyes, which no amount of winged eyeliner could have concealed.

'Thanks, honey. That would be great. If you're sure you don't mind leaving the party?'

Ruby-Grace shrugged. 'I'm not much of a party person, if I'm honest. I get shy in big groups. And anyway, I can always come back if I want.'

'Come on then.' We rushed back to Vivienne, who'd sat down on a chair someone – presumably Craig – had brought for her, her white negligee pooling on the sidewalk around her ankles, and summoned a cab on my phone. It was surge pricing, of course, as it always is in emergency situations in my experience, and there was a seven-minute wait. I just hoped that Vivienne would manage not to pass out or be sick while we waited, but Craig, Ruby-Grace and I kept valiantly chatting to her, even though her replies didn't make a whole lot of sense.

'Here we are,' I said, when at last Bogdan in his red Mitsubishi pulled up a few yards down the road. 'Home time.' Ruby-Grace took Vivienne's arm and helped her to her feet. She was pretty wobbly, and veered from one side of the sidewalk to the other, but

Ruby-Grace, impressively steady on her platforms, kept her in a straight line. I opened the door and we helped her in.

'Thank you, Craig – you're a total legend. Let's speak on Monday.'

'It's not me who's the legend – it's this lady. I can't believe you kept it so quiet that she's a client of yours. I'll be in touch.'

I hurried round to the other side of the car and got in, my mind whirling. In spite of having gone madly over the top on the booze, it had totally been Vivienne's night. It wasn't only Craig, who might – please God, he might – just offer her work. I remembered all the twenty-something YouTubers clustering around her, hanging onto her every word while she regaled them with anecdotes about her acting career; the actor playing Dracula freezing in his tracks when he saw her, like someone had driven a stake through him right there; how she'd sparkled and laughed and lit up the room.

I wondered what had brought on this transformation from the broken, lonely woman in her squalid house to this charismatic party animal. It hadn't been down to me, that was for sure. It was Vivienne herself: her magnetism, the legacy of the work she'd produced before heartbreak had turned her into a shadow of the woman she'd once been – and, of course, whatever the hell had spurred her to transform the way she lived after Max's death.

I glanced sideways at her and saw that she'd fallen asleep, her head drooping forwards, her hands clasped in her lap. The fire had gone out of her and she looked much older, but even sleep couldn't hide the perfect line of her jaw, the jut of her cheekbones beneath her slightly skewed false eyelashes.

The cab inched through endless, traffic-clogged streets. Rain had begun to fall, the windscreen wipers swishing it rhythmically away, the lights of the shops we passed reflecting in a million drops on the side windows.

Ruby-Grace and I chatted inconsequentially about the party and the outfits people were wearing, the entertainment and the food. But both of us, sitting on either side of Vivienne, held her hands. The sight of Ruby-Grace's fingers, with their long coffin-shaped nails, wrapped tenderly over Vivienne's, filled me with deep sadness. I wished I'd been able to hold Mom's hands for longer, that last night – and, more importantly, I wished I'd been able to hold them more often, long before.

At last, the cab turned into Vivienne's road and pulled up outside her house. To my surprise, I could see light gleaming from behind the downstairs shutters (shutters? I was fairly sure those hadn't been there the last time I visited), and through a gap in the curtains in the upstairs bedroom.

I touched Vivienne's hands and said, 'We're home. Come on, let's get you to bed.'

But she didn't stir.

'Give me just a second,' I said to the driver, getting out and hurrying round to the other side of the car.

I opened the door and tried again. 'Vivienne, we're home. Wake up.'

Ruby-Grace said, 'Come on, love. Up you get. Time for beddy-byes.'

I grasped her shoulder and shook her gently. 'Vivienne! Please wake up.'

At last, she opened her eyes. 'Hello, darlings. Where are we?'

'We've brought you home, chick,' Ruby-Grace said. 'You're in a taxi and now you need to get out.'

Between the two of us, we managed to get her out and on her feet, along with her Lady Macbeth props and my own handbag. But there was no sign of Vivienne's house keys.

'Oh God, no,' I said to Ruby-Grace. 'We're locked out.' We stood in the darkness, Vivienne's head drooping onto my shoulder, and as I was wondering what the heck to do next, the door swung open and a woman stepped out.

'Thank God, you're back safely. Oh, Sloane, it's you. Well done for getting Viv back in one piece. Come on then. She'll freeze to death out here.'

I couldn't have been more surprised if a Bride of Dracula had suddenly popped her head out of Vivienne's house. It was Bianca.

Chapter Twenty-Eight

'You know me, Sloane,' Bianca said. 'I do love to meddle.'

She shifted on her high stool, crossed one slender knee over the other, picked up a piece of vegan sushi with her chopsticks, dunked it in soy sauce and ate it. She was looking as smooth and polished as ever, in taupe leather trousers and a cream cashmere jumper, her sleek red bob as glossy as the copper tabletops in the newly opened Asian fusion restaurant where she'd suggested we meet.

I suspected, though, that her casual WhatsApp message (*Hey, sorry I had to dash straight home on Friday before we could chat! Hope Viv got off to bed okay. Shall we do lunch? And by the way, who was that extraordinarily dressed girl with you?*) had as many ulterior motives behind it as there were tapioca pearls in the bubble tea I was already regretting ordering.

Bianca, I reflected, liked to be on the offensive, and since Ruby-Grace and I had turned up unexpectedly at Vivienne's house and found her there, she must have been feeling anything but in control of the situation.

But before I could quiz her about her relationship with Ripple Effect's first ever client, I had an uncomfortable speech of my own to make.

'Listen,' I said. 'I owe you a massive apology. I was completely wrong about you and Myles, and I behaved horribly to you. I was so… I guess my head was so messed up with suspicion and doubt and all the rest. I got the situation completely wrong and I took it out on you – but that's really no excuse. I should have known that you would never do that to a friend.'

'Well, no, I wouldn't. I wouldn't go around shagging someone else's husband, even if they weren't my friend. But I'm not exactly blameless in this situation, Sloane.'

She took another bit of sushi, and I gingerly picked up a tofu skin dumpling and bit off half of it. It was considerably better than the description suggested, so I ate the other half and tried some yam tempura.

'Because you knew about Myles and Charlotte, and you didn't tell me?'

Bianca froze, a crispy soy protein nugget halfway between the conveyor belt and her mouth. Then gravity won and the nugget dropped into her lap, leaving a smear of sriracha mayo on her jumper.

'Shit!' She rubbed it frantically with a napkin. 'That'll stain, and the jumper's new – I just bought it off Luxeforless. It wasn't even on sale.'

'Don't scrub it, just dab gently. Dab, dab, dab. Otherwise you'll drive the grease in deeper and damage the wool. Then when you get home, put baking soda on it and soak it in shampoo. It'll come out just fine, I promise.'

'Really?'

'Really. One of our clients, @CleanQueenJean, did a vlog about caring for cashmere the other day. You should follow her on Insta – she's ace.'

Bianca carefully arranged her napkin to cover the vivid orange smear. Then she looked up at me, half-smiling. To my surprise, there were tears in her eyes.

'It's only a jumper, right? But that's me. Never knowingly under-reacted.'

'God, woman! It's one hundred per cent cashmere. You'd be weird if you didn't freak out.'

Bianca plied her napkin again, but this time it was her eyes she used it on, far more careful about not smudging her mascara than she'd been about her jumper.

'Anyway,' she said. 'Yeah. I'm so sorry. I did know. About Myles, I mean. I've known for almost a year. And I didn't say anything to you, and I feel rotten about it.'

'You tried. Kind of.'

'I didn't try hard enough. I knew what the right thing was to do, but I didn't do it. I was too scared.'

'Scared? Of what?'

Bianca took a deep breath. I could see her bracing herself to say something that wasn't easy. 'I haven't got many friends.'

I ate another dumpling. If I swerved the yam tempura and the bubble tea going forward, I'd be totally winning at lunch.

'But you do, right? Don't you? Other moms at Charis's school and people you meet through work and…'

I tailed off. I realised how very scant my knowledge of Bianca's life really was.

'Yeah. But they're not actual friends. They're just people I see most days. When my brother was getting married I got close to his fiancée for a bit, but then the thing with Myles and Charlotte happened – Charlotte's a friend of hers – and it all went so badly wrong. I made a bit of a scene at their wedding and now Henry's not talking to me.'

To be honest, I could kind of see Bianca's brother's point, but I didn't say that. I didn't need to say anything though, because she was in full flood.

'I just didn't want to hurt you, Sloane. I didn't want to rock the boat. I knew it was over between them by Christmas, anyway, so I just thought if I kind of warned you that he might be… might not be as faithful as you'd want him to be, you might find out for yourself. And then you'd be able to make a decision based on the truth, not on whatever bullshit story he came up with.'

'I see. Well, that's what's happened. I've moved out. We're selling the house. My solicitor and his solicitor are writing loads of letters to each other and it's costing a fortune and I'm renting a house in Walworth for the time being, and to be perfectly honest I have no idea what the hell I'm going to do with my life.'

Her face fell. 'Oh God, Sloane. I'm so sorry.'

'Don't be sorry. It's actually kind of liberating. For the first time in ages, I feel like myself again. Like I've got choices. I can turn my life into anything I want. I can be who I want. You know, for so long I was so engrossed in being Myles's wife, I kind of lost sight of that.'

Bianca nodded. 'Yep. I get that. I've been there too.'

'You mean Michael…?'

'Not Michael. I know people look at him and wonder what I'm doing with him. Don't think I don't know that. But he's a good man, Sloane. He's the best. He supports me one hundred per cent in everything I do, he does his share of housework even though he works full-time and I don't, and he's a fantastic dad to Charis. Which is why we were so desperate to have another baby.'

'Oh. I don't know why, but I thought you'd decided one was enough.'

'Yeah, I know you thought that. Everyone thinks that. But we didn't. We tried for years and years, since Charis was, like, a year old. I was desperate to give her a brother or a sister. Maybe we spoil her – I don't care. I just want her to know how special she is, how loved. And I knew I'd love another child just as much.'

'But you couldn't…?'

'We couldn't. We tried everything. Literally everything. Giving up booze, going vegan, acupuncture, Michael sitting in cold baths every day to boost his bloody sperm count – everything. I've had seven rounds of IVF. You get a free go on the NHS but after that you have to pay. We've spent tens of thousands. They call it secondary infertility. They can't find anything wrong with either of us – I just can't get pregnant. And if I do I can't stay pregnant. I've had four miscarriages. The last one was at sixteen weeks when I thought everything was going to be okay. It's been awful and shitty and it's almost broken us. Not just financially – our marriage, too.'

Almost against my will, I heard my voice trotting out the horrible cliché that infertile couples hate to hear. 'It might still just happen naturally, you know.'

To her credit, Bianca didn't tell me to shut the fuck up. 'It won't. We stopped trying six months ago. I couldn't do it any more – not to Michael or to myself. We've just had to accept that Charis is our precious only child, and there won't be another.'

I said, 'I'm so sorry. It must have been awful.'

'Yes, it was. But you know what, deciding enough was enough was the biggest relief. To just step away from all that charting and all those clinic appointments and all that fucking hope – God, I never want to go back onto that treadmill.'

I nodded and took another sip of my bubble tea. It was tepid now and tasted even worse. I wondered whether, if things had been different with Myles, I would have ended up on that treadmill, too. I wondered whether I might still end up there, on my own, or whether, like Bianca, I'd have to lay that dream aside forever and move on. At least you've had one child, I thought, but I knew that saying it would be even worse than saying a second might, somehow, magically happen.

So I kept quiet, inwardly kicking myself for all the times I'd sneered at Bianca's faddy ways and for never considering that her spiky exterior might be a defence against deep pain.

'Anyway, so I needed a project,' Bianca went on. 'Having a baby wasn't happening. Designing your house wasn't happening. My career – oh God, Sloane, it's pretty pathetic really. Michael's the breadwinner. His bog business brings in more than enough money for us all. But when the fertility treatment started costing so much money I felt I had to do something, and interior design is the only thing I know how to do, really. So I set it up and opened the shop and, if I'm honest, it's ended up costing us money. Michael doesn't mind because he loves me and he knew I needed something that was just for me. But it's a hobby more than a business.'

'I totally understand,' I said. 'I can imagine that when you're going through what you've been through, you need something –

anything – to fill the space around it. You poor thing. Is that why you contacted Vivienne?'

'Vivienne? Oh, God, no. That wasn't me – that was Charis.'

'*Charis?*'

'Well, you know she's started that YouTube channel, where she does Skype interviews with famous people? She's had our MP on there, and a woman who raised twenty thousand pounds for period poverty action by baking biscuits shaped like vaginas, and one of the dancers from *Strictly*. She wants to get Meghan Markle, eventually. I sometimes wonder if I've got the next Fiona Bruce on my hands.'

For a second, I let myself imagine Charis taking Boris Johnson apart on live television, and wished I could see it.

'She's certainly full of ideas,' I said.

Bianca glowed with pride. 'Isn't she? But even I wasn't expecting her to contact Vivienne Sterling. Michael showed Charis an old film of hers – totally age-inappropriate, but what can you do, with a child who's so advanced? – and she found Vivienne's address online. Turns out she's still on the public electoral register, and even in the phone book, which hardly anyone is any more, and she wrote to her.'

'Charis sent Vivienne fan mail? She must have been over the moon.'

Bianca laughed. 'She certainly was. And she wrote back, such a charming letter. Charis showed it to me – it was the first I knew about it all – and so I wrote back, apologising for the intrusion but putting my number in the letter in case she was willing to go ahead with a vlog for Charis.'

I could see where this was going.

'And Vivienne rang you.'

'She did. She was – well, she was a bit tired and emotional, as they say.'

'I can imagine,' I said, feeling a fresh surge of guilt that I hadn't done more for Vivienne myself.

'And the next day I went round to see her, and you know what I found.'

I nodded. 'She wasn't in a good place.'

'It was loneliness, more than anything else. She's not a hoarder, really – she's just let everything get on top of her. And she was drinking way too much, obviously.'

'At the party the other night, she seemed fine and then suddenly she was really out of it.'

'That would be because she's cut down so much, since Charis and I started going to see her. You know how Charis gets on with people from all walks of life. She adores Vivienne. Vivienne's got her reciting Shakespeare and all sorts. Sometimes I think she might have a career on stage herself. With her looks, she could really go far. In fact, I've been taking her to performance classes every Wednesday afternoon, instead of her Mandarin. They're really impressed with her and she's to play the Christmas fairy in the end-of-year show.'

I gritted my teeth and suppressed an eye-roll. That was the thing with Bianca – she'd come up with something entirely surprising and then straight away revert to type.

'That's amazing. You must be really proud. So it was you who did all the stuff in Vivienne's house?'

'Oh no, not at all. It was mostly her. She just needed a bit of a hand getting started. The second time I went round there, I took along a few bin bags and a bottle of bleach and some Marigolds, and just dropped some gentle hints, you know, that she could do with a little bit of a spring clean. And we sort of went from there. It was only once the worst of the mess was sorted that I'd allow Charis to visit, of course. I mean, I know exposure to germs is good for developing children's immune systems, but there's that and then there's – well, *that*.'

'But… I mean, it was like a complete transformation. In about two months.'

'Once Viv got her head around it, there was no stopping her. You've seen her garden. She's got limitless energy. And I brought a few bits from the shop, and from clients' houses that weren't wanted any more, and once she saw it starting to take shape it really inspired her. It's a proper home now, isn't it?'

'It really is. I hope she stays so positive. I'll visit myself, of course. And she's going to be coming into the office later on in the week, because a director we work with wants to meet with her to discuss a potential part in a show he's casting. He's on a tight budget, he says, but Vivienne's name is still quite a draw card and he's keen to work with her.'

And I'd practically bitten his hand off when Craig had called to ask me to ask about Vivienne's availability.

'She mentioned she was looking to get back into work. Keeping busy – that's the thing. It's so important for all of us, isn't it?'

I had another glimpse of the pain and loss Bianca must have been through; the heartache she must have felt when she realised that her family was only ever going to be herself, Michael and Charis. I thought of her filling her days with her unprofitable shop, her elaborate renovations of her and other people's houses, how maybe her determination to create perfect homes was a compensation for what she'd seen as her failure to create the perfect family.

And I thought that Bianca coming into Vivienne's life was probably the best thing that could possibly have happened to them both.

'Honestly, I can't thank you enough for helping Vivienne. You've made a massive difference to her,' I said.

'Oh, please! Don't mention it! She's part of my life now – mine and Charis's. She might have started off being a bit of a project for me, but she's become a real friend.

'Now, I really must dash, Sloane. Charis has Kumon maths at three and then her riding lesson, and then we're going to make a carob and date cake for her to take to the school bake sale tomorrow. It's been lovely to see you looking so well. We must do this again – it's been such fun.'

And she whisked out, leaving me to pay for our lunch, which I found I didn't mind at all.

Chapter Twenty-Nine

My little Mini was the perfect car in many ways, but it certainly wasn't designed for moving house. Even pared down by the numerous trips I'd made to the charity shop over the past two weeks, my clothes still filled its tiny trunk almost to bursting. A tower of shoeboxes was piled on the back seat. On the front seat next to me were my laptop and tablet, a leather case holding a few bits of jewellery, and a framed photo of me with my dad.

In the hired van behind me were my restored armoire, my larger suitcases, my KitchenAid mixer, boxes full of books, pots and pans, as well as all the other things I'd acquired during my life with Myles that I felt were neither his nor ours, but mine.

It was late November and, at four in the afternoon, already almost dark. A thin drizzle was falling, and my little car's windscreen wipers valiantly swooshed the water away. Although the sky was gloomy, the rain reflected every point of brightness: the traffic lights and street lamps, the glowing shop windows and, most of all, the Christmas lights that were strung, sparkling, across the high street, so it looked like the whole world was dressed for a party.

I turned the Mini left into Langdale Street and parked behind the Mazda, with its vanity plate that just about spelled Bianca.

Behind me, Piotr and Gavin got out of their van. I unlocked the front door just as Bianca was climbing down off her ladder, wiping her paint-stained hands on an even more paint-stained sweatshirt. From her perch at the top of the stairs, Beatrice watched her suspiciously.

'I got the last coat on just in time,' Bianca said. 'It's not quite dry yet, but it'll only take a couple of hours. You gentlemen will need to take care when you move the furniture in.'

I thanked her for the millionth time, then hurried back out to my car. Together, the movers and I formed a kind of human chain, ferrying my belongings in and finding places for everything like some kind of giant game of Tetris.

At last, the van and my car were both empty. I handed over a wad of cash to Piotr and thanked him, too, and stood in the doorway as they drove off, warm from my exertions.

'It's starting to look like a proper home,' Bianca said approvingly. 'That pale pink was an inspired choice. It really warms up the room.'

'Yes, well, that's the beauty of living on my own,' I said. 'I can have what I want. And Eileen said it was okay for me to decorate, especially as I'll hopefully be able to make her an offer for the place once the sale on Myles's and my house goes through.'

'I'd better head off,' Bianca said. 'We've got people coming for dinner, friends of Michael's. Are you sure you won't join us? Paul, who plays squash with Michael, is newly single, you know, and he's ever such a catch. He runs his own software company and he's got a holiday home in France.'

I laughed. 'That's really kind of you, but I just don't think I'm ready to jump into a new relationship so soon. I need some time on my own, to settle down and figure out who I am again. I'm not looking to date just yet.'

Bianca didn't know, of course, about the night I'd spent with Edward, or the night he'd spent at mine. Or, in the interest of full disclosure, the other night at mine. And the one after that…

And she didn't know about the conversation we'd had the previous day.

He'd got up before me, and I'd woken up to the fragrance of fresh coffee – a high-end bean-to-cup machine had been my second, and most self-indulgent, purchase for the house – and freshly showered man. I gently pushed a purring Beatrice aside and sat up as he walked into the room.

'Good morning, beautiful,' he said. 'And good morning, Sloane.'

I laughed, and Beatrice jumped down off the bed and started twining herself around his legs. 'Madam here says it's long past her breakfast time.'

'And long past ours. I borrowed your keys and popped out to the bakery up the road. It's seriously good. I got cheese croissants and smoked-salmon bagels.'

'You're an angel, thank you.'

'And I've made coffee. Want me to bring you a cup?'

I shook my head. 'I should get up. Give me a second.'

I quickly cleaned my teeth, showered, pulled on jeans, trainers and a new leopard-print jumper, and found Edward in the kitchen. He passed me a plate of pastries and a steaming cup of coffee.

'So here we are,' he said. 'Saturday, and the delights of London lie before us. We could go to Winter Wonderland and ride on the Ferris wheel and drink mulled wine. Or we could go to a movie.

Or we could go and buy you a Christmas tree and decorate it. What do you reckon?'

I tipped some cat food into Beatrice's bowl and she plunged her face into it as if to say, 'Finally! God, the service in this place!'

I said, 'I should really be cleaning the place. I'm moving the last of my stuff over from my old house tomorrow, and my friend's coming to finish off the decorating.'

'I could help. I'm ace at carrying things and not too bad with a paint roller either.'

I laughed. 'That's an offer I normally wouldn't refuse. But you're right – let's enjoy the day. Winter Wonderland sounds amazing. I'll just straighten my hair and put on some make-up.'

'You look perfect just as you are.'

I kissed him. 'I'm glad you think so, but I need five minutes.'

I didn't bother doing more with my hair than pulling it into a messy up-do, and I didn't need much make-up, either – my skin looked as fresh and glowy as if I'd been slathering on expensive serum. So I did the bare minimum, then considered my shoe collection for a couple of seconds before deciding to leave on my trainers. We'd be doing a lot of walking, after all – I wasn't going to kill my feet to please some idea in my own head of what was expected.

We got the bus as far as the river, and walked slowly through the crowds of tourists in the chilly afternoon, hand in hand. It was a gloomy afternoon – one of those late November days when it seems like it hasn't properly gotten light before it begins to get dark again. But the heavy cloud only served to make the glimmering ice-blue lights bedecking the trees look more magical, the glowing stalls selling gingerbread, candy canes and brightly painted wooden toys more inviting.

We could have caught another bus, or got the Tube, but we didn't – we kept walking, in no hurry at all because it felt like we had all the time in the world. We were tourists ourselves that day in our adopted city, passing through Trafalgar Square, where the giant Norwegian spruce tree sparkled with thousands of golden lights; wandering the streets of Mayfair where the windows of expensive boutiques seemed to gleam with their displays of leather handbags, expensive soap and silk scarves.

'I haven't even started my Christmas shopping,' Edward remarked. 'I'll end up doing it all online at the last minute, as usual.'

'It's the way forward,' I said, remembering how in previous years I'd ended up doing exactly that, for all of Myles's extended family, because if I didn't we'd turn up at his mother's empty-handed and it would be seen as my fault. 'Are you spending the day with family?'

He nodded. 'Going up to my mum and dad's in Manchester. My two sisters will be there with all their kids. It's mayhem but we love it. My youngest niece is two now, so she's just old enough to get the whole magic thing.'

'And mean Uncle Edward isn't going to spoil it by telling them that Santa isn't real?'

'God, no!' He laughed. 'My sisters would never forgive me. Besides, it is kind of magical, isn't it, watching them come downstairs in their pyjamas and seeing their stockings all filled up and going, "He's been!"'

'You leave a piece of cake out for Santa the night before, right?'

'Oh yeah. And a sherry, and a carrot for Rudolph. Last year my sister Rachel forgot to move them, and my brother-in-law was stuffing his face with raw carrot washed down with sherry at seven in the morning to conceal the evidence.'

I laughed, moving closer to him and squeezing his arm. All that – that image of a perfect family Christmas, children turning their expectant faces up to the Christmas tree, their squeals of pleasure as they opened their gifts, them bouncing off the walls with sugar and excitement – was what I'd imagined creating for my own family.

But I was enjoying the day too much to feel gloomy about what I'd lost. Soon, as twilight was beginning to deepen, we arrived at the Christmas carnival and Edward bought us hot mulled wine and pretzels so salty they puckered our lips.

'What do you want to do?' he asked. 'Ice skating? Rollercoaster? Ferris wheel?'

'This is kind of pathetic,' I admitted. 'But I'm shit scared of rollercoasters. I know they're safe and everything, but I just can't.'

'God, I'm so glad you said that. I am too. Ferris wheel, then?'

'That's a far better idea.'

We joined the queue, and soon we were seated in a pod, holding hands as the wheel inched us slowly upwards and the lights of the city spread out below us, blurred by the falling drizzle.

'This reminds me of that first night,' he said, 'when we went to the Shard. Remember?'

'Of course.' I smiled, and I knew that, like me, he was remembering not just the breathtaking view, but those hours afterwards, in his flat, when our breath had been taken away in a totally different way.

'I didn't know then that it would be more than just one night,' he said.

'Me neither.' I looked at his handsome, handsome, smiling face and felt the warm press of his hand on mine, and my heart felt suddenly heavy. 'I didn't expect this at all.'

'Shall we go and get some dinner after this? I know it's early but we'll have lots to do tomorrow, with your movers and stuff.'

'Edward,' I said. 'It's so kind of you to offer to help. I really appreciate it. But I'm going to have to do this on my own.'

He looked at me, the smile gone, his eyes steady. 'When you say "this", you don't just mean moving furniture, do you?'

There was a lump in my throat, and I tried to swallow it away. It didn't work.

'No. I don't just mean that.'

'Sloane, I know it's soon. I know we've only seen each other a handful of times. I get that you don't want to rush into anything and that's not what I'm saying we should do. But we have a laugh together, right?'

'We do,' I said. 'You're amazing, you really are. But I… I'm not even divorced yet. I won't be for a few months. And ending a marriage is a big deal. I just don't know if I'm ready to start seeing someone else yet.'

To his credit, he didn't say, *But you* have *been seeing me.*

'Are you still hung up on him? On your husband?'

'God, no. I'm really, genuinely not. But I rushed into my relationship with him, and it was a massive mistake and it hurt me really badly. I just need time to get over that. Not over him, but over what it did to me.'

'So you're saying we shouldn't see each other any more?'

My heart screamed, *No!* But there was no way to fudge it. If I said I just wanted to keep things casual, and he agreed, and we carried on spending those blissful nights together, the nights would inevitably turn to days. If we carried on yielding to the physical chemistry between us, an emotional connection would inevitably follow.

And that would leave me at risk of reopening the wounds in my heart that were still so raw, still not fully healed.

I said, 'Edward, I'm really sorry. But yes, I think that is what I'm saying. It would be so easy to fall for you, and I just can't let that happen yet.'

His face hardened and I felt a wrench of guilt, knowing I was hurting him. *But better now than later on, when we're both deeper into this*, my head insisted.

'I'm not going to wait, you know,' he said. 'I've loved being with you. I think you're special. But I can't put my life on hold just in case you change your mind.'

'Of course you can't. I'm not asking you for that. It would be a totally shitty thing to do.'

That's what he wanted, though, I thought. *If I suggested that, I'm sure he'd agree.* And it would have been shitty, and selfish and unfair.

'So this is it, then? You're ending it?'

I managed a smile. 'Maybe we'll see each other around. At Fifty-One Wardour, perhaps.'

'I'll be sure to not send you champagne if we do.'

He was smiling too, a smile as sad as the weight on my heart. I reached for him and we held each other for a long time, all the way back down to earth. Then we'd parted, going our separate ways through the crowds. I'd turned and watched his dark blue coat getting further and further away until I couldn't distinguish it from all the other coats any more, and I'd made my way home alone.

'Well, if you do change your mind,' Bianca was saying now, and for a second I couldn't figure out what she was talking about, 'just drop me a text. Paul's coming over at eight. Men like him don't come along every day, you know.'

'I know they don't. But if there's someone out there who's right for me, I guess I'll find him when I'm ready.'

Maybe you already found him, and let him go. But there was no point dwelling on my decision – I'd made it, and now I had to make it work.

I said goodbye to Bianca, then turned my attention to the boxes and bags, all waiting to be unpacked.

By ten that night, I'd made good progress. Plates and glasses were stacked in the kitchen cabinets. All my clothes were arranged tidily in the wardrobe. The abstract painting Dad had given me for a wedding present hung over the gas fire, its brilliant jewel colours lighting up the room. Maybe I would get a Christmas tree, I thought. Make the place feel even more like a home.

But for now, I was whacked and ready for bed. There was just one more thing to do.

I went into the second bedroom, where one day I hoped there'd be a spare bed and a desk for me to work at, looking out over the garden. For the moment, though, it held only my vintage armoire and a box full of odds and ends – bills and paperwork, my passport, games of Scrabble and backgammon Myles and I had bought and never played, old phone chargers and notepads, a framed photograph of Myles and me on our wedding day.

Most of it was junk, and I'd get rid of it in the morning. First, I'd just work through the stuff and pack away anything important in the cabinet, and then I could go to bed. Beatrice, bored of my unpacking, was already waiting there for me, curled up on my pillow.

I sorted quickly through the box, returning most of its contents to take to the recycling bank in the morning. There, I saw with a pang, was a bundle of the letters Dad had written to me when I was at school. They were all twenty years old or more – by the time I was at university, we'd started communicating by email. I rifled through them, smiling as I thought of all the time he'd spent relating the inconsequential details of his life so I'd feel closer to him.

Then, tucked in among them, I noticed a strange envelope, addressed in an unfamiliar hand. The address on it wasn't my school. It was a Manhattan address – the apartment Myles had been subletting when I met him, and it was Myles's name on the envelope.

I should return it to him, of course. It wasn't my property, and it wasn't my business.

But I couldn't stop myself opening the envelope and pulling out the sheets of paper.

They weren't the same pale blue writing paper that Dad used. They were pages torn from a spiral-bound notebook. Whoever had written this obviously wasn't in the habit of writing letters – they'd just reached for the nearest thing and used that. The handwriting was an uneven, awkward script, that of someone who was more used to typing.

There was a date scrawled at the top of the first page – a date I knew well. It was when Myles and I had been seeing each other for about a month, when he'd asked me to move to London to be with him.

Dear Myles, I read.

Writing to you like this feels completely bizarre. I've never written you a letter before – I've never needed to. You always answered my texts and took my calls. It was what you promised, remember? That you being in New York wouldn't change anything, that it was just temporary, and that soon you'd come back and it would be like this time apart never happened.

But it seems something's changed. For two weeks now, you haven't responded to me at all. I've called, I've texted, I've emailed and you've just blanked me. I rang the office and they said you were out at a meeting, so at least I know you're okay and nothing bad has happened to you. But that doesn't mean something hasn't gone wrong. It obviously has.

Obviously, for some reason, you've decided it's over between us. Just like that. After a year together. After we talked about moving in together. After you told me you loved me. Just the last time we spoke, you said everything was fine – you couldn't wait to see me. You said maybe I should come out to New York for a long weekend.

You said you were missing me.

You know, I thought about doing just that. I thought about getting on a plane and coming out there, surprising you at work

or at your apartment. I'm not going to do that. I'm not that
tragic and desperate.

But I wanted you to know how badly you've hurt me. You
won't let me say it to you in any other way, so I'm writing it
down. I don't know what happened to change the way you feel,
but I wish you'd had the courage to tell me.

I guess you don't. I guess you're not the person I thought you
were. I guess it's over.

Have a nice life.

Jess

I read the letter through again. Across the distance of time, I could
feel the hurt, anger and betrayal radiating off the page. I wondered
who Jess was, what she looked like, where she was now. I thought
about the part I'd played in her heartbreak, not knowing.

I thought of Charlotte Bell, bravely coming over to apologise
for the hurt she'd unknowingly inflicted on me. I wouldn't be able
to do the same for Jess – there was no surname on her signature
and no address at the top of the page.

Perhaps, before Charlotte and maybe even after her, too, there'd
been other women in Myles's life. I didn't know and I no longer
cared, I was relieved to realise. But before any of them, there'd been
another other woman, innocently and joyfully flinging herself into
love with a man she believed was only hers.

And that woman had been me.

Chapter Thirty

It was lunchtime on Wednesday, and Megs had brought Ethan into the office. Only Rosie was there, and she'd had a good old coo over him before offering to keep an eye on him while his mum and I retired to the boardroom.

'So,' Megan said, sipping her water. 'I reckon I'll come back three days a week from January, and see how that goes. There's a great nursery just up the road from the flat, and I've taken Ethan there for a couple of mornings already, just to see how he settles in. He loves it, apparently. He's such a cheery little chap. I'm very lucky.'

'Yes,' I agreed, 'you're really lucky.'

Megan's face fell. 'Oh, God, Sloane, I'm sorry. What a dick.'

'Don't be,' I said. 'You know what, if I had got pregnant and then found out about Myles, it would all have been a million times worse. I don't know if I could have gone through with having the baby. That's if I'd found out soon enough to have had a choice. And if it had been too late – I don't know, maybe not having a choice would have been even worse than having one. And having that tie to Myles for the rest of my life, not being able to move on properly – I don't know if I could've dealt with that.'

Megs looked at me intently. 'You are over him, right?'

'I'm over *him*, sure,' I said. 'I mean, I wouldn't get back together with him if he was the only man left on the planet and a nuclear bomb had destroyed all the world's vibrators. As for whether I'm over what he did to me – I'm getting there.'

'That's good to know. Because there's something I need to tell you.'

My stomach lurched and plummeted, and I felt sweat break out on my palms. All at once, I was back there in our spare room, looking at Myles's phone, confronting what I believed was betrayal not only by my husband, but by my friend, too.

I'd been wrong about Bianca. But what if Megan had… Megan and Myles had… surely not. They'd only met on a handful of occasions – at my birthday parties, at restaurants we'd been to with her and Matt as a foursome, at Megs and Matt's wedding. Surely Megan, who I trusted implicitly, not only personally but professionally too, wasn't going to shatter my faith in her?

Not Megan. She'd never do that. You're just being paranoid, I told myself firmly. And although I knew that sensible part of me was right, and I felt ashamed of my brief moment of mistrust, I still dreaded what she might be going to say next.

I took a deep breath, clenching my hands into fists under the table. 'Go on.'

'If I tell you this, do you promise you won't hate me?'

'Megs! Come on – out with it.'

Megan opened her mouth and closed it again. And then, all in a rush, she said, 'I never liked him, you know. I'm sorry but right from day one I couldn't stand the man. Jesus, how can one human being have such a bloody high opinion of themselves? With his arsey suits and his sleazy smile and – oh my God – the way he does that swooshy thing with his hair? It makes me want to chop his hand off and make him eat it, every time.'

It was my turn to open and shut my mouth without saying anything, but I doubt Megs even noticed. She was in the zone.

'He's an utter wankpuffin, Sloane. A twatbadger, a cockwomble, a dickbiscuit. He is a miserable piece of knobcheese and I hope he spends the rest of his life regretting what he did to you. In between farting around with his stupid hair, obviously.'

She paused for breath, but still not for long enough for me to say anything.

'Seriously, if he was here right now I'd be telling him all this, instead of you. I'm frankly amazed you haven't. It's just because you're too fucking dignified, too decent a person, too damn strong and sensible to sink to his bottom-feeder level. You go high, my lovely, but bloody hell, he went low. What a scumbag.'

She paused for another breath, and then went on, 'There, I said it. Now I guess if you ever do get back together, you'll hate me and we won't be able to be friends any more. But it was worth it.'

'You didn't sleep with him?' I finally asked.

'Sleep with *that*? Not a hovering batfuck. I mean, I know you loved him and everything, but – ugh.'

'It's just… I thought you might have been going to say…'

'Oh my God! Oh, no. Of course you thought that. I'm so sorry – I should have known. I really didn't mean to scare you. But that utter slimeball, destroying your faith in everything so badly. I wish you'd unpicked the seams of all his trousers before you left. I wish you'd hidden prawns in the curtains. I wish you'd sold his West

Ham season ticket on eBay. Even that would've been too good for him, the horrendous bastarding bellend.'

'Megs,' I said, 'I'm worried you're bottling up your feelings. Why don't you tell me what you really think?'

'What? But I…' And then she looked at me, and we both started to laugh so hard we ended up collapsed over the table gasping for breath, our eye make-up leaving black smears on its glossy white surface.

When at last we'd composed ourselves, I said, 'Seriously, though. Imagine if I'd ended up staying, thinking he'd change his ways.'

'They never do,' Megs replied sagely. 'Once a shitgibbon, always a shitgibbon.'

'I know,' I replied. 'And if there's one thing I've realised over the past few months, it's that if I end up on my own, I can cope with it. It might not be my number one life goal to end up a bitter old spinster with only a cat for company, but there are worse things, right?'

'Like what happened to Vivienne,' Megan said. 'Staying in a marriage with a guy she loved, who never loved her and messed her around over and over.'

'Like that,' I said. 'It's weird, though. It's like she was trapped in that place, not able to move on, not able to work, not able to even vacuum her carpets or take out her trash, just spending hours and hours in her garden, because that was the one place where she could be happy.'

'And yet when Max died, she was devastated,' Megan said.

'Yes, she was. Absolutely in pieces. But I really think it was his death that helped her to deal with having lost her baby. Juliet. And let her see the trap she'd fallen into, the way her grief about that and her heartbreak over Max had kind of made her get stuck. She couldn't heal and move on. But once he died, it was like she could look at what her life had become and say, "No. I don't want this any more." And Bianca and Charis turning up and making friends with her and her getting the part in Craig's production of *The Cherry Orchard* were just some of the ways that things worked out for her. If they hadn't happened, I reckon she would have worked stuff out by herself.'

'Possibly,' Megan said. 'But it's a brilliant part in a blockbuster production of a great play. Even if it doesn't end up being a springboard to a whole new career for her, it should bring in some money, which I'm sure she'll be grateful for.'

'Well, you'd think so. That's what I thought. But it turns out we're both wrong.'

I filled Megan in on the last time I'd been to see Vivienne. I'd arrived at eleven in the morning and stood outside the door for a few seconds, almost fearful of knocking in case I'd find that something had happened to disturb the equilibrium of her new life.

But I needn't have worried.

Vivienne opened the door seconds after I knocked, wearing an emerald-green velvet tracksuit. Her hair was smoothly blow-dried, and although she wasn't wearing any make-up, her skin glowed. The rich, sugary smell of baking wafted through from the kitchen.

'Darling!' She kissed me on both cheeks, and I could smell some kind of expensive, rose-scented moisturiser. 'Come in! Great timing – I've just taken a batch of mince pies out of the oven. They'll be like molten lava still, but if we wait a few minutes we should be able to sample them without burning our mouths.'

I followed her to the kitchen, where we sat at the wooden table, now scrubbed so clean its pine surface was almost white, and she poured coffee from a cafetière. Outside, I could see that the garden had been pruned back for winter; only a winter-flowering cherry tree still wore a drift of white blossom that reminded me of one of Vivienne's diaphanous nighties. A robin was perched on the back of the bench where we'd sat when she told me about Max's death and the painful, drawn-out demise of their marriage.

'You're looking so well,' I said. 'Working suits you.'

'Honestly, I'd forgotten what it was like to be so busy!' She swished around the kitchen putting milk and sugar on the table, carefully levering hot pastries out of their baking tin with a palette knife and arranging some on a plate, adjusting the angle of the holly wreath that hung from the mantlepiece. 'I have my voice coach twice a week, and I've been doing barre fitness classes to try and get back into some sort of shape, and of course we're rehearsing every day, and then there are all the social things with the cast. Come the weekend I just sleep and sleep! And after the press previews it'll be the opening night and then I'll be working non-stop for six months.'

'It sounds exhausting, but it definitely suits you,' I said. 'Please let us know if there's anything we can do to help. The theatre will send your fan mail to the office and we'd be happy to reply to it for you, and of course we'll handle all your media requests and only say yes to the good stuff. And we can set up and manage your social-media accounts.'

'Oh, you don't need to do that,' Vivienne said. 'I'm already on the Gram.'

'You what?'

'Isn't that what you're supposed to call it? I've got an Insta account now. Ruby-Grace helped me set it up. Such a charming young woman. She explained about hashtags and told me who I should follow. Reese Witherspoon's already followed me back. She's a keen gardener, did you know?'

I imagined Ruby-Grace sitting with Vivienne, right here at her kitchen table, patiently explaining to her about two-factor authentication and filters, and my heart melted a bit.

'Well, it sounds like you've got that nailed. But other things as well – like, if you'd like a selection of frocks sent over for the opening-night party, or anything like that?'

'I already have my frock. I took Charis to Harrods to see Father Christmas, and we had tea there afterwards and then went shopping. It's Dior and it's utterly fabulous. I'll never need to buy another evening dress in my life.'

'Dior? Wow, good for you. You deserve a treat.'

'Yes, well, you see, darling.' Vivienne perched on the chair opposite mine, poured us coffee and pushed the plate of pastries over to me. 'I had a bit of a windfall.'

I took a mince pie, bit carefully into it and found that it was just about cool enough to eat. Rich, brandy-soaked fruit filled my mouth. 'A windfall?'

'That's right. Last week, I had a letter from a solicitor. Turns out I'm the sole beneficiary of Max's will.'

I almost choked on a currant. 'Really? That's wonderful, Vivienne, but it must have come as quite a surprise?'

She laughed. 'I was utterly gobsmacked. He'd written me a letter, too, saying how sorry he was for how he'd treated me, and how much losing Juliet had weighed on his mind all these years. Too little, too bloody late, Max, I thought. I nearly donated the lot to Save the Children in a fit of pique, but then I thought, what would be the point of that? They can have whatever's left when I die. His affairs were in an absolute shambles and there will be death duties to pay, of course, but I need never worry about money again. I can work because I want to.'

I recounted all this to Megan, watching her eyes grow wider and wider across the table. By the time I'd finished, Rosie had brought in an order of salt beef bagels, mustard oozing from their sides, for our lunch. She brought Ethan, too, so Megan could feed him, and then went back to her desk to eat her own lunch.

'So, I've been thinking,' I said, while we dug into our food. 'That as well as promoting Rosie to client relations manager, we should offer Isla a full-time job once her contract ends. And Sam...'

'Yes, Sam.' Megan wiped a smear of mustard off the corner of her mouth and settled Ethan in her lap. 'We really ought to let him go.'

'He did break the rules...' I said tentatively.

'The only rule there is, really. I mean, I like to think we're pretty flexible employers.'

'Except: don't sleep with the clients.'

'And if you do, make sure we don't find out.'

'But it wasn't exactly his fault we found out. I mean, Ruby-Grace...'

'Did you see her on *Naked Attraction*?' I knew that the dating show, where contestants chose a potential partner based on their bodies in the buff, revealed from the bottom up, was a guilty pleasure of Megan's, just as it was of mine. 'My God, that was awkward. I know we get pretty involved in the intimate details of our clients' lives, but not that intimate.'

'I was legit watching between my fingers, like a kid with *Doctor Who*.' Remembering, Megan covered her face with her hands.

'I cringed so hard I almost broke a rib,' I agreed. 'But you have to admit, she totally stole the show.'

'Those legs,' Megs sighed in admiration.

'That six-pack. That booty. That *piercing*.'

'I know, right. I mean, each to their own and all that, but if anyone ever comes near my clit with a jewelled titanium bar, I won't be answerable for the consequences.'

'But that poor guy – what was his name, Robbie? – it was like he was under some sort of spell.'

'And the poor other girls looking for a date. None of them stood a chance.'

'And then he picked her and they went on their date and Ruby-Grace was like, "Sorry, I'm in love with someone else." And basically propositioned Sam right there on TV.'

'He didn't stand a chance, either.' Megs shook her head in wonderment.

'You know what, though, I think under all the superficial stuff, Ruby-Grace is actually a sweet girl. She works incredibly hard – she's in the gym for three hours a day and Sam says Edward Reeves says she's wonderful to deal with and incredibly committed. On the school visits and stuff she's done for Clear Future she's dialled the look right down and been totally natural and approachable. The kids really relate to her.'

Just saying Edward's name made me feel a pang of sadness, and it occurred to me that, if we did sack Sam, I'd have to revert to handling the business relationship with Edward. If that happened, I wasn't sure I could resist temptation.

'So strictly speaking,' Megan said, 'it was Ruby-Grace who instigated the relationship and not Sam at all.'

'That's true,' I said, realising that she was just as keen to break the rule as I was.

'You know what, I'm not in the business of screwing over people's careers before they've even started.'

'I totally agree. And Sam's got so much potential.'

'That's because he's learning from the best.'

Megan and I smiled at each other across the table and then, both at once, our right hands came up and smacked into each other in a high five.

Chapter Thirty-One

Beatrice and I spent Christmas Eve alone at home.

I'd put cheesy festive music on the radio while I baked up a storm: an elaborately iced fruit cake, two dozen sausage rolls and a load of butter tarts, made with my stepmom Maura's traditional recipe.

The little Christmas tree had been up for a week, and I still smiled in pleased surprise when I walked in from outside and breathed in the fragrance of its needles. Beatrice, in contrast, was more interested in trying to climb it and, when that failed, carrying swathes of tinsel around the house and hiding them in random places.

I'd been resigned to spending Christmas on my own – not that you really are alone when you have a cat, as I told Beatrice – but to my surprise I'd been inundated with invitations. Dad had offered to pay for me to fly out to Ontario to spend the holidays with him and Maura, but I'd declined this time, worried that Beatrice might think she'd been abandoned again.

Megan and Matt had invited me round to theirs, but I knew that however warmly they'd welcome me, they'd probably rather spend Ethan's first Christmas as a little new family of three. Gemma had suggested I join her, Raffy and a bunch of their mates for what promised to be a champagne-fuelled and hilarious celebration, complete with delicious food cooked by Raffy and less successful attempts by Gemma herself, but again I'd declined – much as I loved her, I wasn't exactly up for boozy partying.

So Bianca and Michael had won the dubious prize of having me over on Christmas Day. Vivienne would be there, I knew, as well as Bianca's brother Henry and his wife (who'd finally forgiven Bianca for the scene at their wedding) and a few of their friends. Under the tree was a pile of carefully wrapped gifts for them all: an embroidered velvet dressing gown for Vivienne, a hand-knitted cream cashmere shawl I'd bought in a craft market for Bianca, the director's cut of *Blade Runner* on DVD for Michael, and assorted bottles of champagne, artisan gin and perfume for everyone else.

Now, I had nothing more to do except relax in my living room with a plate of smoked salmon, which Beatrice had indicated she expected to share, and think.

Two days before, I'd signed documents from our solicitor finalising the sale of Myles's and my old home. By now a new family – Ben, Harriet and their baby daughter Elsie – would be moving in, filling the house with their furniture, the sound of their laughter, the smells of their cooking. And now, perhaps, I could talk to Eileen about going from being her tenant to being her purchaser. The little house, which had felt like a bolthole at first – a port in a storm – had become a proper home.

Myles and I had gone for a coffee together after we left the estate agency, as if tacitly acknowledging that this might be the last time we ever saw each other. It had been an awkward half-hour; I'd felt reticent with him, the deep wounds he'd inflicted on me too recently healed for me to relax in his company. But he could still make me laugh – albeit silently, as I translated what he said to me into what he really meant.

'So, are you seeing anyone, Sloane?'

I'm seeing someone.

'Not right now. I was, kind of, but I thought it was best if I had some time on my own. How about you?'

'Yeah, I've been on a few dates.'

I'm getting all the sex.

'That's nice. Anyone serious?'

'Well, there's this one girl. I met her at the gym.'

She's ripped. And – go on – ask me how old she is.

'I'm glad you're having fun.'

'Yeah, I am. But, you know, sometimes I miss… us.'

Let's see if I can still jerk your chain.

'That's natural. We were together a long time.'

'And we made a life together. A home.'

That girl I'm screwing won't iron my shirts.

'It's weird how quickly my new place has started to feel like home. Having a cat helps.'

'Sloane? We can still be friends, can't we?'

Tell me what I did wasn't so bad after all.

'I really don't think so, Myles. You see, I've moved on.'

I bore him no ill feeling, though. I remembered Vivienne's words – *Will he hold your heart safe in his hands?* – and I was glad that I'd learned the answer to that when I had. Myles would never keep anyone's heart safe, perhaps not even his own.

And now, I was holding another heart in my hands. And I was going to have to decide what to do about it.

The realisation that something might have changed came to me quite suddenly, when I was doing my Christmas shopping in town. Covent Garden Market was garlanded with wreaths of holly, twinkling with gold and silver pinpoints of light. Giant bunches of mistletoe hung from the roof, waiting for lovers to kiss under them. An enormous Christmas tree gleamed with red baubles.

And there were children everywhere.

In front of me, a woman held her toddler up above her head, encouraging her to look at the pretty lights, while the little girl laughed with pleasure. In a café, a woman was breastfeeding her baby while she sipped a coffee. A whole choir of adorable primary-school kids were singing 'O Little Town of Bethlehem', their clear voices drifting like snow into the winter darkness.

I heard myself say out loud, 'Oh shit!' and I dashed into Boots as quickly as I could.

I needn't have bothered with the test. It just confirmed what I already knew, as soon as I allowed myself to think about it. My breasts had felt tender – almost sore – for the past few days. I'd been ravenously hungry all the time. There was a weird taste in my mouth that I couldn't shift no matter how many times I cleaned my teeth. And my period was AWOL – almost a week late.

It had been two weeks since I'd sat in my bathroom, staring at the digital display on the pregnancy test, feeling alternately elated, terrified and strangely calm. And since then I'd changed my mind over and over again about what to do. I hadn't talked to anyone about the decision I was facing – it felt like it would have been unfair to involve any third party when the second party didn't know what was up. All the options that were open to me felt flawed in their own way, yet the biggest choice that I was making – the choice to have this baby, come what may – was so obvious it was barely a choice at all.

But then. Edward. That last night here in the house, with him, something must have gone wrong. We'd been careful – as careful as two sensible adults caught in the throes of what felt like insatiable desire could be. But still – well, here we were. And this was Edward's baby for sure. Since I spent that last night with Myles, there had been no one else but Edward.

I knew, rationally, that the decision was only mine to make, and I'd made it alone. But now there was a whole other, more complex choice facing me.

I could, I supposed, just go it alone, the way I would if I'd been one of those fiercely independent women who strode confidently off to a sperm bank and said, 'I'd like the six-foot blond semi-pro cyclist with the PhD, please.' That would release Edward fully from any obligations towards me or his child. I could even do it without saying a word to him, so that he could carry on with his life unencumbered by even the knowledge that he was a father.

But that would be wrong. It would deprive him of the choice *not* to be released, if he didn't want to be. And it would deprive our baby of a possible relationship with their father.

I could, of course, inform him that I was having his baby but I didn't want him in my life, although of course I'd be making sure he did the right thing and paid to support the child he could have chosen not to conceive by – well, not having sex with me. And then I could say that if he wanted a DNA test, he was free to bring it on.

But that approach – which I would have fully supported if a friend had told me she was taking it – didn't feel right, either.

Edward wasn't some philanderer who went around impregnating women and then dodging his responsibility towards the children he'd fathered – at least, I didn't think he was.

So, eventually, I'd come to a decision.

I was going to tell him. I was going to say that, like it or not, he was going to be a father – but that it was entirely his decision what kind of one he was. I was going to say that we could take it just one day at a time, see how things worked out, see whether we still had feelings for each other and what they were. Once the baby was born, he could see how he felt about that – and about me.

Whatever happened, I knew that I'd be all right, and so would my baby. Inside me, so tiny it was barely more than a few cells, was what would become my daughter or son's heart – and I was going to keep that safe, come what may.

And I knew that part of that was keeping my own heart safe. I'd seen enough from the experiences of Vivienne, Bianca, Megan and my own mom to know that motherhood had its own, uniquely powerful way of tearing women apart. I knew having a child wouldn't be all gurgles and cuddles. I knew my future could hold pain as lethal as stepping on a Lego brick in the dark.

And I wasn't going to add to that pain by trying to persuade a man who didn't want to be part of his child's life to be a father in any meaningful sense.

I wasn't sure if there was a better way to do what I was about to do. If there was, all my mental gymnastics had failed to come up with it. So I was going to work with what I had.

I picked up my phone and I dialled Edward's number.

I hadn't deleted his contact details and I guess he hadn't deleted mine, either, because there was no mistaking the joy in his voice when he said my name.

I said his back, and then we talked for a long time. By the time we finished, Beatrice had eaten all the salmon.

Chapter Thirty-Two

Ten months later

I woke up from a sleep so deep it had been like falling off a cliff, and the first thing I noticed was the smell of my baby's head. Juliet Linda, named after the daughter her godmother – one of them; of course Megan was the other – had lost all those years before, and my own mother, was still sleeping peacefully, next to me in her cot, the bars dropped down so I could reach for her whenever I needed to, but in careful compliance with the safe co-sleeping guidelines I'd read over and over.

She was lying on her back, her arms up by her head like an angel's wings, her little hands furled like ferns on either side of her peachy cheeks. I sat up as quietly as I could and yawned hugely. Juliet didn't wake, but Beatrice, curled up by my feet, did, and she yawned hugely too. Then she hopped down off the bed, stretched systematically, and trotted out of the room with an air of intense purpose.

It must have been the smell of roasting turkey that had woken me – and my cat, too. But Juliet was oblivious – at just six weeks old, the only food she cared about was what my own body made for her. I leaned carefully over to look at her, wondering as I always did whether I'd ever get tired of admiring her perfect eyelashes, the rosebud pout of her mouth – still and soft now in sleep but able to transform in seconds to bawling fury – and the shock of dark hair that made her look like a tiny emo.

As if sensing my gaze, she opened her ink-blue eyes – and, seconds later, her mouth, too. Before she could utter more than a couple of grumpy squeaks, I gathered her in my arms, feeling the warm, sleepy weight of her and guiding her mouth to my breast. Megs was right – it had hurt like a bastard in the beginning, but Juliet and I were both getting better at this whole being a baby and having one thing.

Soon, she was chonking away like a pro. Careful not to disturb her, I adjusted my position on the pillows more carefully and took a deep, appreciative sniff of the smells coming from my kitchen. There wasn't just roasting turkey – there was bacon, too, and the spicy, buttery fragrance of a pumpkin pie and the savoury, sage and onion smell of stuffing.

'You're not the only hungry one here, you know,' I told my daughter, cradling her head in the palm of my hand. 'Mommy's also taking a keen interest in the catering arrangements.'

There was a soft tap on the door, and a couple of seconds later it swung open, letting in a fresh waft of cooking smells that made my stomach rumble.

'Dean seems to have everything under control in the kitchen,' Maura said. 'So I wondered if you'd like a shower? I could take the little one and then maybe give her her bath? Unless you'd rather…'

When my dad and stepmother had landed at Heathrow two days earlier, Maura had been so overcome by the sight of her new granddaughter that she'd hardly been able to bring herself to touch

Juliet, in case she dropped her or squeezed her too hard or gave her some exotic Canadian virus. And to make things even more difficult, I could see she was terrified of interfering, or giving me the impression she thought I wasn't doing a good enough job. It had taken all my powers of persuasion to get her to cuddle Juliet, change her nappy, give her a bath – all the things I knew she was absolutely longing to do.

So now I said, 'Oh my God, Maura, that would be amazing! I'd love a quick shower and it would be brilliant if you could give her a bath. You're much better at it than me, anyway.'

Maura glowed with pleasure and held out her arms for Juliet. 'Come on then, my little treasure.'

I showered and dressed, then quickly put on some make-up, listening to Maura singing 'Incy Wincy Spider', ready to rush in and rescue her if Juliet cried. But she didn't – she loved her bath and she already loved her grandma – so I left them to it and went to find Dad in the kitchen.

'Hey, honey. Have a good rest?'

'The best. I'm lucky, I guess – Juliet's a good sleeper. But still, afternoon naps are a total lifesaver.'

'Now, I need you to have a taste of this stuffing. Maura says I never add enough sage.'

He held out a spoon and I sampled it obediently. 'It's perfect, Dad. Delicious. And we've got enough food for an army here and there won't even be ten of us. Well, eleven if you count Juliet, but she's not exactly in the market for turkey just yet.'

'It's Thanksgiving, though. If you don't stuff yourself as well as the turkey, you're doing it wrong in my book.'

'I can't argue with that. Although when I invited Megan and Matt for Thanksgiving dinner, she looked at me like I'd gone mad. I think she thought I still had pregnancy brain fog, until I reminded her that Canadians celebrate it in October.'

'I only wish we'd been able to get fresh cranberries,' Dad fretted. 'Linda always said they're better than frozen for sauce.'

'Dad, it really doesn't matter.' I moved closer to him and slipped my arm round his waist. 'Mom wouldn't mind. It's like she's here anyway, you know, cranberry sauce or no.'

Dad squeezed my shoulder, then said it was time he took that bird out of the oven to rest and why didn't we open a bottle of champagne? And Maura came through with Juliet, freshly bathed and dressed in an adorable babygrow with a moose's head on it that was a gift from her grandparents. We put her on the rug for some tummy time and even though she was so tiny she didn't do very much yet except reach her squidgy little hands out for her toys, we were all lost in wonder and admiration at the perfect, wondrous person I'd grown inside me.

'Right,' Maura said eventually, 'I'd better get that pumpkin pie in the oven. And will you push that small table over against the big one, Dean? It's not ideal but we should all just about fit.'

The two of them jumped into action, and a few minutes later Dad opened the door to Vivienne, who'd brought a bunch of golden and orange roses and a copy of *The Very Hungry Caterpillar*. Soon after that, Megs, Matt and Ethan arrived with ingredients for a spiced apple sour cocktail. Bianca and Michael were next, without Charis, who sent her apologies as she was at a sleepover, but had contributed home-made chocolate truffles flavoured with maple syrup.

I sat on the couch with Juliet on my lap, except when someone else wanted to cuddle her, which was quite often. While they were doing that, I just sat, relaxing, basking in the love of my family and friends, sipping a cocktail and chatting.

It was almost dark outside now, and the windows of my little house were misted with drizzle. Beatrice had curled up on Vivienne's lap, full of the scraps of roast turkey Dad had slipped her while carving. I could smell gravy simmering on the hob, potatoes roasting in the oven and the caramel spiciness of Maura's pie. There was only one thing missing.

Juliet started to wriggle and put her fingers in her mouth, telling me she was hungry, so I gathered her close and fed her. She'd sleep again now, quite soon, until two or three in the morning when I'd need to wake up, feed her once more, change her, sing to her – all the little routines that I'd already become so used to that I couldn't imagine what my nights had been like before.

Sometimes, sitting there in the dark with my baby, I felt absolutely alone apart from her, like it was just the two of us in the whole world. But now, looking around the room at all the people who loved me and loved Juliet, and would be woven into the pattern of her childhood, I realised I wasn't alone – I never had been.

I heard the sound of keys in the lock and, with a gust of wind and a splatter of rain, Edward came into the room.

'I'm so sorry I'm late,' he said. 'I found fresh cranberries, but I had to try about six different shops. I tracked them down at a Turkish greengrocer round the corner eventually. I didn't want to let you down.'

I thought of the words he'd said to me when I first told him I was pregnant – that he'd support me in whatever decision I made. I thought of the first, tentative steps we'd made all those months ago towards building a new relationship together: first as friends who were going to be co-parents and then inevitably, joyfully, as lovers who'd created this amazing new life together. I thought of how he'd stayed with me through every minute of my thirty-hour labour, holding my hand, massaging my back, giving me popsicles to suck.

I remembered the expression on his face the first time he held our daughter, which was still exactly the same every time he kissed her or changed her diaper or comforted her when she cried.

I thought of the bed upstairs that Edward had carefully made for Dad and Maura, how he'd insisted on coming with me to the airport to meet them, how he'd introduced me so proudly to his own family at his littlest niece's third birthday party, and how welcome they'd made me feel.

I wasn't sure – I couldn't possibly be – that he and I would be happy together forever. No one can, if you're honest with yourself. But I knew that my tiny daughter, who I passed over now to her daddy so I could go upstairs for the pee I desperately needed, would always have a father who loved her, just like I had.

'You'd never let us down,' I said.

A letter from Sophie

I want to say a huge thank you for choosing to read *No, We Can't Be Friends*. If you did enjoy it, and want to keep up to date with all my latest releases, just sign up at the following link. Your email address will never be shared and you can unsubscribe at any time.

www.bookouture.com/sophie-ranald

No, We Can't Be Friends is my eighth novel (I don't count the one that's stashed away in a digital drawer somewhere on my hard drive, never to see the light of day), and so I feel I'm qualified to say this: it doesn't get any easier!

There are those wonderful days when the words flow and the characters come alive and I think, 'YASSS, I've got this!' – and then the next time I sit down in front of my keyboard imposter syndrome kicks in again and I can't believe I was ever stupid enough to think I could do this job.

Just me? I don't think so. All the authors I speak to online and in real life say the same – writing, then letting our characters and their lives loose in the real world, is a scary business. It's like the people, places and even animals we've spent hours creating aren't ours any more – they're products to be put out there, packaged, marketed and reviewed.

That's daunting – but it also leads to some wonderful interactions. Over the past year, I've had so many readers reach out to me on social media or through online reviews to tell me that my characters have resonated with you, made you laugh and even brought tears to your eyes – or even just that they've helped to pass your time on a long-haul flight or provided some distraction when you've been ill in bed.

I'm so enormously grateful to every single one of you who've got in touch to share your thoughts with me – and of course for those who haven't, but have taken the time to read my books and comment on them on Amazon, NetGalley or Goodreads. I hope you've enjoyed spending time in the world of *No, We Can't Be Friends* and, as always, I'd love to hear from you.

Love from Sophie

Acknowledgements

If some novels are a marathon to write, *No, We Can't Be Friends* was a sprint – and I'm no Usain Bolt! Writing on tight deadlines requires the support of a team with absolute ninja skills, and I am extremely lucky to have just that.

At The Soho Agency, the amazing Araminta Whitley, Alice Saunders and Niamh O'Grady have looked after me throughout this process, answering my questions, dispensing advice and being there to provide digital pats on the shoulder and 'there, there' noises when I threaten to go into meltdown.

I'm also unbelievably fortunate to have the best people in the business supporting me at my publisher, Bookouture. My editor Christina Demosthenous worked her magic on a very rough first draft, taking a scalpel to redundant storylines and pointing me in the right direction to transform the book into something I can be proud of, and which I hope my readers love.

Noelle Holten, Kim Nash, Peta Nightingale, Alex Holmes, Lauren Finger and Alex Crowe have also provided invaluable support behind the scenes on publicity, production and promotion. Rhian McKay, an absolutely forensic copyeditor, took a deep dive into the manuscript and eliminated countless errors and glitches. Caroline Young has come up with yet another cracking cover that totally captures the spirit of the book. Thank you all.

At home, I've had love and cuddles from my darling partner Hopi, and Purrs and Hither the cats. I love you all very much.

Made in the USA
Middletown, DE
20 May 2020